THE BEYOND NOW DEVICE
A Fictional Exploration Of Time

by
Mark Hollock

The Beyond Now Device, A Fictional Exploration of Time
Park Hollow House First Edition January 2018

This is a work of fiction. Persons, places, and situations are used
fictitiously. Statements about time, even the ones claiming to be true,
are a product of the author's imagination and should not be used
when facing crucial decisions.

ISBN-13 Number: 978-0-9996620-1-4

Cover image and design by Joan Parks

In appreciation of the dedicated modern researchers who have made it possible for my life, and the lives of so many others, to be productive and longer than God may have intended

How did it get to be so late so soon?
It's night before it's afternoon.
December is here before it's June.
My goodness how the time has flewn.
How did it get so late so soon?"
-- Dr. Seuss

CHAPTER ONE

June 7, Minneapolis

Time. As an unemployed teacher of English to junior high school students, Alan thought of time in terms of periods. He was currently in his sharing-an-apartment-with-his-younger-cousin period. In his bedroom, leaning against the headboard with a rolled pillow tucked at the small of his back, he heard their voices, Sanger's and Em's, coming from the living room. Over the top of his reading glasses, he stared at his closed door.

"I'm not going to say it," he heard Em say. "You'll hear it and think you've got me now, can do what you want. Get my phone turned back on, bring me job applications, text me just to see where I am. No."

"I've said it," Sanger said. "I know you do. What's wrong with saying it?"

"It's meaningless. People say it as casually as 'great' or 'awesome'. No, I won't do it that way."

Alan imagined his younger cousin, Sanger, standing not quite square to Em, elbows at his sides and his open palms imploring. He thought Sanger loved too easily, wanted to love with all the energy he possessed.

After a long moment of silence, Em spoke again. "You don't have to take your uncle's call. Turn off your phone. He just wants to pull you into some petty crime, something he'll walk away from and leave you holding the bag."

"He's family, Em. And it's not like that."

Alan knew Em wouldn't stand for it, liked to be contrary, and was rarely able to contain her feisty nature.

"You can't get pulled into things you know will end badly. Where is he, anyway?"

"Chicago," Sanger said. "Uncle Bill's a bar and pool hall kind of guy. He said he'd call again this morning. He said this is the big one, a scheme to lift him out of the company of car salesmen and pimps."

"And you believed him?"

Alan dogged-eared a page of his paperback and tossed it to the foot of the bed. Lonely, a word he rarely applied to himself, preferring instead to see a dark absence of responsibility while visualizing a cup he could no longer fill with purpose. He intended to step out and referee their fight. Yet he sat, fingering the loose ends of his good intentions.

Ten years earlier, at twenty-nine, he'd grown distant from the family, from the rest of his cousins and aunts who drank too much, laughed too loudly, and spit disdain toward anyone they deemed couldn't take a joke. It was good for him to have left, gotten married, and protected his wife from his relatives' shady behavior. The only familial keepsake he harbored was a propensity to tipple in the evening. For that heirloom, he eventually lost his job as a teacher, then his house through a faulty mortgage, and his wife by her own choice. Ambition and confidence evaporated as he sank deeper into lethargy. Two years earlier he had dropped a knapsack in Sanger's second bedroom, moved in, and stopped drinking.

Footsteps on the other side of the door. Sanger paced as he said to Em, "You only knew Uncle Bill when we were in high school. But you're right, he's not a very good criminal."

Alan counted Em's predictable one-two pause before she said, "Oh, Sanger. Not very good criminals do time in prison. Don't get pulled in to whatever scheme he's cooking."

"I'm already in. He's family."

"Don't take his call."

"Why are you being like this?"

Alan sat on the edge of his bed. It was a small apartment with both bedrooms directly off the living room. Ready to stand and open the door, he hesitated as he heard Em respond, "I want the best for you. And your Uncle Bill isn't what's best for you."

"Thanks," Sanger said. "I'm taking pretty good care of myself. But it's nice to know you want the best for me. Even if you won't say…you know."

"I do." Em said.

Alan heard it and counted two beats for Em's response.

"Um," she said. "Don't take that in the matrimonial sense. But I like you plenty."

"I'd feel better if you slept with me because you liked me, not in lieu of rent."

"I like you, Sanger. But if you don't see it by now you probably never will. Not until I can afford my own place. Is that it? Would me moving out make things more clear. Is that what you want? For me to move out?"

Alan rolled his eyes as he stood with his hand on the knob of his bedroom door. He knew Em didn't want to move out. She didn't have current rent let alone the upfront cost of a new place. And Sanger didn't want her to go. As frustrated as he might be with her, he would let her stay as long as she wanted even if the new-born pup of sex had never squirmed between them.

~ ~ ~

Sanger startled as his cell vibrated across the coffee table. During the time it took him to step, reach, and pull the phone to his ear, he closed his eyes and visualized what would remain if Em was gone. He saw his bed as a flattened field of wheat he'd created alone through the night. A quarter of his closet would hold uninhabited hangers, waiting for her return. And the prime top drawer of his dresser, pulled out, hollow. Taking Em in after her eviction wasn't a problem. Exchanging rent for a slice of her passion, although never his intention, was. Sanger blinked, wishing he trusted her affection.

"Hello? Uncle Bill?" Sanger said to his cell.

There was a pause as if no one was on the other end. Sanger pressed his ear to the phone. It was ten-thirty Saturday morning. Uncle Bill said, "The package is at the Amtrak station. Pick it up at baggage claim."

Sanger heard the quiet static of Em shifting position and felt her open disapproval. He glanced for help even though she hadn't heard what Uncle Bill said. To Bill, he said, "What's that tapping noise? Where are you?"

"Billiard balls kissing on green felt. Someone just broke a rack. But you'll pick it up?"

"I will," Sanger said. "Of course I will. But why the station, why not deliver it right here?"

"Who knows what UPS does, x-rays, sniffer dogs. The railway has no security. It's there now. It arrived last night. And Sanger, it'll take a few of you to carry it so take someone along." Another round of silence until Bill added, "This is great of you, you're helping me out a lot. Call me when you get back with it."

Sanger put down the phone and stared at Em. He liked her looks, adored the spray of freckles across her nose, and the reddish highlights in her straight black hair as it hung to her shoulders. She wore no makeup and her dark clothing draped loosely over her naturally toned body. He didn't understand why she thought she went unnoticed when out in public.

Alan stood in his bedroom doorway. "What's Uncle Bill got you doing?" he asked.

"A package arrived at the train station," Sanger said. "He wants me to pick it up."

Alan shook his head and as he walked toward the kitchen said, "I'm going to scramble some eggs. You two want any?"

Sanger hadn't minded taking them in, letting them eat the food he bought or use the electricity he paid for. He liked the feel of giving; if he had it, it was meant to be shared. He never kept track of rent owed and turned a deaf ear at any promise of repayment. Yet he occasionally glimpsed the effect of his generosity on them, on Em, on Alan, especially when he wanted something from them. He felt the slow erosion of their autonomy, hated their feelings of dependency when they had to hit him up for pocket money. It was Em who once told him that she resented the special treats he brought home, feeling the obligation to thank him even if it was something she didn't especially like or want. Alan was his cousin and tolerated more from Sanger…yet Em, she could tolerate only so much.

Fifteen minutes later, as Em continued drawing with

pastels on paper and Alan forked eggs into his mouth as he sat on the arm of an overstuffed chair, Sanger waited for just the right moment. When the others were attending to themselves, he said, "Let's go pick up that package for Uncle Bill."

Alan said, "I think I'll just wait here. Okay?"

Em raised her eyes from her drawing and said, "Me, too. I'm involved in this." She lifted a pastel stick and waved it in the air.

Sanger sighed. "Uncle Bill said it's heavy and I'll need a few people to help lift it. What do you say?"

~ ~ ~

Alan met Em six months earlier, just before Christmas, when Sanger brought her home, claiming she had nowhere else to go in late December's sub-freezing air. Strung out, Alan recognized it right away; unkempt clothing, and looking closer to a wet kitten than an accomplished adult.

Evicted, Em had told Sanger and Alan an abridged version of her adult life: too many drug-infested nights as her remaining friends simply shook their heads; parents standing shoulder to shoulder, pointing her away from her childhood home; and finally being escorted from her job as a hollow-eyed teacher of third-graders while the end of her rope flailed wildly from her loosening grip.

Alan had been clean for over two years, Em just these last six months. It was something they shared and never talked about. Since Alan already occupied the second bedroom, Sanger had been willing to rearrange the walk-in closet for Em. But she refused and slept the first four weeks on the couch in the living room. Then one night after laughter and goodwill, she slept in Sanger's bed, worrying in the aftermath if a sex-for-rent agreement had been established.

~ ~ ~

Em donned the borrowed jacket she'd been using and they piled into Sanger's duct-taped sedan. Em up front, Alan in the back. Even though it was early June all across the country, the upper Midwest was under an errant high-pressure system of cold Canadian air, dazzling their eyes with a cool, white sun. Alan rolled his window down and Em hoped the car's heater would soon warm.

Em looked at Sanger's profile and knew he took driving seriously, considered cars dangerous and wanted life protected as if they could all live in a huddle of Emperor penguins. As if seeing marriage stenciled across his forehead, Em didn't know how to tell him the degree of mundane she thought forever coupled would be.

"You need some other way to view what's between us," Em said as she stared out the windshield.

As a single child under the custody of indifferent parents, Em never understood Sanger's tightly knit symbiotic relatives. She had never wanted more people in her life, especially not those who watched too closely or gave serious advice on how to shape up and pull herself together. Even the thought of one special person caused worry about being under another's wary eye, needing to keep secret the space and time she needed on her own.

"What?" Sanger asked. "Oh, yes, maybe. Aren't all relationships a series of large and small deals leading to compromise?"

"I think it's less about deals than about definitions. I say we choose to exchange sex, do it together. But you only see it as a commodity."

"A gift in return for a gift is open trade. Unless it's

something else."

Em understood Sanger's financial gifts as the burden she must live with. Yet she reacted by stretching her meager influence over him, testing, teasing, pushing him to question whatever she cared to hold under the light.

She knew Sanger refused to accept a sex-for-rent agreement, saying from his side that he was simply offering space with no strings attached. So Em had continued to reply, "Me, too. Take it or leave it. It's my free offer." Even as Sanger was uncomfortable buying sex from her, Em was neither ashamed nor disgusted by her choice. Other than acknowledging Sanger's negative feelings when he thought of it too deeply, she made herself comfortable with the situation.

"Why does it have to be something else? See. That's just what I mean." Em looked behind her at Alan who shrugged and remained distinctly quiet. She wanted a witty refrain but when none came, she said nothing. They had arrived at this conversation station before and Em had each time been surprised at Sanger's faith in the idyllic state of perpetual coupling.

~ ~ ~

As they stood at the St. Paul Amtrak baggage storage room, Alan grew impatient with his younger cousin and pushed Sanger out of the way. Leaning on both arms over the counter, Alan stared at the absence of luggage on the shelves, a reminder of the dearth of belongings in his own life.

Slow to make decisions yet anxious to get the package and leave, Alan asked the attendant if there was anything for Sanger Duncan. When the attendant pointed, Alan's eyes took the scenic route: dropping from the attendant's visor cap, down the uniformed shoulder, around the elbow, along the forearm, and over the hand to the end of his index finger. Then his eyes took the leap to the steamer trunk against the wall to the right. Once revealed, the package grabbed his attention like a fly circling the room.

As Alan slipped behind the counter and approached the trunk, he mumbled, "Do you think we'll be able to lift it?"

It was nearly knee high and as wide as his regular spot at the end of Sanger's kitchen table. Leather handles were riveted to the ends. A flush-mounted spring lock closed front and center. Two more latches were evenly spaced across the brow. The trunk was old, battered, with only shreds of labels still attached.

Em came beside him and tapped the trunk with her foot, just as though she was inspecting the tires of a car on the lot. Alan leaned down and took one long sniff, imagining fruit or meat or anything that might rot during transport.

With fingers to his lips he wondered what the trunk might contain. Touching the top, he reached down to one of the leather handles and lifted. "Lots of weight. Too much maybe. It's heavy."

Alan was stronger than Sanger and Em combined, so after a minute of debate Em and Sanger each had a hand through the leather loop on one end of the trunk. Alan was similarly attached at the other end. They picked it up together and aligned themselves to the space through the counter with tiny steps. Once ready, the attendant raised the drawbridge and they stepped through.

It was a hefty load and each took a stab at the contents. Em called to Alan, "Books. Novel novels, pristine publications. Valuable volumes."

Alan looked back and smiled before he added, "Lead. Heavy as lead. Axe heads. Bed of lead. Body of dread. A dozen dead Rhode Island Reds—"

"Whoa," Sanger interrupted. He and Em released their handle, letting their end drop to the polished floor as an echoing thud rang through the cavernous station. "Alan, why do you say that? Don't even hint that there might be anything dead in this trunk."

Senseless to hold any longer, Alan let go, too.

Em said, "Could be a dead, decomposing body. It's heavy enough. I wouldn't put it past your Uncle Bill to send us something like that."

"Uncle Bill," Sanger said, "wouldn't send a—"

"Ha," Alan said, staring at Sanger. "You can't be sure. Uncle Bill could stuff a body in a trunk, laugh about it, call us wimps, blame us for not seeing the humor in it all."

They picked up the trunk again and carried it to the car. The car's trunk wasn't big enough so Sanger reached in and pulled out two elastic cords, securing the steamer trunk in the car trunk. Then they slowly drove away.

Alan worried during the trip back. Even though he wasn't driving, he scanned the road for potholes and waved following cars past with a long arm out his back window. He was uneasy about an accident, a rear-end collision attracting the police who would stand with them behind the car examining the damage, while the steamer trunk's oozing contents dripped to the ground at their feet.

~ ~ ~

While Alan, Sanger, and Em drove home, Henrietta Sauk sat on the foyer floor in Sanger's apartment building. With her back against a wall, she stared at the five apartment doors that opened into this foyer. Up the stairs were five more doors, and five more, and five more on the top floor. She'd already explored every floor, gently turning each knob in hopes of finding a vacant unit. The floors were the same: run-down, harsh florescent lighting, pale green paint, and a thin carpet with threadbare patches along the trafficked paths. She sat in the foyer with her jacket zipped and her fingers fiddling with her bangs.

Her hair was between styles. The purple streak down one side no longer started anywhere near her scalp. She could have snipped it right out, as she had cut away the bleached ends of her bangs, badly at first, and then shorter each time to repair a previous mistake. The remaining fringe hung as a partially drawn window shade across her forehead, sloping and as lopsided as she thought she was.

The boys of the night before, only her second in Minneapolis, had taken her in. Or so she thought. She met them in a downtown park and realized only later that her fanny pack reminded them more of a tourist than a runaway. They called her 'newbie' and 'streetster wannabe' with such laughter and smiles that she felt included. They told her they'd show her the ropes, teach her what she needed to know. They led her away from the park, explaining they knew another place, more urban, more *street* than any expanse of park lawn. They took her just a few blocks south to where two thoroughfares merged. At the actual merge point, these two roads formed twelve lanes of crazy traffic, fed and overpassed by ramps to an inter-state, east and west. Plus a pedestrian/bicycle flyover. The land beneath was cut into mismatched triangles and trapezoids of infrequently trod territory, even too dangerous for rabbits or raccoons to risk their lives crossing the silver roadways. This area was, in fact, a small and easily comprehended space. Yet to Henrietta's new view, it was like a video game's rich gothic environment.

Henrietta wanted to kick herself. *Should've never let any of it out of my sight,* she thought. *What was I thinking?* It didn't take long for one of the boys to rifle through her backpack that contained the bulk of her one hundred and thirty-six dollars, and her iPad, and her small collection of cosmetics, and her clothes, jewelry, soap, toilet paper...*stupid, stupid, stupid*. She pulled at her bangs harder. They took everything, leaving only what was in her fanny pack: wallet, twelve dollars, library card as ID, journal, and cell phone but not her charger. *Stupid.*

After being abandoned she had climbed the hill to the back of a large apartment building. All the doors were locked. She crossed the street and tried an even larger apartment building, a brick behemoth built in the early twentieth century. One of the doors was propped open with a wooden wedge, smokers perhaps. She had slipped in and taken the stairs to the basement where she slept, uncomfortable and fully clothed.

Unkempt, hair a mess, she was pulling on her bangs again when she heard a commotion at the outside entrance.

She watched a man step in, leaving his two companions, a man and a woman, to stand in the doorway. He looked around the door and entry area. When he didn't see what he sought, he said to the woman, "Third time lately that the door stop's gone. Do you think people steal them?"

Henrietta fiddled with her fingers, only glancing occasionally at the man as he looked around the foyer. When he caught her eye, she lowered her head and pulled on her bangs.

"Hey," he called. "Will you hold the door open for us?"

She got up but said nothing. With her back to the open door, she pressed herself out of their way as they carried a trunk through and stopped at the bottom of the stairs.

Two of them had their hands on the leather handle at the back of the trunk. The other man was alone at the front. Henrietta was still leaning on the open door when the front man said, "You can let it close now. Thanks. But if you have a minute, I could use some help on this end carrying it up the stairs."

Henrietta wasn't sure what they really wanted. She suspected she might stupidly walk into another sour deal. Wordlessly, she approached and put her hand on the leather grip, needing to half cover his hand with hers to make the fit.

As they carried the trunk to the third floor, Henrietta ventured quietly, "This thing's heavy. What's in it?"

The three chuckled the laugh of those in the know. The man whose hand she was touching smiled at her. He said, "A tawdry body packed as dead weight freight."

Henrietta furrowed her brow and didn't believe him. Once in the apartment, they all stepped into a medium-sized living room. Directly across the dingy hardwood floor was a kitchen separated from the living room by an archway. As Henrietta stepped farther in, she craned her neck and saw more of the kitchen: appliances to the right and a small dining area to the left. Other rooms opened into the living room. One bedroom to the left and one to the right. Another door opened to a walk-in closet, where a desk and chair looked overly large in the small space. Two upholstered chairs, a couch, a coffee table and a few side tables with reading lamps furnished the living room. Accustomed to matching furniture, the rooms reminded her of rats and cockroaches and bugs that bite in the night.

Henrietta stood in the middle of the living room and didn't know what to do next. She watched the three take off their coats. The woman hung hers from the back of a kitchen chair and then called, "I'm making a sandwich. Anybody want one?"

Henrietta was hungry, had been feeling the grumblings in her stomach for hours.

"Not for me," one of the men called.

"Me neither," said the other.

Henrietta wasn't sure. She thought she should just leave, wander out as the three were busy with their own activities. The moment to go unnoticed was fleeting, the same moment that will soon pass and take with it her opportunity for a sandwich. She said quickly, "I'll have one. If it's no trouble."

"No trouble," the woman called again from the kitchen. "Come sit at the table."

Henrietta pulled a chair and sat. Soon one of the men joined her. She was wary of being tricked, lured into ill-advised trust by the promise of some ham on rye. The man asked, "What's your name?"

She leaned back, gaining perhaps three more inches of space between them, and countered with, "What's yours?"

"I'm Sanger. We need to call you something. So what's your name?"

"I'm Em," Em called, still working at the kitchen counter.

"And I'm Alan," Alan barked from the living room.

They're all listening, she thought, and became immediately cautious and pleased and suspicious. She pulled at her bangs and said, "Rooster. That's what people call me. Rooster."

"Rooster?" Sanger said. "Your parents picked that?"

"It's a nickname. In third grade I won the calling contest. I like it better than what my real name shortens to. And my mom didn't pick it, but nobody calls me anything else."

Sanger smiled and adjusted his chair. "Well, Rooster, how old are you?"

Rooster half-laughed, sounding more like a snort. "Old enough. What difference does it make? How old are you?"

"I'm twenty-nine," Sanger said, "and you're right, doesn't make a difference."

Rooster raised her eyebrows. "God, you're as old as my stepdad. My mom's a little older and literally swoons about what a treasure he is. But I don't think so. He's like, like a little kid. Stupider than a little kid."

Em brought glasses of water to the table and asked, "And

you're…how old?"

"Fifteen. So?"

"Your mom was young," Em said, "when she had you."

"Twenty. Not so young. And no, I don't want to have a baby younger than when she had me. Why does everybody ask that? Makes me think they think I'm stupid."

Em touched Rooster's shoulder and said, "No one asked that and no one thinks you're stupid." Em paused. Rooster felt the hand's weight on her shoulder as Em added, "You from around here?"

Rooster lowered her head and said, "I live here now. Or will. Soon. Got to get settled."

Em walked to the counter and returned with the sandwiches on plates. She looked down at the table. "Rooster," she said, "what do you do from here? What's next on your schedule?"

"Nothing. Why does everyone have to fill up their days with plans? Can't we just play it by ear, see what comes, let the universe have its way sometimes? Live free or die."

"Would you like us to call your parents? We could perhaps talk to—"

"No, no, no. Don't do that."

Em took a deep breath. "It looks like you've been sleeping rough. Where did you sleep last night? Where will you go tonight? If you need a toilet or want to wash your face, where will you go?"

"I heard at the university you can just walk right in and use the women's rooms. No one will stop you. They keep the toilet paper locked in these…" she shaped something invisible with her hands, "but someone gave me a key-like thing to get them out so I can at least carry a roll around with me." Rooster looked back and forth between Em and Sanger and imagined they were thinking something about her, judging, evaluating, appraising her worthiness. At the same time, though, she'd just spent two nights on the street, been laughed at, stolen from, and endured more hours of cold than ever before. A warm bed, a shower, another sandwich. She knew her twelve dollars wouldn't last long.

Then Em said, "Give us your parent's number and you can stay here until they come and get you."

Rooster stood straight up, knocking the chair out from behind her. She picked up her second half of sandwich and said, "No. I'd rather die than go back to those people."

Rooster had an impulse to run for the door. Instead she watched Em pat the air with her hands as she said, "Okay, okay, settle down. Sanger, she can stay here for a while, can't she? Until some plans are made, gets on her feet."

Sanger reached for Rooster's hand but she pulled it away. He said, "Sure, you can sleep on the couch tonight, take a shower, drink a gallon of milk. No problem."

Rooster sat and wasn't sure who should speak next. She wanted to trust them. But after last night's debacle, she worried she was really as stupid as she's been told.

CHAPTER TWO

December 22, Chicago

Six months earlier, Niko Talek stood beside a table in a restaurant. He stood so long that his attorney finally said, "Niko. Oh do sit down. It's not as bad as all that."

Niko Talek had walked over a gravel path from the parking lot to the restaurant dreading the upcoming meeting. Winter sun had coated the bald spot on the crown of his head and he imagined vitamin D passing through his interstitial tissue. But it did no good. He couldn't shake his foul mood. Physicist and lecturer at a local university, Niko viewed the world as it ought to be viewed, shunning the poetry of a breeze in the wake of dragons' wings and instead raising his face to icy winds streaming from a high-pressure system north of Lake Michigan to a tightly-wound low over North Carolina. If he had known the ways in which the coming months would rouse his life, he wouldn't have been so despondent through the Christmas season.

Niko sat and asked, "Are they taking me back?"

A woman, also seated at the table, looked away. The man shook his head and said, "Right up front…no. How can you expect them to?"

"Well, I do."

The attorney pointed his beer bottle at Niko and said with a lilt of humor, "But you stole a box from the medical lab."

"I didn't steal it. I picked up the wrong one. Mine is—"

"Yes, I know. You've told me this all before."

Two months earlier, Niko had shared an office in the university's medical-science building. He had been expecting a package and when one arrived, Niko tucked it under his arm and took it home. Later that evening he discovered it wasn't addressed to him. No problem, he would return it the next day.

"A mistake," Niko said. "Why are they being so harsh with me?"

"Someone almost died," the woman said. "The package you took nearly cost a woman her life."

"Niko, this is Donna. She's assisting me in negotiating with the university. But the bottom line is they're not going to take you back. It just wouldn't look right."

Since the early indications from the disciplinary committee Niko had let himself falter. Beneath his coat a stain marred his shirt. He needed a haircut, exercise, and a healthy meal; none of which had he had lately. "What's next?" Niko took a swallow of his beer. "Can I sue?"

"You could. You'd lose. As an advisor and a friend, why

not publish the paper you've been talking about. Something splashy in a reputable journal and get some post-fiasco cred."

Red and green lights blinked over an area where a band might later play. After staring too long, expecting to decipher a seasonal code, Niko said, "It wasn't my fault. It's just their excuse. They've always wanted to get rid of me."

The woman stood, shook her head, and walked away without comment.

"I'm sure," the man said. "But they're still calling it irresponsible."

"I'm fifty-nine years old. What am I going to do? Would an apology help?"

"To the university? Maybe. But do not contact the injured woman's family."

Niko put both hands around the beer bottle and pressed his forehead to the top of it. "And other universities?"

"Not yet. Maybe after some time. Focus on writing, get that paper together and submit it. You're close to done, right?"

"No, no I'm not." Niko raised his head. "I got out only six samples before they took my privileges away. And I have no field studies. I wanted to use students, but now that's...out of the question, I suppose."

"What was it? Something about time?"

"Yes, it's..." Niko faltered. Telling anything serious to those without a scientific mind was like preaching the Gospel to insolent children—pleasant stories, perhaps, but no feel or faith in the content. "A fantastic product," Niko said, "that will revolutionize our view of time."

"I'm sure it will."

Unable to help himself, wanting to explain, Niko continued, "Everyone thinks time is like the background music in an elevator, surrounding us continuously."

The man rose and stepped away from the table. He

signaled to his assistant who was returning from the restroom.

Niko jabbed one finger into the palm of his other hand. "Here and now, inseparable. But what if they were separated? Could it be—"

"I've got to go." The man stepped farther away. "Publish. That's the best you can do for yourself right now."

With both hands around his bottle of beer, Niko watched his attorney leave. Within minutes he tipped the bottle upside-down one last time and stepped out into the cold. He stared at the dappled surface of Lake Michigan to his left and the weight of Chicago's skyline looming to his right. He couldn't publish without data, couldn't get data unless others used it. Friends were out of the question, notoriously unreliable. An ad in a newspaper? And ask for what? He needed unbiased subjects willing to use the device before they knew what to expect. And then provide objective impressions even though their experiences would jar their senses and leave noteworthy imprints on their lives. But most of all he needed randomness.

Over the following weeks, Niko's plan coalesced. He would conduct his own study and publish in a reputable journal. He only needed to get his device into the hands of unsuspecting subjects.

One day in January he bounded up the outdoor steps and continued another flight up to his apartment. The art store had been colorful and the sales assistant pretty. *Art*, he thought, *creative similarities. I am still that guy with a PhD in physics. So what if I picked up the wrong delivery? Why only blame me? The courier shrugs his shoulders and I get fired. I'm sorry about the woman because her medicine sat in my apartment. But the company should have labeled it bigger or stamped a medical alert warning.*

Card stock, a tin of India ink, and a small silkscreen frame with squeegee. He worked for the next hour cutting the pattern for boxes of his own design. Six of them. Eight inch by four inch by four inch. He dipped the lower half of each not-yet-folded box into a bread pan half filled with diluted ink. Above the color he silkscreened a name, 'Beyond Now' and then folded the boxes. While they dried he printed his *Treatise on Time* in tiny 6pt font on continuous-feed paper.

Having his lab privileges snatched away so suddenly, Niko secured only six completed compounds before his identity badge was taken. He didn't regret taking the aggregate, which by contract may not have been his at all. After scouring second-hand stores for atomizers able to spray the minuscule solids that were at the heart of his mixture, Niko felt ready.

As the earth tilted on its axis into spring, Niko kept one device for himself. Wanting as much random exposure as possible for the results to be taken seriously, and wanting them found by people who soon had important decisions to make, he left one on the fifth floor of a Chicago trading company, one in the locker room of a professional baseball team, one in the international airport near baggage claim, one in the waiting room of a marriage counselor, and the fifth in a seedy pool hall.

Whether picked up by a stock market pundit or a pool hall scamp, Niko knew their understanding of time would be ordinary and unexamined. Most believe time is made up of past, present, and future. Time's continuous, without gaps between this now and the next. Time flows in one direction. Time is one way to measure change, change being one way to recognize time. Yet considering only change and measurement, people have argued for centuries about the 'realness' of time, imagining an unchanging place where time dallies pointlessly among unmoving objects that neither age nor die. Others, like pulling apart a flower in search of its source, called the past passed and no longer in existence; the future not yet upon us; and the present but a mere point marking the end of the past and the beginning of the future, and without duration can't be a part of time. It isn't crazy to wonder if time itself exists at all.

Niko didn't fool himself, he knew most people easily conceded the existence of time. In a changing world, time was still elusive, perhaps only a figment of an imaginative ordering of events, a puff of smoke, gone before it's captured. Of time, what can be certain? When Niko last called a colleague across the globe, it might have been evening for him but late the next morning for his friend. Niko's day was quietly nearing bedtime while his friend was surrounded by the bustle and car horns of Bangalore. Yet when they referred to 'now' they knew what they were talking about. An immediacy to 'now' exists that supersedes clocks or location. Even when a companion in Chicago walks by and says, "Do you want to join me (now) for a glass of wine?" Niko knows she's referring to that moment and so does his friend in India, understanding that wine is appropriate even though it's only late morning in the state of Karnataka. A perception of time exists that ignores the ticking and declaration of clocks.

Through human history people didn't consider that there might be any play in the when/where of now. People didn't dismiss the idea but rather didn't even consider it. For most, there has been a reliable clock at the center of the cosmos ticking away and setting a universal time, encompassing everything in every direction. The future isn't yet. The past is gone. Now is assumed to be moving through time at the same rate for everyone. Some people may run faster but no one thinks they're entering the future any sooner. With a steady rate through time, few are fooled when a moment of consequence passes through their fingers. We know when now is.

~ ~ ~

After Em and Rooster finished their sandwiches, Sanger

kneeled in front of the trunk and pressed the lever beneath the center hole of the circular plate. It popped open with a tiny sound of spring-twang. He lifted the tongues of the latches on each side. Em, Alan, and Rooster stood around and watched over his shoulders. Sanger slowly lifted the lid while imagining an incandescence emerging, washing their faces in a glow of golden light.

Instead they saw a battered box resting atop a pile of clothing. Similar in size to a large boxed bottle of cough syrup, it had a name on the front and the simple two-tone color scheme of an ancient hospital's hallway. Sanger thought of an elixir from the 1950's.

Sanger placed the box aside and then used both hands to dig into the top layers of clothing. "Nothing in here but old shirts and coats."

Em lifted the box with experienced hands, the way she might examine a flower or the dead, hollow carcass of a Japanese beetle. "I like the simple design even if it's a little...primitive. I think someone silkscreened this on card stock and then folded it into a box." She opened the lid, reached in with forefinger and thumb, and pulled out an atomizer.

Rolling it in her hands, she said, "It could be perfume. Definitely a bulb-pump atomizer, like an old perfume spray bottle. But this," she indicated the reservoir sack, "this sure isn't a bottle." She held it up for the others to see. "This pouch is really thin and soft, like holding a man's warm scrotum."

Rooster reached and touched the pouch. "Thin-skinned."

Em continued. "But what's inside the pouch is really odd. Not a liquid but more like a slippery powder." She presented it toward the others for them to feel.

Rooster touched it again. "Like mud."

"Yeah," Em said. "And it holds the shape you squeeze it

to."

Em put the atomizer on an end table. She reached into the box again and pulled out a thick wad of folded paper, like what might be used under a table's shortest leg. As she unfolded it, opening it once, and again, and again, she laughed. "It's like an accordion of paper. But it's gotten wet and then dried again. It's brittle and the ink has blurred."

Once fully open, Em added, "Look at this. There're some bold headings but the rest is in tiny font. I'll need a magnifying glass to read much."

"What's the product?" Sanger asked. "Is it perfume?"

Em pressed the paper flat to the floor and read an introductory paragraph. "Beyond Now. Thank you for your participation in the study of this product. Pouch reservoir, directional stem/nozzle, squeeze-bulb. Support pouch in palm, aim nozzle toward face, squeeze bulb lightly. Odorless mist. Absorption through inhalation. Please use the contact information below.

"Then an address and phone number. After that are the dense paragraphs of fine print. Let's see if I can make any sense of it." Em squinted with her face close to the paper. "Okay, here's one. 'In the depth of your experience, do not eat or drink. If injured, do not seek or accept medical treatment. While you…' Hmm. I'll get that magnifying glass later."

Alan tightened his eyebrows as he said, "Perfume? Why does it say don't eat or drink?"

Em started her haphazard fold of the instructions, but Rooster grabbed the sheet from her and carefully refolded the paper as she would correctly prepare a highway map for storage.

"Well, my curiosity is satisfied," Sanger said. "Should we call Uncle Bill? Tell him we have the trunk. Get it off our hands."

"Not so fast," Alan said. He touched the atomizer as it

rested on a side table but didn't pick it up.

"Yeah," Em said. "Whoa. What if this is one of those perfumes people find irresistibly attractive? Beyond Now is probably its name. Nice. What do you think? A hint of erotic nights. The possibility of love in the arms of a stranger?"

"Or a spray," Alan added, "to clear your sinuses."

"Why would it say," Rooster asked, "don't eat anything? That's just odd. And don't seek medical treatment. That's dangerous."

Sanger stared at them. "I don't care what it does. It's not ours. It belongs to Uncle Bill and I want to get rid of it as soon as possible."

"It's got to be worth something," Em said, as patient as she had ever been with Sanger. "Your Uncle Bill wouldn't send it if it wasn't worth something."

"That's right," Alan agreed. "It's got to be worth something."

"Maybe it's just an advertising ploy," Rooster said. "Look at that box. Weird. They just want to draw people in. Shitty perfume in a shitty box, someone will buy it. It's just lies. I'm tired of being lied to. It's just a gimmick. The company doesn't know whether it's got something worthwhile and you're their guinea pigs. Then you use it and imagine something. But nothing happens even though you think your cold went away twelve percent faster or your teeth are a shade whiter. So you report your good news and they shape a new product with a big sales campaign for something that doesn't do shit. Probably won't end up with anything more than a new and improved box, which it surely needs."

"Yow!" Alan said. "Don't be shy about sharing your opinion." Still, not wanting to be the lab rat of some unknown manufacturer, Alan stepped away from the atomizer as it sat on a side table.

The Beyond Now Device

~ ~ ~

June 7, Minneapolis

Later that evening Em showed Rooster the kitchen and pointed out where things were kept. Alan lay on the couch reading. Sanger pushed the trunk against a wall to get it out of the way. He was the most cautious of the four but his curiosity had been piqued, regardless of the warning not to seek medical attention while using it. He stepped to the end table and fingered the atomizer's box.

"It's clearly meant to spray something," he said, even though no one was listening. After pulling it out of the box, he added, "Look, there's a cap on the nozzle. Remove cap; that should have been part of the instructions." But perhaps Rooster was right. Whoever made this had something up their sleeve, soliciting free trials for their money-making scent.

Holding the atomizer waist high and at arm's length, he looked once more at Alan who was reading and absently scratching his foot. Em and Rooster stared into the open refrigerator. *How good or bad could it smell?* He uncapped the nozzle and squeezed the bulb. A small cloud of dry mist floated up. In it he saw the top of a roiling thunderstorm with tiny sparks of lightning in the nebula of miniscule granules. *What the…* He leaned closer and the first particles entered his nose. He blinked and looked up toward…

*

…the car's interior ceiling. Sanger felt the low thud of rain on the roof, a deluge that might have included hail. He was in the passenger seat while Uncle Bill sat behind the wheel. Sanger slid a hand over the car's leather interior. Uncle Bill noticed and said, "Ain't she a beaut? 1931 Auburn 8-98A."

Sanger looked over the dashboard and saw the vivid blue of a digital display. July 01. 10:06 AM. "There's a digital clock in here. Nineteen thirty-one?"

"So it's a replica. Borrowed it from that buddy I mentioned. Nice though, right? But you've got to get going. I'd wait but I've got places to be."

Sanger didn't know what Bill was talking about, neither who the mentioned buddy was nor why he had to get out in the rain. They were parked as one among many in a line of cars along the curb. The rain continued pelting the hood as Sanger watched through the nearly vertical windshield. "Can't I wait until this lets up?"

"Gotta go now," Bill said. "There's the bank, back there. I'm expected somewhere else."

Half a block behind them was the National Trust bank and Sanger realized that's where he was supposed to go.

As Sanger opened the door, Bill added, "Don't forget this," handing Sanger the envelope that rested in the open glove compartment.

Sanger wore a light spring jacket. He slipped the envelope inside and turned up his collar. With one last glance at Uncle Bill, Sanger stepped out of the car. He held the envelope to his ribs with his right forearm but within a few puddle-splashing steps, and certainly by the time he stepped through the bank's revolving door, Sanger was soaked. He traipsed with squeaking steps across the cathedral-like expanse to a wide staircase.

The ground floor was open to the roof and the second floor ringed it like a balcony. Overhead, the large Plexiglas cupola thundered with the downpour of rain and was as loud as two trains speeding past. Once up the stairs, he stepped to the wooden railing and looked down. His thin spring jacket hadn't kept the envelope dry.

The Beyond Now Device

Sanger circled the balcony once and didn't find the name that was written on the envelope. Hugh Gardner. Unsure exactly why he was there, confused about the unfamiliar name on the envelope, he felt sure he was in the right place and would deliver the envelope. Standing along the balcony, Sanger looked down and saw a man pacing the lower level, shoulders wet, one shoe untied, and a gait similar to a child taking stairs slightly too large for him. He avoided the kiosks of information, the islands of withdrawal and deposit slips, and addressed no one in particular. But with one arm in the air, he said, "What the fuck. This close." He brought his thumb and forefinger together. "Can't trust anyone. No one will come through. What's another day when they've waited this long already? Bastards!"

Mesmerized, Sanger watched as the man shouted, "Fuck you," at the woman nearest him. The noise of the rain on the roof was deafening and the man's shouts were only heard by the few people near him.

Sanger stood behind a row of glass panels that connected the banister to the floor. The man dropped his arm and looked up to the level above him. When he saw Sanger, he stopped. They made eye contact for a second, and then another, until Sanger dropped his eyes and turned away.

With sidelong glances, Sanger watched the man who was no longer screaming but still muttering to himself. At that moment a security guard appeared at the top of the stairs. As the officer used both hands to pull his gun from its holster, the man at the bottom waved his arms forward in a dismissive gesture. He walked backwards, continuing his wave-like display of arms. Near the revolving door he grabbed a woman by her neck and pulled her to his chest. The security guard screamed and hurried down the stairs. Sanger saw a shiny flash, metal, a knife or small gun near the woman's neck, he wasn't sure. The guard ran across the wide bank floor. Customers who hadn't heard the noise were surprised by the commotion.

The crazed man, now with hostage, backed through the revolving door and to the street, disappearing from Sanger's view through the gray rain. The guard soon followed.

Startled by these events, Sanger stood at the balcony's railing for a few minutes. Then he pulled the envelope from his jacket. He read the addressee again. It was his own script, heavy block lettering. There was no return address and no postage. At first this meant nothing to him, and then with a realization, he couldn't catch his breath. He stared at the envelope, both sides, and knew something important was about to change hands, something he was offering, releasing with a finality that froze him in place.

Thinking he should open it, and then thinking he shouldn't, Sanger just wanted to find the correct office door and slip it under. Or drop it on the floor right there and hope it found its way to the correct pair of hands.

Walking again around the balcony, Sanger saw the frosted glass panel of the correct office. *Specialized Loans* and a list of occupants. Sanger knocked and walked in. An attractive woman sat at the reception desk. "I have something for Hugh Gardner," Sanger said.

"Have a seat. I'll let him know."

Sanger twirled the envelope with his fingers, eventually touching all of it. On impulse, no longer wanting to wait, he rose and dropped the envelope on the desk. Turning, stepping toward the door, he heard the voice behind, "Here's Mr. Gardner now," as Sanger pushed through the door without looking back, and…

*

...stood in his living room, as the mist that had been squeezed out of the atomizer drifted to the floor.

Holy shit! Sanger thought as he returned the atomizer to the side table. He turned in a circle. Alan was still on the couch, his leg propped over his raised knee, scratching his foot. Em and Rooster continued to stand in front of the open refrigerator. Unable to help himself, he said to Em, "Why are you holding the fridge open so long. You're just letting all the cold out."

Em turned her head and gave Sanger a stern stare. "We just got here. What's your problem?"

"I...I don't know. Sorry." *They didn't notice me gone,* he thought. *It's like I wasn't. No time passed. A dream? I hallucinated it all.*

Sanger dropped into an overstuffed chair, exhaling an overstuffed breath. No one noticed. Did anything really happen? *Uncle Bill was there, but he's in Chicago; deliver an envelope; why would I hallucinate that?*

He considered telling Em and Alan of his experience. Perhaps he'd channeled a past kidnapping, something that happened years ago. Then he remembered the car, Uncle Bill's 1931 replica. *That's why it feels like the past,* he thought. *And it was an old bank, decorative. What happened to the grabbed woman? Maybe my vision is the needed lead to a cold case, some air bubble of history finally rising to the surface.*

Yet the clarity of perception. Maybe not a vision, but real. Either way, the police had records of crimes and his story might match one. The date of the crime was the first of July. Last year, the year before? It shouldn't be hard to search and find abductions at the National Trust. He wondered again if he had any momentous responsibility to tell the police. *Only if it matches a real crime.*

Within an hour, Sanger felt weak and oddly empty. A headache grew and then pounded. His breathing was shallow and rapid. He could barely tell the others how bad he felt. With both hands to one side of his face, Sanger indicated that he was going to bed. Em soon joined him and rested on pillows to read. Within minutes, Alan told Rooster that he, too, was going to read in his room.

~   ~   ~

Rooster couldn't believe how quickly everyone called it a day, wrapped things up, brushed their teeth, put their dishes in the sink, and scurried off. Practically orchestrated. These were not party people. She sat on the couch where she would eventually sleep. Looking at her phone that rested calmly in her palm, she decided not to turn it on. She wanted to call friends, well, friend, but didn't want to be located by modern telephone technology that she wasn't sure even existed. A sheet and a blanket were folded on the floor at her feet. There had been no more talk of staying or leaving or parents or police. She squirmed lower on the couch and casually reached between the cushions in search of coins: a quarter and a nickel. It just wasn't worth it. She put the two coins on a side table.

After spreading the sheet and blanket on the couch, Rooster angled toward the table where the atomizer rested. She approached it obliquely, as was her sensible approach to anything she didn't understand. If only she had always thought twice and watched her step. Still, she sensed there was something odd there, as her memory of the instruction sheet reminded her. She thought about smelling a squeeze and then slowly shook her head, prudent to be satisfied with a warm and soft space for sleep.

CHAPTER THREE

June 8, Minneapolis

The next day Alan picked up the atomizer and held the weighty reservoir sack in his palm. Sanger, Em, and Rooster watched. Alan didn't know why Sanger was pushing him to use it—Sanger certainly wouldn't if the mister was a tumbler and the pouch a bottle of whiskey.

Alan pressed the atomizer's uncapped nozzle point into the pad of his thumb. It marked him with an indented circle and an upraised center. He was curious what it will smell like. Alan didn't like the odor of perfume. Any sweet fragrance reminded him of the derangement he felt at the funeral parlor where his wife was displayed on lay-away, waiting for her ascension into heaven. He furrowed his brow as he brought the nozzle close to his face. His not drinking had been demanding, asking more of him now than at the beginning. He knew the pouch didn't contain alcohol but still wondered why Sanger wanted him to sniff it. "Why are you pushing me to use this thing?" he said.

"Just humor me. It doesn't hurt." Sanger paused and rethought all the ways something might hurt. "Listen, you'll be right back in a moment."

"Right back? What do you mean?"

"It's nothing, just a figure of speech. You'll see. You might even like it."

"I don't believe you," Alan said. "But let's say I try it, how does it work?"

"Hold the pouch, squeeze the bulb, and stick your nose in the mist that comes out the nozzle. And Em, you count to ten."

Alan held the atomizer high over his head and squeezed the bulb. He heard Em say, "One…two…" A small cloud of powder hovered above him. Alan saw the shape of a translucent cauliflower hanging in a hydroponic garden. Then he…

*

…stood before an elevator and read: Enter Floor Requested. He touched-in the number thirty-five. He didn't know how he knew what number to enter. It wasn't memory, it hadn't come to him as realization, nor did he pick that number from a set of possibilities. The display changed to: Proceed to Elevator C. Of the six elevator doors, C was behind him. Inside, there were no columns of floor buttons, only a display that already knew where he wanted to go. The ride up was swift as his weight pressed down on his soles, slightly spreading each foot wider. When the bell dinged and the elevator came to a quick stop, he was momentarily projected skyward, his soles ascending inside his shoes.

The doors slid open and he stepped out. To his left a large window overlooked the city of Minneapolis with its collection of old two- and three-story brick buildings surrounded by the growth spurt of tall glass towers. To his right a T, with corridors left and right. He followed the signage to thirty-five eighty, all the while knowing he had never been here before. The doors on each side of the corridor had gold numbers painted on their frosted glass windows. He stopped in front of thirty-five eighty. William Meyer, Attorney at Law, was inscribed on the door with frill and embellishment. Alan touched the flourish of print and a curlicue of paint came off on his finger. His as-yet-unseen companion materialized behind him and slipped a heavy object into the right pocket of his jacket. Uncle Bill patted Alan's shoulder and said, "Go ahead, Alan. You know what to do. When you're done, I'll see you back at the car."

Alan opened the door and saw an empty reception area. Behind and to the right was an inner office containing a large desk covered with hillocks and drifts of loose papers. The forced, conditioned air from floor ducts pushed wisps of breeze to the warrants, wills, and citations dangling over the desk's edge. In a moment Mr. Meyer came up from behind the desk holding the folder he retrieved from a bottom drawer.

"Oh," he said. "You Bill's messenger? Good. Everything's set. This here is," pointing to the other man, "eh, doesn't matter."

The other man, tall enough to rest an elbow on the top of a four-drawer filing cabinet, tapped the meat end of a baseball bat into his right palm. He said, "Did you bring Bill's forty thou?"

Alan didn't answer. He wanted to understand what was being said, where he was, and why. Confusion ruled and he believed a drink would settle his nerves. As he looked around, his thinking was captured by the window behind Mr. Meyer. A sliver of sunset rushed through the wooden Venetian blind, casting horizontal stripes across Alan's chest. Mr. Meyer's face was in darkness from this backlighting effect. On the desk was a day scheduler, upside down, and open. The print and handwriting was incomprehensible, like a foreign language, and Alan mumbled the title at the top of the page, "Oh eee, three you, en, tee". Raising one hand to his forehead, discovering sweat, Alan wiped those fingers across his chest like a third-base coach signaling a bunt.

William Meyer looked up. "Empty? What's that you say? Got nothing to say? Nothing's a bad word today. A valise, a briefcase. Something decidedly not nothing that has Bill's forty thousand dollars in it. I've got to show up-front capital, make my pitch, let them know I can handle their product. They're not the type to wait. Let's have it."

"I...I...I'm from Bill. But I don't know what you're talking about."

William Meyer looked at his bat-toting companion and said, "Get a load of this shithead. Stepped in the wrong door; needs directions to her beauty parlor." Then he turned back to Alan and added, "Why would Bill send you if you don't know what I'm talking about."

Mr. Meyer stood in one smooth motion, pushing his wheeled desk chair behind him with the backs of his knees. He was a large man around the center and his suit jacket was too small in the shoulders. "What are you? An idiot? Who'd come into this office without knowing what's going on? If Bill thinks I'm going to just send you out again, he's wrong." Mr. Meyer looked once again at his companion and with a flick of his head, signaled him to step toward Alan.

When Alan saw the baseball-bat guy take a step, his

stomach grew tight with fright. In past times of confusion he'd kept his mouth shut and shrunk away. This time, though, he remembered Rooster's audacious conclusion that they were being used as lab rats, pawns in a game in which they weren't really invested. Alan raised his left hand toward the bat-slinger and said, "I don't have Bill's money."

"Beat the crap out of him," William Meyer said.

Alan reached into his right coat pocket and his hand fit over the heavy object as if hand and gun were made for each other. *It's time to not do nothing,* he thought. *No more lingering over her death; no more disaster over losing my job.* He knew it was true. *Got to get on with it.* He felt an immense sense of satisfaction as he lifted the gun. His spine tightened as he stood larger— stronger—more decisive than ever before. He was suddenly absent of equivocation, understanding that doing something was always better than doing nothing, nothing being a deep hole impossible to climb out of.

"I do have something for you," he said. Then he pointed the revolver at Mr. William Meyer, shooting him twice in the chest.

Astonished by Mr. Meyer's surprised stare, Alan watched him fall forward over the desk. Alan's skin tingled, like a thousand miniature bees stinging his face. He wiped his nose and saw red on the pad of his finger. A uniform pattern of blood-spray also coated Alan's glasses. He took them off but they were slippery and squirted from his fingers, sliding under William Meyer's desk.

He thought of Em and her enjoyment of their word game. He pointed the gun at the other man and said, "Two lead slugs, a dignified rhyme of accuracy and crime."

Alan turned toward the door and then back to the man with the baseball bat. "Get out of here. Beat it."

Alone in the office, not counting the corpse of William

Meyer, Alan lifted the desk phone and tapped in 9-1-1. He was ready for all of this to come to a conclusion. Shaking, voice cracking, he told the police he had killed a man in the Capella Tower and has set a hostage free. He said he had other hostages and will be waiting at the main entrance, ready to negotiate. He didn't understand why he told the police these things. He imagined only one outcome if he stepped onto the street with a gun.

As if in a stupor, Alan took the elevator to the ground floor. Police cars lined the street, colorful lights as if looking down a fair's midway. More cars arrived, sirens and more lights. After a deep breath, he pushed the door open and raised his gun toward the sky as officers crouched behind their cars. He heard harsh voices commanding him to…but he didn't make out what they were saying. The world slowed. The shouts of the police sounded like groans and their movements took forever. Alan, without aiming, shook the revolver toward the police. More voices…he shook the gun again…and then he saw a bullet emerge from a marksman's rifle, traveling directly toward his head. He knew it would hit him even before he heard the explosive crack of gunpowder. He understood this all at once and reached with his left hand to block the bullet, unable to relinquish one last attempt to change the course he had set.

He heard a moist sludge, reminding him of grape jelly dropped to the floor, but assumed it was the bullet penetrating his skull…

*

…as he let the atomizer drop from his hand. He heard Em say, "…three…four…" as the pouch landed with a thud on the hardwood floor.

Stunned, Alan wrung his hands as Em said, "…five—"

"Shut up," he interrupted. "That's not funny. Crap."

Alan dropped into an upholstered chair. As the experience rushed back, he kicked the atomizer away and said, "I killed him, I just…" Alan pointed his hand toward the wall, like a gun. "Two to the heart."

Sanger reached and put an arm over Alan's shoulder.

"Uncle Bill gave me a gun," Alan added. "I kept thinking that doing something was better than nothing, so I shot him. Blood sprayed everywhere, got all over me. I can't believe I killed him."

Sanger asked, "Uncle Bill? You killed Uncle Bill?"

"No. William Meyer, Attorney at Law, frosted glass, thirty-fifth floor."

"When, Alan? When did you do that?"

"Just now. Not now. Just before now. A moment ago. And a guy with a baseball bat was there." Alan pressed his face into his palms.

Em twisted around so her face was close to Alan's. "It was just a dream, Alan. Some crazy imagination, that's all. It couldn't have happened. You've only been here."

Alan mumbled, "Forty thou. He thought I was bringing Bill's money."

"Bill's money?" Em asked.

"I sent the guy with the baseball bat out then called the police to turn myself in. No. That's not right. I called the police so they'd shoot me when I stepped out. And I did. And I pointed the gun at them. And they did. I saw the bullet coming at my head."

"Whoa," Sanger said. "Back up. You were in an attorney's office?"

"Yes. I don't know why. Well, yes I do. I was to deliver Bill's money. But I didn't have it. It was like a dream. I just did stuff and didn't know why." Alan looked to the ceiling and added, "Oh eee, three you, en, tee. I saw it in his day planner, Russian or something. But I saw it. Oh eee, three you, en, tee. Do you think it means something?"

"Maybe a license plate?" Sanger suggested.

"Maybe. I saw William Meyer and the guy with a baseball bat. Then the police were out there when I went down."

Em brought a pen from her pocket and pulled one of her drawings close. She turned it over and said to Alan, "Write it down. That oh eee thing."

Alan wrote block letters on paper. OE 3uпt.

Across from Alan, reading it upside down, Sanger recognized it. "Oh my God, June 30. That's the day before the date I saw."

"You saw?" Em asked.

"I used the device yesterday and had a pretty weird experience." He opened his palms toward Em. "Uncle Bill took me to a bank. Don't you think that's odd? That we'd both have Uncle Bill in our experience."

Rooster, still sitting on the floor, took the paper from Alan's hand and held it upside down, right-side up, and upside down again. "Cool," she said.

Sanger added, "I was at the National Trust bank and watched an angry guy complaining about bank policy. Then he scooped up a woman and dragged her out of the bank. Maybe with a weapon. I don't know why I was there. Oh, sure I do. I delivered a letter to…to…Hugh Gardner, a banker. But I think I saw a crime from the past. Clairvoyance, crystal gazing, hindsight."

"And you think," Em asked, "that Alan also saw a crime from the past, watched someone other than himself shoot this lawyer guy? Or do you think Alan really killed someone in the past and the memory of it is surfacing now?"

"It's something the police will be able to corroborate; if

the lawyer's name is someone already dead. And if so, Alan might know who did it."

"No, no, no," Em chided. "Alan said he killed someone and you want to tell the police? They'll think you're both crazy. One type of crazy if the guy's not dead. And another type if he is."

"Okay, well maybe not tell the police. Not yet. I see what you mean. We'll make the best of it." Sanger looked at Alan. "Together, Alan. You'll see."

Alan, feeling the first waves of nausea, nodded. In the next moment a spiking headache pierced his skull. He leaned forward with his chest on his knees and let his hands fall to the floor.

"Alan said he killed a man," Em repeated. "Then he wanted the cops to kill him. Why would he hallucinate that? There's no best of it to be made."

"No," Sanger replied. "He never said that. That's not what he meant. Maybe he's confused." Sanger paused, torn between the excitement of their stories slightly matching and trepidation for the one Alan expressed. "No," Sanger mumbled. "Alan wouldn't do that. Not kill someone. And he wouldn't want to be killed by the police. No. But don't you think Alan and I are having similar experiences? Bill taking us around, maybe even telling us what to do? Don't you think that much is true?"

~ ~ ~

Rooster squirmed at the ideas. *Suicide by cop? Da?* She looked down and privately rolled her eyes. *Then Sanger,* she thought, *won't believe it, says it never happened. It's just a drug. Can't they see it? I've probably done more drugs than them combined. Sanger with his short strict hair, button down shirt, he's probably never imagined what the mind can create. The truth of the matter, brain matter. Surprised how*

real it seems. Da! He says it never happened. But got to believe yourself.
Even when he swears. Don't ever come in my room again. And he says,
'what?' Like he doesn't know what I'm talking about. Pig. Asks what
I'm talking about. Says it never happened, I must be imagining it. Tells me
it's my wish, a fantasy. Like I fantasize about him! And he's whispering,
that breathy hot hissing, 'I think you like it. You sure are ready. Check
yourself out.' Like shit I am. Never want to be ready for you. 'Never
happened, Hen.' Don't call me that. 'You worry like a mother hen. Ease
up, enjoy life. Your mom knows how, take it easy. Here, Hen, have
another toke.' Asshole. It never happened! And mom believes him. I just
want—

"Rooster," Em said, waving a hand in front of her face. "Rooster, look at me. You're going to pull your bangs right out of your head. Are you okay? What's going on?"

Rooster blinked a few times. "I'm okay. Yeah. It's a…I mean…it's a drug. Sounds just like a drug trip. Sanger and Alan hallucinated the whole thing."

"But you're all right?" Em asked.

"Yeah, sure. Never better."

CHAPTER FOUR

Same day, Minneapolis

Over the next several hours Sanger walked near the mister, touched it, stepped away, and was short with anyone who asked what he was doing. He found something intriguing about his previous experience. And hearing of Alan's episode piqued his interest even more. By evening he was impatient with the pull and push of his own attraction and reticence. Finally he picked it up and without announcement squeezed the bulb, ejecting a cloud of mist that hung before him. The spherical collection of particles coalesced into a framework of geodesic dimension. Wanting a closer look, Sanger leaned forward, letting the first grains enter his nose, as his eyes…

*

…burned from the thick car exhaust on that humid evening in downtown Minneapolis. Sanger was in his own car and adjusted the fedora on his head as he made a right turn onto South Sixth Street. He knew the fedora was Uncle Bill's and wondered how he got it. Stopping in front of the Capella Tower, he killed the engine, stared, and waited in the 'Deliveries Only' lane without knowing why, scanning for clues through the drizzle-filled air. The city had pools of bright neon lights reflected in the wet street. Rainclouds absorbed the tops of buildings taller than twenty-five stories and through his rear-view mirror Sanger saw a sliver of sunset stretching between buildings across the western horizon. The bobble-head compass and clock on his dashboard said June 30, 8:55 PM.

Sanger rested his chin on the steering wheel, acutely aware of wasting this precious moment. Before using the atomizer a second time, he had told himself to explore, pin down the year, bring something back from his unique experience. He stretched his neck to look at the sky and then it hit him. *Step up, wave my hand, prevent an abduction. I should've used my skull, called out to clear the door.* It seemed simple. And if he ever returned to that time and place he felt sure he could make a noise, holler, warn the customers.

But this wasn't there and it wasn't then. Sanger looked at the clock on his dashboard again. June thirtieth; the day before he witnessed the abduction while delivering a letter. If his current hallucination was in the same year, which made the most sense, he was remembering an incident that happened tomorrow. Shaking his head, Sanger swung his legs out of the car and stopped with his foot over a puddle. The reflection of the bottom of his shoe caught his attention and the unusual moment struck him, his foot looming large from that unique perspective.

Looking to his left, he saw Alan emerge from the Capella Tower. As Alan burst through the door and ran, his long plastic raincoat splayed behind him. He stopped abruptly at the passenger door of the car but didn't open it. Instead he turned back toward the door out of which he came.

Sanger then saw Uncle Bill rounding the corner of the building at full speed. Bill grabbed the handle of the back door and jumped in. He said, "Gotta go, boys. Gotta get a move on."

Sanger depressed the clutch, turned the key, and started the car. "Open the door, Alan." Sanger leaned to open it for him, lifting his foot off the clutch and stalling the engine.

Looking again at Alan, Sanger said, "You've got red paint sprayed on your shirt and face. What've you been doing? Is that blood?"

"No time for dawdling," Uncle Bill said. "We need to get out of here."

As Alan jumped in the front seat, Sanger saw a man burst through the doors of the building. He held a baseball bat in one of his churning arms. As he ran, the bat lurched forward and back like the wheels' connecting rod of a steam locomotive.

When the man reached the car, he let the bat slide so the handle's knob slap-stopped on the meat of his palm. Raising it over his head, he looked for a moment like a lefty at home plate waiting for a strike. Then he swung, reaching for an imaginary pitch, high and outside. The windshield in front of Sanger didn't break but dented with a mosaic of tight cracks radiating from the point of contact.

Sanger started the car but couldn't get it in gear. The man's second swing punched a small hole through the windshield from which glistening shards of glass fell on Sanger's knees and to the carpeting of the car's interior.

Sanger engaged first gear and they jerked away from the curb into traffic. He made a guttural sound of relief and then said to Bill, "Shit, who was that guy?"

The sky opened and a deluge of rain dropped. The wipers were faulty, jerking up just an inch and then flopping back down. Sanger couldn't see through the lucent reflections of neon in the windshield's dense web of cracks. When he leaned his head out of the driver's window, the fedora lifted from his head in the breeze as they picked up speed. He reached for it with his left hand but was too late. Looking back through the side-view mirror, he saw the hat land in a puddle, and farther back, the man with the baseball bat standing in the middle of the street.

Sanger turned back to the interior of the car and said to Bill, "What was that all about?"

"Plenty of time to talk later. Keep your eyes on the road."

Disappointed in the loss of the hat and frightened by the memory of the bat crashing into the windshield, Sanger raised one hand as if reaching to lower the driver's-side visor and…

*

…realized he was back in his apartment, feeling like a daydreaming fourth-grader pointing at an incomprehensible math problem on the blackboard.

Sanger heard the others speaking, just as before, and was surprised at returning to the exact time he left—interrupted by a dream-like, automotive experience. Sanger caught Em's eye and said, "That was odd. I mean, really odd. I sniffed the atomizer. How long have I been standing here?" Sanger was disoriented, but smiling. His eyes shimmered with the recent excitement of driving Uncle Bill's getaway car. Only the returning memory of blood on Alan's face tempered his exhilaration.

"What do you mean?" Em asked.

"How long have I been standing here?"

"Only a moment. You picked up the atomizer. Put it back down. Nothing more."

"It happened again. I hallucinated. Or dreamed. Or vividly imagined."

"Hallucinated?" Em asked. "Is that what you're calling it?"

"I don't know. Maybe."

Rooster sat up straighter. "Hallucinated like sparkling colors and seeing a mountain village in a bowl of cottage cheese? Or like snarling wolves ready to attack you?"

"No, more like a dream, maybe like a dream. I was totally there. I don't know."

"A dream," Rooster asked, "like being—"

"I don't know," Sanger's harsh words pushed Rooster back. After a pause, he added, "Em, come sit with me."

As he pulled Em to the couch, Alan dragged a chair close and Rooster slid across the floor. Sanger told his tale of torrents of rain, Alan running, the security guard churning down the stairs, and the guy with the baseball bat. Even as it rolled out of his mouth he realized he was comingling his two experiences.

Sanger spread it out before them and noticed his arms aching as they motioned his explanation. He was reluctant to mention the blood on Alan and the attorney he must have killed. Unsure how to…then a headache crawled up his neck.

Murder took up too much space in Sanger's mind. Poetic moments. Somewhere a gun was fired, a bullet pushed, a heart pierced, and blood made aerosol. Every time Sanger followed that trail, he believed Alan had pulled the trigger to initiate the particle propulsion that pierced the flimsy skin and sturdy bone, erupting the heart, and leaving it beating no longer. Bursting to spray Alan with blood.

Alan said he had killed on the thirtieth of June. And Sanger had watched a wild man abduct a woman in the bank on the first of July. Yet he'd seen the July episode first and then learned of Alan's later, even though it really happened the day before.

Confused, the headache behind his eyes worsening, Sanger reminded himself that he hadn't seen Alan kill anyone, only believed it because Alan had said so. He knew his cousin was a troubled man. That's why he'd taken him in two years earlier. But who knew when Alan's murder might have happened, or how long Alan has kept this secret. Hiding a murder could eat someone from the inside; denying it could make anyone feel like a fraud. Perhaps Alan's hallucination of the crime was a sign he was ready to talk about it, confess to a priest, or let it out with a counselor? Alan taking his turmoil to a therapist might put him on the road to a new start. Something could be done. Blocked content rising like spring shoots…take ownership of his actions…confess to the crime…forgive himself. *The police weren't the answer*, Sanger thought. *Family was. We'll handle this together.*

Then he ran to the bathroom and threw up.

~ ~ ~

Alan leaned back on an upholstered couch, his arms outstretched, crucifixion-like. He thought of his own scene in William Meyer's office. Quick images returned out of order and he strained to follow. Details escaped him. Other man, maiming man, bat tap to palm slap. He tried to run his spool of memory like a reel of film but was unable to find the beginning or keep the scenes from leapfrogging. William Meyer, his wish consisted…of riches for pitches or stitches in britches or twitches of fishes? *Killed him dead*, Alan thought. *Face itched from stinging bee kisses. Never right, took a life, offered mine to a marksman's plight. Something's wrong. Explosion of gun, expecting a stun. And then a moment of blankness, less than a moment, a sliver of no-time to find myself exactly where I'd left.* Dizzying.

~ ~ ~

Rooster watched Alan without let-up as he slumped deep into the couch. Sitting on the living room floor, arms resting on her knees, she expected one of them to break out of character, laugh, and admit this was all a ruse, just trying to yank her chain. Their denial of Alan's experience. No. Killed someone? No. Couldn't have, wouldn't have. Wanting to die? Never happened. She thought they were crazy, all of them, looney. If it was a drug, couldn't be a very good one. *Who'd pay money*, she thought, *for a drug you take on one step and have the high over before the next step? It's got to be a dream or a drug to enhance dreams. A drug to exaggerate dreams inside an active imagination.*

Rooster was sure if they offered her some, she'd say no. On her list of lessons learned was never to take drugs with strangers. She'd learned it so many times that she didn't want to learn it again. But she suspected they won't offer. Contributing to the delinquency of a minor by pushing sandwiches was a lot different than offering drugs. She wondered what it was like, though. Sanger came back smiling and excited. But Alan must've had a bad trip.

Scratching the top of her head, Rooster speculated that it might not be dream or hallucination. *Maybe a daydream*. She remembered times in class of putting her head down and daydreaming of sunny weather, fields of tall grass undulating like the sea, and a world just waiting for her to enter. But it had been a long time since happy-go-lucky daydreaming. A year? Two? Since she started hanging with Smitty and his friends?

Now when she put her head down, she relived how things ought to have been, regretting a word spoken here, an objection not voiced there, the way she would have boldly launched that stinging retort, for sure. How had things gotten so bad? She knew fixating on what had already happened wasn't daydreaming. She wanted a word for conversing with someone who wasn't really here, for composing a text never to be sent. Those thoughts were like living in the past, but not really a memory. Like imagining a different past without any expectation of changing it.

She suspected Em was nice and she and Sanger together had to be an item. She glanced at Alan on the couch. Brooding? Why was he so troubled about killing someone only in his imagination? So troubled he'd want the police to execute him? Rooster wanted to kill someone and felt only the frustration of knowing she couldn't. One side of her brain said, *go talk to Alan.* The other side said, *no. Go ahead—no. He might like to talk about it—so what? Just ask him—no, I don't want to talk to anyone. I don't want to be here.*

She realized she thought too quickly, knew she had no place to go, which made this place okay, better even than a lot of other places.

Rooster got up and sat on the couch with Alan. Not too close but not hanging over the far arm of the sofa either. "You're a lot older than Sanger. How can he be your cousin?"

"What?" Alan said. "Oh. My grandfather had four kids. My father was the first born and Sanger's father was next but not for quite a few years. Then Bill. Our Aunt Rose is the youngest."

"Bill's the one in Chicago who sent the trunk and the atomizer?"

"Yeah." Alan smiled. "But the way we say it, Bill's the one who left. I was about ten or so when Uncle Bill left, all of a sudden, big to-do, a lot of heads together whispering. That was months before Sanger was even born. Bill comes back now and then, a lot more now than then. I hardly ever saw him through my teenage years."

"Is he nice? I mean, an okay guy?"

"I don't know." Alan paused to think. "I really don't know him. You'll have to ask Sanger. Whenever Bill was in town, he doted on Sanger. Took him to ball games, the zoo, movies. Let him hang around when he met with his cronies in backrooms and toasted deals over handshakes and shots of whiskey."

Alan leaned back and let out a weak laugh. "I don't think about Uncle Bill much. He used to have a thing for Sanger's mother. I overheard talk about it plenty of times. Drove Sanger's dad crazy. Bill's always been a…a character. Sanger told me he smoked his first weed with Uncle Bill. Do you kids still call it weed?"

"You can call it anything and people know what you mean. Doobie, joint, vegetables, hey you wanna smoke some shit? Who'd ever say yes to that unless they knew what you meant?"

They were quiet for a minute until Rooster said, "Your family sounds nice. All those people around. My dad came to Minnesota from some place in California. Bought a farm. Who'd want a farm in Cold Country after growing up in California? But he had to go and die. Then my mom married that dipstick, my stepdad."

Rooster rubbed her face and bit one of her nails. "My mom came here from Oklahoma. She has family down there. I've heard some names of aunts and cousins but I've never met them. All my grandparents are dead." She reached for her bangs and then put her hand back in her lap as she added, "I'd like to be a bright-faced sunflower in a huge field of other sunflowers."

~ ~ ~

Em sat in the kitchen that evening with the others. They each had a muffin and a cup of coffee. Em stared at Sanger. He was a nice, stable guy and she appreciated him like a faithful dog. Not as a faithful dog appreciated its master but more how the master appreciated the dog. He was steady and solid and stumbled through any situation with determination.

But there were elements of his and Alan's slipping away that weren't adding up. Sanger said hallucination, relaying what it felt like to him. Alan clearly didn't have time to shoot someone, he wasn't gone for even a moment. It was so out of Alan's character that Em was tempted to dismiss it. Yet Alan's depression over the last few months was obvious to her, even if he and Sanger never mentioned it. Was this a crime Alan had committed long ago, now filling him with remorse? A man who'd already committed a crime might grow depressed. Or a depressed man might commit a crime in order to die by police barrage. Which was it? Depressed first and then a suicide wish? Or crime first and then depths of depression?

"Sanger," she said, "what do we know about these experiences? We know you went to the National Trust bank one day. And then the next day you and Alan both went to the Capella Tower downtown."

"Actually," Sanger said, "when I went to the bank it was the first of July. Then when I went to the Capella Tower it was a day earlier, the thirtieth of June."

"I'm not sure any of that matters. I've been thinking of—"

"I want to look up that lawyer," Alan interrupted. "I'll do it now."

"And do a search for abduction at the National Trust," Sanger suggested.

Em ate her muffin and remembered times of drug use when she forgot the events preceding sleep and then woke to a future she hadn't known was coming. How often upon waking had she asked herself, 'Where am I?' And then a seedling of thought struck her. Each night people passed through time without effort. Carried by time to wake in a future they didn't see coming. *Could it be*, she thought, *that time travel is—*"

"That lawyer's not dead," Alan said as he returned. "And I didn't find anything about abduction at your bank. But get this. The attorney had an office in one of the suburbs. Then he moved downtown this year. March. Look." Alan held the laptop so the display faced Em and Sanger.

Em made an exaggerated motion of scratching her head. She pointed to Sanger and said, "You saw July first as the date you were at the bank." She pointed to Alan and added, "You saw June thirtieth as the date you shot William Meyer. How can that be? This isn't something that happened in the past. Not last June or any time before. William Meyer wouldn't be on the thirty-fifth floor of his new downtown office."

Sanger looked at her. "No. What are you saying?"

"Just that—"

Sanger's phone rang. He commonly left it for anyone to use since Em and Alan had their plans terminated. He suspected it was Uncle Bill. He should have called the same day they'd picked up the package when it would have been easier to simply say, 'Yep, we got the trunk.' Sanger wanted to let it ring, have Bill leave a message. He held a hand up to Em, stopping her from answering it, even though he knew she wasn't intending to.

Pushing caution aside, Sanger waited through a suspenseful number of rings until he finally pressed a button to answer the call. Touching the speaker button, he held his breath while Uncle Bill's voice burst forth.

"Hey Sanger, sorry I didn't call sooner but I got…hell, it doesn't matter. So, you've got the package. Like I said before, don't open it. It's not interesting, just some old clothing I'm delivering from Guy A to Guy B. They're both forking over some cash for the service. Sweet. You'll get a cut and I'll get it off your hands as soon as possible. Don't worry. But, um, you picked it up, right?"

"Yes," Sanger answered too quickly. "I said I would, didn't I?"

"Hey, why so testy? Picking up a package and taking it home isn't the favor of the century. I mean, I could've asked you to deliver it to Denver."

"No, no, you're right. The trunk's pushed against the wall in my living room."

"Behind a couch, I hope." Bill made a chortling sound, indicating laughter. "So, good. You haven't opened it, have you?"

Sanger paused and looked at the others before saying, "No, of course not. You said not to."

"You had to think of that answer, didn't you? If you can't tell the truth, keep your mouth shut. Anyway, yeah, good. And about not opening it, it's just because it's locked and I don't want the lock broken."

"No, that's okay. It wasn't locked."

"Shit."

Sanger waited in silence until Bill said, "I'll be out to your place in a couple of days, a week at the most. I'll take the package then. This is great of you, Sanger. Considering everything, you're great."

And then Bill ended the call.

~ ~ ~

After a few minutes of silence, Em tilted her head, weighing different options, stalling a moment longer. Finally she said, "I've been thinking, not thoroughly but listen. Everything happens in time. There's stuff in the past, stuff in the future, and stuff right now. Your experiences didn't happen now. We all saw you go nowhere, do nothing, and come back with an experience. But it didn't happen now. So, if it didn't happen now, then what you experienced was in the past or in the future."

"Why not an hallucination?" Rooster asked.

Sanger wiped his face and said, "It felt like the past. Uncle Bill's 1931 car seemed old. I'm assuming we're going back to an old crime and channeling it."

Em paused and stared at Sanger. She thought he'd be happier with a jaunt to the past. But she suspected it wasn't that way. "The car was a replica," she said. "Alan didn't find any old abduction reports during his internet search. And the lawyer, William Meyer, he's not dead. If it was in the past, he'd be dead by now."

"Yeah," Sanger said, scratching his head.

"I don't think," Em continued, "that travel to the past is possible. It's the wrong direction than everything else. And it's terribly dangerous. If Alan went to the past and killed that guy, whole limbs of the family tree would disappear."

"Not if he's remembering having done it in the past," Rooster said. "And his memory is now surfacing."

"No," Em said. "The attorney's not dead. It hasn't happened. We've been thinking that Sanger and Alan traveled to the past and saw some old event. Something they feel destined to change. But no. Travel to the past is just plain crazy. We'd never be able to depend on what's now. Sudden surprises would pop up everywhere because some yahoo we don't know changed past events that we weren't privy to. Today's world would be a very crazy place if travel to the past was possible."

Rooster raised her hand and said, "I've heard that travel to the past is possible but it's really hard to change anything."

"I don't know," Em touched her forehead. "If we could go to the past and change anything, no matter how minor, we'd have seen evidence of it by now. No, without a durable past we'd never know anything for sure about now, never be able to trust that what we knew yesterday will still be around today."

Sanger rubbed the back of his neck. "So if it didn't happen now…and I get that, I understand. And if travel to the past isn't possible because, if it were, we'd never have a secure present. Then we're left with, ah, I don't believe you."

"It makes sense. We're constantly going in that direction anyway." Em took Sanger's hand and added, "Let it sink in. Roll it around your brain. Why not travel to the future? Like they say, it's only a matter of time before we're all there."

"And changing things in the future?" Rooster asked.

"I suppose we could," Em said. "Change things that haven't happened yet. If the future is set in stone, then we'd only be changing things to what they're eventually going to be. And if it's not predetermined, then we're changing things that might not happen that way anyway. Sounds safe."

"And the idea," Sanger asked, "that no time transpired in our experiences. I had a vivid experience that seemed to take ten, fifteen, twenty minutes but no equivalent time took place here. What's that mean?"

Em took a deep breath and sulked for a moment. "No," she said slowly. "No, that makes sense, too. Why should time transpire? That now, the now in the future, hasn't happened yet. Why should it take up time in our time if it hasn't yet happened? It's not going to take up time twice: once in the future when it happens for real, and again now when you're future-projected to it. So you spent time in the future but it really shouldn't take any time up now, here. You see?"

Sanger smiled as he said, "Maybe we could take advantage

of this. See coming trends in advance, predict earthquakes. Em, we're sitting on a gold mine." Sanger stood. "Pictures. That's it. I need to take some pictures. And newspapers, I've got to bring back the sports section and—"

"Sanger," Em said, "you're forgetting something. In the future, you see an abduction. And what else? Deliver a letter. And the day before that Alan kills someone, just before offering himself up to be killed. We don't want any of that to really happen."

"No, of course. Of course you're right. That's our first priority."

The four silently exchanged glances. Em touched Sanger's hand and said, "We've got to call the number on this thing's instruction sheet, find out what this atomizer is all about."

"Sure. Yes. Okay." Sanger stood and went into the living room. Em followed with his phone and Rooster and Alan followed her. They sat around a coffee table with the phone staring back at them.

Sanger reached for the instruction sheet and touched in the numbers. They each heard the ringing and eventually a male voice said, "Yes, yes. What do you want?"

CHAPTER FIVE

June 9, Chicago

Niko Talek sat in a leather club chair at his local public library. He stared at the book in his lap. His own use of the Beyond Now device had filled him with uncertainty, vacillating between a future that already existed and was waiting for him to fill the footprints he'll eventually leave in the sand, and an open future where all his imaginings held equal chance of arriving.

Since being fired from the university, he had waited through a dismal winter and a wet spring. After leaving his Beyond Now devices around the city he'd heard nothing about any of them. Had not even one been found? If found, had they been tossed in the garbage? Had they been repackaged and re-gifted without the treatise on time he'd tucked in each box?

Returning to the book in his lap, he began again reading the first act of the play. Just as before, Niko missed a word here and there. He retraced the preceding paragraphs to recollect the meaning and tone of the dialogue. But within minutes, mind adrift, full soliloquies went unabsorbed. Before he knew it he was deep into act three, having missed the trail of action that brought him there. He let the book fall closed and realized the epiphany of what he'd just done. It was exactly as he had experienced it. Using the Beyond Now device was as if an actor fell asleep in act one and reawakened in the middle of act three. Confused, for sure. Lost, perhaps. But someone on stage knew what was happening. The other actors' cues, their dialogue, their actions swirling around him would provide the clues he needed to fit into whatever timeframe. Act three was already in the making as act one commenced.

This would be obvious when well-meaning people unwittingly used his device. Niko needn't help those users grasp the content of their future experiences—a thankless task since the possibilities were endless. He could only help them understand the true nature of time, just as understanding the elements of drama helped an actor fall asleep in act one, wake in act three, and continue to follow the story because the elements—conflict and climax and resolution—followed a motif set with the first words of the first act.

Niko took a deep sweet breath. Even as a professor he had never been a very good counselor, disliked office hours, and often closed his door during times when students expected him to be available. But understanding the true nature of time; that was right up his alley, something he'd been doing all his years of teaching.

He tapped the back cover of the book in his lap. When his

phone rang, Niko reached into his pocket, touch connected, and said, "Yes, yes. What do you want?"

"Ah. I'm putting my cell on speaker. There are four of us here." Sanger spoke although it would be a few minutes before Niko learned his name. "I don't know who I want to talk to. I got this number from the instruction sheet that came with—"

Stunned, excited, impatient, and suspicious, Niko said, "Please wait. I will transfer your call." Although it was only him, he had a burning desire for a steaming hot espresso, aromatic in a demitasse cup, saucer, tiny spoon to—

Niko interrupted himself by noticing not an inch of movement in the other library patrons. Their stillness struck him as exactly right because Niko, waiting so long for this call, was just where he should be. 'Here' was his personal spatial location and 'now' was his personal temporal moment. Time was all around, like space, and Niko felt this moment as the opening of a future he richly coveted and deserved. Yet space and time soon lost their similarities. Here was right where he was. Here for a friend a thousand miles away was also where that friend stood. They both claimed 'here' without disrupting the other. One of them could even walk away from here, claim a new here, and return to the previous location and be here again.

Not so true with time. If Niko drifted away from now, his portal to success might close and he'd never return to this moment again. They were now on the other end of an invisible connection. He was now on this end. *Is it currently now everywhere?* he wondered. *Are all who inhale now doing it at the same time? Are all simultaneous events, far and near, happening now?* It seemed true. But Niko wasn't convinced. Use of his device demanded these questions. He rolled a hand before him, knowing these questions came more easily than answers, and he wondered if believing all simultaneous events happened at the same time was as self-centered as thinking he stood at the center of the solar system and all heavenly bodies swirled around him. It simply looked that way.

Niko returned his mind to the patrons, to the library, to the callers on the other end of his connection. Deep breath. With a cheerier voice he said, "Thank you for waiting. My name is Niko Talek. How can I help you?"

"My name is Sanger and I have Em here, and Alan and Rooster."

The four were silent for a moment until, "I'm Em. We have one of your products and we're not sure what it is…or what it does…or is supposed to do."

"Yes, yes," Niko said. "No matter. Where did you get it?"

"We didn't buy it," Sanger said. "We, ah, found it. But this phone number was on the instruction sheet."

Niko wanted to identify where he had left the device, thinking he would learn something about the recipients. "There's a number on the back of the box. What is it?"

"Okay, just a minute," Sanger said. "Number five."

The pool hall, Niko thought. His expectation was that those calling with device number five would be small-time hoodlums. But so far these people didn't sound—letting his bias show—slow or moronic. They sounded hesitant but articulate, educated. "Shit," Niko said, louder than he would have liked.

"What?"

"Nothing. Sorry. Okay. Have you used it yet?"

"Yes," Sanger said. "But we just want to know what it is. What's it supposed to do?"

Niko cleared his throat. "Give me your names. And where you are. Your number is in my phone now. Tell me and then we can speak of specifics."

Niko listened but heard no response. He continued. "The device is harmless. You're free to stop using it at any time. But first, what do you think it is? And then, I'll answer all of your questions."

Again there was no response over the phone. Finally the younger woman, Rooster, said, "You mean you've got a factory in the Midwest somewhere and you're cranking these things out but you still want us to tell you what it is?"

Niko rolled his eyes, acknowledging that he had approached this from the wrong direction. They were confused. He was tired and often distracted. But she was right.

"Yes, yes. It's like that," Niko said. "But please, I want to help. Start by telling me your names and address."

Niko heard some mumblings and a very faint, "Don't answer."

After another moment of silence, Niko said, "It's simply a formality. Record keeping. This way I'll follow-up with you and—"

The call died on the other end. Killed on purpose, Niko assumed. Definitely not suicide and unlikely an accident. *No matter*, he thought. *I'll return their call after I get home.*

~ ~ ~

They stared at the phone as Alan pulled his finger away from the End Call button. Rooster got up from the floor and said, "You guys can stop now. I didn't find it funny at first and I still don't find it funny now. Travel to the future? You must be kidding me. And that guy on the phone…where did you dig him up? I just don't know how you put this act together, unless you've lured others in before."

Alan waved for her attention. "No, we didn't lure you in. We had no idea you'd be downstairs when we got home with the trunk. Or that you'd move right in. I mean, need a place to stay. Don't get me wrong, you're welcome to stay."

"Thank you?" Rooster stared at Alan, wondering if he was as nice as he almost sounded.

"We're just trying," Alan added, "to figure out what happened when we used the atomizer."

"Get off," Rooster said. "You can't believe you're traveling in time. It's a drug. You hallucinated."

Sanger asked, "How do you explain that Alan shot someone and I saw the blood that was sprayed on him?"

Rooster leaned over the coffee table. "You listened to each other's stories and…it just can't be…you're not…no, it doesn't make sense."

Em waved a hand to get their attention. "Let's just for a moment pretend that it is travel to the future and Alan killed, will kill, then be killed. Then Sanger witnesses that abduction the next day. Let's think, just for fun. Is there something going on here we should worry about? And if so, what can we do about it?"

"Just don't do it," Rooster said. "Why are you thinking so hard? Don't go to that office building. Don't go to the bank."

Sanger said, "Rooster's on the right track. On that day we keep reminding Alan that he mustn't kill, mustn't hold hostages, and mustn't call the police on himself. He goes to the Capella Tower, supposedly with Uncle Bill, and makes sure not to kill anyone, hence no need to call the police."

"So you're saying," Em repeated, "we know what's going to happen. And when. We don't let it by just saying no."

"Right," Sanger nodded. "Then we take a trip and not come back until after my incident at the bank."

"After?" Em asked. "And you'd be okay with that? Don't you think delivering that letter is important? Weren't you going to try to scream and warn that woman by the door?"

Sanger hung his head. "Look, I was there once and didn't stop anything. And who knows what that letter's about? What makes you think I'll do any different on the real July first?"

"There's something missing here," Em said. "Not missing, inconsistent. You can't have it both ways—tell Alan he's able to control his future by just saying no, while you're uncommitted, incapable of doing anything different than what you've already done. Which is it?"

Sanger couldn't answer.

Em pressed on. "How is this playing out in your whole life? I know you see a future out there, a house on the lane and some toys on the lawn and a dog greeting you home? That's the future you want. Is it out there, as solid as rock, and it'll happen? Or do the decisions you make today tip the scale either toward or away from what you envision?"

Sanger wiped his face. "I'm frightened of going back to the bank. I don't want to go there again. I don't want to warn people and I don't want to be responsible for delivering that letter."

"You're missing a lot of what the future is made of," Em said. "The future is thousands of tiny steps leading to it. Threads."

Em patted Sanger on the knee and added, "Your experience as Uncle Bill's getaway driver started years ago with your devotion to family. You'd really like to be under Bill's wing, careening your car away from a crime, doing what he says."

Sanger shook his head. "No, no, no, I'm not Uncle Bill's stooge. I won't let that happen. I know what's going to happen. Uncle Bill would have to hold a gun to my head for me to go along with what he's got planned for Alan."

Em took a deep breath and let it out slowly. She thought Sanger could be so…narrow when it came to imagining possibilities. She exhaled again and said, "Or your uncle tells you a sob story about the trouble your mother is in. Then he tells you he knows just what to do to solve everything."

"Hmm, a good story might have me following him. But, Em, you're here. You won't let this happen."

Em got up and stepped to the side table where the atomizer patiently waited. Distracted, she said, "Maybe."

~ ~ ~

Em picked up the atomizer and held it in one palm. Curious, wanting to know what the hubbub was all about, she figured after listening to Alan's and Sanger's tales she'd be able to sniff the mister and keep her cool. She knew what it was, what it was supposed to do, not a chance she'd be blindsided the way Alan and Sanger were.

"Don't," Sanger said. "I think we've had enough of that thing."

"I think not. Just a tiny pinch."

Em squeezed the atomizer's bulb, similar to her caring fingers pinching the supple weave of cloth. She looked up at the emitted mist and saw a single bowling lane and a whirling ball of cotton speeding toward the pins. As she lifted her nose toward it and inhaled...

*

...she discovered herself walking along the side of a midtown building. With each step she felt the tight pinch of her skirt. Bill walked beside her in a dress shirt and tie, his suit coat hanging over one shoulder.

Glass reflected her image and she saw a silver barrette on the side of her head holding whips of hair that had already escaped her stern pony tail. Her skirt was black, above the knee, with a slit up one side to mid-thigh. In her hand was an envelope clutch purse. She saw herself as a no-nonsense business woman even though she regretted the tight dress that sharply accentuated her figure. *Not my preference, but...* she thought. In French heels she still wasn't as tall as Uncle Bill. After a few more sidelong glances, she liked what she saw.

They approached a massive revolving door and Em recognized this as the National Trust bank. When installed, the door was the largest of its kind, so delicately balanced that a child could push it with ease. As they walked she felt Bill's hand on the small of her back, not so much directing her as simply an act of reassurance.

"Don't you worry at all," Bill said. "You're just here as enticing decoration."

She wanted to be put off by his narrow view but, as she took one more look, it was true, she was enticing.

Reflections slid and glass flashed as they both half-circled through the revolving door. Inside, the ceiling was two stories high with a balcony rimming the oval-shaped room. The bank was old, built in the 1920s. A vast marble floor spread in front of her with mushroom-like writing stands receding in two neat rows. Customers gathered in clusters, while above, workers traipsed from one office to another along the balcony's railing. Armed guards fought boredom at each end.

Uncle Bill cupped one of Em's elbows and said, "I'm going to show a man our pictures. Keep your cool. I'll play along with him, even if he acts stupid and denies the whole thing. I'll let him believe what he wants, doesn't matter. Follow my lead. He'll be confused, won't know what's hitting him. Just don't get flustered."

Em sensed there were things to remember, items of orientation. Sanger's Uncle Bill was coming to town. No, already here? "What day is it?" she asked, groggy and uncertain. Although she knew where she was, she didn't know why or when.

Bill rubbed her back. "What day is it? Are you on drugs or something?"

Em scanned the walls and saw a calendar that displayed June 30, but no year was shown. She thought about last June thirtieth and realized she'd been living somewhere else then. And next June thirtieth was a few weeks away.

"Listen," Uncle Bill interrupted her thoughts. "My sister, Rose, was to come with me today but she couldn't make it. She'd twist this guy around until he couldn't rub two coins together." Bill let out a little laugh. "You two look enough alike, same size, dark hair. It won't be a problem. Just show him what's in your purse and say nothing more. I never intended for you to do this part." He looked around the bank lobby. "Here, here he comes. Just say what we've practiced." And then he added in a whisper, "You're a sweetheart for doing this. Just keep your goods in mind and look beautiful. We're in a bank, you know. Let your assets earn some interest."

They had an appointment with a specialized loan officer, Hugh Gardner. He approached the information desk and accompanied them up the wide staircase. Em was surprised by how young he was. He wore an expensive suit and filled it well. In the privacy of his office, he directed Em to sit in the chair to the side of his desk. She immediately understood that he will better see her when she crosses her legs.

Em knew what to do although had no memory or expectation. Her fingers tingled as elation rose from sweet rumblings in her center. Her chest grew warm. Pushing aside loose hair, Em made and kept eye contact with Mr. Gardner. She pressed her lightly painted lips together and knew more than ever that she was pretty and Mr. Gardner liked what he saw. The power she had over him astounded her and she smiled with the sense that the meal Uncle Bill offered had been cooked just right.

Mr. Gardner pushed aside papers, straightened his keyboard, touched his tie, and glanced at the bare skin showing above Em's knees. He said, "Miss…" and let his glance drop from her eyes all the way to her sturdy French heels. "I'm Hugh Gardner. And you are?"

Blush formed around the base of Em's neck. She touched her right clavicle with her left hand and said, "Just call me Em?"

"M, that's mysterious. What can I do for you and…?"

His bright smile led her to believe if she dropped a doo-dad—handkerchief, lipstick case—Mr. Gardner would jump out of himself to retrieve it. She looked at her knees and knew she was blushing. Intriguing heat or embarrassment over clothing she wouldn't ordinarily wear? "My uncle," Em stammered. "I have something to show you." She lifted her clutch from the floor and opened the triangular front flap. She pulled out a manila envelope and handed it to Mr. Gardner.

Em was impressed with the ease of Mr. Gardner's smile. He must have been her age, maybe a year or two older. She suspected he was expecting a form request, a notarized document, or any of a hundred contracts on which his working life floated. His smile faded, as too did Em's, when he understood what the large, glossy photographs showed.

Uncle Bill stood behind Em and said, "She's the picture of innocence, don't you think? Dress her up a little, slap on some lipstick—she's still just a magical image of innocence."

Mr. Gardner stuttered, "How? When? Shit. You people…"

Bill responded with, "It's all make-believe, nothing's as it seems. But I'll tell you, I've got a few underage girls who are willing to sign statements about you. No photos, but statements. These pictures are enough…she looks young, doesn't she? Take her out of this outfit, out of any outfit, and all your employer will see, all the judge will see, is she didn't deserve this."

"I never...never...underage girls? They're lying."

"Doesn't matter." Bill opened his arms, smiled, and said, "By the time you clear your name the damage will be done."

Em looked from Mr. Gardner's face to the photographs and back. She couldn't place ever having seen him before. But the photos? The woman in the pictures looked like her. Nausea rose in Em's throat as she believed she must have done what the photos showed. Reluctantly, she could live with that. But worse, she felt tricked and manipulated, highlighting every ugly thought she'd ever had of Sanger's uncle. Em wiped glistening sweat from her throat with the back of her fingers, giving a wet shine to her nails.

"Go now, Em," Uncle Bill said. "I've got forty thousand dollars' worth of loans to arrange with Mr. Gardner."

Em left the office and walked to the wide staircase. She passed office workers but barely noticed. At the top of the stairs she wasn't sure where she was, didn't know where to go. She didn't comprehend what just happened. Em wished she hadn't come, wished she'd never seen the pictures, didn't like what was now. Was that her, naked with Mr. Gardner? Had Uncle Bill tricked her? She hadn't seen Sanger's Uncle Bill in years. She swore then and there to discover for certain if she'd been used in this way by Bill.

At the top of the bank's staircase, Em sighed and stepped to the edge of the balcony. She grew slightly dizzy and placed her hand on the banister...

*

...as her legs became weak and she leaned on an end table in Sanger's living room. She let the atomizer fall from her hand. "I...I..." She looked around the room. "I don't feel so well."

CHAPTER SIX

June 9, Minneapolis, continues

Sanger watched her sniff the mist and then drop the atomizer. Nothing more. "What happened?" he asked.

"I hallucinated," Em said. "I was...Uncle Bill and I were...blackmailing a banker. June thirtieth. Damn him. He used me. I mean, naked pictures of me. He had them, me nuzzling up to the banker...together, naked. I'd never seen him before. Or done that with him. I didn't know him or remember him at all. So how could Bill have the photos?"

Sanger didn't want to believe it. Yet he secretly suspected she'd do it with anyone, on a lark, to satisfy a whim. He imagined a glimpse of her enthusiastic body skin to skin in the photos. At that moment he believed in both fate and destiny. Sickening bile climbed his throat as though the future Em experienced had both already happened and was sure to happen again. "I've been thinking," he said, "and this future thing sucks. It's just our belief it will happen that's going to make it happen."

"I don't know," Em said. "It felt so real. And coherent. It was a lot more," she moved her hands as if shaping the outside of a ball, "contained, self-fulfilled. What if it's like skipping a stone across water. The first touch of stone to water is now. Then we get a brief exposure to the future when the stone next touches water. But whatever happens during the skip is just a blank to us. I could have posed for those pictures in a future I haven't experienced yet."

Em furrowed her brow. She added, "But to think I had sex with the guy just so your uncle could blackmail him? Why would I do that?"

Sanger opened his mouth but no words came out. He, too, wondered why Em would do that. What would compel her to have sex with the banker and let photographs be taken? He opened his mouth once more and a single word came to mind—money. Instead he said, "I don't know. It doesn't have to be that way. You're the one saying the future has all these threads. We just need to make new threads. Or stay out of town the whole time my uncle is here."

Em rubbed her forehead with one hand. "It felt so real. He had pictures to prove it." She reached for one of Sanger's hands and added, "Why would I do that?"

Sanger knew better than to say it. But the word mixed with the bile of jealousy, rose up his throat, and crawled to the tip of his tongue. He couldn't help himself. "Money," he said, dropping his head and closing his eyes tight.

~ ~ ~

"Money!" Em pushed Sanger's hand away. "You don't really think I'd sleep with someone simply for the money, do you?"

Em immediately regretted letting her anger say it out loud. Of course he'd think she'd sleep with someone just for the money. He already thought she was having sex with him in exchange for rent. But Em had her own homegrown ideas about sex. She knew the intimacy she felt when she decided to open herself to another person's interest, curiosity, attention. And in return risked asking the questions usually too difficult to ask. *Have you ever been caught in an embarrassing lie? Have you acted and walked away deeply ashamed? Have you ever rescued someone?* She had watched men's public persona either evaporate or noticeably stiffen as they answered questions like those.

Her thoughts were interrupted as Sanger took her hand again. "What if a week earlier than your hallucination Uncle Bill offered you $6000 to sleep with the guy so he could later blackmail him? Let's say he had a convincing story about why doing it was a good thing. Maybe you agreed. Six thousand dollars is a lot of money. You'd probably move out, get your own second story apartment, listen to your own music in a window seat that overlooked an interesting street scene. And then rarely see me again. You've never expressed any reason to stay. Never."

"Oh Sanger."

In the silence that followed, Alan and Rooster mumbled to each other. Em was sorry they heard her and Sanger's resumption of their perpetual argument: Sanger's inability to trust her affection and her stubborn refusal to show him in a way he recognized.

Rooster asked Alan, "Don't you ever jump in and tell them how stupid they sound?"

"Nope," Alan answered.

Em suddenly wanted to cry as she realized the damage of their headstrong attitudes. *We should be talking about my whole future experience,* she wanted to say to Sanger. *How the date fits, what's the money all about, not just the part that disturbs you.* She knew she could easily share with him the anger she felt toward Uncle Bill. Yet to also tell him she felt attractive and her whole body blushed? No, it would only turn to focus on Sanger's reaction, how he felt, where he hurt.

"Listen," Sanger said. "By the time Uncle Bill takes you to the bank, you might've already moved into your new apartment. Once there, you may no longer care if Alan kills someone and then sets himself up as a target to be killed by the police. No longer like me enough to discourage my collusion with Uncle Bill."

"Oh Sanger. You're making things up. There's no six thousand dollars. I never said that. And I didn't see anything like it in my future exposure."

"You just haven't experienced it yet. But you might."

"Sanger, don't do this. This is the way the future is cemented. People say it first or think about it too much. I'm going to stick that gymnastic trick. I'm going to ace that test. I'm going to blow it. It's lost forever. Oh, boo-hoo, no one likes me."

Em's knees grew weak and she edged toward a chair. Nausea welled and she swallowed it back down as she added, "Sports experts say imagine an excellent performance. But the same is true for all those negative thoughts, too. And now you're doing it, imagining me having sex with that guy for $6000 and then moving out and never seeing you again. Is that the future you want?"

Sanger blinked. With a long exhale, he slowed himself. "Em, I like you a lot. I'm already committed to you. What's wrong with that? I'm here for you. And I never wanted a *quid pro quo* around sex and rent."

Em took her own deep breath. "I know, and I like you, too. You're smart and dependable. More generous than anyone I know. You think a lot, and care a lot, and I'm never afraid you're going to hurt me. Other than this...whatever it is...insecurity. You think I'd jump at a six thousand dollar ticket out, slamming the door as I leave. None of it's true. You're making it all up."

"Uncle Bill wouldn't do what you saw, those pictures, blackmail. I can't believe it of him. But you, who of us knows where you'll be in the next couple of months as the warmer weather arrives? Or what you'll feel about any of this? How can I trust you to be here, to help Alan not kill and be killed? I need...I can't live day by day. I want a guarantee of the future. I want to count on you and know I can."

Em paused and held Sanger's stare. She knew she didn't see Uncle Bill the way he did, hadn't had his family's influence color her life. She looked down to where she was touching his hand. Under a furrowed brow, she said, "None of us knows the future, I could promise you a lifetime, but we all know there's no guarantee in vows. A pledge like that just keeps us living as though nothing will change when we know a lot of things will change."

Em slid away from Sanger to get a better look at him. "I promise," she said. "I promise I'll stand beside you at the end of June to keep Alan from killing William Meyer. Okay? But right now I'm ready to call that help desk guy again. Niko whoever he is. I've got some questions."

Em took Sanger's phone and touched in the numbers. Her nausea remained and she didn't know if she could get through another conversation. She placed his cell on the table. As an afterthought she pressed the speaker button. Alan pulled up an upholstered chair and Rooster sat on its arm.

No answer. Eventually Em ended the call. "Wrong number?" she mused.

"It worked last time," Alan said.

Rooster looked at the phone's log and compared the number to the one previously dialed. The same. "Do you think it's been disconnected?"

"Since last time?" Alan challenged.

"Sanger did hang up on him," Rooster said. "Maybe that's how they roll. People say, 'Hang up on me and I'll never talk to you again,' don't they?"

Alan tapped the table. "It's a business. They make a product. There's got to be someone there. Call again."

Em remained quiet, seriously wondering what she would ask, or tell, or how she would explain her experience. Losing confidence about this call, wrapping her arms around her uneasy stomach, she touched in the numbers and waited while it rang.

~ ~ ~

June 9, Chicago

Niko stepped into his apartment, dropping three books by the door. His phone buzzed first and then chirped. He tapped the front of his clothing in an unnecessary gesture of identifying the correct pocket.

He sat and touched his cell. "Niko here. How can I help you?"

Rooster and Em were pleased to hear Niko's voice again; Sanger and Alan less so.

Em began slowly, "Niko, we've got a problem. We've used

the device and…I've used the device and saw myself do things, things I've done already, photos, things I wouldn't ordinarily do, but must have done." Em listened carefully but heard nothing. "Are you still there?"

"Of course. Yes."

"And that's just me," Em continued. "Alan used it and shot someone."

Rooster added, "And then wanted the cops to kill him."

"And Sanger," Em said, "witnessed a crime. In a bank!"

"Stop," Niko said. "Don't tell me of your experiences. Listen, if time is fabric, the future is the stretchiest and the past is the stiffest. If the past can shock and surprise, the future can horrify and sicken. When we see a disturbing event in the past, have no doubt that the future holds something worse."

Em leaned close to the phone. "You're scaring me. Some of us thought we were going to the past. Or the past was bubbling up out of history like dinosaur bones rising to the surface. But now we believe we're experiencing the future. You've got to tell us what's going on."

Niko paused, took a deep breath, and wondered how best to approach the truth about time. He said, "First things first. Do you believe the future exists?"

The four in Sanger's apartment looked at each other. Em said, "Sure it does. I mean, not yet. But soon. Is that what's really happening?"

"It's important how you believe," Niko said. "Is the future before you, fully stocked like a hotel refrigerator? Or is it out there as a translucent image, wispy and unfurnished, ready for a futon from your friend's basement to make it your own? Perhaps the future—"

"No," Em said. "It's got to be more like a stocked refrigerator. How else would everything get there? We don't carry our belongings into the future like every moment is moving day."

"Yes, that's so," Niko said.

"This is Alan talking. Are you saying the future already exists and is filled with the events that will inevitably come to pass?"

Sanger touched the phone. "That can't be right," he said. "We make choices, decisions. We shape the future we walk into. This moment retreats to the past as the future approaches."

"Approaches from where?" Niko asked. "Do you watch it approach out of a background that doesn't yet exist, out of thin air? Time is closer to walking in a dark tunnel with the flashlight pointed behind you."

Sanger groaned. "But what about the choices we make? Even if we're blind to what's coming, we still make choices."

"How do you know…oh, this is Em. How do you know, Sanger, that the choices we make aren't the choices we're destined to make?"

When no one on Em's end spoke, Niko said, "Choices…of course. Choices play a part. But perhaps not as much as some think. There are profoundly retarded people, and those with severe brain damage, and others in comas. They don't make choices the way we do, but they're still carried by the tides of time. Choices matter but—"

"The future," Em interrupted, "has a life of its own. Is that what you're saying? It doesn't depend on whether we participate or not."

"Yes…no. Listen," Niko said. "I want to tell you all you need in one magic moment. I want you to understand in a blinking epiphany. But learning isn't the same as appreciating a beautiful sunset. Understanding time is…like reading a poetic paragraph where the expression clings to your soul because you suddenly have words for your feelings. Knowing time is the dog-eared iconic paperback carried by a devoted student."

Niko paused for a response, then added, "Perhaps others read the same paragraph and have only inarticulate feelings, freeing them to appreciate the meaning through image, or smell, or the lightest touch of finger to cheek. Only by using both of these methods will time be understood properly."

"We just want to know," Sanger said, "how to avoid the things we've seen."

Niko cleared his throat. "That isn't for me to tell. It would do no good if I did. A First Event, the Big Bang or a wave of God's hand, set all things in motion. Then began predictions of the future life of stars and the motion of planets and where our moon will be on a certain date so an earthly craft can land on it. From the First Event, the entire dance of the universe was created, including the end of time.

"So, does the future already exist? Is time a real substance, like an earth-moving machine whose massiveness will swallow any wrench we dare throw into the gears? Could we predict the whereabouts of our moon accurately if the future didn't already exist? Is the time beyond now already out there, taking up space, while heavenly bodies run their inevitable courses?"

Niko waited for a response. "No matter," he continued, "I may ask the question but the nature of time isn't decided by popular vote. Some want a future that already exists, trusting the promise of prediction. Others a future that comes to exist with each step, believing we control coming events through the choices we make. And you, are you more comfortable with a future of divination and foresight? Or is your life richer by the uncharted territory of serendipity and chance? Those are the important questions when it comes to understanding time."

Niko hung up, quietly pressing the End Call button. He scratched his head, feeling the fatigue of speaking extemporaneously. He dropped onto his couch and slumped. Teaching the ins and outs of time over the phone was ridiculous. A full semester of basic assumptions was needed. Time was continuous, no gaps existed between this now and the next. Past and future and present constituted the entire spectrum of time. We traveled through time in only one direction. Now was filled with simultaneous events. When two non-simultaneous events occurred, one precedes the other. *Just look.* Niko imagined himself standing at his lectern before the rising rows of students in a lecture hall. *It all appears true. But none of it is. Don't be fooled. None of it is as it seems.*

As Niko's mind drifted, he leaned farther back and stared at the ceiling. But he did not see it. His open eyes filled with a past that came to life. A classroom full of students sat before him. His voice droned on. "The universe is a container for things and events. Space is the box in which things reside. Time is the carton in which events evolve. Long ago, before events surpassed things in our evaluation of reality, people lived in a thing-centric world. Their expression of things was easy; pointing to an object caught others' interest. Naming it brought the thing to mind. Thing-centric people assumed apples fell because it was in the nature of apples to fall. Apples decayed because it was the way of apples. One apple may decay more quickly than another, but this had nothing to do with time. If time existed at all for these thing-centric people, it was a property of the apple as it decayed. Time was seen as a part of things the same way we view water as a part of apple juice.

"When events became the primary source for understanding reality, people told stories around campfires of magnificent hunting trips. These stories carried no elements of time. They could have happened before, or they could have been what was in store for them tomorrow. The story possessed the magical element of letting the listeners believe it was happening now.

"Soon, though, they discovered the difficulty in describing

the slaying of a mammoth during a simultaneous thunderstorm while a fatal accident injured one of their party. Were these events connected? Was there rhyme or reason to be made of them? It would have been better to tell these incidents in separate stories. Language was a clumsy tool for retelling simultaneous events.

"Even though these people understood life as a perpetual moment, conveying their experiences through language demanded the separation of events into before and after. A thumb over the shoulder indicated then. Rolling a hand forward signaled later. One-after-another became the standard method to describe events. The world occurred in series. Time moved and flowed. And 'now', even the perpetual now, lost its magic, becoming a moment among many, a transitory instant between earlier and later."

When Niko returned to his present moment, he wondered how he would explain all of that to his telephone compadres. Does later emerge out of now? Does later pass through now to become then. *Does the future already exist?*

CHAPTER SEVEN

June 12, Minneapolis

A few mornings later, Alan ruminated over his murderous experience. Killing bothered him more than being killed. Yet even in the explosive moment of killing there was something satisfying about the power of the gun, something definite and decisive. He wished he had been so persistent in acknowledging his wife's problems, listened more gravely, and believed her exhausted foreboding of the ill will she saw over every horizon.

Alan stood under the arch that separated the kitchen from the living room. Rooster contemplated her darkened cellphone.

Sanger and Em were in their room. Stepping to the atomizer on the side table, Alan lifted it and placed it in the palm of his left hand. The early sun came through the east windows and Alan watched tiny sparkles of dust float in the air. A prism hung in the window, Em's contribution from her special box of favorite things, and split sunlight into its constituent parts. Alan momentarily caught the purity of blue as it struck his retina. *Only through a prism, blue's true hue.*

He was surprised that even for a moment he had drifted away from thoughts of the power residing in the atomizer. And if not that, then regret over the heinous way he had cast his wife aside. Not through affairs with other women or gambling their savings away, but by not taking her seriously and disregarding both the least and grandest of her concerns. He felt the atomizer's pliable reservoir sack in his palm, saw again William Meyer's heart burst, and was momentarily filled with satisfaction, reassured that he was capable of action and doing what needed to be done. In contrast, the memory of his wife was a never-ending smudge of impatience and shameful inaction too indelible to erase. He couldn't reconcile the two. He wanted forgiveness for his passive dawdling over his wife's concerns yet was still uneasy about his decisive execution of William Meyer. He thought of these images and knew he could have forced a better outcome with his wife. *Just like I killed William Meyer,* he thought, *I could have been there, listened, taken it as seriously as she. I could have.*

As Alan prepared to squeeze the bulb of the atomizer, he heard Sanger say, "Alan, let's not do the mister alone. I mean, let's have others in the room with us. A safety measure. And agree to talk about it afterwards"

Em, too, had stepped from the bedroom into the living room. "Are you sure?" she said.

"I can't stop thinking about it. I need to know more." Alan

squeezed the bulb, and as he reached through a cloudy shroud to replace the atomizer, he sniffed the mist…

*

…and his hand filled with the cool metal of a door knob. He turned it, pushed the door open and saw, through the empty reception area, William Meyer sitting behind his office desk.

"What can I do for you?" Mr. Meyer called, raising an eye and continuing to finger through a stack of papers.

Alan said nothing. He looked to the left and saw a bank of chest-high filing cabinets with leaning towers of papers atop. Above, an overhead fan twirled listlessly, regularly blocking the ceiling's reflection of the low setting sun. His eyes received light, shadow, light, shadow and his mind slid toward a winding mountain road, hairpin curves, and his brakes unable to slow the car as he pumped them with shadow and light.

"Come out with it, I don't have all day. I'm expecting someone."

Without thought or understanding, Alan said, "Uncle Bill's without ill-will. Still, if needed, I'm able to kill."

"What?" William Meyer raised his head. "You Bill's nephew?"

Alan nodded.

"Good. Everything's all set. Did you bring the money? Where's Bill's forty thousand dollars?"

With control just out of reach, Alan said, "Bill will give, but he needs an alternative. It's a dilemma for him to borrow, maybe tomorrow."

Mr. Meyer leaned forward on his elbows. "What are you saying? What's this rhyming crap? Give it to me straight."

Alan stood still, knowing Mr. Meyer expected Bill's message some other way. But Alan just wanted everything to slow down. He said, "Bill's got no intention to hinder, just wants you to reconsider."

"Reconsider what?"

Alan was mute. What lay ahead seemed clear but he wanted events to pan out differently. His wife's voice spoke through a veil of depression, *'You don't understand? There's a big difference between unable and unwilling.'* Mr. Meyer was insistent. Alan craved a simple instruction. *What do you mean? Tell me how.* Confusing this future experience with past situations, Alan spoke to his wife by addressing William Meyer, "I'm doing my best. Can't we give all else a rest?"

Alan covered his mouth and coughed, desperate to slow this speeding car from crashing. His wife had grown tired and he, angry. Then he added to William Meyer, "No money from Bill, so hold the shrill. I'm serious."

"Serious?" William Meyer leaned on his hands as if he would stand. "What's the matter with you? Rhyming imbecile. Tell Bill now or never. Today. I need his money today. Look at the time. I've got to orchestrate things. Tell Bill plans've been made. There's no backing out. You got all that? Now get out of here."

"Give me some credit for as hard as I've tried. I'm not being sleazy, it hasn't been easy." Alan's wife never believed the pale, inauthentic ring of his plea. Alan pulled the gun out of his pocket and held it near his thigh.

"Yeah, yeah...whoa, whoa." Mr. Meyer said when he saw it.

As if it was the only thing Alan knew, he said, "Bill's got no intention to betray, just can't borrow today. Maybe tomorrow, okay?"

"Sure, I understand. Just put the gun away. Nobody's got to get hurt."

Alan raised the gun and pointed it at Mr. Meyer's desk.

Mr. Meyer stopped stone still. Yet his words rushed out a

little too rapidly. "I get you now, I understand. But listen, it's not as simple as that. There's a chain of events leading to today and will pass right through into tomorrow and next week. You understand? I can't just stop the conveyor belt. I need all the money now, not just promises of getting it soon."

"Why can't you believe me. There's no money now. Don't furrow my brow."

Mr. Meyer raised his hands in a frustrated display of palms. "Holy crap. Where did Bill get you? I need to talk with someone who can tell me what's going on, not some rhyming lunatic."

Alan raised the gun higher. He pointed it at Mr. Meyer's chest. "Would it be so hard to believe I'm serious? No, not so hard. Not even mysterious."

"How can I take you seriously? I don't even know—"

"Bang, bang. Gun rang," Alan said as he pulled the trigger twice. "Bullets sprang, didn't mean to harangue, but you should have—"

Alan was interrupted by the mist of blood that exploded from Mr. Meyer's chest. The blood stopped in midflight, leaving miniscule specks of red hanging motionless in the air. The drifting motes reminded Alan of home and the dust particles in his living room. The smell of gunpowder stung his nostrils. Mr. Meyer fell forward onto his desk and Alan backed toward the door. He looked at the gun in his hand and then tossed it toward William Meyer. The effort was weak and the gun hit the floor in front of the desk. Alan squatted to reach for it and in his haste knocked his glasses off. They dropped to the floor and skittered under William Meyer's desk. Alan stepped backwards, wanting out of the reddest room he'd ever seen. Losing his balance, he reached…

*

…and caught himself on the side table as he replaced the atomizer. His current moment felt expansive while the remembered experience shrank to the size of a pebble, BB, grain of sand. "Literally hideous," Alan said. "Mysteriously vicious, satisfyingly delirious." He lowered his head and added, "She only wanted me to know how serious."

"Alan?" Em asked as she stepped into the living room.

"I killed him for a dime. What a crime. I can't believe I talked in rhyme the whole entire time."

Rooster raised her head and furrowed her brow, suddenly wanting to pay attention to others in the room.

"Oh no, Alan." Em said. "What happened? Did Uncle Bill want you to kill him?"

"No. Negotiate. Bill's money's not steady, should've had it already. Bill's in a pinch and his deal can't be cinched. He's trying to borrow, thinks maybe tomorrow." Alan wagged his head so hard his lips flapped. "I want to stop rhyming. Why can't I stop rhyming? William Meyer thought I was an idiot. I just couldn't get past my own thoughts of…my mind was fixed, it was she who needed to change, not me, I couldn't hear her…him. Hers was no way to live. She had to see the tailspin I was in. And still wouldn't see it my way. He see it, I mean him."

Em opened her mouth but no words came out. Then she said, "So you killed him? Made him see? Her see? See what?"

What? Rooster thought. *What's he talking about?*

Alan stared at Em as pain behind his eyes spread to his temples. "Oh hell."

Then he walked to the couch, nearly sitting on Rooster's legs as he plopped down. He hid his face in his hands and mumbled. "Oh God, just like with my wife. They were both talking about things I couldn't understand. I should've listened longer. Asked more questions. Put a hand on her shoulder. I feel like I'm going to be sick."

Alan felt jiggling on the couch. Rooster looked at him and asked, "Because your wife finally divorced you or something, ran off with the computer repairman?"

Alan's auricles tightened from helix to lobe as he heard the sudden absence of sound in the room. He knew Sanger or Em wouldn't mention the truth, knew it was his to speak or hide.

"What?" Rooster said, breaking the silence that hung electric among them.

Alan lifted his head and said to Rooster, "My wife killed herself. And I didn't do anything to stop her. I got tired of her complaining, her inability to enjoy the things we used to enjoy. I quit listening, no longer asked her any questions. I gave up. There was a time I thought I could help, but you need some success to grind on. Eventually I wouldn't hear her, refused to understand her. Just like me today with William Meyer. I kept coming back to the idea that the money's not ready. He wouldn't hear me. So I shot him. Given a few more minutes I probably would've called the police again. Let them do me in. Or just do myself in." Alan paused and took a deep breath. "Maybe next time."

"No, Alan," Sanger said. "You did everything you could. Your wife was depressed, had been for years. You're being too hard on yourself."

Alan twisted his lips. "You don't know, you weren't there, didn't see how we were."

Sanger patted Alan's shoulder and said, "You're a good guy. I'm sure you did all you could. Everybody blames themselves after a suicide."

Alan listed to his left as Rooster bounced up straight from the couch and said, "Sanger, why won't you listen to him? Why are you telling him it didn't happen? I'm going crazy listening to you spew that mush."

Alan got up, nodded to them all, and went to his bedroom.

Sanger gave Rooster a sharp look.

Em said, "What do you think Alan meant by 'maybe next time'?"

Sanger tapped the table, thinking of Rooster, but saying to Em, "He just needs some time alone. He's not in good shape, hasn't been since...that's why he came to live with me."

"Should someone talk with him?" Em asked.

Still angry at Rooster's ridicule, Sanger said to Em, "What do you know? You don't know. What do you know about family? You've got no one and you think you can understand what Alan needs."

Em dropped her head and said, "Sanger, I'm sorry."

Sanger stabbed a finger to the table and then spat words. "Who have you ever taken care of? Not even yourself half the time. Damn it, he's opened himself for police target practice. And he's killed twice now."

"Technically, killed only once," Em said, "only one person. And technically-technically, he's never even done that yet."

"Oh, Em, what world have you dropped out of? Say it any way you want, but he's experienced killing twice. He's progressing toward homicide. Or suicide."

Out of the silence that hung over the table, Rooster said, "Don't you think maybe someone ought to be in there with him? Instead of out here arguing about it."

"Shit." Sanger stood and looked at Em and Rooster. "Shit."

~ ~ ~

After Sanger left the room, Em looked at Rooster and gave her a weak smile. "Sanger can be," she said, "a little slow to see the big picture. But he's nice and kind and wants to do the right thing. From what I know, Sanger will never kick you out. Stay or leave, the decision will be yours. He took me in. He took Alan in. He doesn't think about it. He's just like that."

"Good, I guess." Rooster paused. "No, that's good. But you don't really think you guys are traveling to the future, do you? I mean, come on."

"The word 'traveling' makes it hard to imagine what I think. I've been trying to think through it. When we travel, we actually go somewhere. Travel is a place-oriented term. But time might stretch and shrink like an accordion."

Rooster rolled her eyes. "I'll listen but I don't buy it. I see three people hallucinating and returning with a story. And the story you've got may mix and match but it's because you know each other. Now I've been dirtied with the story so if I do the atomizer I'd probably go to where you guys have described."

Em nodded. "I see what you mean. Once we've shared what we experienced, it's hard to get a clean assessment. But listen to this for a moment. Now is when we all exist. Now lasts about, say, a second. But now could be half that or half that or half that again. Different kinds of races time events to the thousandths of a second. Our idea of when now is can be made infinitely small."

Rooster looked back and said, "You're saying we could have had a thousand nows in the last second. But who can deal with that? Who wants to break up their day that way?"

"You're already doing it. Blood flow, brain activity. But not consciously. And I'm less interested in the very short now. I'm interested in making now longer. If we can think of now as either one second or one thousandth of a second why can't we think of now as a day and by extension, a thousand days? Why can't now be two to three years long?"

"And if we could, you're thinking we could see into the future?"

Em leaned forward and said, "I don't know. I think now

overlaps the last moment of the past and the first moment of the future. Now doesn't only touch the past, it's got to extend a little into the future also. Now overlaps that moment when the future becomes the past."

Rooster rubbed her forehead and said, "That's beyond me. Maybe you're right but it's hard for me to—"

Sanger's return with Alan in tow interrupted Em's and Rooster's discussion. As they sat, Alan said, "Sanger doesn't want me to be alone. So now I want something to eat."

~ ~ ~

With the clatter of Em and Alan preparing food behind her, and Sanger motionless across the table, Rooster thought about what Em had said. Now was tricky. She rubbed the tip of her thumb over the nick in her ring finger's nail. *They're going to make food now,* she thought. *They're making food now. They just now made this superb food.* Rooster assumed each of these nows extended over a different length of time. How was that true? She pulled her lower lip. *The past is stretchy, yesterday or last year or all of time since the first Fender guitar. And the future is variable; in a moment, give me a sec, just wait. Is now like a monumental taffy-pull?*

Rooster furrowed her brow. But generally she thought now was momentary. *By the time I even think it, that now is passed. If now's made smaller and smaller until the most immediate past butts heads with the nearest edge of the future…there's no time at all between the past and the future? Can that be?*

If now is as short as that, she thought, *then everything I do is either already done or not yet started.* Still, Rooster knew that during doing she was neither in the past nor in the future. She was in that peculiar spot called now.

Yet if now took any length of time, then it was flexible rather than rigid. A disturbing thought lingered in the back of her mind: *what if now's got no standard length? What if it's an un-spanning moment between what happened and what will happen? What if all of my time with these people is wedged between getting away from my step-father and whatever I do next? What if now is simply the time it takes for me to move on?*

Rooster scratched the top of her head and said, "Em, maybe you're right. Now has got to span a period of time. If it does, then it's got to be contractible and expandable. If we stretch now to include the next three weeks, will you guys experience it all just like it's happening now?"

As Rooster stretched her mind to encompass the next three weeks, she wondered if she might still be experiencing the previous three weeks. Might her stepdad still be coming to her room? Was there equilibrium so that as far as she stretched time into the future, she also had to endure an equivalent amount of the past?

~   ~   ~

Later in the afternoon, Alan only peripherally recognized the passage of time, and only sporadically at that. Rectangles of sunlight didn't crawl across the kitchen floor but rather were in one spot one moment and jumped to another spot when Alan next raised his head. He didn't actually detect their movement, but they had moved, like his wife's slow descent into depression, jolting him aware only when her stony gaze broke through his unwillingness to notice.

He sat at the kitchen table with Em and Sanger and Rooster. He was only vaguely listening as they talked about now and then, this and that, here and far. He was clear with himself; he wasn't inclined to think that his personal beliefs about time, or space, had any relevance in reality. It mattered not what he believed about the thickness of now, whether it was paper thin or wafer thin or as thick as toast. How could his beliefs influence the reality of time? It was out of his hands. Time was the way it was, no matter what he thought.

He had no jurisdiction over the flow, flux, flight, lapse, or unraveling of time; had no control over killing William Meyer; had even less sway over the suicide of his wife; and destiny's closing remark might be a police bullet to his skull. As a lackey to the ravages of time's forward march, Alan felt helpless. And worse. The feeling was familiar, this absence of prerogative, without choice but to kill, unable to speak other than in rhyme. He was incapable of understanding what his wife needed, and even when he could, he was inept at providing it. Without authority over the unfolding of the future, how could he hold himself responsible for any of it? Yet he did, and it nauseated him.

Alan raised his head to hear Em say, "Maybe it's something about us, the secrets in our pasts. That's the experience we get with the mister."

"You mean the future is emerging out of us?" Sanger asked.

"Whoa, you guys," Rooster said. "First you talk about the future as streaming toward us, something big and fast coming our way. Then you talk about it as though we're the ones walking toward it without any choice but to enter the future with each step we take. Now you think it's coming out of us, that the future is shaped by the content of my past. Which is it?"

Em closed her eyes. When she opened them, she said, "You're right. We need a good picture of our relationship to the future. But isn't it true that all we've done has led us to this moment, now? And if we're all agreed that we're experiencing the future—"

"Not me," Rooster chimed in.

"Okay," Em said. "You're right again, and our voting on it won't make it true or not. But we've got an ability to interpret these future experiences. What if instead of some random future, we're transported to a future that we need to experience, something that comes right out of our past?"

Alan groaned and dropped his head back into his folded arms. "Need to experience?" he asked. "What is this, some kind of therapy device?"

"I needed to experience," Sanger asked, "being Uncle Bill's getaway driver?"

Alan pointed at Sanger and laughed. "For as long as I can remember you've wanted to be noticed by the family, seen as a stand-up guy who'd do as much for them as you think they'd do for you."

"Yeah," Sanger said. "So?"

Em shrugged and added, "Look at it. Sanger, you liked the thrill of it. Maybe you need the taste of it in your not-yet-actualized march into the future. Maybe now that you've sampled it, you'll have more information to make a judgment."

"That makes sense for you, Sanger." Alan turned from Sanger and said to Rooster, "You should try it." And then addressed Sanger once again, "Makes sense for you."

Rooster shook the table with both hands and addressed Alan. "I don't think I want to try it. But I will, if you tell me why you got so teary-eyed over imagining killing William Meyer." She paused half a beat then added, "And how your wife fits into it all."

"Well, don't hold your breath," Alan said. "It's not easy for me to get a clear picture."

Em spoke up, pressing Sanger one more time, "Don't you think? That it has something to do with us?"

"Yes," Sanger nodded. "Sure. Maybe. I did like the feeling of driving a getaway car."

Em smiled. "Well then, I've got a confession to make."

CHAPTER EIGHT

June 12, Minneapolis

Em stalled by looking at the table and then reaching to touch the salt shaker. "My experience," she started slowly, "confused me, brought up a lot of emotion that left me uncomfortable. My body reacted and I felt things I'd only felt on drugs. I'd like to go back, learn more about the experience, explore my feelings."

Em knew this would be hard for Sanger. She watched him hesitate as he tapped the table a couple of times before saying, "What do you mean, explore your feelings?"

"You came back," Em said, "and said you felt exhilarated."

Sanger nodded, but only reluctantly. "I said that," he answered. "Behind the wheel. That guy with the baseball bat. It was exhilarating."

Em took one of Sanger's hands. "In my experience, in the bank with the manager...I was dressed nice and I looked nice. I felt sexy. Oh, not just how I was dressed but the way the bank manager looked at me. He'd've been willing right there to...it caused a little turmoil inside me. My feelings surprised me and offended me and intrigued me. Now I'm curious. I want to know more."

Sanger pulled his hand from Em's and stared at the table. "I think you're pretty and sexy and I like having sex with you. I never thought you wanted to be leered at like that. I thought you thought it was crass."

Rooster made a T with one palm over the fingertips of her other hand. "Too much information, guys," she said.

Alan stood and took Rooster's arm. He said, "Come in the other room with me."

"Just kidding," she responded. "I want to stay here."

"Come on," Alan said.

Chairs scraped the floor and feet padded away, leaving Em and Sanger alone in the kitchen. She thought of what Sanger had said: pretty, sexy, leered at, thinking it's crass. "I do," she said, "think it's crass. Did...do. I can't help it. I don't want to have my kitten purr every time a guy looks at me with starvation in his eyes. It's just that—"

"You got turned on by him?" Sanger slumped and covered his face with one hand. "Okay. Sure. That happens. But you want to do it again? Where does this all lead?"

"It wasn't like that. It wasn't him. I felt sexy and it was okay. It was nice. I felt glowing and alive."

Em knew offering her tentative feelings before they were ready for presentation was risky. Sanger could jump to conclusions long before she had explained herself. Looking at Sanger's face, she thought it was already too late. Wanting to extricate herself from this discussion before it turned into a debate, she said, "I'm going to put some water on. Do you want a cup of tea?"

Em stepped to the sink and held the kettle under the tap. She felt Sanger slide behind her and press his chest to her back, his hips to her buttocks.

She twisted at the waist, saying, "Oh Sanger, cut it out. I just want to watch water boil, be alone for a minute."

"I'll watch, too."

Em felt his eyes on her and knew she hadn't been completely honest. Revealing sexual feelings involving another man, even if he was a stranger with whom she had only one-sided contact, even if he was part of a future she might never experience, wasn't all of it. There was more, about Sanger. Their relationship was good, sex was good, companionship was good, everything was...Em pursed her lips and said nearly aloud, just good.

She knew Sanger was attentive without grudge and patient without irritability. She could depend on him without surprise. In their monochromatic existence, even having his down-and-out cousin around added a degree of color and interest. Her experience with Uncle Bill and the bank manager had shown her that she missed startling revelation. In the quiet of the kitchen, waiting for water to boil, Em had a sudden longing for spontaneity. And maybe a good fight to clear the air.

~ ~ ~

In the living room, Alan sat on the couch with Rooster. He looked around, stretched his arms, and rested his hands on his knees.

"So?" Rooster said.

"So? What?"

"Are you going to tell me? I didn't mean what I said about your wife. I didn't know she killed herself. But I want you to tell me about it. Didn't you say you would?"

Alan scratched his head. "Did I? I don't think so. Maybe you should sniff the atomizer." Alan pointed. "It's over there."

"Tell me anyway. I'll sniff it after you tell me."

"Hmm." Alan sat up and turned a quarter toward her. "Has anyone ever called you galling?"

"I don't know what that means."

"Pesky, irksome, vexing. Annoying."

"Oh, maybe sometimes. But I know what you're doing. You're changing the subject so you don't have to tell me."

Alan rubbed his mouth back and forth with one hand. "I've never felt in control of my life. Ever since I can remember, everything has swirled around me and I've just been swept up by it. My wife got depressed. I should have seen it sooner. By the time I did, I didn't like it. Then I did what I do with things I don't like, I avoided it."

Alan stopped, looked at Rooster, and expected her to say something. When she didn't, he added, "It's not like I didn't want to help her, not at first. It's more like it didn't cross my mind. I didn't try, didn't put myself out, didn't pursue other avenues like Partners of Depression support groups. I just continued to be me, work-a-day, bought a house, considered children, washed dishes, mowed the lawn. Nothing out of the ordinary, except there *was* something out of the ordinary. We talked like any other couple but she kept a lot from me, probably what was most important, she kept from me."

Alan paused. Rooster waited and then broke the silence with, "She's got to take some responsibility, don't you think?"

Alan chuckled a false laugh. "Sure. But she's dead and I'm

still here. I've tried, but there's very little satisfaction in blaming the dead. They won't take their fair share, won't apologize, won't offer a hand in comfort."

Rooster burrowed a hand beneath one of his. Before he could lift it away, she said, "You need something to hold on to. Not my hand, but something…you need a conclusion."

Alan closed his eyes. That was easy, he knew what it was, had been, and will always be. As he pulled his hand from hers, he said, "I have never felt in control of my life. That's my conclusion."

~ ~ ~

Only in the past year had Rooster considered that lives might be in control or out of control. Since she first dyed her hair and got a smart phone, she'd felt her life grow more and more out of control, even as her grasp had grown increasingly desperate. She believed running away from home was the act of a girl at the helm of her destiny. But fending for herself was difficult, people were not always nice, and she longed for a pint of ice cream softened by a burst of microwave.

She said to Alan, "Well, I guess I should open my nostrils for some rockin' mist."

"No," he said. "You don't have to do that. I was only kidding."

"I think I should. Like I'll live up to my side of the deal, be responsible, build up your trust in girls again."

Alan smiled. "Okay, but let's get the others out here. Sanger, Em," he called, "Rooster's going to sniff the mister."

Sanger and Em stared at Rooster as they came into the living room.

Stepping toward the side table, Rooster said, "I don't think I'll go where you guys went. In the same story and all. Uncle Bill doesn't know me, how could I be in his story?"

"I'm not sure you're getting how this works," Em said. "If Uncle Bill meets you any time before the end of June, you could be woven in to whatever's going on."

"Yeah but I'm doing the mister now."

Em sighed. "But you'll be transported to the end of June."

Rooster picked up the atomizer. "Maybe. But I don't see why." She held the pouch in one hand and gave the bulb a healthy squeeze. As the mist rose from the nozzle, its shape coalesced into a megaphone with a man screaming through one end and smoke rings of sound drifting out the other. Just as her face entered one of the rings...

*

...she turned in the living room. No one was there. It was dark with only street lamps illuminating the ceiling. A thick summery-hot breeze came through open windows. She plucked at the sleeveless sun blouse clinging to her sweaty skin. Across the room, a digital clock displayed July 01. 01:23.

A trapezoid of cold moonlight shone before Alan's bedroom door like a bright welcome mat. The door was ajar. Of course it was, she wanted him to be expecting her, hoped he was hoping for her.

She stepped through and saw him on his back, alone on the bed, one arm tucked behind his head, and the other across his naked chest, coyly hiding his breasts. She saw a tiny flutter of his closed eyelids and knew he knew she was coming. She wanted him to anticipate her, absorb her insistent presence into his quiet acceptance.

Sitting on the edge of his bed, she placed a hand lightly over his femur. She felt a slight movement of his leg, a faint spreading of his thighs. "I know you're awake," she said.

"I can't hear you."

"You're awake," she said a little louder.

"Yes."

Of course yes, what other answer was there? Comfortable? Yes. Sleepy? Yes. Ready? Yes.

Rooster leaned forward, her hair tickling his chest and her breath in his ear. "I'm so tense."

"Talk to my other side. I can't hear in this ear."

She leaned across his chest, lips nearly touching his. "I'm so tense."

"Running away from home," Alan said. "Away from friends, away from school. It's a big change."

"I don't mean any of that. I mean tension. Like in my muscles. I'm growing so tall I don't think my skin will stretch enough."

She sat up and lifted her blouse over her head. "I need some relief."

Alan raised a palm between them. "Rooster, no, don't. I don't want—"

She pulled the sheet from his waist—"Let's have a look"—dropping it at his knees. "Look at that. It doesn't look like you don't want this."

"Really, don't, you're only fifteen."

Rooster leaned, her lips at his ear again. "It'll be all right," she cooed. "Just relax. I'll do everything. You'll enjoy it." She hummed for a moment, touching his face. Then she added, "I think you want it. Look how you are down there." She reached and made a callous pinch of the skin over his right clavicle.

"Ow!"

"You still feel it," she said, "don't you? Lingering after-feel, that's what we want. Put your mind there now. It hurts less now. But you'll be able to find it any time you want."

She smiled, feeling sure she understood him, even as he

denied what he obviously wanted. "Trust your body. Everything will be all right." She stroked his thigh, reassuring him. "Spread your legs now. Move your arm away from your breasts." She put a finger to her lips and said, "Don't tell Em or Sanger. This is our little secret."

Her finger caught the odor of her breath. It stank like sharp alcohol. Something was wrong. She leaned farther, hot breath making Alan's ear moist, and nonsense came through her lips. "You'll like this. You sure are ready. You'll thank me later. You're so very special. You were born for this. It's like you've always known how. No, don't be stupid, just lay still. You little shit. You're nothing but a..." Rooster drew back her hand as if to swipe dishes from a table. Intending her fingers to whip across Alan's face, she...

*

...dropped the atomizer and felt the soft pouch land on her bare foot. She leapt back as if the pouch had burned her skin. Bent at the waist, slinking away from the devilish thing, she took more steps back. Rooster was again in Sanger's living room. When she looked up she saw Alan, Em, and Sanger staring at her.

"What is that?" she screamed. "Why did you think I'd like that?"

Alan took half of a pace toward her. Something wild in her eyes convinced him to freeze in mid-step.

Good, she thought. *Don't come near me.* Anger at them, him, rose and turned her face hot and swelled her brain, pressing the matter tight to her skull. She looked at Alan and said, "Why did you do that? That wasn't my future, it was yours. Why would you do that to me?" A dull pain in her head throbbed.

"What? What did I do?"

"You, you, you came on to me, made me think you wanted it...no, I wanted it...sex. It was obvious, you were already ready. Waiting for me to come into your room. Stupid, stupid, stupid." Rooster clenched her fists and turned away from them. Her experience was rapidly disintegrating, growing hazy, becoming a memory and mixing with other memories.

Rooster sat on the front edge of the couch and held her grousing stomach. She raised her head, looked at Alan, and said, "You told me I'd like it, wanted it, our little secret, relax, spread your legs, just be still. Oh...oh my God. I said all that, I did all the talking, repeating what that asshole said to me." Rooster pushed herself deep into the sofa, curled into an egg and shuddered.

Em sat next to her, wanting to keep her talking. "Where were you?"

"Here," Rooster said. "I walked into Alan's room. He wanted me to."

Em looked at Alan. He shrugged his shoulders and showed his palms. Then she touched Rooster's shoulder and asked, "When was that?"

"Late, no one else was around. At night. He was on his bed and I knew he wanted me to come in." Rooster sniffed before adding, "I knew he was waiting for me. You know how you just know stuff. In dreams, I mean. It was like that, like a dream. But then it turned ugly and it was my step-dad coming into my room."

Em stretched her arm farther around Rooster. "Did you see a date?"

"I went to the past," Rooster said. "Why would I go to the past when you all went to the future? It doesn't make sense."

"Did you see a date?" Em asked again.

Rooster pointed across the room to where the digital time-and-date alarm clock stood. "July first."

Sanger took a step toward the others. "That's the date I took the envelope to the bank."

Rooster wanted the memory to disappear, the tightness in her stomach to ease. She visualized the clock in her mind. "No," she said. "No, it was after one in the morning. We'd still talk about it as the night of June thirtieth. But that can't be right. It was just like when he came into my bedroom. Everything he said…I said. It was like going to the past and I was him and Alan was me and I knew you," addressing Alan, "wanted me there, knew you wanted it because…you even had a stiff cock. I saw it. But why would I see that? Why would I go to the past when all of you went to the future?"

Then she dropped her head between her knees and vomited on the hard wood floor.

~ ~ ~

June 14, Chicago

Niko Talek stood in his tiny apartment in the Bucktown neighborhood of Chicago. He wanted to get it right, explain time to the recipients of his device in a way that would help them understand what they were going through. Although his intentions were sincere, his technique, most of his former students would agree, fell far short of his goals.

After one more glance out his window, he began a fictional lecture to pseudo-students at a university where he was no longer allowed to tread. "We function better," he said aloud, "when time resides in a larger context. Any context will do. So imagine running. Each step makes contact with the ground, a burst of opposition between sole and soil propels us forward. Only through contact with solid ground is a pace maintained. Think now, the same movement on a floating log. We run, that's clear, but the log rolls. Although our toes grip the log, the log doesn't grip anything."

Niko stopped, thinking that was enough, point made, concept understood. But he imagined some lethargic students at the back of the lecture hall. For them he added, "Can the future be seen this way? No. A springboard diver starts his acrobatic trick before he has left the board. Arm and head movements begin while there is still a solid opposing force from which he can propel. If the diver leaves the board prior to initiating the trick, he will flounder, no matter how much he waves his arms or throws his head. This solid out of which the future is propelled is the past. Yet when a past is poorly supposed—as through amnesia, inattention, denial, rejection, or complete replacement with fantasy—we run the risk of stumbling instead of gaining traction."

Sweat ran down Niko's chest. He felt his imaginary students pining for more. It wasn't like him to want to tell others what to do. He was more prone to offer the facts and let others determine an action. Still, he added, "Fortunately, we have this solid ground from which to push off. Through our lives we are awash with concepts: ideas, morals, prejudices, fears, compulsions, and ill-formed conclusions. Some people set themselves in motion with a pleasant stroll out of a pleasant past. Others cast off from a history of hardship and woe. The past is nothing more than solid ground on which we walk. Some struggle with their context, painful as it might be, until firm footing is found. Others opt for a whimsical ride, fabricating the scaffolding of context with soda straws, and hoping it will support the weight of the future they will enter."

A breeze through the window fluttered the curtains. Sweat still rolled down the sides of his face. He would have never taken the time in a real classroom to press his point, instead believing that those who drew their own conclusions were far better off. He cleared his throat and said, "We need solid structures from which to propel into the future. Stand on roller skates and push a door shut. It is as likely you will roll backwards as it is for the door to close."

That's the problem, he thought, *I'm repeating myself.* With arms perched on an imaginary lectern, Niko took a deep breath.

"Yet knowing this," he added, "some ignore firm footing when embarking on a journey. Without acknowledging influence and context, some set their sight ahead and believe they will never again deal with what they are hoping to escape. But a future isn't built this way, out of thin air, miraculously appearing because they have turned their backs on the past. No. Without an honest recognition of the past we tend to sprinkle our futures with repeated mistakes. And defiantly call it free will."

CHAPTER NINE

June 15, Minneapolis

Rooster's distaste for the device slowed any enthusiasm the others had shown. One morning before work Sanger sat at the kitchen table with Em. He rested his chin in his palm as he waited for Em to coat her question with words.

Em opened her palms and said, "So there's an explosion, the Big Bang, and everything is streaming outward from that point. Behind the outer ring is the slower debris from the explosion. But ahead of the outer ring is nothing. So where does the future fit into this picture?"

Sanger nodded. "I see what you mean. Time is hard to visualize." He took her concern seriously even though he preferred to think there had always been a future. The first moment of the Big Bang created an instantaneous now. In the next moment a past was begun. But how did a future ever come to exist?

"I don't know how it works," Sanger answered. "A new now is created every instant, a past as soon as the current now elapses. The future is what the universe is expanding into, a space that doesn't yet exist. Is it so wrong to just take it for granted?"

Em said, "That's okay for most people most of the time. But we're stepping into a future that might or might not exist. Look at it, other than my expectation, I don't know where to look for evidence of a future. What if there's only now?"

"Things change," Sanger said. "We notice these changes and—"

"Do we? Notice, I mean. We have the illusion of smooth movement but what if it's like looking through a flipbook. Or the still pictures of a movie."

"Are you saying," Sanger asked, "that there's only now? And when we perceive we only perceive it now. So our only perception of movement is through our memory of where something last was?"

"No," Em said. She thought of Aztec temples discovered after all living memory had vanished. "There's evidence of a past," she added. "Temples and books and sketches on cave walls. But I want something as concrete as dinosaur bones as evidence for a future."

Sanger stood and reached for his wallet and keys. "Scientists say when the Big Bang exploded it spewed out stuff that wasn't nothing…solids, gas, stuff that took up space. But it also cast forth energy, like light, taking up no space but something to be reckoned with anyway."

"Yes, sure," Em said. "But did the Big Bang spew out time? Did time begin as soon as the Big Bang expansion started? And if that's the case, did it come with a future already built in? We can't be experiencing trips to the future if there's nothing beyond now."

"Hmm," Sanger said. "I've got to go to work. See you later."

"Do you promise?"

Sanger stopped at the door and stared at her.

After a moment of silence, Em wiped her hands across the kitchen table and said, "I don't know these things about time. I only know that without faith in the future, we'd never put so much trust in promises?"

~ ~ ~

Rooster had heard Em and Sanger quietly talking in the kitchen. She couldn't make out what they had said and didn't care. She fell back asleep and dreamed of waking in a strange city situated in the geographic center of North America. She was nothing but a speck on a planet spinning into a new day while orbiting an average star as it bustled through empty space, light years from its nearest star neighbor. Rooster's star was on the outer edge, revolving around the black hole at the center of its galaxy. This whole galactic collection streamed alone through empty space, thousands of light years from its nearest galactic neighbor. In the quiet she lifted her lids and saw a billion smudgy galaxies as far as her eyes could see.

Rooster listened carefully and didn't hear anything. She was alone. No one knew where she was. She didn't have enough money to simply start buying a new life. There was no environment she could step into and immediately belong. If she had brought her clarinet she might have found a marching band looking for a new member. Or maybe there was a dark poetry club who had their own crash pad and shared evening meals. She didn't believe she could stay here with Sanger, Em, and Alan. They were weird and they believed they were traveling into the future. Also weird. Even if her single dalliance with the mist was really a step into the future, it wasn't one she wanted salted away where it will patiently wait for her arrival.

She sat on the couch, holding the blanket around her legs. Unmoving, only her eyes roamed to the left and to the right. Her mouth tasted thick and she smacked her lips. The muffled sound of traffic drifted into the room, monotonous with an occasional higher whine of an accelerating engine. Birds must have been in nearby trees because even through the closed windows she heard their chirping. The refrigerator hummed in the next room. *Something to drink.*

In the kitchen, Rooster found a note from Em stating that she had gone out, Sanger went to work, and to make herself at home. The remains of an earlier pot of coffee were being kept warm by the coffee maker and Rooster poured the last of it into a cup. She sat at the table and stared, unable to wrap her mind around the situation she was in. She noticed Alan walk into the room but couldn't quite muster the energy to respond. Nor did she want to. Her episode with the atomizer had shaken her sense of integrity. She intellectually knew Alan hadn't accosted her. Yet the emotional weight was like carrying saddlebags. On the one side she felt Alan was the aggressor and she the victim, a pattern she knew too well. In the other bag was the memory of her crawling up his chest, whispering in his ear, raising her summer blouse over... She wanted to disappear from the kitchen, hoped Alan hadn't seen her. She grew warm and squirmed in her chair as embarrassment smoldered from her body.

"Hey," Alan said. "Rooster. Did you drain the pot?"

When she turned, he was holding the clear glass pot at arm's length toward her. She didn't answer.

Alan poured the dregs into the sink and said, "When you finish a pot, make a new one. Social grease."

"I don't know how."

"Enjoy your coffee. I'll show you how next time."

In a few minutes Alan sat at the table across from her. He glanced at Em's note but didn't say anything.

Rooster raised her head and said, "I'm sorry about before." She knew a good apology was coupled with an answer to the question, 'what are you sorry about?' She had heard 'I'm sorry' a thousand times from her mom but never with an explanation attached. She wanted to try harder.

She cleared her throat and said, "You know, before, when I accused you of trying to get it on with me. I didn't mean it, it wasn't you. I got confused by sniffing that atomizer and thought...I...it just wasn't right."

Alan's silence unnerved her. She hung her head and thought, *He's staring at me. He knows. He knows everything. I wonder what his favorite name for it is, what he's calling me right now. But he doesn't know crap, not really, only that one thing, like all I am is just that one thing.*

Alan reached across the table but didn't touch her. "Tell me if you want," he said. "I'll be on your side."

Rooster remembered her mother screaming in her ear. *Tell me, don't just cry. Tell me what's going on. I've got to get to work, I can't sit here all day. Tell me.* And when she did, her mother was definitely not on her side.

"When you," Rooster asked, "when you get a stiffy? Do you make it happen because you want? Do you make it go away because you want?"

Alan interlaced his fingers and put his knuckles to his lips.

"When I was your age," he said. "In school, this happened in school to me a few times. We, my little subset of kids, wore tight pants, I'm talking really tight, pockets were useless, couldn't get our hands in. So a couple of times in class I got an erection out of nowhere. I wasn't trying or anything, it just came on. If the bell rang and I had to change classrooms, I had to hold my books in front of me so everyone wouldn't see what I'd sprung."

Rooster wanted Alan to say something she could apply to her own life, a rule perhaps; if that happens, do this. She wasn't sure what he said or what he meant to say. "If that happened in school, how'd you make it go away?"

"Without stimulation, it eventually goes away on its own." Alan smiled. "It's a fond memory now but back then I was extremely embarrassed. I think it's like taking a race horse out for training. Some days the horse gets the smell of grass up its nose and wants to run at full speed. Something just got into it. When I was your age, I felt a lot like that. Who knew why or how my body responded to anything?"

Rooster shook her head and pulled her short bangs. "I responded, you know, down there. Not with you but in the time I got confused about. Not because of what was happening. I didn't want what was happening to be happening." Rooster pursed her lips. "But isn't my body the real measure of me? Then my thinking part is like a coat over that? Aren't I first the girl who got all horny? And then just some kid pretending to be good?"

"No," Alan said in the gentlest voice Rooster had ever heard. "No. It's like...like a five-year-old who believes there's a monster living in her closet. That's not the time to leave her alone with a shotgun and rat poison. It's not the time to laugh and ridicule. It's certainly not the time to push her into the closet and slam the door shut."

Rooster looked at the kitchen table directly in front of her. She followed a line in the wood to a few sturdy grains of spilled salt. "I don't...I don't get it. What do you mean? Gun, poison, sounds okay to me."

"No," Alan said. "I mean that kid shouldn't have to decide alone what to do about the monster. But if she's ridiculed or pushed into making a decision right away, well, the kid's simply not yet equipped to do it."

"You're talking about me, aren't you?"

"And me," Alan said. "My erections in school were just mine, my body was just mine. If anyone knew, I felt sure I'd die of embarrassment. You shouldn't have to decide today or last week what you're all about. If it was just you and your body you might not be hounded by those questions of whether you're a pretender or not."

"Too late now. I've got those questions."

Alan took his glasses off and placed them on the table. "Well, we all do at some point in life. There'll be time to sort things out. I know it's difficult when everything's got to be hidden away. Especially difficult when someone you don't trust knows your secret."

Rooster rolled her eyes directly at Alan. "Again. Too late now. That's where I am."

"I'm sorry."

Rooster heard a rattling at the door, leaned back, and saw Em enter the apartment. She and Alan were quiet as they watched Em walk past with a small bag of groceries. Rooster turned in her chair as Em put jars in a cupboard.

Em said, "While Sanger is at work, I thought we three might sniff the atomizer and then talk about our experiences. The end of June will be here before we know it and we've got to learn more."

Em finished putting things away, stepped to the table, and

said, "I thought we could go out after and get some lunch. My treat. Well, Sanger's treat as it will come out of the grocery money. Oh, Rooster, I have a toothbrush for you."

Rooster raised her eyebrows, making her bangs wiggle. "You bought me a toothbrush?"

"No. We have some spares. New. Still in their containers."

"You have spare toothbrushes? New ones? Who has spare toothbrushes?"

Alan reached across the table and touched the back of Rooster's hand. He said, "People who go to the dentist."

~ ~ ~

Same day, Chicago

In the end, they didn't go out for lunch that day. Nor did they use the atomizer. Something happened that gave each of them a lot to think about. They received a call from Niko Talek.

Niko was on a roll, pacing from his little kitchenette, through the living room, on to the bathroom, and back. Thoughts swirled in his head and he wanted to get them out in an order the recipients of his device would understand. He lit up his phone, scrolled through his contact list, and touched to make the call. Even before saying hello, he was speaking at full speed. "You've got to know that future travel is nothing like going back in time. Past has already happened. Even tiny changes during a visit to the past will register snowballing effects, larger and larger changes as time goes on, disrupting the now in which we currently live. The standard example, listen carefully, it's easy to understand, is accidentally killing your youthful grandmother, leaving your own mother never born, and the unique genetic stew of you never created."

At that point Em interrupted Niko and asked, "Are you on amphetamines?"

"No, no, no. Caffeine. I have a small espresso machine." Niko stood tall and took a deep breath. "Future travel poses different problems than travel to the past. We live in a world where order comes through cause and effect. There are no actions that do not produce an effect; you might wish so, but it's not so. There are no effects that have no cause. No spontaneous eruptions, no appearances out of nowhere. I'll say it again. Nothing happens without a cause, no actions free of effect."

Niko rolled his hand in front of him as if to encourage the rest out of his mouth. "By following the snake trails of cause and effect, any future visited is the result of actions before it. To go to the same future-time and future-place more than once, the interceding events mustn't change to be sure the visited future will contain the same content."

"Why are you telling us this?" Alan asked.

"I thought you might be confused about—"

"Might?" Rooster leaned close to the phone. "I'm saying this with extreme sarcasm."

Niko wiped his forehead. "Assuredly confused. But why am I saying this? Why must you know there's a difference between past and future excursions? The problem is human desire. Some want to guarantee the future unfolds exactly as they've seen it, to live again what was briefly tasted."

Em felt again the sensuous episode of sitting beside her banker's desk. She squirmed in her chair and hoped Alan and Rooster hadn't noticed.

"Others," Niko continued, "want the future they viewed never to be seen again."

At this, Rooster stabbed her finger at the phone and said, "That's the ticket I want to buy."

"Yes," Niko said. "Of course. But how best do we guarantee a future promised? How best to dissuade a future unwanted? When there is only an endless series of now, again and again and again, what to do? Establish a routine, never vary, set your eye on a goal, stick to a plan. Can that be right?"

"Maybe," Em said. "We pave the future with choices. Is there an alternative?"

"Sway," Niko said. "Sway with the vagaries of serendipity and chance, worry nothing for what an unpredictable future holds, bend like a willow, reach your destination when you get there. Either method is a choice. Stick to a plan or abandon all expectations. Choices are imagined and regretted, but all are confined to our influence over now."

Pacing again, Niko added, "Do you comprehend now's pitch and yaw and the dangerous reach into darkness on the far side of now? It doesn't matter in a deterministic timeframe. What will be will be. Let go and let God. Yet you want change as a possibility. You want to control that change through personal will, well-considered choices. The past is locked. The future is not yet upon us. Now's rich potential can be squandered by considering only it. But to understand all of time, all of time must be included in the composition. Journeys to the future are very tricky business."

~ ~ ~

After Niko ended the call Em sat quietly at the kitchen table. Regardless of what Niko said, or meant to say, Em still felt excited when thinking of using the atomizer again. There was something about banker-Hugh that intrigued her. The hairs on her arms stood on end as she thought about sitting near him. Passing her hand over the raised hairs, she reconsidered. It was something about herself that caused this reaction, something she wanted to experience again. Small eddies of contrition rolled in Em's stomach when she thought of revealing her thoughts to Sanger. *He won't understand,* she thought. *He won't see it from my point of view. He just doesn't see the advantages of experiencing life to its fullest. Without seeing, I'll hurt him.* Nonetheless, she wanted to sniff the mister again and wanted to do it soon.

~ ~ ~

Rooster, too, sat at the table, just as confused as Em. She was sure she didn't want to use the take-me-to-the-future device again. Her singular experience had soured her taste for it. Even her cryptic talk with Alan hadn't encouraged her to use the vile object again. She envisioned her experience with the mister as a whale surging above the surface, her past coming up for air. She wanted not using the mister again to discourage any future containing that content. She wished it had never happened, willed it to never happen again. Didn't even want to think about it, thank you very much.

CHAPTER TEN

June 15, Minneapolis

That same afternoon, Sanger sat at his desk in the offices of Tri-canter Advertising Agency. He didn't have a regular job but billed hours for the projects to which he was temporarily assigned. His specialty was writing instructional pamphlets in bad English for 'authentic' foreign companies. They shipped their product to the United States where gullible Americans wanted the genuine article, right off the boat. A generation ago, Italians could write bad English all on their own. Today they sent polished prose that rivaled that of the Indian subcontinent.

Sanger hacked it up so it read like a village scamp wrote it with a short pencil on the side of a cardboard box. He told people it was easy, butta it's a not.

Sanger's desk rested in an open space he shared with a rotating list of interns, currently Mellissa. He sat unmoving, leaning back in his chair, while time overfilled his palms and dripped to the floor.

"What are you doing?" Mellissa asked. "Do you even need to be here?"

"I'm thinking. And no, I don't need to be here." Sanger paused. He knew saying no more was best, but was unable to stop himself. "What's nice about here," he added, "is thinking is encouraged, fostered...not interrupted."

"Point taken. I'll leave you alone."

Sanger leaned back and closed his eyes. He wondered if he could take something to the future and leave it there. A single sock; a set of keys; cufflink, earring, shoelace? *Will it be there,* he thought, *when I finally arrive in real-time? Maybe that's what lost items are. Perhaps tiny trips to the future are commonplace and I simply don't notice. Maybe lost objects are things I've taken to the future, left there, and find again when I approach in the forward-marching present. I swear I looked there, how many times have I said it?*

He leaned forward with his chin in his palms. He stared, unseeing, directly at Mellissa.

"What?" she said. "You're staring at me."

"Sorry, sorry." Even though he thought it was best not to talk about the atomizer, he wondered if he could cloak the whole idea in absurdity. "Listen for a second, though." Sanger paused, collecting thoughts. "Let's say you could travel one week into the future, could you bring back something that hadn't yet been made in the present you're returning to?"

"What?"

"You time-travel ahead one week, go into a bakery, and

buy a loaf of bread that was made that morning. Could you bring it back one week to your normal present which is before the loaf was made? Could you do that?"

Mellissa sat up straighter. "You're working on that shoe account, aren't you? The tag line, what is it? Run your future times now in Kon-form shoes. And it's not bread but ideas. I get it. Assume your times will improve, believe you can run those times now with our shoes. Incredible. You're not as dull as you look."

"Thanks. But back to the loaf of bread. Can we bring it back from the future, to a time before it's been made?"

Mellissa scratched her head. "I'd say no. If it wasn't yet made, it couldn't exist in its own past. All the ingredients would be what they were before they were bread. Can a loaf of bread really have a past?"

Sanger ignored most of what she said and continued, "Think about bringing the bread back. In that same way, can you have a totally original thought in the future and bring it back, even though you've never had that thought before? Or learn something in the future, something that couldn't yet be known in your normal present. Could you remember that when you returned?"

Mellissa twisted her lips. "I see the analogous relationship between thoughts and bread but don't you think they're different? Isn't it about the nature of ideas? Do we create them out of nothing, whimsical insight? Or do we discover them, assuming they've always been there and we finally notice. If they've always been there, we should be able to bring them back from the future."

"Yes, yes, I like that," Sanger said. "But if all ideas already exist, that's getting awfully close to a predetermined world. Like destiny, kismet, fate. World-changing ideas will eventually be thought because they're out there in the future waiting. Is that what you mean?"

"That's what I mean but I don't personally believe it. I don't believe in destiny, there's no preplanned way it has to be. I make decisions, I determine my own future."

"There's no soul mate out there you're destined to meet? There's no reason you were put on this planet, nothing you're illogically drawn toward, no calling?"

"I wish there was. Everyone wants something to give their life meaning. By making choices, I take on personal responsibility. Without it we just let the poor take care of themselves and let injustice have its day because I wasn't drawn to changing it. It wasn't in the cards for me. That's what believing in fate brings us."

"Okay," Sanger said. "So you're saying that believing in a set future already out there, where there's nothing new under the sun, is substantially different than believing our choices force one future over another."

"Yes, of course. I just said so. We're responsible for the choices we make. No one's responsible when destiny's in charge."

"Okay, sure. But back to my original question: if we could travel to the future, could we bring back the loaf of bread that hadn't yet been made in our normal time? Could we bring back ideas, solutions even, we hadn't yet hatched?"

Mellissa stood and leaned her hip against her desk. "I'm voting no. Just like the loaf of bread. There are so many tiny movements and nuances. There are a thousand things we notice and another thousand we ignore in any moment. Fragrance, puffs of wind, uneven pavement, so many things to notice and remember. A memory from the future? I don't know. I wonder if we'd return with any memory of it at all."

~ ~ ~

A day or two or…later, Minneapolis

Earlier than usual in the evening Em pulled Sanger toward their bedroom. "We need to get some sleep and let all we've experienced sink in."

"I don't get it," Sanger said. "How can we be jumping into a hole that hasn't yet been dug?"

Em sat on the edge of the bed and slipped her pants off. "What do you think is up about Uncle Bill bringing all that money to William Meyer? And is he getting the money by blackmailing the banker?"

"I know." Sanger nodded and slipped under the covers. "Sounds crazy, blackmailing the banker right in his office. And why does William Meyer get killed, what's the advantage in that?"

Em rolled on her side and said, "How are you going to ask Uncle Bill questions without tickling his suspicion?" She snuggled deeper into the mattress and doubted Sanger heard her.

An hour later, Em and Sanger were on their backs, side by side. Even though Sanger turned his head and cleared his throat, Em knew he was asleep. She slid from under the sheet and snuck into the living room while pulling a long T-shirt over her naked body. She wondered if it mattered how she was dressed when dipping her toe into the future. Will underwear be supplied because she usually wears them, or not because she doesn't always. Rooster was asleep on the couch and the atomizer lay on the side table.

Em picked it up and wondered if it was fair to use it without telling Sanger. Then she closed her eyes and decided he didn't need to know everything. Rolling the mister in both hands and running the nozzle along her cheek, she thought of seeing the bank manager again, but didn't know how to control her next experience. Nonetheless, she squeezed the bulb and pushed her nose into the cloud of particulates that took the shape of an open umbrella. One good inhale and she…

*

…lifted her head to see 'Grain Belt Beer' in neon, backwards in a window. The booth was dark while pendant lamps hanging over the bar cast cones of bright light. Men and women lined the bar, most with their backs to her. Her very short skirt rode high on her thighs and she unsuccessfully attempted to pull it down with first one hand and then the other.

Across the booth's table was Uncle Bill, who said, "Here, we're in our own private booth now and not up at the bar with those ditch-diggers. How can you say I don't respect you?"

Em didn't know what caused her to say that to Bill, but she trusted it and replied, "You just wouldn't be the way you are if you respected me."

"It's nothing, just this once. I've got two rooms booked upstairs. You take him to one and I'll snap a few pictures from a tiny hole in the adjoining wall. Just leave the light on. He'll love it." Uncle Bill stared. "Listen, a tiny hole, I'll hardly see anything of you, he'll be on top."

"Are you crazy? Why would I do that with some stranger?" Em had a vague memory of photographs mixed with someone being tricked and of someone suffering for the deception. She couldn't make the connection but suspected…she didn't know. Lowering her voice, leaning across the table, she whispered, "I'm not going to do it."

"Oh, sweetie. He's a nice man. It'll be okay if you want it to be. I know he'll be gentle." Bill put an envelope on the table. "An inducement, a little reward."

Em slid to the edge of the booth, picked up the envelope, and tossed it into Uncle Bill's chest.

"Wait, wait, wait," Bill said. "I'm sorry. I'm just a crusty old man, forgetting what's important in life."

"Yes you are."

"Of course you don't want to do it with a stranger," Bill said, rolling his eyes. "I understand. I'm sorry. Stay."

Em slid back to the middle of the bench.

"Okay, how about this," Bill continued. "There he is up at the bar. Hugh Gardner. There's an empty stool beside him. Just go up, sit, talk. Ask his name, where he works, ask him to tell you a joke. Laugh real sweet and touch his arm. Tell him you have a sore shoulder and ask him to feel the lump in your muscle. When he touches you, lean your head to the side and let your mouth open a little. I'll take a few pictures and then we'll be done."

"You mean flirt?"

"Yeah." Bill pulled his index finger from the web of his other fingers and pointed. "There's no harm in that. He's up at the bar."

Em sighed. She recognized the man Uncle Bill indicated. He was the guy from the bank, a man she hasn't yet met. She wanted to talk with him but was offended by Bill's outlandish request.

"Do it, sweetie. You're so beautiful in those clothes. Undo one more button at the top. No one will get hurt. Listen, in five minutes I'll come get you. I'll walk up and say, 'Hey, there you are, gotta go, gonna be late.' How's that? Five minutes and I'll come rescue you."

Em felt cornered by Bill. A few pictures in a dark bar were better than a peephole to a guy's white butt. As she approached the empty stool beside her target, Em stumbled and grabbed Mr. Gardner's arm.

Mr. Gardner caught her and asked, "Are you okay? Lean back on this stool."

Em teetered with one hand on the empty stool and took a closer look at him. He still wore his suit but the tie was loose and his shirt's collar button undone. His hair was mussed, as though a friend walked by and tossed it, giving him a boyishly rogue look.

He smiled easily and then cocked his head to the side. "You're staring but not talking." After a moment he added, "I'm Hugh. Are you okay? I mean, if you haven't swallowed too much alcohol already, I'll buy you a drink. I'd usually measure that by how you pronounce your words but you're not saying anything."

"Sorry. You look familiar. Do I know you?"

But of course she only knew him through a future encounter that hadn't yet happened. Her memory of it was on the tip of her tongue but couldn't be fully recalled.

Hugh eyed her closely. "You don't look familiar. I don't think I know you." He paused and then added, "Would it be too forward of me to say I wish I did. Know you, that is."

Em felt her cheeks glow warm and couldn't remember the last time she blushed. "Well Em, I'm Hugh." She extended her hand to shake his. "No. That's not right. I'm Em. You're Hugh." She laughed and slid more firmly onto the stool. "We've got to keep at least that much straight. Right? I'm Em and you're Hugh. Yes, please buy me a drink. I mean just order it, whatever you're drinking. I can pay for my own drinks. It would be way out of line for me to assume you'd pay for my drink. The line of equality has to be drawn somewhere." She took a deep breath and added, "Why can't I stop talking?"

"Are you sure you're not already a little tipsy?"

"No, I haven't drunk anything...drank anything. Is it drunk or drank in that case. I get them confused. I don't confuse a lot of words but just…. Oh, why am I doing this?"

"It's okay." Hugh signaled the bartender for two more of what he had. "Maybe you've had a hard day."

Em nodded but couldn't remember anything about her day. She imagined climbing a ladder as the rungs just out of reach disappeared…and then here.

"Do you come here often?" Hugh asked. "Well, I guess you don't or I'd have noticed you before."

"No, not here," Em answered. "Not often. But I like the place. How about you?"

"A couple times a week. Just a drink or two before I go home to a cat and a sparsely filled refrigerator. And you…live around here?"

"An apartment," she was quick to volunteer. "With my…friend. He, my friend, has an unemployed cousin. He lives there, too. And he, the cousin, stays out of the way a lot. He does some cooking, tidies, grocery shops, takes the garbage out. Hmm, Alan does a lot."

"Sounds like a good deal."

"Yeah, a bit like that." Em took another deep breath, felt a bead of sweat on her forehead, and had a vague memory of wanting to explore something. Or express something and understand. She stared at Hugh's gentle smile and felt heat radiating from her chest. "I'm twenty-six years old," she blurted, "and sitting here totally flustered. I want to just talk and keep talking, tell you everything, but I know I should play my cards better than that. I've been the recipient of too much information and I know how disturbing it can be. I mean disturbing to find the talker a disturbing person and then try to get away politely or at least without arousing suspicion. And it's not like I've never met a nice guy before. Of course, I'm just assuming you're nice, I don't really know that yet. Besides, can we ever really know—"

Hugh lifted a hand, held it in midair between them, as he said, "Hey, listen. I like what I see of you so far. There's something in your face that speaks honestly to me. You're a lot like someone I've never yet met, if you know what I mean."

"Like someone you've expected but haven't yet met?"

"Yes, exactly like that. Not everyone...forget everyone. You're right, it's hard to trust first impressions. Let's just slow down, drink our drinks, and see."

Em closed her eyes and nodded. Fuzzy music on the juke box, odor of beer in the air, her fingers around a narrow glass, and a feeling like there was no place else she'd rather...

*

...be than in her living room, Sanger's living room, nodding her head like a schoolgirl listening to her best friend's favorite band.

Distracted by the disappointment of no longer blushing in the bar with Hugh, Em placed the mister so close to the edge of a side table that it slipped and plopped to the floor. It was still the middle of the night and the others were sleeping. Em stepped into the kitchen and stood behind a chair, supporting her weight with stiff arms. She stared and thought. *A future flame? Hugh.* She liked his name. *Will Bill blackmail him with innocent pictures of us in the bar? How so? What's missing here? Ohh! Will I sleep with him before going to the bank and Bill gets pictures of that? He liked what he saw of me and I like that. So why would blackmail work? Is he married, omitting that fact, and possessing a wife who is possessive of him? Like I should complain! Why did I lie and call Sanger only a friend? It all happened so quickly. But I've got to see him again, for his sake. Got to warn him of Uncle Bill's despicable plan. Got to keep him from seeing me as Bill's accomplice.*

Em sat, pushed aside Sanger's cell phone, and dropped her

head to the table. Her face felt even warmer than blushing. She placed the backs of her fingers to her forehead and felt herself burning up. As she thought of warning Hugh, her body tingled with the prickles of fever. Goosebumps formed on her arms and as she stroked the standing hairs the sensation spread through her whole body. *Wow*, she smiled and thought, *why do I want him to be doing this to me?* Then a wave of post-future nausea overcame her.

~ ~ ~

Same night, Chicago

Niko Talek was also awake. He had received a postcard from one of the department secretaries encouraging him to renew his efforts at reconciliation with the university. In tiny longhand script, she had filled the text area so densely that it looked like a square of QR code. He had read it once and put it away.

Unable to sleep, he pulled the card out and read it again, this time with a magnifying glass. He was sure she had said she'd act as his advocate in the promotion of his case. Yet reading it again, she hadn't exactly said that. He examined her words carefully, trying to detect the hidden cipher she had used to lay out the steps he needed to take. Unable to unravel her meaning, he paced the room, attempting to place his mind anywhere else.

After rummaging through some boxes, looking for an old group photo to clearly identify the postcard sender, Niko picked up his cell and phoned those kids with device number five.

The phone in front of Em vibrated and performed a counter-clockwise dance. She recognized his number and even though alternating between sweats and chills, she picked it up immediately. "Niko, I'm glad you called. It's like synchronicity or something. I mean, I wasn't thinking of you but I used the device just a few minutes ago. I was with a man, someone we'll get into a lot of trouble unless I warn him. So I've got to—"

"Don't tell me," Niko said. "I don't want to know. I can't help you that way."

"Niko," Em began again. "I just want to know how to direct the mister."

"I don't know. It's only through understanding time that you'll make sense of this."

"Well I'm not understanding," Em shot back. Fearing she spoke too loudly, Em walked to the sink, the farthest point in the kitchen away from the living room. "I'm confused all the time."

"Back to the beginning then." Niko was privately pleased. Dredging up the basics of time allowed him to immerse himself in something other than his hopeful return to the university. "I've told you that our senses only know now. There's nothing else when it comes to time. That is the truth."

"Only now?" Em asked. "You told us there's also a past. That there's evidence for it and we do what we do because of past influence."

"Yes. That's true too. But previous influences from your past happened to you when it was now. Even as you reconsider the past, draw new conclusions, it's now when you do it."

Frustrated, Em leaned back against the sink and said, "I want to go back, ahead, to the future, and warn this man. Harm will come to him if I don't. And I want to do it now."

"Of course. No problem. You see, it's not really the existence of the future we debate, it's the content."

"That's not helpful. How do I use the atomizer and pick the time and place I want to go?"

Niko looked at the postcard on his table. He picked it up and held it at arm's length. "Common to all our views of time," he said, "is now's specialness, a precious moment, unique and unrepeatable. Now happening always and forever, that's our most stubborn intuitive idea about time. But false. There is no sliver of time that the future crosses to become the past. There is no moment more unique than any other. Make no mistake, this is the reality of time. Abandon what time feels like, developed while humans first walked across the African savannah, and enter the twenty-first century. Now is your opportunity to do it sooner than others."

"I don't get it," Em said. "How can…why…of course now is special, it's the moment of our presence."

"Do you think it's now everywhere now? All across the universe, is it now at this present moment?" When Em didn't respond, he added, "Do you?"

"Yes. Now is the middle point, the…what do you call it…the fulcrum. When time goes through now, it enters the past. When the future approaches now, it's divulged. How can now not be unique and precious?"

"Clocks on a spacecraft traveling very fast run more slowly than stationary clocks on the ground. Not just clocks, but evaporation of water, growth of hair, the entire aging process slows. Anything we measure with time, slows. Those on board the spaceship don't notice, time passes normally to their intuitive eye. The same is true for those closer to a source of gravity. Time runs more slowly the closer you are."

Em said nothing. She stared at the kitchen floor and knew she wasn't in a spacecraft and didn't believe she was close to any gravity fields.

Niko looked again at the postcard. At this distance he saw an image in the ink. It was of Kersten Hall and the trees in front of it. The trellis of flowers climbing the corner, and the upper left window, his—

"How can anyone know that?" Em asked. "It's just, what,

math or something?"

"Yes," Niko said. "It's good to be skeptical. But it's true. Global Positioning Satellites have clocks on board. They measure time and beam the information to computers on Earth. The satellite clocks are adjusted for the time difference between those clocks and the clocks on Earth. Adjusted twice really, once for the slower running GPS clocks since they're traveling very fast, and again because the clocks on Earth run slower because they're closer to a strong source of gravity. If the computations weren't done just right, locations would miss by feet and miles."

Em said, "That's…"

"Yes," Niko said. "Isn't it? Now is not simultaneous for race car drivers and their crew sleeping on the infield. The width and breadth of time isn't dictated by pen on paper. Still, it's important how we think of time."

Niko tapped the edge of his phone. "Are you listening?"

"Yes."

"I have a small story before I go. Each mammal on Earth gets a billion heartbeats for its lifetime. Large animals, elephants, who live longer, get a billion. Small animals, mice, also get a billion. Elephant hearts, ka-thump, ka-thump, beat more slowly than mouse hearts, ticca, ticca, ticca. They each get a billion beats but elephants use them up more slowly. It's easy to think of a large animal, large heart, beats more slowly, lives longer, of course. Yet the difference might not be in the physiology but in time itself. Might time run more slowly in the massive than the diminutive? Does time adjust itself for the gravity of an elephant?"

Niko hung up and Em took a few tentative steps to the kitchen table. Sitting, she dropped her head to her forearms, feeling confused, exhausted, and ill.

CHAPTER ELEVEN

That same night, Minneapolis

Sanger woke to the sound of an overnight truck rumbling past. He had one arm over his head and felt the vibrations in the headboard. Then he heard the atomizer plop to the floor in the living room. He noticed Em's absence and knew if she sniffed again, she was probably already back. He wanted to enter the living room and question her, demand of her, insist on...something. Restraining himself, he rolled onto his side, facing the door, and waited.

Within twenty minutes Em stepped into the bedroom, backlit by the streetlight streaming through a window behind her. Startled by the effect of light through her clothing, clearly seeing she wore nothing beneath her T-shirt, he still couldn't make out the expression on her shadowed face. She could have been anyone, a nearly naked stranger entering his bedroom. The thought both disturbed and aroused him.

"What's up?" he said.

"I talked with Niko again."

"When?"

"Just now. I just got off with him."

Sanger wanted to question what she meant but knew it was just a figure of speech. "Did you learn anything?"

Em sat on the edge of the bed. "No. Maybe. Satellites and gravity. There's nothing special about now. It's not all as it seems. And…do elephants really live longer than mice?"

"You sniffed the perfume again, didn't you?" Sanger asked.

"Why? Why do you think so?"

"I heard it fall to the floor. I figured someone dropped it. I figured it was you."

"So? So what if I did?"

Sanger pinched his lips together to calm himself. "Don't be like that. I'm not interrogating you. I just want to know what happened. Did you—"

"Sorry, Sanger. It was unnerving. I was in a bar with Uncle Bill. He wanted me to take the banker up to a room and have sex with him while Bill took pictures. I said no."

"Good for you. That must have happened before you went to his office and confronted him with the photographs. So, we're not necessarily experiencing the future in sequential order. I guess the confrontation with the naked pictures won't happen now. And you, good for you, proof you can change the future."

Em shook her head. "It's not changed by much. The larger

dynamic is still there. Camera, pictures, blackmail, loans. I don't know. The banker's in the bar and he's still Bill's target. It's just that this time Bill is settling for a flirt rather than a strumpet."

Hairs on the back of Sanger's neck stood on end. He knew he had no right to be jealous or possessive. But he was both. In that moment, he agonized over every aspect of his relationship with Em, unable to find anything recognizable. They were living together and having sex even before he knew her favorite color, turning intimacy upside down, and leaving him wanting to start over so he could woo, charm, and beckon. Instead, he was jealous of a mirage and he impulsively wanted to demand she never see him again, as if that would solve what concerned him. *If there were no others,* he thought, *no other men who could capture her attention and lure her into...* Nothing Sanger knew fit the picture of them living together and having sex before dating and long talks on the phone and hesitant presents indicating more than he could say. Try as he might, he didn't know how to slide a foundation of trust beneath the sheets on which they had already sweat.

Frustrated by Em's inability to understand his desire for holding hands and Saturday night movies and friendship notes left for no reason, Sanger lifted himself on one elbow and said, "Uncle Bill settles for a flirt? You? That's pretty lame. Who'd pay to keep pictures like that secret?" Sanger heard it come out wrong and knew that Em had, too.

With arms crossed in front as her hands held the hem of her T-shirt, ready to pull it over her head, Em froze. "You mean who'd be jealous of plain old me?"

"No, no. I mean...compared to being naked in bed with him." Sanger sat up. "You're edgy. Did you do as Uncle Bill asked? Did you flirt?"

"Yes. But I was nervous and giddy. I suppose that's what flirting is for me. I talked too much. Babbling."

"You? Talked too much? And giddy? I've never seen you giddy." Sanger slid away from the edge of the bed, making room for Em.

Em pulled the T-shirt over her head, held it with both hands under her chin, and said, "I can be giddy. I can be coy and flirtatious and pretty. He likes me, that banker guy, likes what he saw." She slid under the covers and curled on her side.

Sanger looked at the back of her head and said, "I'm sorry, Em. I think you're pretty."

"You never say it, you don't act like it. Oh God, I still sound like the gaga girl I was in the bar."

Gaga girl, Sanger thought, *you don't do that with me.* "I'm sorry Em. I'm stuck in my thoughts of you and a banker. What could you and he possibly have in common?" Sanger stopped. Dark intimidating thoughts rose. Whenever he'd told Em she was pretty, she had scoffed in return and disregarded his remark. Whenever he'd pushed for more commitment, she had always redirected the conversation. Sanger blinked, struck by what she was giving the banker and not giving him. He said, "You're attracted to him, aren't you? Not just turned on by him, but *want* to be. And like it. Attracted, I mean. That's what you've got in common. Are you going to have sex with him? I don't mean because Uncle Bill wants you to, but just for yourself?"

"Sanger. I don't even know him. We've never really met, other than in those—"

"If they're snippets of the future, you will meet him."

"You can't be sure. How do I know what's going to happen in the future?"

Sanger leaned close. He pressed his forehead to the back of her shoulder and asked, "Do you want to have sex with him?"

Sanger felt Em's pause, noticed her absence of breath.

Motionless, he asked again, "Do you want to have sex with him?"

"He's vapor. It's like he doesn't exist."

"But he will. He might."

"Listen to yourself." Em pushed his head away and rolled to her back. "That's true in any relationship. Who knows who'll step into our lives over the years? Who I'll be attracted to and who'll magically be attracted to me at the same time?"

"People make vows to guard against that."

Em rolled to her side again and pulled the covers over her head. "There you go," she said, "that's the answer. Put human nature in a straightjacket; lay the groundwork for cheating and lying; protect secrets from your partner behind public vows. Sanger, who knows what the future will bring? And I don't care. I'm going to embrace the future rather than guard against it."

Em wanted to cross her arms over her chest as an exclamation point to her last statement. Yet she knew she was being more theoretical than practical. People made vows to bind themselves to another. She could do that, and receive someone else's promises, while still knowing that the words were just the intention and not necessarily the destiny. She wanted to believe she made choices, had free will over her future, and these choices really made a difference. Yet just two years earlier she'd been a captive in the microcosm of street drugs. She'd felt herself completely out of control, often unable to handle her highs and poorly equipped to cushion her tumbling lows. She had no influence on the world around her and eventually refused to make choices, accepting the flow of events as if that flow and those events were God's indifferent will. In response to whatever was asked of her, she more often than not had answered, "Sure, why not?"

She curled on her side and took a deep breath. On the exhale she pushed Sanger's worry aside, leaving her with the cozy feelings of sitting with Hugh. She wanted a second opportunity with him and she got it. *Nothing wrong with that,* she thought. Now she wanted a third chance. *I'll try it again tomorrow.* Then she felt Sanger roll out the other side of the bed. *Why is it so hard for him,* she thought, *why can't he be happy for me?*

~ ~ ~

A day or two later, June 17 or 18, Minneapolis

Before eight in the morning, Rooster brewed her first pot of coffee with Alan monitoring, and the four sat sluggish around the kitchen table.

Sanger said, "We've got to thwart Uncle Bill's arrival. That's the easiest. Put him off coming and all we've seen won't happen. He's the key to these unfolding events."

"Maybe," Em said, standing.

"Alan," Sanger went on, "you wouldn't kill that guy without Bill pushing you. And Rooster, you don't want to use the thing again. I'm okay. I've had my experience of being Bill's getaway driver. I don't need to do it again in real time." Left unsaid, but closer to the pin prick of his worry was his desire that Em not go any more rounds with her banker.

When he heard the phone ring, Sanger glanced at the display and couldn't identify the number. He made a shh-sound to the others and whispered, "It might be Uncle Bill."

"Focus," Em said, "If it's Bill, you'll want to know what to say. What are you going to say?"

"I don't know." Sanger picked up the phone and once it was to his ear he heard, "Sanger? Sanger, is that you?"

"Yeah, Uncle Bill, it's me."

"Good. Listen. It'll be another couple of days before I see you. No problems, just some loose ends."

"You've already called and said you'd be a few days

longer."

"That was a few days ago. I'm calling again to say it will be a couple more before I'm there."

Em touched the mute button and said, "Tell him not to come."

Sanger gave Em a stern look and unmuted the phone. "Uncle Bill? I was wondering if I could deliver the package, the steamer trunk, the rest of the way."

"Why would you want to do that?"

"I want to get closer to your operations. You've offered. I want to do more, always have."

Bill laughed. "If you've always anything, you've always been reluctant."

"No, no," Sanger stammered. "I wouldn't say that. I want to save you the trip all the way out here. That part sounds like it's been troublesome for you."

Bill was silent. His pause lingered. "Well, it is hard to get away right now. Not a good time. This and that and then something else. But Sanger, this is for important people and you should replace important with dangerous. You get me?"

"Yeah, yeah. I do. But a delivery's a delivery. What's it matter if I do it or you do it? I just want to help, take a little of the load off your shoulders."

"Thanks. But I don't think so. When I arrive I've got other places to be, other people to see. The bigger picture is more complex than you know. But thanks. I'll remember your offer and keep it in mind in the future."

Looking down at the phone, Sanger raised his eyes to meet Em's. In that moment he knew he'd rather do anything, including reveal they had used the futuristic device, than allow the future Em will experience become real. "No," he blurted. "I don't want you to come here."

"What?"

"Just don't come."

"Why?"

"Don't come. We opened—"

~ ~ ~

Em slapped Sanger on the back of the head and called to the phone, "Bill, we opened a checking account at the National Trust bank."

"Em? Hey, how's Sanger's favorite squeeze?"

Em breathed deep and imagined pulling a cool, damp blanket over her chest. She didn't want to extinguish her hot coals, just temporarily muffle the heat of her anger. "I don't know. When I see her I'll tell her you said hello."

"Good for you," Bill said. "Keep the peace. You're always a kidder."

"Well I'm not kidding now. I ran into someone I know who works in the bank. Hugh Gardner."

Bill paused. "So? That's got nothing to do with the package. Worlds apart."

"Hugh Gardner?" Em said again. "Do you know that name?"

"Should I?"

"Yes, you should. He was trying to chat me up. Knew me a few years back when I was into drugs. Still thinks I'm impressed with the dark side. He said he's got a scam going. Mentioned a lawyer, William Meyer. Do you know that name?"

"I might. You know, I know a lot of people. Names fly by me like billboards on a country road."

Em paused, hoping by now Bill was wiping the sweat from his brow. "You're being set up."

"Hey, don't you worry about me. Thanks for the tip, but you really can't know what your friend was talking about. Men say all sorts of things to impress pretty young things."

Em rubbed her forehead, thinking of what a man stuck on himself might say. "He said, exact words, 'easy as pie. Got a chump on the line. You ought to come around my place and I'll tell you more.'"

Em felt Sanger's stare. She added to Bill, "He said he and his lawyer friend have four bozos who swallowed the line all the way down their gullet. Said these bozos will walk into an office and plunk down forty thousand dollars and then just walk out again. No receipt, no paper trail. But if you don't think that's something you'd ever do...well, just forget it."

Bill was silent. In a moment, he cleared his throat. "I don't know."

Em detected a hint of defeat in his voice as she added. "Bill, don't come out here. Let Sanger deliver the package. Let me gather more information about this scheme against you."

When she heard nothing from Bill's end, she added, "Isn't the delivery of the package getting to be late? Isn't the guy waiting for it getting impatient?"

Em held her breath until finally Bill said, "Okay. All right," along with a few more mumbled words under his breath. He added, "I don't have the delivery address with me but I'll get it to Sanger. Em, you get that information. I won't come out. We'll keep in touch."

"Good," Em said, "that's best." And then she hung up.

After the call, Sanger said, "That's good, right?"

"I don't know," Em said. She turned away from Sanger and pulled on her lower lip. When she turned back, she said, "Bill doesn't come here. No blackmail, so I don't meet Hugh. No delivery of the money, so Alan doesn't kill William Meyer. Sounds good. But what worries me...don't you think convincing Bill was too easy?"

The Beyond Now Device

~ ~ ~

Later that same morning, Minneapolis

The news of Bill's continuing absence swept relief through Alan, followed by disturbing eddies of disappointment. Killing William Meyer had been satisfying for its confirmation of what he could do, although it still lacked the authenticity of the present moment. Compelled to pull the trigger was a mere shadow to really squeezing the gunmetal already warmed by his hand. He needed free choice for the act of murder to convince him he was the man he could be. For a fleeting moment Alan considered his future experiences as nothing more valuable than a false memory. What might be, compared to what might have been, both bolstered by the power of belief.

Alan sat at the table, not knowing he was suffering from the weather dilemma, where prediction carried less weight than the present and led picnickers to embark because it wasn't raining now. Decisions of murder were too weighty to make in the span of a moment, no one should have to—

"If Bill doesn't come," Sanger said, interrupting Alan's thoughts, "none of what we've seen will happen."

"Why not?" Rooster asked. "You could still be the getaway driver for Alan even if your uncle isn't there. Alan could still go visit that lawyer. Em could still go to the bar and sweet talk her honey."

Alan wanted Rooster to shut up. None of those possibilities needed to be said aloud. Bill not coming took away none of their ability to make choices. Even unstated, secretly-desired futures sometimes materialize. He said, "When Bill doesn't come, have we really changed the future? Will none of it happen?"

"We don't know for sure," Em said. "Why couldn't it?" Em stood and held the back of her chair. "All of it could still happen. Lifting Bill away doesn't change us, we're still people who want something and make decisions to get there." Frustrated, Em repeated herself. "All of it could happen. Well…not the gun he gave Alan. But the rest. I know where Hugh drinks. I could go and meet him. Why not?"

There it is, Alan thought. *Em wants the future she's seen. Is it all tied together? Is me killing the attorney the only way for her to meet her banker? Can one future survive separate from the futures around it?*

"Here's a thought," Alan said. "Bill doesn't come. He doesn't hand me a gun. I've got no reason to go to the attorney's office, or any way to kill him even if I do. No need for Sanger to wait on the street and drive a getaway car. No need for Em to meet her banker, no need to blackmail anyone. All this stuff around June thirtieth won't happen. Okay? So now if we use the atomizer, what will happen?"

~ ~ ~

June 21, Minneapolis

How they decided to use the atomizer again was a bickering mess, filled with soft accusations, meaningful groans, and half sentences meant to indicate full paragraphs. To say they made a conscious decision was a conclusion they drew after the fact. Eventually Alan and Em cast strong votes to use the mister again. Sanger was as strongly opposed. Rooster sat at the table with the grownups but still had a foot in childhood. More than the others, she felt a pull toward the familiarity of the past, even a past she was currently trying to escape. For a moment she believed there was nothing in the future she would strive for, not like what the others had in mind for themselves. So they would do what they wanted, her voice even less than a pesky fly buzzing around their ears. At most, decisions only for herself. And hers was a cautious wait-and-see.

The next morning after Sanger went to work, Em, Alan, and Rooster sat with dirty breakfast plates still on the kitchen table. Alan touched the mister as though it was a joint ready to be plucked and lit.

"Well, here goes." He gave the bulb a healthy squeeze. In the particles drifting toward him, Alan saw a line of coconut palms silhouetted from the sea behind, leaning sharply in hurricane winds, the fronds pointing away like a row of feather dusters. He reached one hand to touch the apparition and...

*

...hesitated, hand held ready to open the door to William Meyer's office. Once in, he stood in front of the large desk and groaned at the familiarity.

Mr. Meyer looked up. "You from the courier company? Where's Andrew?" He paused and then added, "Doesn't matter. I don't have anything for you."

Alan sensed something familiar about the office. He pushed his glasses up his nose and then coughed once, twice, and with the third he barked under his breath, "Doesn't matter." An irresistible urge of echolalia set in. Once named, Alan was unable to stop his next statement. "I don't have anything for you."

Having suffered intermittent bouts of it after his wife died, Alan's control then had been to replace the repetitive phrases he felt compelled to voice with off-the-cuff rhyming, others finding rhymes slightly less annoying than echolalia.

Alan's urge overwhelmed him and more words burst forth, as though expelled by Tourette's. "I don't have anything for you." And then he added, in a vain attempt to control his mouth, his words, his environment, and his miniscule presence in the entirety of the cosmos, "Doesn't matter if letter or lacquer or smatter of liquor."

"What?" William Meyer said.

"What?" Alan repeated.

"Oh God, if you're not from the courier's, you've got to be from Bill. Do you have it? Do you have Bill's forty thousand dollars?"

Alan watched William Meyer eye him up and down, feeling as if every inch of him was being covered with the paint from a spray gun.

"You got the money?" William Meyer asked again.

"I don't have anything for you." Alan repeated, now stuck on a handful of words, a distinct subclass of the whole English set. Words were scrambling to get out of his mouth and he needed to distract them. "...anything for you. I mean, favors in lieu of Bill coming through with what he's got due."

"What?" William Meyer wiped his face with his left palm and looked at Alan again. "I've got...listen, Bill needs to bring that money. People need it now. Very, very serious people."

Alan put his face into the crook of his elbow as if to sneeze, but the words escaped anyway. "Doesn't matter."

William Meyer sat up straighter. "Doesn't matter?"

"Doesn't matter?" Alan repeated, mimicking Mr. Meyer's inflection.

William Meyer caught Alan's tone and pounded a fist on his desk. "Don't mock me. What's the matter with you? This is important. I need Bill's money."

"I don't have anything for you," Alan said again.

"Get out of here. Tell Bill I need that money as soon as possible. Sooner. I need it today. And tell him to answer his goddamned phone. Tell him that."

Alan put his hands in his jacket pockets to stem their shaking. He lifted his face toward Mr. Meyer and said, "Anything for you."

The Beyond Now Device

William Meyer, Attorney at Law, stood behind his desk. "What did you say? Nobody makes fun of me like that. The next words out of your mouth better not mimic me." He put his hands flat on his desk and leaned on his shoulders. "You better squawk something I haven't already heard."

"I don't have anything for you," Alan said. His right hand artlessly wrapped the handle of the gun in his pocket and his index finger naturally slipped between guard and trigger. He lifted the handgun and fired twice into William Meyer's chest. He did it without debate, without consensus, without considering alternatives or consequences. In that rote moment, the seconds were as familiar as putting his face under a warm welcoming shower. Spots and flecks of blood filled the air. He reached to wipe his face and knocked his glasses to the floor.

After a stunned moment, William Meyer fell forward across his desk.

Alan turned and believed he needed to report this to the police. Make the call, wait for them at the front entrance, hold the gun high for them to see, and wait for their response. As he reached for the phone…

*

…he placed the atomizer at arm's length on the kitchen table. Em and Rooster stared. He was momentarily disoriented by pain in his fingers but still knew what they wanted to know. "I was in his office again," Alan said. "And I shot him. I was back here before calling the police, but that's what I was going to do next"

Em said, "I'm sorry, Alan. I'm sorry you had to do that again."

Alan shrugged. "Like a kid putting his head under water, it's a little easier each time."

"That can't be good," Rooster said.

"I couldn't help it. I felt out of control, compelled. I had a bout of echolalia, couldn't overcome it. Echolalia! It really put William Meyer off."

"Eco-what?" Rooster asked.

Alan ignored her question, covered his mouth to keep from vomiting, and said, "I dropped my glasses, kicked them under his desk."

"I'll get them for you," Rooster said. "Did you touch anything else? I'll slip in and get your glasses."

~ ~ ~

Before anyone could counter her move, Rooster grabbed the atomizer. "Fingerprints? Did you put anything down, pick anything up?" A future she had never seen or imagined opened before her and she was swept by an overwhelming desire to help Alan. She felt it as jaw-clenching determination and set her face in a mask of resolve. She straightened her chair and said, "I'll take care of it."

Rooster aimed the atomizer's nozzle up and squeezed the bulb. A cloud formed in the air above her head, then drifted down so her face was in the middle of it. During the first half of her blink…

*

…she reached for the door whose frosted glass displayed in gold lettering: William Meyer, Attorney at Law.

She hesitated and then knocked on the door. Rooster didn't expect an answer, wasn't he dead already? "Mr. Meyer," she called.

Pushing the door open, she stepped through the reception.

The odor of rust and stale books struck her, initiating peristalsis in her intestines. In the office a man sprawled across the large desk. Through the room's sticky humidity a few buzzing flies lazily circled the body.

She didn't like buzzing, an annoying sound, and wondered where they came from, how long he must have been there for flies to have found him. She waved a hand to disperse them and thought Mr. Meyer's name was familiar. After a deep breath, she looked at him more closely, confirming she will not be able to wake him.

Flies always tell the tale of success. She couldn't imagine where that came from or even what it meant. Yet she had a feeling of success, buoyant ease growing toward satisfaction. Words circled the room as a great sense of...she tried a few of those words, giving them life by saying them aloud, "Satisfaction, serenity, ease, right." *Yes, that's it. All can be set right. Come on then, let's put things right.*

A pleasant hum filled her chest and she liked how putting things right felt. Rooster looked at the piles of books and strewn papers. She especially noted the bottle of whiskey and three shot glasses. There was a lot of blood spreading on the desk and seeping into the man's clothing. Startled and sickened and satisfied. *Let's clean up. He'll make no more messes.*

She stepped behind the desk and after a moment of listening for footsteps, opened the bottom drawer on the right. She knew what to do but couldn't remember instructions. In the drawer rested a leather briefcase. She lifted it, first with one hand and then with both because of how tightly it was wedged in.

Rooster opened the briefcase and saw bundles of paper money. *Holy smoke. That's a lot of loot.* She placed the briefcase on the floor and remembered Alan's glasses. Bending at her waist, knees stiff, hair grazing the floor, she saw them under the desk…along with a handgun. Crawling, she retrieved the glasses but was unable to touch the gun.

The gun brought Rooster to appreciate the seriousness of what she was doing. Much of her world had taken place in the nether land between what she wanted and what she actually did. Although the two seemed side by side, she was occasionally struck by the gap that separated them. Rooster took a deep breath and thought she couldn't stop in the middle, had got to carry through. With a pen from William Meyer's desk, she bent again and pulled the gun toward her. Then she slipped the pen through the trigger guard and lifted, just like in a police drama.

She dropped the gun into the briefcase and then used thumb and index finger to pick up Alan's glasses, sticky with blood. She placed them in the briefcase.

Getting up and standing behind the dead man prone over his desk, she took another deep breath and pushed his rolling office chair to the back of his knees. From behind, she reached and wedged her hands under his armpits while pressing her body to the back of the chair. She pulled him but he didn't budge. *He's heavy.* Then with great effort, she hefted him back and he landed with a plop, slouching in his chair. *Comfy now, Mr. Meyer?*

She grasped the top of Mr. Meyer's abundant hair and pulled him backwards toward the corner of the room, leaving her space to walk around his desk.

Rooster stopped for a moment, compelled by confusion to assess her situation. The opportunity to help Alan was like fate. *Everything past*, she thought, *and all that's to come is part of my destiny. It's led me to this moment—where I'll truly help someone.*

After sliding the back of one hand across her forehead, she stood with thumbs in her waistband and evaluated her progress. She next emptied a plastic shopping bag from a local department store. When she stood up she was struck by a quiver that ran through her, a jiggling of time perhaps. She sat for a moment and questioned the complications of destroying evidence in the future. Not destroying. Reshaping an event so the next to see it would interpret it not as it happened. Acting in the world suddenly felt very serious. It all held responsibility, anything from releasing her bad mood on others, to tossing cigarette butts behind the school. Her recognition of unforeseen consequences slowed her movements.

It was dark through the window and she heard no sounds in the office. *Alan didn't deserve punishment for what he'd done. Even if he killed someone?* Rooster paused as if looking at a fork in the road. *Even then.*

Thinking it likely Alan had touched them, she put the bottle of alcohol, upside-down and stuffed along one edge, plus the shot glasses, in the briefcase. She looked for any other fingerprint-prone items. Last she examined the open surfaces of the desk, newly sprayed with a fine mist of blood.

As she secured a good grip on the briefcase she could still feel her fist full of William Meyer's hair. Looking up and back at him, she froze for a moment at his purple-pale face and his hair standing on end. Turning away, beads of sweat ran down her ribs. Parts of her sleeveless summer blouse were already damp and stuck to her skin. She looked around the room and shivered as the hairs on her arms stood on end.

With the briefcase in hand, she stepped into the corridor. While walking, another wave of prickliness undulated over her skin. She wasn't sure where to go. Turning quickly, she lost balance, reached for the wall…

*

…and found herself placing the atomizer back on the kitchen table. She looked at her torso. No briefcase handle in her grip. No featureless office corridor surrounding her. Rooster was at the same time relieved, disappointed, confused, and nauseated.

"I got your glasses, Alan. I put them in the briefcase."

"What briefcase?" Em asked. "Did you go to William Meyer's office?"

"I did, I did, I did," she said smiling. "I helped Alan. The guy was already dead. Dead when I got there."

"William Meyer?" Alan asked.

"Yes. I found him all dead and bloody. Flies circling around. I..." she covered her mouth. "I did all I did to help you. But—"

"What did you do?" Alan asked.

"I put your glasses in the briefcase with the gun from under his desk. I took the bottle of alcohol, plus the three shot glasses. I brought it all out."

"What alcohol?" Alan asked. "What glasses?"

"Listen," Rooster said. "He was dead, bloody, flies, smells." She swallowed hard. "I feel sick." Rooster pulled her bangs. "Jesus, what have I done?" But after a quick pause, she added, "He was dead. So I got rid of evidence. That's right. It's now like you weren't there. You won't be arrested, no trial, no one will ever know." Rooster looked at Alan as pain in her temples caused her eyes to blink rapidly. "I didn't think it through. I just wanted to help. I mean, he was smelly. I think he crapped his pants."

"Oh dear," Em said. She sat and put an arm around Rooster's shoulders. "I'm sorry you had to...felt you had to...will do…"

Rooster sat taller in her chair and said, "I put things right. That's what I did. I fixed it. I cleaned the office. I got Alan's glasses. I got the gun. And I got all that money in the briefcase."

"Money?" Alan asked. "What money?"

Rooster wiped sweat from her face and returned her focus to Alan. "It was in the briefcase in the lawyer's desk drawer. I was supposed to get it. Or no…that's right. I knew I was supposed to get the briefcase." Rooster rubbed her forehead.

Alan added, "You stole money? I never took money to William Meyer's office. Whose money did you take?"

"Maybe," Em said, "maybe sometime you do take Bill's money to the attorney."

"I hope so," Rooster said, "because Alan's glasses are in with the money now. Or will be then."

CHAPTER TWELVE

Third week in June, Minneapolis

Over the next couple of days, for as little real-time as it took to journey to the future and return—a tease of fragrance, a sudden glance, glint, blink, no time really—it was surprising how much time these episodes consumed afterwards, most of it done privately rather than with the input of others. When they did speak together, half sentences, reconsidered statements and bewildered, open-mouthed non-utterances filled their conversations. They knew they were tinkering around the edges rather than diving into the thick of their concerns. Rooster, who didn't want Alan's future to appear, suggested a rubber band around his wrist, or string tied around his finger so he wouldn't forget...forget?...she wasn't sure. Em considered wearing the clothes she wore in the bar, hoping for time to recognize her and slip her to that moment again. But how to control coming events, welcome or not, eluded them.

There was one thing they all agreed upon, and Em said it first. "Do you know we're all coming back a little sick."

Alan wiped his forehead. "It's not like a disease. Just disorientation, motion sickness. Don't you think?"

Em stared at the atomizer. She looked forward to re-meeting her banker and her mind had regularly toyed with the thought. "I'm going to take a turn," she said, expecting her keen interest to appear as just one of the gang, another volunteer at taking her turn.

She squeezed the bulb and a white cloud, less dense than fog, formed in front of her. As she pushed her face through it, inhaling as she went, she had the impression of dew on her cheeks and the gentle touch of feathers. She began a blink and...

*

...opened her eyes while walking, stumbling with her first step. It was a warm night and a gloss of sweat formed on her forehead and between her breasts. She shrugged out of her light cardigan sweater as Hugh Gardner loped to catch up with her. She assumed they met in the bar and were now walking to...where? She wanted to ask him but knew it would sound peculiar if she was bewildered by what she should already know.

Em held her clutch purse close to her stomach and reached in, hoping to find a phone, especially the date-display. She dug farther and saw a one hundred dollar bill. Surely it was Bill's contribution to what she and Hugh were expected to do next. She clicked the purse shut and considered her mixed feelings. She didn't want to do it with Hugh simply to further Bill's crazy scheme. Yet it wasn't that she didn't want to do it with Hugh at all.

They walked together in silence and Em worried their absence of banter might cause Hugh to wonder if she still wanted to go where they were going. "I swear we've met before," Em said, risking sounding foolish or, worse, idiotic.

"No," Hugh replied, "not until you bumped into my barstool. I'd have remembered."

Em still felt the easy pleasure she had felt days ago in a previous future-projection. Yet for Hugh, he was surely remembering an encounter that took place only minutes ago. She slipped her arm under his elbow and raised his forearm level with the pavement.

He placed a hand on hers and said, "I feel like an old European couple out on their nightly promenade. When I was in Italy I saw old couples walking like this. They looked like they'd been together forever."

When Em didn't say anything, Hugh added, "This friend's uncle of yours who wants to meet with me tomorrow…might he be a future uncle-in-law?"

The question made Em's heart pound. At the intersection, she felt as if she'd run full speed to the edge of a precipice and stopped on a dime. On the far side she saw the free woman she wanted to be, triumphing in the world as she wished it was, telling Hugh the truth about her relationship with Sanger, vowing all was possible as long as insistence was honey and an open mind the tea to put it in. With the toe of her shoe hanging over the edge of the curb, the other side was too far for the leap she considered making.

Pausing for traffic, she looked down the imagined precipice and watched a cluster of women struggling to accommodate common expectations; women who understood only baby steps brought real change; women who regretted the bruises they pressed into the delicate feelings of those closest to them.

It can't be as simple as that, Em thought. *Struggle together inside our roles or go alone with my own beliefs. Can't be only this or that.*

"Em," Hugh said. "Your uncle?"

What was the question? Uncle-in-law? "No," she said, knowing even the slightest hint of uncertainty would leave the impression that paragraphs of later explanation wouldn't supersede. She wanted to tell Hugh, be as direct and earnest as the woman warrior would be. Yet everyone had delicate feelings protected by the familiarity of their relationships. In her mind she tried. *Sanger is to me…I am to Sanger…he understands me, accepts me…doesn't he?*

"My place is just a few blocks ahead," Hugh said. He turned chatty and Em listened with only one ear. The returning image of women struggling to hold their place on the steep precipice monopolized the rest of her attention. *It can't be as simple as struggle with others or dream alone. Why can't I be with two men? Love them for different reasons. Who'd want me to love them for the same reason? Yet it's the part of me I might give to Hugh, and not give to Sanger, that will hurt Sanger most. Shit, I've got tears in my eyes. Can't look up.*

Stroking her lower eyelid and smearing wet across her cheek, she felt Hugh's grip on her arm tighten as he said, as if from the far end of a tunnel, "Hey, you okay?"

A man had once told her there's nothing more attractive than a woman crying. He had meant it as a post-pummeling delight for himself and Em had sworn to not let tears have their way with her again. She blinked a few times and when she lifted her head…

*

...she looked into the eager faces of Alan and Rooster. Un-worded images streamed through, cascading over one another. *Hugh knew me*, she thought, *we must have met in the bar.* Em shook her head. *He was walking me home, to his home. That's...is that good or not?* Em wished she didn't have a connection with Sanger's uncle. *And Sanger*, she thought, *I withheld information about Sanger. There are no plans for Bill to become my uncle-in-law. But that doesn't mean there's nothing to share with Hugh about Sanger.*

"Well?" Rooster said. "What happened?"

"I stood on the edge of a deep ravine. On the other side I was a feminist warrior, rejoicing for the world I wish we lived in. Alone. And—"

"That sounds great," Rooster said as she leaned closer.

"But halfway down the ravine," Em continued, "a group of women worked together to make the world a better place. They were slower, accommodating, compromising. But together."

"So you didn't go," Alan asked, "to the saga of Uncle Bill? You weren't in that story at all?"

"That's not true. I met with the banker. It was earlier than our appointment in his office but later than first talking to him in the bar." Em paused. "I need some time to figure this out. And, yow, have I got a headache."

~ ~ ~

June 24, Chicago

Niko pinned the postcard he had received from a coworker high on the wall farthest from his couch. By reclining on pillows and squinting, the tightly packed script displayed an image of the main grove of trees on campus. How could she know his feelings for that spot? What more was she saying in her cryptic phrases? He considered it a magical postcard as the sensations of the university came back to him in the dense text of her penmanship. He knew it wasn't what she said with words, her encouragement to keep his chin up, her conveyance of well-wishes from others. There was something unstated but essential cleverly hidden in her subtext.

He got up and walked half circles in front of the hanging postcard, cupping his forehead or scratching his scalp. When his phone rang, the hairs on his arms stood on end with expectation of a call from the university. He picked it up before noting the calling number. "Yes," he said, like the first chirp of a morning bird.

"Niko, this is Em."

Immediately disappointed, Niko replied, "Oh. Yes. Yes, of course."

Instead of asking the questions that might have been on her mind, Em began with something general and open for any type of answer. "It's well known that a square is a rectangle with its four sides the same length. Why isn't there something about time as clear as that?"

Niko looked at the postcard again and all of what he'd seen remained. He knew he was no longer there but could smell the autumn leaves on the lawn, the exuberance of a new academic year beginning. It felt as real now as it had been then.

He took a deep breath and said, "There is something as clear as that. The present moment exists. It's during now all of our sensory capacity is available. Recollected feelings are happening now, the warm glow generated by past experience is as real as the original. And we experience it right now. The person I was fills me. The person I will become grows from the roots I plant now."

With the phone in the center of the kitchen table, Em,

Alan, and Rooster looked at each other, suspicious. It was Em who said, "Niko, are you all right?"

"Yes, of course. I am...I just woke from a dream. Let me have a minute. No, I'll ring you back." And then he ended the call.

Niko settled himself by getting out his small espresso machine, filling the tank, grinding the beans, putting the grounds in the portafilter, half filling the frothing pitcher with milk, and screwing, sliding, locking everything into place. After turning the machine on he looked away and focused on now. But thoughts brought his fingers to stroke his face and he didn't stop until he heard the popping of the drip. Stooping, he watched the crema spiral from the spout into his cup and smelled the aromatic espresso.

Shifting the controller from pressure to steam, he held his frothing-pitcher under the nozzle. When hot and foamy enough, he poured the milk into the shot of espresso. Coffee in hand, Niko walked back to his phone and called Em.

When Em answered, she said, "Niko? Are you okay?"

"Yes. I composed myself. I'm ready for your questions. Let me first say that though there may be disagreement about the when and how of the future, we surely agree on the existence of now. Now is the pocket in which we hold every bit of our anticipation. The same pocket where we do all of our waiting. Like it or not, we're all keenly aware of anticipatory waiting. Curiosity encourages hunch. Apprehension heightens surprise. Foreboding trashes hope. We long to foresee the future and wish to control what will be shown. Is it too much to ask when we're perpetually stuck in now? Always now, of course, when else could it be?"

"Niko," Em said. "Now's okay with me. No problem. But I want some control over what's going to happen."

"Yes, yes." Niko shook his head back to the present.

"Predict the future. Determinists know everything appears through a series of causes. If the stream of causes is known then the future is obvious. This assumes a future already out there because the line of events all point to it. When time has a Super-beginning—God started it all or the Big Bang set it all in motion—the beginning of time and the end of time were locked at the moment of birth. Discovering God's will, or knowing every previous cause, that's the key to knowing what the future holds. Through those eyes, even the choices you make appear inevitable upon looking back."

"Okay, determinism," Em said. "Fate and destiny. How do I make what I know of the future happen?"

Niko laughed. "What makes you think it won't?"

"But maybe change it a bit."

Niko laughed again. "Change it to what? But yes, I see. You want to try your hand at free will. But here you've got to believe the future is not already out there. You've got to have faith in something that doesn't yet exist. You've got to assume it's created with each passing now, one instance coming into being out of a range of infinite possibilities. So think of time as a gigantic rope-making machine where various strands of future are collected and twisted together during now. Bind tightly those moments, twist them into events, enfold them into action, and spew them out behind as a braided past. It's a good story."

"That's the one," Em said. "Future's not out there, yet. We make decisions now to have the future we want. Is that how it works?"

"Almost." Niko took another swallow of his latte. "Of the decisions we make each day, we only make a few. Potentially, many could be made. Of the decisions we don't make, they are every bit as important as the decisions we make. As you follow an indecisive road, you'll set the future through lethargy as much as with energy. And, too, remain responsible for all the unintended consequences. Free will. Phew! Who's so willing to accept full responsibility when choices are half-hearted, lackadaisical, or you simply refuse to choose?"

"I thought you said," Em asked, "that it didn't matter what we thought of time. The truth of time would be whatever it is no matter what we thought."

"Yes, of course. Time doesn't care what you think. But how you think of time makes a world of difference. Educated, entrepreneurial, reasonable, TV-watching people are at heart determinists. They see predictable planetary orbits. They schedule their next haircut. They order causes like ducks in a row and assume the inevitable future is a consequence of those ducks. They believe truth exists, all can be understood, and we are better-off knowing it. These are the beliefs of a determinist, someone who knows the future exists and it is out there waiting for our discovery upon arrival."

"I believe those things," Em said, "But I'd have said I believe in free will. Not determinism."

"Yes, yes," Niko said. "You're a product of the modern world. Of course you prefer free will. But let me finish with a story. It goes like this. Time is the ultimate illusionary elixir. As I sit across the table from my heartthrob, we pick up our wine glasses at the same time. We sip together. Through the fluke intertwining of our movements, I feel a connection. We smile, thinking of ourselves as one. Through the coincidence of this shared moment, I feel close to her.

"Others in the restaurant may tip their glasses simultaneously with us. Perhaps hundreds in the city, millions on the planet may tip their glasses right now. But now has never had the power to connect us all, at least not on its own. Through all of human history we have needed 'here' for us to get the most out of 'now.' If a million sip wine right now, I only care about those with me, and in particular the one across the table from me, right here. As we tip glasses at the same time, we appreciate the magic of the moment. That's the ancient view of destiny—that which happens by serendipity and chance must have been destined to happen.

"Since the beginning of time, time has been taken for granted and only considered important when coupled with 'here.' I know only a little of what's happening thousands of miles away right now. Never has it been possible to know the content of now unless that content was also right here. Until recently.

"The telegraph opened minds to the magic of currently knowing a distant now. It was soon followed by telephone and radio. Short wave enthusiasts sprinkled the globe. Telephone lines were originally sparse and limited to a few populated areas. Currently, anyone with a smart phone and an instant-messaging account can know that right now in a faraway land a demonstration is being crushed and the police are now pulling their night sticks out. It can both be happening and I know about it at the same time, regardless of whether here or not.

"A revolution in our understanding of time is near. Now's tight connection with here has made it difficult to understand time. Yet as we stream into the future, we must square ourselves with the intricacies of now as thoroughly as we appreciate the spatial dimensions of here."

Niko sat back with his cup of coffee and thought he was done, explained enough, and conclusions would be obvious. "Do you get it?" he asked.

"Not quite," Em said.

"Okay," Niko said. "One more time. A leap in our concept of time has taken place. For us to keep up with new thought we must dig our explanation of time out of the fifth century and reconstruct it with knowledge from the last hundred years. I recently sat on the edge of a small lake with a child. At dusk, she said, 'I like sunset the best.'

"You see. Already she was misspeaking what we watched, as though the sun dipped lower and lower, settling itself into a nice warm bed. Reality isn't always what it seems.

"I used a ball we had with us as a visual aid. As I rotated the orb I pointed out the shadow that crept across it. I explained we revolve around the sun to make a year. My half-sized companion knew that. And we spin on an axis, like a ballerina, to make a day. She knew that, too. Even though it looked like the sun was dipping lower and lower, it was really us upon the earth, spinning dizzily backwards. Horizon-rise before our very eyes.

"We nearly lost our balance just thinking about it. It is this quality of change that radicalizes my imagery of sunset, making me put a layer of intelligence between my understanding and the intuitive feel of time."

CHAPTER THIRTEEN

Same day, Minneapolis

Later that evening, Em sat on the edge of the bed, staring at nothing. The sound of traffic was as quiet as ever. Sanger tinkered in the bathroom. Em wasn't tired and focused on the mister and her experiences with it. *Have we all time-jaunted into the future? Could any good really come out of changing the future?* Em felt as though her thoughts were sitting at the bottom of a pool and wished they'd come up for air.

She slid into bed, curled away from Sanger's side, and pressed her head into the pillow. After Sanger finished in the bathroom, he clambered into bed. Em felt him run his hand just above the skin of her arm. He cleared his throat and she knew he'll soon speak. She sensed his hand over her skin again, as though his hand was filled with static electricity and drew her hairs upright.

"You, uhm," Sanger began. "You...are you hoping to see the bank guy again?"

"Why do you ask?"

"Alan mentioned he thought you were keen on your future. So, do you want to see him again?"

"How can I do that? There's nothing we can do to control the whereabouts or timeframe."

"That's a little harsh. Don't you think we have to keep believing we can control things?"

"Maybe so. But we can't control everything."

"Still, that doesn't answer my question. If you could, would you...want to see him again?"

Em pressed her face into the pillow. "Want to see him again! You make it sound like we've been on a date. I don't know him, I've never met him."

"You will."

Em felt flustered by her indirectness. She regretted not telling Hugh about Sanger and now couldn't muster the courage to tell Sanger about Hugh. "I might see him again. I don't know how it works. Who knows where the future will take us?" Em slid closer to the edge of the bed.

She felt Sanger move away. The tingle of the hairs on her arm disappeared and she knew he was on his back.

"Just tell me what you want, what you imagine," he said.

Em sat up and dropped her feet to the floor. "I don't know these things. I'm going to the kitchen." She stood and pulled on one of Sanger's dress shirts.

The Beyond Now Device

Sanger felt the spit and pop of a boiling caldron in the pit of his stomach. He had never felt the need to distinguish between feelings he generated for no good reason and those he felt due to a legitimate cause. He assumed all he felt was well-founded. He trusted his body. Yet he had watched Alan feel useless when there was nothing to be done anyway. He had listened to Alan's convoluted description of the forces out to get him and the situations lined up to thwart his intentions. Sanger understood Alan believed it was all true, but also knew it was Alan's own mind developing the picture. Sanger's current nauseous feelings were validated by his suspicions, his suspicions nourished by Em's reluctance to talk. He covered his eyes with his forearm and thought, *she'll soon be having sex behind my back; doing things with him she's never done with me; enjoying his silvery fingers beyond anything I've ever made her feel.*

Sanger rolled to his side and curled into a loose fetal position. His thoughts were the type that should never form physical vibrations in the real world. "I'm jealous," he mumbled quietly to himself, "because I love her. If I didn't love her, I wouldn't be jealous. That's how it works. Shit." Sanger clenched his jaw and then relaxed in his assumption of love, no matter how bad it made him feel.

Same day, Chicago

At about the same time, Niko sat on his couch and stared at a bright rectangle of light on the opposite wall. Streaming through his window from the streetlight outside, it made no sound but he stared at it as if it was screaming. Losing his professorship had stunned Niko. His life had grown unbalanced, pushing him to wonder about the essence of real. The light was real, measurable and detectable. But was dark real? *If dark was merely the absence of light, could I see it reflected from the floor or wrap myself in its cloak? Could I really fill a box with it?*

Niko's mind was saturated with gaps of absence and the edges of dark thoughts he couldn't render. *There's only now*, Niko repeated. *There's only now. Only the present moment exists. This moment is my sensory capacity. Nothing is as vividly startling as this present. Now is self-evident. Only what happens now is real. Everything beyond the will or was of now is whimsical mirage, unsubstantiated notion, a dangerous glance into the precipice of nothing.*

Niko stood and raised his arm into the line of light, casting a shadow of a bird with his hand. *A moment ago the shadow wasn't there*, he thought. *Now it is, but then it wasn't. Then is as real as now, the absence of shadow as real as the current shadow.*

He made the shadow-bird nod its head a few times. And then a memory from his childhood came to mind. *Is the past as real as unicorns, as real as a story's meaning? As real as the kitchen table...*in his childhood home where his older brother once threw a fork that stuck in his sister's forehead. Just as she turned, the tines approached, piercing her skin, bruising her skull, but leaving no lasting damage other than four diagonal dots above her left eyebrow that never went away.

Even the memory didn't compare to the real event as his father stormed across the room screaming, "Jesus, Petr, Jesus," throttling his neck with dirty, calloused hands, as his mother shrieked, and his sister stared, and he, amazed at the graceful choreography of tines and forehead, imagined the slow dance of moons colliding. Graceful wasn't real, not as real as choreography, which wasn't as real as a fork's single tine. The notions used to organize thought were not as real as the objects that filled those thoughts. And this memory was a pale substitute for the real thing, a thing that destined his future.

If he could return to that moment and raise a hand in the flight path of the fork, the cascading consequences wouldn't have occurred. But there was no going back. Hot coffee cooled to air temperature without any greater effort than patience. Hot tempers dissipated and frightened onlookers absorbed the dissipation. Ordered states vanished into disordered states. A glass of milk teetered on the edge of a counter. Once it fell and broke, it was impossible to predict where each shard would stop or each bare foot would tread. There were just too many possibilities, too much disorder.

Physical laws work mathematically, regardless of the direction of time—except the second law of thermodynamics. Entropy dictates the direction of time. A cooling cup of coffee will not absorb heat from the room and begin steaming at a temperature higher than the ambient tepidness of the room. A natural law. And Niko believed it. There was no going back.

Niko stood in the dark while his thoughts were on fire, finally separating the chaff from the wheat and setting it ablaze. *Now exists and is real. The past is real because that had been the start, the initial condition.* But he couldn't let his mind rest there. There had been no rest there. Now. Then. Now then.

As an escape he thought, *only light is real. Only things made of light are real. Coal and ferns and silicon and lithium. The list is endless but not infinite. Everything isn't real. There's no law against speaking of things that aren't real, of filling the heads of children with resurrection and living forever and compound interest and tomorrow. Tines in her forehead. Four diagonal dots. The sign of...* Hope survived in refusing what he knew, never knowing it again.

To trust that tomorrow will be substantially like today ignores tipping points, critical moments, earthquakes tearing the skin, tornadoes whisking the atmosphere, and epiphanies that rocked worlds and set Niko on a new course. *The past is real,* he thought. *The present is real. The future is real. The course was set by my past, turned toward a momentous now, and has carried me into this particular future. I can't think about it.*

The imagining, the memory, paled in light of real events. *There's only now,* Niko repeated. *There's only now.* Niko wanted to anchor himself to others who also speculated on the reality of time. He touched in the number of those four with his device and listened for its ring.

Simultaneously in Minneapolis

As Niko touched to make the connection to Sanger's phone, Em stepped straight to the middle of the living room. She stared at the atomizer and thought it should animate, turn toward her and snarl. Or perhaps wink, tilt its cocky head and whisper, 'Come on, I know you want to squeeze me.' Em took two steps and picked it up. Wearing only Sanger's shirt that hung to mid-thigh, loose and airy, she felt suddenly self-conscious, as though wrapped in nothing more than an after shower hand towel. She held the heft of the atomizer's scrotum in her left hand, a substantial weight-to-size ratio that drew her closer.

Em didn't know what to tell Sanger. She was attracted to these future runs, intrigued by a set of physical and emotional responses that felt truly her own. Sexuality had always been utilitarian, good for the peaceful coexistence of herself and the impulse-enhanced men she had too often known. But if she had to strive, strut, and swagger the way men did, she wouldn't bother. She had never groomed for a special *him*, never thought much about the back and forth of flirt and response.

She believed these feelings embedded in a future event were worth exploring. She wanted to explain it as simple as that to Sanger. *Nothing personal,* she thought, *no reflection on you, nothing to do with you. Can't you see that?* But she knew he couldn't. He had no skill at pulling himself out of a situation and observing it from a distance. That was her attraction to Sanger-the-Reliable. He was one hundred percent immersed in whatever caught his attention. She found it attractive, the boyish way he pulled on his ear while reading, or methodically cut tomatoes as if listening to a metronome.

Em held the atomizer and gently stroked the pouch as if it was a badly bruised peach. *Now or never*, she thought. She looked toward the bedroom and squeezed the bulb, dispersing a cloud of dust into her face. Her eyes watered. She held her breath and for a fraction of a second she saw a painting by Claude Monet, The Japanese Bridge, melting out of its frame, an image unusually thick with paint and nearly unrecognizable. As she drew in breath, she heard Sanger's phone buzz and…

*

…recognized a noisy bar, a booth, and Uncle Bill's moving lips, "…don't cry, sweetie, we won't do it that way. Okay? No big deal. But you got to know, it was worth asking. You understand? So, forgive me."

Not understanding, Em reacted from what she knew of Bill and rolled her eyes. Wearing one of Sanger's dress shirts, she pressed the collar and brought it tighter around her neck. She knew Uncle Bill had made some foul request, but couldn't place what it was. Sensing a momentary fear that Bill might force her brought a prickly sensation of challenge and strike. Without identifying Bill's request, Em said, "I don't know how you can even think I'd… I mean it, that's degrading and you shouldn't insult me like that."

"Yeah, yeah, I hear you. Okay." Bill slid his beer bottle from one hand to the other. "I'm running out of options here. He's just up at the bar, looks like a nice guy, don't you think? Go up and talk to him. Just talk. And take this with you." Bill held a small black plastic rectangle, half the size of a credit card. He reached and slipped it into Em's shirt pocket, gathering a feel of her left breast with the back of his fingers.

"Hey," she said. "What's that?"

Bill spread thumb and forefinger about two inches apart, indicating the size of the object, and said, "It's a small—"

"No, I mean copping a feel. What do you think you're doing?"

"Just a mistake, sweetie. Clumsy me. Thick fingers. I meant no harm. But I dropped an audio recorder in your pocket. Just go up and talk to him. Record the whole thing and take it home with you. I'll come around to Sanger's place...I'm sorry, yours and Sanger's place tomorrow. Give it back to me then."

"I don't know. Why should I?"

Bill pulled a hundred dollar bill from his pocket and said, "Tomorrow. If you record his voice saying anything, anything at all, I'll slip this into your underwear drawer."

"Ew. You're sick."

Bill smiled as he got up from the booth. "It's up to you. I'm just asking a favor. Talk nice to him. Let him talk nice to you. Flirt. You're young, be happy."

Em pulled the audio recording card from her pocket and stared at it, assuming it was already on, and then returned it. Looking left, an empty stool stood beside the guy. She left her beer on the table and sauntered over. After climbing on the stool she turned to him and said, "Hey."

When he only stared at her, she added, "Aren't you?" pointing at him a few times. "You're..."

"Do I know you?"

"Oh," Em said. She put her elbows on the bar and leaned. *Shit*, she thought, *he doesn't know me*. She looked at him again, wondering if she could supply a reminder of something that for him had not yet happened. He caught her glance and she turned away.

Hugh asked, "Waiting for someone?"

"No, just thinking." Em lifted her elbows off the bar and dropped her arms to her sides. She turned toward him, but without his recognition she still felt immersed in the dirty wake of Uncle Bill. She didn't feel attractive, couldn't even muster a flirtatious smile.

"I'm Hugh," he said, extending a hand. "Can I buy you a drink?"

"I'm Em. Yes, I'd like that. Whatever you're drinking."

Hugh signaled the bartender and then faced Em again. "Do you come here often? Well, I guess you don't or I'd have noticed you before."

"No, you're right. Not often. I'm here as a favor to my...my friend's uncle, I'm on a secret mission."

"Oh? Tell me about it."

"No, Hugh. It wouldn't be a secret then, would it?"

"You're right. So what do you do when you're not on secret missions?"

"Between jobs, you might say." She liked his smile and wanted to tell him enough while still maintaining some mystery. "I used to be a school teacher but had some life problems and took time to recover. I was an art student in college and now audit some classes locally."

"That's very interesting. Is studying art like going through a Liberal Arts course, get a taste of a lot of things?"

Curiosity piqued, Em appreciated his ability to skip over her hardship and ask about what was once good in her life. She turned one hundred and eighty degrees and leaned her back against the bar. "Some schools are. Mine was more for people who already knew what they wanted. We were given a lot of freedom. The best thing I learned was how to set up a studio, materials to buy, amount of space needed for sculpture versus painting versus printmaking. That type of thing."

Forgetting Uncle Bill as she talked, leaning back relaxed, Em felt the rise of blush climb her chest. She didn't mind. Without thought, she undid the top button of her shirt. "What do you do, Hugh? When you're not lurking darkly in neighborhood bars?"

"I work in a bank. Some people call me a banker. Now, before you tar and feather me, or run for the door, give me a moment." Hugh reached with his index finger and touched the back of Em's hand. "I like what I do. I'm good at it and I'm fair. Even honest."

"I bet you bankers say that to all the pretty girls."

"You *are* pretty. But…."

Em felt her rosy blush climb higher up her neck. Embarrassed, she wondered if Hugh will feel the heat radiating from her.

"You've picked up a little color in your face," Hugh said. "You can't be embarrassed about being pretty. You must have heard it a thousand times."

"I think it's…it's only…never from a banker. That must be it."

"Bankers," Hugh scoffed. "Now-a-days we frighten the world." Hugh slid a little closer to Em. "In all your freedom at art school, what kind of art do you do, or hope to do?"

Stunned for a moment, his question brought back her college dreams of grand openings, interviews, explaining her art to an attentive audience, the public life of fame rather than the work to get there. Blushing now well into her cheeks, she said, "I'm guessing I'll change styles. You know, like Picasso, have different periods. I don't mean that I'm like Picasso, he was really talented and a genius. I'm neither but would like to…problem solve. I'd like to have a pile of viscous color in front of me and dip my hands in and shape the blues and greens over here and pull the reds across to hang and throb, then press my fingers into divots of yellow that appear and disappear, bursting across the poly-luminous sky-scape in front of me."

"You saw all that," Hugh said. "As you spoke, you saw all that, didn't you?"

Em lowered her head. "Yes," she said. "Of course."

Hugh reached and touched the side of her head, pushing a few hairs behind her ear. "I think it's amazing that you saw all that in your head. But you know what? I did, too. A little bit. I saw a pot of soup. Don't laugh. I know the soup colors of green peppers and red peppers, carrots, and tomato paste slurry. The colors I saw were clumsy, blocky, and sharp-edged. But your description was enough to let me see at least a hearty vegetable soup."

Em held her fingers to cover one cheek. She ran her other hand through her hair, touching where he had touched, letting a few strands fall over her ear. "Enough about me," she said without looking at Hugh. "What do you do at your bank?"

"I'm a loan officer." Hugh paused and collected his thoughts. "I analyze loan requests, help people shape their request, approve them when I can." He sat up straighter and added, "But you. You're like an art elf."

Em wanted to pause and bask in his flattery. She needed to fan herself. Or take time to walk to the women's room where she'd look intently at herself in the mirror and splash cold water on her face. She bit her lower lip and was pleased to remember what he said about himself, pleased she could still organize an intelligent response. "I thought car loans, even home loans, were on some kind of conveyor belt. Punch in the numbers and get a result. You either get the loan or not, no room for appeal or special circumstances."

Hugh waved his arms, indicating the whole bar. "Most of it's like that. My department is a little different. On the organizational chart, I'm represented by an asterisk, with an explanation on the next page. We represent entrepreneurs, risk-takers, innovators, anyone with a crazy idea they think might work. Only crazy ideas, though. I service only ideas that don't fit the conventional loan market. And only up to two hundred thousand dollars. Starter money for a lot of what I see."

Hugh put one elbow on the bar and leaned close to Em. He spoke breathy, nearly whispering. "We help people reach their dreams. No kidding. Sometimes inventors come with an idea but haven't a clue about money. I get to work with them, talk with them, creative people, and then I present a plan to get them what they need to bring their idea to market. People feel good when they get what they need, even if the whole thing fails later. They feel good. I help people feel good."

Em felt his excitement as her own and moved her head closer to his. "I bet you're good at making people feel good." Em spread the collar of her shirt wider, hoping to release the heat surrounding her chest.

"It's one of my greatest pleasures." Hugh touched her hand as it still held open her collar.

Em felt an electric connection from his hand to hers. It jumped to her chest, where it circled as a pleasant hum. Concentrating on it made her dizzy. She noticed that Hugh had finished his drink so she gulped the remains of hers. "How do people find you?" she asked. "Is there a way you could help me feel good? If I need a loan, that is."

"Of course." Hugh pulled his wallet from a back pocket and slid out a business card. He began to give it to her but stopped. Looking over the bar counter, he didn't see what he sought. Patting his suit coat, he added to Em, "I need a pen. I'll give you my numbers. Listen, we're done with our drinks. I have plenty of pens at my place. I can show you where I live. It's not far. Will you come with me?"

Em slipped the business card from his fingers, even though he hadn't written any numbers on it. She noticed his full name, Hugh Gardner, his email address, and memorized his business number before placing it in the front pocket of her shirt. Looking up to answer his question, she simply said,

"Yes."

Dropping from the stool to her feet, she turned to take his hand, thinking…

*

…*yes, what a powerful word, yes.* Goose bumps grew on her arms and she noticed the absence of beer odor in her apartment. Across the room, she heard a phone buzzing.

Em put the atomizer on the side table. Her body tingled. Wherever she touched—ear, side of neck, clavicle—her skin was sensitive. The phone buzzed again. She glanced at it but didn't fully recognize the noise as having come from there. *If that instance of the future is continuing,* she thought, *have I entered Hugh's living room by now, accepted a glass of wine, already removed my shirt?* She worried he might not have meant, 'Let's go and do ourselves proud.' He might have only meant what he said, that he needed a pen. No matter. She heard it that way, pens not even distantly on her mind, and said yes. *Are we doing it now? No, not now, but in a future that hasn't yet unfolded?*

CHAPTER FOURTEEN

Concurrent with Niko's call, Minneapolis

Still bewildered from her recent future excursion and Hugh's enticing charm, Em looked at the phone as it buzzed on the coffee table. It was the last thing she heard before her journey and now it was still ringing. But she knew, no matter how long she felt she was with Hugh, it had only been a moment. She picked up the phone. Before she could even say hello, Niko was already talking. "…and then they all said it never happened. But I saw it, still remember. My brother stuck a fork into my sister's forehead. It dangled down her face before my father pulled it out. It left four dots above her eyebrow. But now, no, now they…"

Disoriented, Em's mind drifted and her skin tightened from chill. Her thoughts returned to the bar and the man who showered her with compliments. But he couldn't have meant it, probably rained sweetness on every girl he wanted to take home, his words no more than a lure in a trap. Em attempted to believe she hadn't fully made up her mind; that cautious consideration might prevail; and she wouldn't crawl into bed with Hugh just because her blushing skin was sensitive to touch. *That's not like me,* she said to herself, *I'm not like that. Anymore. Not since the oblivion of my drug days.* But after a moment of introspection, she thought, *and just recently with Sanger. I hopped in the sack quick enough with Sanger.*

"…and we believe all sorts of untruths," Niko continued into the phone. "Myths and fairy tales. Oh, we call it symbolic representation! The truth of all men, not just one man. Still, we live in a new world where the pressure to be alike is present, only the demand less insistent. People today long for a personal history, a story they can call their own."

"Niko," Em said, "what are you talking about?" In the silence of his thought, Em drifted back to her recent future experience and admitted, *if my future-voyage had lasted longer, I'd be sliding skin to skin with Hugh all the way home.*

"All through my childhood," Niko said, "I believed my sister had a magical mark, four diagonal dots above her eyebrow. And I believed my brother had cast that spell, made her into something she wasn't. Tines through skin. It was no different than witchdoctor's dust hanging in the air, or the hand of a deity stirring stormy seas."

Em didn't understand what Niko was talking about. Her concern convinced her that returning him to the present was better than…whatever he was doing. "Niko, listen to me. I just had a stint with the mister. I was with a man, we talked, liked each other. Will he have a corresponding experience just because he was with me? A dream perhaps of an unknown woman hanging from his shoulder. By bringing him into my experience, have I given him a tip-of-the-tongue image? Will he have an upcoming moment of *déjà vu*?"

"*Déjà vu*?" Niko asked. He paused and then continued as if he hadn't heard. "I turned from sprites and pixies to get away from what they were. My brother and sister had a relationship filled with bewitchment, sorcery, taboo. It frightened me. They looked at each other whispering the secret incantations only they intuitively knew. I turned from their beliefs. Like kings and popes, they claimed they had a secret reservoir of knowledge the rest of us weren't privy to.

"I turned to facts in the physical world. Truth for anyone who cared to look. No more conjecture, innuendo, or hunch. I devoted myself to measuring acceleration, the span between stars, and the relationship of time and light."

Em, confused, reached three fingers into the front pocket of the shirt, hoping to find Hugh's business card. The pocket was empty, of course. The card, the giving, the accepting, none of it had yet happened. Em sat on an upholstered chair as Niko went on. She thought about going to Hugh's office, for real, in the present tense. She knew where he worked. Maybe leaving a note, for his eyes only, predicting they'll soon meet, explaining their captivation, an allure best expressed through poetry. Their secret.

"We believe," Niko said, "so much that isn't true. A misperception can shape a whole life. We are the victims of unreliable assumptions, prone to exaggeration, and comforted by denial. The truth may face us but we turn away. When it comes to time, now is present and exists. The past is present and exists. The future is present and exists. It's all contained in the universe, just as we are. But the uncomfortable truth is this. Now is not unique. There is no unique moment called now that holds any more relevance than any other moment. We only want there to be."

Em held the phone closer to her ear and thought that if he could whine, she could divulge. Interrupting him, she said, "Forgive us for who we are. I'm nothing but a schoolgirl, Niko. I want to write 'Em loves Hugh' on the cover of my notebook and spend the rest of the day drawing kittens and butterflies in the margin." She paused and held the silence for two beats. "I should have outgrown this silliness. I'm having palpitations, sweat for no better reason than a pie-in-the-sky longing for a man I may never meet."

"Yes," Niko said, not knowing what she was talking about. "Yes, of course."

Hearing the indifference in Niko's voice, Em said, "I can't talk to you anymore tonight. I'm..." Suddenly nauseous, Em cradled her stomach and added, "I'm struggling and you aren't helping at all. I don't know what to do."

She thought she heard the first sound of a word from Niko, but she hung up so quickly that it wasn't legible.

~ ~ ~

June 25, Minneapolis

Early the next morning Alan and Rooster sat on opposite ends of the couch, she with her back on the armrest playfully kicking and squeezing him to the other end. Although smiling, Alan wasn't as captivated with the game as was Rooster. His internal sense of time was running amuck, hours shrank while days stretched, until unsure it wasn't already tomorrow.

Soon Sanger and Em entered the living room. When Rooster saw them, she pulled her legs back and calmed herself.

Em announced that she needed coffee.

"Rooster made it this morning," Alan said and then added, "If Bill's not coming, why are we still going to a future where he plays a role?"

Rooster kicked him and Alan didn't know why. He gave her a stern look and said, "It's got to be that he'll still come even though we said otherwise. Do we know when he'll get here."

No one answered and Alan thought Rooster was pouting. With Em and Sanger in the kitchen, and Alan on the couch with Rooster, he thought about how different a future trip to William Meyer might be if he had the money Bill owes. In one smooth motion, he stood, stepped to the atomizer, and picked it up. It was a comforting weight, a solid presence, and an inviting promise. He squeezed the bulb and saw in the hovering mist a small boy waving from a window. Alan drew his head back and his view drifted farther from the window, seeing the whole house and then the street and the neighborhood and the entire city as though standing above a map. Drifting farther away, Alan reached forward. As his hand tore through the atomizer's cloud, the image disappeared, and...

*

...he grasped a door handle while his other hand surrounded the grip of a briefcase. He opened the door and stepped through a portal that grew more familiar each time. He stopped in front of William Meyer's desk. Flexing his grip on the briefcase, Alan smiled. Looking down, he was pleased to see the leather case dangling on the end of his arm. His smile broadened and he released a short chortle.

"You come in here," William Meyer said, "and laugh. What's that about?"

"I've got your money. That's a little bit funny."

Alan groaned inside, fearing this was the start of another episode of rhymes. He kept his chin near his chest, waiting for a barrage of abuse from William Meyer. When none came, Alan felt a wave of relief.

"Put the money on the desk," Mr. Meyer said. "Pull up a chair. Seems you're a poet and don't even know it." William Meyer stood, anticipating the briefcase's final delivery. He said, "That's the only poem I know. Nice to get a chance to use it."

Alan put the briefcase on the desk and pulled a chair. He didn't say anything, fearing his next words would push their poetry connection too far.

William Meyer opened the briefcase and looked through the contents. Alan knew it was money but hadn't seen it. He watched Mr. Meyer open a bottom drawer and retrieve a bottle of liquor. Plus two glasses.

"Have a drink with me," William Meyer said as he splashed a couple of fingers worth into each tumbler. "Bill called and said you were coming. I've known him for ages." He pushed one glass toward Alan. "Salute."

Alan picked up the glass, without any intention of drinking from it, and extended his arm toward William Meyer's extended arm. Neither of them reached far enough to make the distinctive clink of glass to glass.

"Tink," Mr. Meyer said over the absence of real sound. "Bill and I go way back. About the money, I say better late than never. But it's not late, just barely not late. Classic Bill, though. Even back in school he'd turn in projects only minutes before they were due. We used to call him Deadline. Frustrated the hell out of us. 'Hey Deadline, you done yet?' But he always was, barely, and never late." William Meyer indicated laughter with a few breathy snorts through his nose.

"What's it for?" Alan asked, tilting his head toward the

briefcase.

William Meyer stared before answering. "No harm now in telling you. I need up-front money to get the ball rolling. I'll show Bill's money, along with more, to people who have contacts in a part of the world I won't mention. Those contacts will purchase and supply arms to...ah, people standing up for what they believe. Once they're paid, my money is returned, plus some profit, and I'll put it up as collateral again. With some luck I'll leap-frog ahead and ahead and ahead."

"You trust these contacts?" Alan asked.

"Enough."

Alan patted his right jacket pocket, making the weight in there shift over his hip. "And those arms are going to righteous people?"

"Who's righteous now-a-days? One man's preference is another man's tyranny. Can't get too involved in what people are willing to fight for. Doesn't make sense to judge how others choose to spend their precious time on the planet."

Alan reached into his coat pocket and wrapped his fingers as though hand and gun were made for each other. He thought this man was on the verge of deserving to die. A quick flick of the gun, a practiced draw, a smooth pull of the trigger. But it wasn't real, not the same real as it will be when now, the genuine now, was also present. Alan could lift the gun, aim it at William Meyer, and pull the trigger twice. Still, it wouldn't be real, not as certain as it will be if the past was just a moment ago and the future just a step ahead. He knew he was in a moment out of time, in a future before it was meant to be. He could do what he pleased with no certainty that what he did will be what he'll do in the future when he and the authentic now walk hand in hand. As tempting as it was to deliver two lead slugs to the heart of a deserving man, Alan lifted his empty hand from his pocket and said, "I've got to be going. When will Bill get his money back?"

"That'll take months," William Meyer said. "But Bill knows all that. We're good."

Alan turned and stepped toward the door. He thought one last time about lifting the gun and shooting this arms peddler. But he wouldn't be dead, not really dead. Instead, Alan reached for the door and...

*

...placed the atomizer on the side table. He felt calm, as calm as knowing right without doubt. Looking around, he noticed Rooster staring at him. He showed her his palms, flinched his shoulders, and said, "I didn't kill him this time. I sure wanted to...but I didn't."

"That's good then," Rooster said. "Right?"

"I suppose. I already want to go back, I mean forward again, and do it. He's not a good man. But I know if I sniff the cloud again so soon nothing will happen. It would be good for me to kill him. This time for who he is, what he's doing, not because he made me feel small."

"Wow. That's super. What happened?"

Since Alan was gone only a moment, Em still hadn't poured her coffee. Sanger, too, hadn't noticed Alan's departure.

"This one I need to think about more. I'll tell you later." Alan sat on the couch beside Rooster and leaned his head so far back that he was staring at the ceiling. He grew an earache and relaxing his neck like that felt good.

Rooster slid closer, leaned on his shoulder, and said, "This is good for you. Right?"

~ ~ ~

Later that day, in the middle of the afternoon, they all went out for pizza. It was a small pizza shop with a pickup counter and no table service. Rooster stood at the counter, steaming. *Sanger just expected,* she thought, *that I'd wait here while they all sit. I will, I am, it's the least I can do. But Sanger flicks his wrist and says, 'Rooster, wait here for the pizza,' then turns away like it's his command, nothing less. I don't know what Em sees in him.*

Rooster toed a piece of pepperoni stuck to the tiled floor. *I could have sat down with them,* she thought, *and then got the pizza when it was ready.* She turned her attention to the counter and picked at a crater in the Formica. *I'd've been glad to, volunteered, jumped up first and said I'll get it. But that flick of his hand, turning away. I'd've had to push the back of his shoulder and say, No, why me? Who are you to tell me what to do?*

Like I'd say all that. He wouldn't hear me. He'd wave his hands and deny it all. I've been watching you, Sanger-the-turtle. Get called out and you just cover your head, throw out apologies like they're candy tossed to kids in a war zone. Then looking with those sad brown eyes and saying you didn't mean it, must have come out wrong. But you did and should have known. You're just like how Em describes your goddamned uncle, squirm and squeeze. Probably runs through your whole family.

Except Alan. Rooster stopped picking at the countertop after prying up an edge of the Formica crater. *There, I've made a cave at one end of this ancient meteor strike where cave people will band together at night and build a fire to warn animals from attacking the warmth and comfort of our bodies entangled for sleep.*

Rooster looked up and saw the teenaged counter clerk watching. Embarrassed by her thoughts, she covered the Formica crater with her hand and said, "Isn't it done yet?"

"Another minute or two."

She turned away from him and leaned her back on the counter. She took a deep breath and thought, *who'd suspect they're cousins? Alan's quiet, polite, considerate, understanding. He's treated me like an adult from the first moment.*

Rooster looked left and watched them. *Look at Sanger talking with his 'inside' gestures, hands and fingers only, close to the table, while Alan and Em, what?, are they sleeping? So what about Sanger. I don't care about him. Em's okay. No, she's nice. But if I have to take sides, I'll choose Alan every time.*

A bell dinged behind her and the counter help prepared their pizza; out of the oven to the counter, swipes across with a rolling cutting blade, and... "Use these mitts underneath. The tray's hot."

As Rooster slid the pizza on the table, she heard Em say, "What right do we have to change the future? Can we even do it? Look, if Isaac Newton hadn't discovered calculus, Gottfried Leibnitz would get the credit. If Columbus hadn't sailed west, someone else soon would have."

"What are you saying?" Sanger asked. "We might as well let Alan kill William Meyer because if not him, someone will?"

Em looked at Rooster, as if for help, but Rooster was thinking, *if the future is stuff that will happen, events that got to be performed...can I pick who does what because if William Meyer has to die, I could do it instead of Alan. I could do it better, too.*

Em replied to Sanger, "No, I didn't mean it that way. I meant, what if there's a greater good to the way we're seeing the future pan out? Ought we really to be tinkering with it?"

Alan waved a hand over the table, getting their attention. "I didn't kill him this time. I sniffed the magic earlier today and didn't kill him."

"Was anything different?" Em said.

"I had his money. Bill's money to give to William Meyer. Everything flowed more smoothly with the money on William Meyer's desk. It was almost pleasant except that he's an arms dealer who will use Bill's money to promote death and destruction."

"Oh," Em said. "But should he really be killed for it?"

Alan stared at her. "I didn't do it this time. But yes. Yes he should."

"No," Em said. "We should get the money, deliver it and walk away from this whole thing without any more trouble. We've got to get Bill here and get his money."

Listen to her, Rooster thought, *what an...advantagist, no, opportunist. She just wants to get back to flirting.*

"Em," Sanger said, "maybe borrowing the money from your banker friend isn't the best course?"

Rooster smiled. *There you go, pull the curtain wider.*

"You're going to," Sanger added, "blackmail him? Embarrass him? Is that what you want? Make him ashamed of what he'll do with you."

Whoa. Rooster sat straight. *Throw that barn door all the way open. Poor Em. Lift your head. Don't back down now.*

"No," Em faltered. "I think by now I can talk him into helping us. Voluntarily."

Huh? You don't even know him yet.

Sanger had almost taken his first bite of pizza a couple of times. He dropped the piece, leaned toward Em, and said, "Well, you better get started. He'll never suspect he's being used, enticed into an illegal deal that could lose him his job."

Pow, pow, Rooster thought. *But what a joke. He's as narrow-gauge as she is. He just wants her to boogie with no one but him.*

"You don't have to get sarcastic." Em, too, dropped her piece of pizza. "It's the only way. We've got to tell Bill to come, follow him through borrowing the money, and have Alan deliver it so he doesn't kill the attorney."

There you go, Rooster thought. *Don't lose track, whatever it takes to boogie with whoever catches your fancy. Jeepers, I run away from home straight into a zoo.*

The Beyond Now Device

~ ~ ~

Alan took a bite of pizza and weighed the consequences. He had only been able to follow an unknown script in each of his future jaunts. It felt familiar. All his life he'd been influenced by the hype of decisive men who called the shots, grabbed what they wanted, and shaped the future in their own capable hands. Alan wasn't such a man but suspected he should have been. If he'd tried harder and been more patient with his wife. Or paused judgment over her inability to recover. But now a future charged toward him and there was no escape.

Alan listened to Em and Sanger quarrel, knowing their main concern was for themselves. His was too. But what they risked, time travel or not, was what they would risk in any modern relationship. Alan wondered again why Sanger wanted such mundane things from Em: never-failing faithfulness, relentless dependability, and the vows to make it so. Instead he could get her creativity, surprise, and her deepest affection if he set her free to finger through the music store's back racks even if she occasionally brought home the musical equivalent of a dud.

It dawned on Alan that he wanted Uncle Bill to come, wanted the money delivered to William Meyer, even if it meant blackmailing Hugh Gardner. Even if it meant Em being photographed having sex. He took another bite of pizza. Sanger and Em spoke in spurts of non-verbal articulation. Rooster nudged Alan's shoulder and tossed her head to the right. She did it again and then slid into the chair next to her. Across the table, Alan moved, too, one seat away from Em and Sanger.

"What's going on?" Rooster whispered.

"With them?"

Rooster rolled her eyes. "I know what's going on with them. What about the rest of it? Murder, money, meandering into the future?"

"Is it that different than what we already do? See into the future. I know the door over there is closed. From across the room, it will take time to walk over there, and I already know the door is closed."

"Okay." Rooster pulled her bangs to think. "But you're seeing the door shut now, not next week. And looking across the room at the future is one thing. But traveling there and experiencing it?" Rooster dropped her head near the table and whispered, "In my future with you, I smelled you, I almost touched you. It was a lot more than looking both ways before crossing a street."

Alan stretched his fingers toward her but stopped his hand in the middle of the table. "You're right. I'm sorry. I shouldn't make light of it. I'm just trying to figure it out, too."

"No," Rooster said. "It's me. I'm jumpy. I'm confused. I know none of it's your fault. But they," Rooster tilted her head toward Em and Sanger, "they have their own little soap opera going. I don't know what I'd do if I was only thinking about me. I almost ignored you when you said no. Why would I do that?"

"They say of current molesters, nearly all of them were molested."

"You mean because it happened to me, I'm destined to do it to you?"

"No," Alan said. "Not at all. But you've got a head start. You know what it's like for someone to ignore what you want and only focus on what they want. It's like growing up in a circus family or with a suicidal parent. You've experienced it, know how possible it is."

Rooster stretched a finger to within an inch of Alan's hand and said, "That's harsh."

"Sorry. I've done a lot of thinking about the future lately, maybe more than ever."

Rooster smiled. "Sounds silly for me to say the same thing. But me, too. Alan, you're the only one I can really talk to. Thank you. But, what are we going to do?"

CHAPTER FIFTEEN

June 25, Minneapolis

At home that evening, the four lounged in the living room. "Telling Uncle Bill to come will just confuse him," Sanger said. "We've already asked him not to. We can handle the future. I'll bet we stop seeing Bill's plans really soon."

Easy for you to say, Em thought. *If Bill doesn't come all you lose is an opportunity to play with your criminal fantasies, one more lost chance to be under Bill's welcoming wing in a life of petty crime. You're too tied up in family already.*

Em dropped her head, resenting the sacrifice she'd been asked to make. Bill not coming would change the future of her meetings with Hugh. She might never meet him. She had already said yes and been giddy with pleasure. She'd already blushed and talked with an unusual self-consciousness. She still longed for the stimulation he provoked and saw no reason to quit seeing him. When they told Bill not to come, she had risked all that, changing a future she was growing to welcome. Now if they asked Bill to come, for Alan's sake, Em was ready to support the plan, even convince others of its validity.

Alan slipped deeper into the couch and thought about the benefits of Bill not coming, not bringing his grand scheme, and not bringing his guns. *That was the best plan yet,* he thought. *I'll be extremely okay never again going to William Meyer's office, never discovering a gun in my pocket, never pulling its trigger.*

Yet there was something intriguing about the atomizer and the future. Alan was sure he could kill William Meyer dozens of times and the rude lawyer still wouldn't be dead. In time he could master the power he felt in the murderous act, let the kick of the handgun travel up his arm, course through his heart, and vibrate in the soles of his feet. And then, if he liked, do it again. Where but in this odd wrinkle in time could he repeatedly feel a power he had never felt before? Where else might he knowingly fulfill his destiny and shoot a man twice in the heart? On purpose. Just for the thrill of it. Where else might this act have no lingering consequences? *Once more,* Alan imagined, *take a sniff of the atomizer and grasp the experience with both hands, as if I'm throttling the neck of...feel okay about it, act like I know what I'm doing?*

~ ~ ~

On the couch, with her shoulder grazing Alan's shoulder, Rooster felt him grow as still as the tail of a storm where leaves flipped once or twice but were no longer whipped faster than the eye could see. She liked how he explained his last trip to the future, but suspected he might drift back in regret, sorry he didn't take action when he had the opportunity. She thought she ought to keep his mind here by distracting him from any meandering ruminations. Tickle him, punch him, kiss him. Stand up and dance, juggle three oranges... *I'll just annoy him*, she thought. *He's already called me pesky and irksome.*

Instead she talked, hoping to keep him from sinking into sorrow. "I think I'm getting addicted to that thing. Just hearing what little you're saying stirs me up to do it again. It's pretty weird, don't you think? Pretty weird to have experiences you can't explain to anyone, dare not tell anyone. Anyone besides those who've been through it, don't you think? I mean, who'd understand going to the future? Who'd believe it? No scrapes, no bruises, they just got to take your word for it. Who'd believe it? Even bringing it up will rock the boat, crumple everyone's sense of right and wrong. Don't you think?"

Rooster pressed gently into Alan's shoulder, just enough to secure an imaginary egg between them. She added, "Can't really blame my step-dad for wanting no one to know. I blame him for doing it, but I get not wanting anyone to know. Mom, too, for sure, didn't want to see things that way."

Rooster sniffed and wiped a tear from her eye. "Have you ever wanted to do something you shouldn't tell others? You know, something to keep secret even if it was okay with the person you did it with? You and me are maybe alike in that way. You know what I mean? Something pleasant but no one would understand? I'd think it was okay if you... you know? And me...because I want to." When Alan said nothing, Rooster heaved an oversized breath and said, "Jesus, listen to me, caring about something I might want to happen when I'm not sure the future's even real."

As she felt Alan's arm pull up from his side and drop over her shoulders, a well of tears seeped into the bottom lids of her eyes. Rattled by her wet response, she sat up straight and pulled away from him, determined not to let him see her cry. She stepped to the side table, picked up the atomizer, and said, "Yeah, I'm really getting addicted to this thing. See you again in a moment."

She squeezed the bulb and put the atomizer on the table. The mist rolled toward her. From a high vantage point she saw a tiny carnival—Ferris wheel, pony ride oval—in a heavy rainstorm under dark clouds. Peering more closely, she…

*

…opened her eyes to a busy downtown street. Rain. Her cloth jacket was already wet through to her shoulders. She stood with her back pressed tight to the side of a building. The fresh odor of humid air rose from the pavement and her hands rested on the top of a baseball bat that stood vertical between her feet. Turning her head to the left, she saw Alan's Uncle Bill running from around the corner of the building to a car parked at the curb. The car looked old, not old, shiny and bright, old-fashioned.

She took a step in that direction but stopped when she saw Alan stumble out of the main door, head down, with his right hand over his right ear. She called his name once, then again louder, and finally a third time even louder.

Alan stopped and squinted at her. She saw the spray of blood on his face, the skin around his eyes still white where his glasses must have been. Beyond him, Rooster saw Sanger wave from the window of the antique car. "What are you doing?" she said to Alan.

"I can't hear you," Alan said. "What?"

"What are you doing?" she said too loud, embarrassed, and looked to see who else might have heard her. Sanger reached farther out the car window and waved again. Rooster pointed toward Sanger and said to Alan, "Sanger wants you."

"I can't hear you," Alan said again. He followed her pointing arm and saw Sanger gesticulating even more wildly.

Alan stepped backwards toward the getaway car. She followed a few steps behind. Seeing Uncle Bill in the back seat brought anger to stomp its booted feet in her brain. Blood on Alan's face. Bill had pushed Alan into killing William Meyer, she knew it. Following just a few paces behind Alan, Rooster strode to increase her speed. Then she ran to get to the car first. Near the car's headlight, she saw the back of Sanger's head as he said something to Uncle Bill behind him. Anger spread to the ends of her arms and her hands tightened around the neck of the baseball bat. She raised it over her head and...

*

...stood in Sanger's living room as if changing an overhead light bulb. Discovering her hands empty, she dropped her arms and took a wobbly step that bumped her hip to the side table. She turned to Alan on the couch and said, "A baseball bat? I had a baseball bat."

"What happened?" Alan asked.

Rooster, too, saw the value of thinking twice before explaining once. She wanted to wait for...for. But there was something else, something had happened before her most recent future venture. Only the emotional remnants of unwanted tears remained, the content lost, and her skin prickled with a tinge of fear, if whatever it was returned.

Rooster blinked, her eyes feeling swollen and fat. She said, "I'm going to think a bit. It's a good example you're setting." But as she remembered her experience, she thought about how Alan couldn't hear her, how blood trickled from his ear, more blood covered his face, and how much she liked him.

~ ~ ~

Later that same day, Chicago

Niko roamed through his apartment in turmoil. Although he wasn't very good at assessing a situation in the moment, he excelled at post-analysis. Regretting having mentioned his family or their influence on him, he was most remorseful about his inability to listen to Em's confession. Finding no one else to blame, it wasn't difficult for shame to surround him in its directionless darkness.

Later that evening, Niko called and asked specifically for Em. "I'm sorry for speaking about my family when we talked last night. I suppose you've all gotten a good laugh about my brother and sister."

"I haven't," Em said, "told anyone about it. It seemed personal and private."

"Thank you. That's kind."

With the phone on speaker at Em's end, Sanger spoke. "We're assuming visiting the future is very much like remembering the past. The more we do it, the more solid our impressions grow. We think we need to change what we do in those future episodes, prepare ourselves for the now of that moment. Is that how it works?"

Niko needed a few moments to fully recover. He coughed and then said. "No, of course that's not it. Your thoughts of the future, even your *memory* of it, are of little consequence."

"I'm," *hoping, dreaming, looking forward to,* "concerned," Em added, "that we're loading the deck with assumptions of our future. When we look to the past with this or that expectation, it won't matter because the past will be what it was. Aren't we strengthening the possibility of a certain future each time we experience it?"

Niko stared at his own phone before saying, "You're joking, right?"

"I don't like it," Rooster said. "Seeing that bloody body was bad enough." She hung her head and looked at Alan through her eyebrows. "I'm really sorry I crawled into bed with you. I keep thinking I imagined it because I can't face the idea that I'm going to do it. It wasn't you, the worst was the way I thought of you." Rooster shook her head and added, "It doesn't have to...the future, I mean...doesn't have to happen the way we're seeing it, does it?"

Em said, addressing Niko, "All we're doing is remembering our experiences. Doesn't matter if they're past or future. The direction in time doesn't matter."

Alan mulled over the conversation so far. He added, "My past is just a story I'm telling myself, the story as I remember it. Then I interpret it and get a sense of who I am—the person influenced by who I've been. We're worried we might lock ourselves into a particular future based on what we've already experienced. Can you help us?"

"I am helping," Niko said.

"No," Em said. "No, you're not. The date's approaching and you're not telling us what to do."

"Okay," Niko said. "You're not ready. But the dates you've mentioned are approaching. Let me go into more detail about now."

"No," Rooster said. "Please. You've already said. Perpetual now, constant. It's the only time anything gets done. We need—"

"Listen," Niko said. "There are two common ways to think of our journey through time. The first is like driving a motor scooter, steering this way and that, hurtling into the future. This is the captain of one's own ship approach. People believing this want to take control. They prefer the world as is, expect it to be as it's been. They decorate their homes with matching furniture and appreciate a schedule. They believe, at college or Ikea, they can place an order for a pleasant life. They're steering on a highway into the future and trust the next moment will be very much like the last."

Niko paused and the four on Em's end looked at each other. When he resumed, Niko said, "Others consider themselves standing on a cliff and time is a mighty wind plastering their shirt to their chest and blowing their scarf horizontally behind. Time is blasting past them. They're overwhelmed at the prospect. Gusts and shears make life unpredictable and they feel pummeled by options and choices and too many brands of laundry soap. These're the addicts and grumblers among us. They're the excuse-makers and blamers. They sense the world is not for them because they are regularly clobbered by circumstance."

"That's the one," Rooster said. "Does a big dose of confusion come with that one?"

"Yes," Niko said. "Yes it does. But time's not a cruel ruler. For those living by happenstance, there's a chance their wild emotions can run free, letting slip the mask so they are truly seen. Spontaneity invites danger by having so little regard for the future. Once a heart-felt emotion escapes, there's no taking it back. And once seen, others will never forget."

"Oh," Rooster said.

Niko ignored her and continued, "Others, standing at the helm of their ship, grow protective of what they're controlling, territorial, risk-averse, and dare not let themselves be seen, especially by their raw emotions which they know can never be taken back. They're more comfortable in the company of those who break horses, of those who value dignity and esteem, status and place, and the brittle strength that comes from adhering to the prepared path chosen years earlier when the known glinted and gleaned far more brightly than what remained unknown."

Sanger turned the phone so it was facing him and said, "What's that got to do with us?"

"Everyone must decide. This is understanding time. Is life better lived at the helm of your ship, steering clear of troubled waters, carrying enough ballast to dampen the pitch of any storm?"

"Or?" Rooster asked.

"Understand and accept the consequences of your actions. Live robust. Appreciate that your friends know you because you're hiding nothing. Face the wind and let insects get blown between your teeth."

Sanger leaned close to the phone and said, "No one lives that way."

"Which way?"

"Either."

Niko paused. "I spoke in extremes. Sorry. I let a grain of sand tip the scale. It's all in balance, of course. Who could argue with that?"

~ ~ ~

Not long after getting off the phone with Niko, Sanger called Uncle Bill. Hesitancy coursed through his body. Still, on the scales of consequence, getting Bill to come and blackmail the banker might save Alan from killing anyone. Of course, getting Bill to come and blackmail the banker might push Em into bed with the banker so the photographs would exist. Alan's murderous behavior was worth avoiding, even if Em had to woo the banker, even if Sanger suspected she was enjoying her role in the scheme far too much.

Sanger watched Em gently slide the phone across the table,

encouraging him to do as they agreed in the pizza parlor—get Bill to come. Em mouthed, *for Alan's sake*, as Sanger waited for Bill to answer.

"Uncle Bill? This is Sanger. Listen, last time we talked, I got it wrong. You really do need to come out here as soon as possible."

"I am. I'll be there in a couple of days."

"Em was mistaken. I don't even know where she got all that. Just come out as soon as you can."

"I am. You didn't think I'd change my plans over something Em said?"

"Oh."

"I'll get my flight information to you. Pick me up at the airport. Two days from now. Okay? Gotta go."

Sanger watched the connection end. Now it made sense why they were still going to Bill's upcoming story. Telling him not to come hadn't changed anything. Sanger kicked a throw pillow across the room. "He's coming," he said. "Never intended not to." Sanger couldn't look at Em, afraid he'd see the satisfaction he assumed she felt now that her future will unfold with her banker in the picture. He thought of himself at the helm of his ship and didn't want to show Em how steeply he leaned forward into the oncoming wind. Wishing he could hide his jealousy while knowing it filled him to bursting, he said, "There you go. Let Bill lead you into whatever coercive blackmail he's got planned."

Sanger, wanting to exert any narrow independence remaining over Em's sudden windfall, stepped to the atomizer to show her that he, too, could...something. He lifted the mister, squeezed the bulb, and saw in the mist an overgrown path leading farther into the forest. He reached ahead to spread the leaves as...

*

…his hands rested at the hours of 9 and 3 on the car's steering wheel. *Uncle Bill's car,* Sanger thought, remembering the dashboard, clutch pedal, starter…*but is remember the right word for something that hasn't happened yet? Recalling an experience in the future is…* The rear door slammed, the car bounced, and Uncle Bill said, "Gotta go, Sanger. Get a move on. Gear her down. Gas her up."

Sanger turned. Bill's face was red and sweaty. He swiveled toward the front of the car just in time to see the meat of a baseball bat fracture the windshield, sending a spider's web of tiny fissures through the glass.

"Run," Bill called as he opened the rear door and crawled out.

By the time Sanger was on the sidewalk, Bill was fifteen feet away. Bill pointed to Sanger's right and said, "Meet me at the diner. You go that way."

Sanger kept his eyes on his feet as the pavement passed beneath him. Knees churning, feet smacking, he was running as fast as he could. After two and a half blocks, he stopped and leaned on a wall next to an alley. He didn't hear the slapping of frantic footsteps behind him. He slowed his breathing, oriented himself, and wondered which diner. Sanger tucked his chin to his chest and walked rat-like as close to the side of the building as possible.

This was the part of Uncle Bill's gang Sanger liked least. Set adrift with minimal instructions, cast loose to fend for himself. The pavement passed beneath him as if he was on wheels and it was the earth that spun. Abandoned, in the back of his mind he heard Bill's voice, "I gotta go this way. But you can't. You've got to go that way. My way's not right for you. It'll be okay. We'll meet—

*

"Sanger!" Em called, interrupting his thoughts.

"Wait," Sanger said, straining to hear the rest of what Bill was saying. He looked around and saw Alan and Rooster putting plates away in the kitchen. Em stared at him.

CHAPTER SIXTEEN

June 25, Minneapolis–Chicago connection

Thirty minutes after Sanger retold his most recent future journey, Em picked up the phone and called Niko. Sanger and Em sat on the couch in front of the coffee table. Alan sat in a chair to their left. Rooster crossed the room to sit on the floor at Alan's feet.

"It's us again," Em said when Niko answered his phone. "All that stuff you said earlier about the movement of time. You know, it's rapidly approaching and knocking us off balance. Or we're charging into it like the captain of a ship. We like it but don't quite understand. How does it help us change the future?"

Niko, in the midst of making tea and washing dishes, turned the gas flame off, dried his hands, and sat on his couch. After a moment of thought, he said, "I once told you, Em, that there was nothing special about now. I was distraught that night. I'm sorry. We do hold a special place for now. We know when now is and we're not long fooled by an experience that feels like now, but isn't. We refer to the past with a tilt of the head and indicate the future with a pointing of our chin. We all know these motions and understand what they mean.

"Remembering the past can be profound. It can feel as true as living it again. A reassuring palm on the shoulder gets meaningfully woven into a life's story. Then, too, there was that awful evening when mom got too drunk to keep dad from stumbling into the candle and the ensuing flames changed the family forever. The details will be argued. But the gist of it will be remembered, the emotional distillation of those striking events."

Thinking she knew what Niko was talking about, Em wondered if the hankering she felt for Hugh was enough, if her desire, kept to herself and hurting no one, indicated an essence of which she could be proud—or a fleeting moment missed, gone hither without her even touching it.

"Stroll through an overseas market," Niko continued, "with odors, colors, music blaring, merchants calling, children scampering. It is the pith and nub remembered more than any particular odor or the exact number of children. The take-away impression might be the similarity between people all over the world, encapsulated in a thriving market. Or instead, the mind's highlight might draw on the diversity of people through the common gestures in a dusty bazaar. Nonetheless, it's the inner conclusion that gets tucked away, carried forever as meaning."

"Yeah, yeah," Sanger said, impatient with Niko's perpetual

display of subtleties. "We get the picture. We want to change it."

Niko continued as though he hadn't been interrupted. "Remembering the past is similar to imagining the future. There isn't much difference. How then does a remembered past come to mind without prompt while an imagined future needs nudged and wooed to unfold into a full scene? We can remember whole situations from the tiniest detail. Yet when we try to imagine a specific future event, we either picture the edges, failing to see the substance, or repeat one element over and over, hoping to get a whole story from a single image."

The hairs on Sanger's arms stood on end. There was something familiar about what Niko said. He couldn't shake the vision of Em naked in the arms of her banker. It was the only image he had, refusing to imagine them talking or laughing or strolling side by side. As Sanger was about to...Niko continued.

"Here's what you need to know. A child wishes to be a cowboy. A teenager swoons for her wedding day. Many dream of the chance to make money. These are the common pictures from which we draw a recognizable self. Yet we who listen to these childish longings often surrender the opportunity to ask what is meant by that, who will she be as time stretches beyond the honeymoon? Who remains when more money is no longer enough? Instead of the clothing by which others will know them in the future, we could query them about their inarticulate inner essence, encourage them to know their deep-seated motivator."

Until the last few days Rooster had never seen such a clear divergence of paths ahead. Her destiny might be to crawl into bed with Alan and touch him as she had been touched. Or ignore any chance of that happening, never speak of it, bury the itch that might follow her through life beneath a construction of propriety and decorum. She understood Niko was making a recommendation, felt sure he was pointing both at her and to another possibility.

Niko leaned on both arms over his coffee table. "When past experiences are squeezed into an emotion and that emotion is later extracted into words, the details may be lost but the tone, relevance, and coloring will be remembered. That's the basis on which the future can be seen. Instead of imagining a cowboy hat, chaps, and spurs, the future might be imagined as the gist of things without detail, a direction without destination. It's worth asking: Who is the girl behind the cowboy vest?"

The four were quiet in Sanger's apartment. Rooster murmured and then said aloud, "Okay. But is it even possible to carry a gist of the future rather than an expectation of its details?"

~ ~ ~

After the call, Sanger grew increasingly disoriented. Over the preceding days he had missed work, meals, and often tossed through the night rather than slept. He at times didn't believe he was traveling into the future. Alternately, he believed with just as much certainty that he was. True or not, he worried that anyone beyond his apartment wouldn't believe him, or they'd think he'd gone off his rocker, or was trying to beguile them with a fantasy.

He walked listlessly around the apartment. Em retreated to an overstuffed chair, while Alan and Rooster sat on the floor, leaning against the couch. With Niko's conversation still in mind, Sanger called to Em through the humid air, "Uncle Bill said when he's arriving. I'll pick him up at the airport the day after tomorrow. I'll bring him back here and then we'll take it from there."

"What about the atomizer?"

Sanger walked to the steamer trunk and sat on it. "He'll take the trunk away, deliver it."

"What about the atomizer?" Em asked again.

"If we keep it, Bill will open the trunk and know it's missing."

Em adjusted her position on the chair. "We could lie. Say there was nothing like that in the trunk."

"I don't know. Seems risky."

Rooster coughed to get their attention. "Is he the kind of guy who'd throw lamps, kick the furniture, or punch holes in the walls if he feels tricked?"

"No, of course not." Sanger waved a hand, remembering the concert Bill had taken him to as a teenager, the altercation in the alley near the stage door, and the bloody face of some guy Sanger thought just wanted a cigarette. "Not with us," he added. "He wouldn't do that around us."

Sanger wondered about the special relationship he had with Bill, wondered if that same accord extended to all of them.

~ ~ ~

June 27, Minneapolis

Em slipped out of bed in the morning earlier than the others. She was drowsy and unsteady on her feet. In the kitchen she retrieved bread from the freezer and dropped two slices in the toaster. She didn't need to eat, wasn't really hungry, yet thoughts of thick honey and pools of butter made her mouth water. She pressed her lips together, imagining sweet satisfaction on her tongue. Such a personal act, done with her lips, kissing, licking his neck, the intimacy of taking something inside her. Did she really want toast? Yet this far along, it wasn't worth resisting.

Walking past the toaster, she noticed she hadn't pressed

the lever down. *Maybe I'm not meant to have toast today. Maybe it's not toast at all that I want.*

In the living room, Em stared at the atomizer. *Innocent little atomizer*, she thought, *cute even, antique-ish, standing proud, taunting, maybe malevolent.* Em stopped and wondered how her attitude toward the mister had veered so quickly. She knew she'd been losing time lately, staring out a window until surprised by cold coffee, getting out of bed to discover she had only gotten in twenty minutes earlier.

Em lifted her head and looked at the mister again. She imagined it tossing its own head, nozzle up, a clear 'come hither' motion. Although she despised her inability to say 'no more,' it was familiar.

Stepping to the side table, Em fondled the atomizer as if being kind to it would...but she didn't know what she wanted. Her mind slid smoothly to Hugh Gardner. She recalled the episodes as savory and lush and questioned the caution she had shown lately. Each battle to not sniff the atomizer took her back to her drug days when 'what will one more time hurt' was her favorite mantra. With the mister in hand, she thought of Hugh's willingness, and all she needed was a tiny squeeze of the bulb. When she did, miniscule particles rose toward her face. In it she saw herself prone in the street, clinging to a curb, exhaust streaming toward her as a car sped away, knowing her friends were leaving her behind. She reached...

*

...for Hugh's hand as they left the bar by the back door. The air was fresh, warm and balmy. She felt Hugh tug on her arm, pulling her to hurry. But she wanted to go slow, savor the moment.

"It's not far," he said, and she knew he meant his

apartment.

They walked arm in arm a few blocks to his place, stepped through the outer security door, and up the stairs. Em was excited, pleased that he was pleased. Yet there was a knot in her stomach and she knew it had to do with Sanger. She didn't want to hurt him, yet she would. Thoughts to justify her behavior, old and tired truths, came to mind: *no one owns me; I can make my own decisions; life is short and pleasure is precious; why deny my appetites, an occasional fatty bacon burger won't kill anyone.*

She remembered why she was doing this. Bill needed the money to give to Alan in order not to shoot William Meyer. *Whew!* She wasn't cruising in Hugh's arms for only her own pleasure. It was her contribution to the team, her willingness to do what needed doing.

Consumed by these self-serving thoughts, time slipped beneath her. Em had always found it impossible to be self-conscious and pay attention to what was around her at the same time. The next thing she knew, Hugh was pulling her into his bedroom and she was kicking off her shoes. They stood face to face, him fumbling with the buttons of her blouse. Centered again, she asked him to breathe, bring the warmth of the moment back. He did and pressed his forehead to hers.

Em found giving advice easier than taking it. She will talk with Sanger about her role to help Bill get the money. But she knew they'd also speak of her unrealistic need for independence. Was it though, unrealistic? It was a need like any other on a continuum with some needing more and… Time suspended, lost motion, and when it resumed Em discovered herself in bed on her back, Hugh above her, absorbed in their lingering kiss. Startled, her lips stiffened and she knew Hugh felt it. He pulled inches away and pressed his forehead to hers exactly as it had been moments earlier.

"It's okay," Hugh said. "I'm glad you're here."

She raised her head and met his lips. When she stretched her tongue to his teeth and beyond, she felt his hips shudder and recognized the totality of their connection. With slight thrusts of her hips, she wondered if Sanger could feel what she was doing with Hugh; if he was thinking of her at this moment as she thought of him; a now not shared.

Through drifting thoughts, Em's time sputtered. She liked...she wanted...she tried...then she let the dark of the room surround her as she drifted deep into the mattress. Passing through an unmeasured moment, Em kicked her legs in a surprised start. Her legs didn't move far, entangled in something flexible and frightening.

"Hey," Hugh said, "you must have fallen asleep for a moment. It's okay."

Em looked around the room. The sheet over her was too much for the warmth of the night. As Hugh leaned down, she put a hand on his chest, remembering they were naked.

Hugh placed his palm to her cheek and pulled her ear between fore- and middle-finger. "That was nice," he said. "You were right to slow us down."

"Yes," Em said, even though her fractured memory didn't feel slow and she had a remnant of panic in the deepest part of her stomach. She wanted to move away from him, get up, get dressed, or at least sit in a chair. Panic that the sex was unremembered, against her will? No, out of context, unable to fit into her larger life. But the initial jolt soon passed and she moved closer to him, smelled their sweat and didn't want to talk, would rather stretch a shoulder and twist her lower back awake.

Hugh sighed. "I had a cat like you once. Small, slender, she'd curl up beside me and seem happy. I called her Pat, Patty, because..."

Em stopped listening. She remembered what was on her

mind, remembered making an appointment for herself and Bill to meet Hugh in his office. Was remember the right word? Had that happened yet? Bill will show pictures to Hugh. *How will I face him? What will I say when he sees those photos? He'll hate me.*

"I better go," Em said.

"Okay, if you have to. I'll call a taxi."

Before she climbed out of bed, Em pulled herself to the warmth of Hugh's body. She liked it. She wanted to believe everything will be okay. Yet when she closed her eyes, she was filled with foreboding.

She dressed and looked around the room for anything she might have left behind. Turning to Hugh, who was still in bed, she saw him pointing to the nightstand. "Don't forget my card. And don't forget your pen."

"My pen?" Em said.

"Yeah. You got it out for me to use but we were...things moved quickly. So you just left it on the nightstand."

Em picked up his card, slipped it into her back pocket, and collected the pen. It reminded her of Uncle Bill and the secret audio recording device. The pen was fat, a spy camera? She began to feel sick, wondering if she had recorded something. As she stood on one foot and then the other to pull on each shoe, a vague image materialized of crawling in a gutter as the exhaust from a receding car surrounded her and she was too far gone for even her friends to help. She listed to her left as she...

*

...continued to sway on her feet in Sanger's living room. She was still holding the atomizer. Early birds chirped beyond the open windows. The apartment was every bit as quiet as it had been a moment ago.

Within ten minutes of Em's return from her future sojourn, Sanger got up and announced he was going to the airport to collect Uncle Bill. Other than knowing Bill would fly in, she didn't know what day it was. She stood in front of the wall calendar and stared. If she knew the day of the week, the date would be limited to four or five numbers. Knowing the date would inform her of the day of the week. She turned and watched Sanger leave. She wanted to ask the date of him. She thought to say goodbye.

Em watched Sanger leave and regretted that, *what's gone is gone. The past is filled with a lack of possibilities, any potential already exhausted. Decisions are made in the present. Regrets and promises pale in comparison. Once this moment passes, there's no retrieving it.* Just as she regretted not saying goodbye as Sanger pulled the door shut, she mourned the missed opportunity with Hugh. Time hadn't been continuous, it had been filled with holes, might have even run backwards. Sex with him had been like appreciating the appetizer while the aroma of the main course only drifted in from another room. *Sand through my fingers. But that's silly. I never really experienced him. I just feel like I did.*

Rooster entered the kitchen and pulled a chair to the table.

"There's something very special about now," Em said without explanation. "Yet in my future journeys, I thought it was now. Wherever we are in time, does it always feel like now? Are we capable of feeling any other way? Isn't it more like…oh it makes me feel crazy."

When the phone rang, Em saw that it was Niko. Pleased, she touch-connected and said, "Niko, is losing track of now a major mental disorder?"

"If I say yes or no I really haven't answered your question."

"Errg!" Rooster said. "It's hard to get a straight answer from you."

"But I do have a story, and maybe an answer."

Alan came into the kitchen and poured himself coffee. He looked at Em, pointed to the phone, and indicated 'what's up?'

"Niko," she said.

"What?"

"No," Em added, addressing Niko. "I mean Alan just walked in. Go ahead with what you've got to say."

"Everything so far has been straight-forward," Niko said. "But from here on it will grow more complicated. Imagine an enormous ship, fifteen stories tall, a thousand feet long, 50,000 tons, and able to carry a thousand passengers. How can a monster like that float? It floats because of displacement—the weight of the water, displaced by the ship, is greater than the weight of the ship. I've said before, objects occupy space. They displace whatever was there before. Something was always there before, space holds no vacuums. And no two objects occupy the same space simultaneously."

"So?" Rooster said.

"So, time on the other hand is filled with events. But unlike space where there's a well-defined volume imposing a maximum load, time accommodates any number of events in the period we call now. Time swells for many events and hangs loose for few. Now is always filled with all that's happening. The fit between now and its content is perfect. There is no losing things in the emptiness of now, nor is there any need to squeeze more in, as if it's an overflowing suitcase needing to be closed one last time. Now accommodates it all."

Niko paused and Em, Rooster, and Alan waited.

"We all know this," Niko continued. "When we see now as empty we often sense it to be dragging. Yet when we see it as full, it seems to speed by so that among travelers it's often heard, 'I can't believe it was just this morning when we were in—'"

"Niko!" Em said. "Get to the point. We're nearly to the day Alan kills—"

"Don't tell me," Niko said. "I don't want to know."

Em blew out a deep breath. "Just get on with it then."

"Stretching our concept of time," Niko said, "defining our world with time in mind adds insight to topics we already take for granted. Depression is replacing a robust now with a now appearing empty and shallow. Psychosis is overlaying now with a non-current now. Greed ignores now's satisfactory content and instead wants it all, now. Selfishness is shocked and annoyed when someone else's now must be accommodated. Lust focuses on a tiny subset of all that's happening, giving it undue dominance. Sloth is postponing now's demands."

Niko paused and waited for a response. When none came he added, "Is losing track of now a major mental disorder? Of course."

~ ~ ~

Still June 27, Minneapolis

At 9:45 am Sanger stood behind a row of chairs at the Baggage Claim area of the Minneapolis-St Paul International airport. The row of seats was bolted to the floor and Sanger felt secure leaning against it. Carousel 12, incoming flight from O'Hare. He wondered how he'll explain the situation to Bill. Or what parts to explain. Rooster drifted through his mind and he smiled, believing that harboring a runaway teenager, not informing her parents, letting her come and go as she pleased, plus offering visions of the future, was the least unusual ingredient in this swirling stew. Yet Sanger's smile turned to dismay. They should have phoned the worried woman and assured her of Rooster's safety, well, as safe as can be surrounded by potential pornographic photos, blackmail, murder, and an open example of relationship infidelity.

Perhaps we could have, Sanger thought, *kept Em's future fling a secret, hidden, as the majority of infidelities are. Not known, not imagined. Rooster needn't think stepping-out is normal in committed relationships, which it*, Sanger paused, *isn't…is, is it?* He knew he was too focused on Em's role in the unfolding fiasco. But why not— that's where his thoughts had blown, settling into drifts, and left his precious notions of faithfulness and family even more challenged than they were before the atomizer entered his life.

He looked to his left and was brought back from his musing to see Uncle Bill striding along the polished floor. Bill was a big man, husky through the shoulders and just as thick in the waist. His gait was steady and clean, not like a man who had recently gained weight, but like one who had always been whopping. Sanger saw the fedora on Bill's head and was momentarily angry. *That's my hat*, he thought, *mine to wear and lose when I gassed your getaway car from the curb*. But faster than a blink, Sanger knew the hat was never his. He only wore Bill's fedora because he wanted to follow Bill, walk tall under his wing, and warm himself in the intermittent glow of gangster.

"Hey Sanger," Bill said, extending his right hand.

As they shook, Sanger said, "Here's your carousel. Baggage?"

"Carry-on only. Baggage is for rookies." Bill had a canvass carryall rolled under his arm and a knapsack over one shoulder.

"Let's go then. My car's in short-term parking."

As they walked to the car, Sanger asked meaningless questions and made inane comments even though he knew there were more important topics to discuss. Once they were off airport property, Bill adjusted his seat, settled back, and said, "We've got a lot to do and not enough time. We'll have to write it down, make a schedule."

"We?" Sanger asked.

"Yeah, you. The way we last talked on the phone, I thought you wanted to do stuff for me, I mean with me."

"Sure," Sanger said. "That's what I meant."

"Good. First we have to go to this address." Bill dug into his pocket and handed Sanger a scrap of margin from a page of newspaper with an address written on it.

"Okay. I can get us there. Why? What do you need to do?"

Bill didn't answer the questions. "About that snake of a lawyer. I do know him. And the banker, not so much. I'm involved in a deal."

"Why get involved if he's a snake?"

"Even snakes sometime guarantee a good return on investment. And that's where the steamer trunk comes in. I'll deliver it, get paid, and that'll be part of the money I'll give Meyer, the lawyer."

"Part?" Sanger asked.

"Yeah, part. I'll need more. And that's where you come in. You and Em and the banker. She's still living with you, isn't she?"

"Yes. What's she need to do?"

Bill lowered his head to look through the windshield at street signs as they drove. "Em? Not much. She's got a pretty face and that's something to work with." Bill paused and then asked, "Is this the right street?"

"Yeah. Next block down. But about Em. What will you need her to do?"

"Not much. Don't concern yourself. Nothing's written in stone."

Sanger slowed the car, unable to drive safely while his mind circled through flirting and jealousy and the perceptive fingers of a banker who counted money all day. He turned to Bill and asked, "Are you lying to me?"

Bill twisted in his seat, opened his palms, and put an

incredulous look on his face. "No. Sanger, have I ever lied to you?"

Stunned to see himself in Bill's actions, Sanger was mute. He saw an uncanny resemblance of clan, inheritance, genealogy; parentage and offspring. He imagined a bevy of times he'd opened his hands in the same exact motion, believing once he'd shown his palms he'd be seen as credible and trust-worthy. Of course.

"Besides," Bill added, "if I need more of Em, I'll negotiate directly with her. You've heard the crime theory of compartmentalization? Everybody's duties separated. Need to know. That sort of thing. Is this the right street?"

"Yeah. I told you I'd get you here. Next block down."

When Sanger pulled to the curb, Bill opened the door and said, "Wait here, I won't be a minute."

Sanger leaned his head on the steering wheel. He was despondent about the need-to-know philosophy. Yet when he thought of the future he had already experienced, and heard from the others about theirs, he saw the separation Bill mentioned, unaware what the others had done until they returned to the present and disclosed.

Drawn out of his thoughts as Bill jumped into the front passenger seat, Sanger saw a shoebox on Bill's lap. "What do you have?"

"Take a quick glance. I won't hold it open long." Bill lifted the lid.

Sanger saw a pair of handguns resting peacefully, like a six and a nine, the barrel of one coddling the handle of the other.

CHAPTER SEVENTEEN

While Sanger is collecting Bill, Chicago

Niko unrolled a silk Persian carpet, woven in Pakistan and bought in Nepal. He'd purchased it on a Katmandu side street after a few days of haggling. Then the store owner rolled it, wrapped it in brown paper, and tied the ends with twine. Niko carried it all the way home, convincing customs agents that it wasn't a weapon. On his living room floor he spread the soft two feet by four feet carpet evenly with his palms. Standing, with the windows behind him, the background shone ultramarine blue with its filigreed borders lighter. He walked to his desk and dug through a drawer for a book. Returning, with the windows in front of him, the silk reflected the light differently, making the background silvery gray and the filigree darker.

He sat beside the carpet and from the inner cover of the book retrieved three coins. They felt warm and worn and within a few minutes he had tossed them six times, recording each configuration. He hadn't consulted the *I Ching* since undergraduate school where he had also read the words of Timothy Leary and Richard Alpert.

The first hexagram, according to his third edition, Richard Wilhelm translation, was 'Decrease' with transforming lines in the 5th and 6th locations from the bottom. Changing those lines from broken to solid and solid to broken turned the hexagram into 'Limitation'.

Niko quietly studied the words of interpretation. Decrease combined with sincerity brought good fortune. Decrease rounded the bend to increase. Decrease came in its own time. Decrease encouraged character formation. The transforming 5th line promised increase in its time. And the changing line in the 6th place specified increase without harming others brought supreme good fortune.

Niko recognized the signs of his own instability. Or perhaps exhaustion. The memory of his brother's and sister's taboo relationship—their magical incantations, their private arrogant knowledge—had been enough to send him to the extremes of psychic theory. The *I Ching* had been a stepping stone toward science, a wayward outpost where claims were made on how to become a better person.

He flipped through the dense book, lingering only a moment at the fractured spine and frayed cloth cover. The hexagram his transforming lines indicated became Limitation. The trigram above was danger, Water. The trigram below was joyous, the Lake. The lower lake resided within borders, water from above was limitless. When too much water filled the lake, channeling the overflow carried its own reward. The superior person controlled their craving.

Easier said than done, Niko thought. He looked around the room and saw no way out of the depression into which he'd sunk. Desperate to squeeze a respectable article from those using his device, he realized that he had left them out of the equation. Time was a delusion, a mirage in exquisite detail. Even Albert Einstein said, "…the separation between past, present, and future is only an illusion, although a convincing one." A construction of consciousness?

Niko stared at the *I Ching* and wondered if everyone actively fabricated time. Or had long forgotten, imaginative people established the tool of time and passed it on through Darwinian sequences? The illusion persisted, the misperception perpetuated. But how? Why?

Niko had not yet told them of time's leap from the conventional, and regretted withholding that information. The *I Ching* reminded him of the better person he had once wanted to become. He rose from the floor and sat at his writing desk. The treatise he had enclosed with each device had been unreadable to those four. Lost in thought, he intended to set things straight.

Less than an hour later, he called them and without waiting for polite greetings, he said, "Twentieth century thought redefined time like no other era. A table isn't wholly itself in this moment, and then itself again in the next moment. It extends through time just as its length extends through space. Quantum physics upended time like an atomic blast disrupting space. It's left us with an understanding of time that's nothing more than—and."

"a-n-d," Alan said simultaneously with Em as she said, "And…what?" while Rooster chirped in, ""What's that mean?"

"Just the simple conjunction," Niko answered. "And. But the authority of it, the base of quantum thought is the double-slit experiment."

"I've heard of that," Alan said.

Niko tapped his phone. "Listen. Drop a pebble in a placid pond and concentric circles of peaks and troughs spread from the center. If the pond-space is limited by a wall, the waves bounce off of it, interfering with the waves still approaching. When an opening appears, the waves continue through, emerging to fill the space available, a half circle beyond the wall. The wave-properties exist even when the wave is chopped up. But if instead of waves through the opening, a gun is fired. The pellet travels a straight line and hits the target at a predictable spot. Instead of wave-like properties, it possesses particle-like properties."

"Okay," Em said. "So?"

"These two sets of properties are generally incompatible. Sound does not travel like a dart through a blowgun straight into my ear. And a line of cars on a one-lane mountain road will not wander beyond their particle-like borders to spread up the hill and into the valley.

"Yet there is one befuddling example that will explain more than can be initially comprehended. The electromagnetic spectrum spreads from long, low-frequency radio waves to short, high-frequency gamma ray waves with visible light a small portion near the middle. Yet we also know light as a particle. When a single wavelength of visible light, blue's true hue for instance, is shined on a mirror it behaves more like a tennis ball against a wall than it does a wave of water against that same wall."

Em, Rooster, and Alan looked at each other without comment.

"Shining photons of the truest blue through a single slit

produces an expected particle-like pattern on the wall behind. A single line. (|) Yet when two slits exist, a wave-like pattern produces bright lines where the wave's peaks meet peaks and troughs meet troughs. (| | | | |) A pattern of multiple lines from only two slits."

Alan scratched his head. "A wave of light goes through the single slit and doesn't spread out. So?"

"Physicists are weird and they found these results weird. Here's why. Through the double slits the waves interfered with each other's peaks and troughs. But even when only one photon at a time was shot through the slits, the interference pattern emerged. When they tried to determine which of the two slits the photons went through, the pattern on the back screen appeared as two clear strips as if tennis balls had been thrown through. Not like a wave as seen before. But it gets even weirder. When they quit observing so closely, the results returned to the interference pattern. The mere act of measuring ruled, and turned the wave properties into a particle-like phenomenon. So there you have it. Most of it."

"You mean there's more?" Rooster asked.

"Always more," Niko said. "Weirdness ensued. If a single photon was shot through either of the slits one at a time, they still produced the interference pattern. How can that be? A single photon-wave interfering with itself? A phantom twin? Or maybe the single photon traveled through this slit *and* that slit, traveled all possible future paths available and interfered with itself as if all those futures already existed."

"You're joking," Em said. "Right?"

"No," Niko answered. "This wasn't just true with photons but also with protons, neutrons, electrons, et cetera. Imagine yourself as an electron orbiting a nucleus. Before anyone looks, you have the superposition of possessing all possible attributes, of becoming all possible versions of yourself. So you are left-handed *and* right-handed, tall *and* short, blue-eyed *and* green-eyed. Then someone comes along to measure you and you're at that moment a tall, left-handed, green-eyed person. There are probabilities of what attributes you will become but no certainties."

During the pause, Em asked, "Niko, are you falling off your stool."

Alan shook his head and added, "I've heard all this, I'm a teacher, but Niko, has your stool ever had more than two legs."

Rooster pulled on her bangs and asked, "Is this science or something? Should *I* have learned this in school?"

CHAPTER EIGHTEEN

Moments later, Minneapolis *and* Chicago, Microwave telephone connection

Em picked the phone from the table as if holding it closer to her lips would emphasize her next words. "Sanger's gone to get Bill. We need some answers before Bill arrives. Before this last bit about tennis balls and waves of water you told us that misplacing now causes psychic slippage. We're all loosely tethered lately and need something to ground us again."

"Okay," Niko said. "I know it's confusing. Time is the great evolutionary furnace. A dozen thousand years ago peoples of the Fertile Crescent grasped a sense of time. They casually watched grains drop to the ground and carried them home. They soon, within a few hundred years, cut the tops of grain stalks and carried them to their migratory hunter-gatherer settlements where they shattered the ears in a careless spillage of oat and barley seeds. Years later, as grains grew in their previous settlements and not in the area where the stalks had been cut, these people made more permanent dwellings. But agriculture didn't hold the immediate reward that hunting or gathering did. A guarantee that the planter would also be the harvester necessitated patience, foresight, and the early stages of ownership. Designated duties followed as cultivation became more labor intensive: tiller and planter and waterer and harvester and store keeper and permanent buildings and protectors of the storage and planners and animal husbandry and spreaders of fertilizer and childhood diseases transferred from living side by side with domesticated animals and as egalitarian hunter-gatherer groups lost out to agricultural communities, private property, specialized roles, leaders, and soldiers, and clerics imploring rain, passed their skills from generation to generation."

"What are you talking about?" Em asked.

"Did you know," Niko asked, "the earliest writing wasn't of personal experience or imaginative thought, but was of record-keeping and exchange rates and taxes. Surplus and want, supply and demand, trade routes and colonization. War. All because some clever people noticed the illusion of time and then ran with it. The world is shaped by the image we knit. Not exactly accurately, we value impression more than realism. When two events occur one after the other and we see it that way, no problem. Still, we're sometimes fooled into seeing an after-event as happening before."

"Okay," Alan said. "We misperceive the world. Can we

jump to the point?"

"No. It takes more than rote acknowledgement. The world is real. Sound waves vibrate our eardrums, stimulate nerves, send current to the brain, where that stuff in the air, nothing more than waves in a medium, is processed. Yet one of a group might say, 'What's that sound?' unable to distinguish a snap from a step from a switch. A few offer their interpretations and one or two might reply, 'I didn't hear anything.'

"The world is not something that only exists when you're paying attention. Assuming the world is real, it must be distraction or lackadaisicalness in the person who doesn't hear a particular sound. When refocused, they suddenly hear the sound that had been there all along. This is the consciousness we trust to pass along a message, follow detailed procedures, or carefully wash dishes in a restaurant. This is also the consciousness willing to ignore unchanging patterns, give scant attention to what's not new, and, well, daydream. "

"I daydream," Rooster said.

"Yes, of course." Niko added, "Think of thunder from a lightning strike. We know sound and light travel at different speeds and reach our ears and eyes at different times. If someone stands less than ninety feet away and claps, we hear the clap and see the hands whack at the same time. We know this isn't true. Our brains are able to process the small difference but our consciousness creates an easier to understand picture of reality.

"If the person steps a few feet farther away and claps again, it's just too much. We hear and see the clap as non-simultaneous, able once again to distinguish before and after."

Impatient, Alan said, "So?"

"Yeah," Rooster added. "So it didn't look like they happened at the same time. So what?"

"So what nothing. Our sense of time was developed when

running was as fast as one could go, throwing as far as a projectile could be sent, and a few words, a handshake, and an exchange of items was as quick as a trade could be made. While cooking in my kitchen I may not need to so finely differentiate time and events. Yet crossing a street, driving a car, piloting an airplane, or assessing the data about an incoming missile? It makes me wonder if our illusion about time is keeping up with the new realities in the world."

"And you're thinking it's not?" Em said.

"I'm sure it's not. Our understanding of time is at best a convenience where we piece together various parts to make a whole we think we understand. Time might not flow. There might be gaps between this now and the next now. Yet we have no idea how this now dissolves and the next now appears. To us, it's always now, even though soon it will be tomorrow and we're streaming into a future that does, or doesn't, already exist."

~ ~ ~

June 27, Minneapolis

Just as Niko hung up, Sanger and Uncle Bill entered the room. "Hey everyone," Sanger said, still in the doorway and receiving quiet stares from the others.

Bill stepped in behind Sanger, nudging him out of the way. He stopped short, looked around the room and said, "What is this, some kind of convention? Are the neighbors coming? Who's that?" pointing to Rooster.

"No, Bill," Sanger said. "Everything's all right. Don't get bent out of shape."

"Who's that?" Bill asked again, pointing at Rooster.

"I'm Rooster," she contributed, raising her fists in a boxer's pose.

Bill pulled Sanger across the room, even as Sanger resisted. "What's going on here?" Bill asked. "Why do you have a stranger here?"

"Don't worry. Let's just settle in and see where we are. Everything's okay."

As Sanger and Bill returned to the center of the room, Rooster said, "Hey, new guy. If you're Bill, I'm telling you, you better leave Alan alone."

Rising to her taunt, Bill said, "Holy hell, Sanger, who is she?"

"That's Rooster. She's okay. Don't worry."

"Rooster?" Bill said. "What kind of name is that?"

Rooster again tightened her fists on the ends of cocked arms. "It's my name. You want to make something of it?"

Bill took a step toward her while saying, "And what if I do?"

Sanger and Alan stepped between Rooster and Bill. "Slow down," Sanger said. "Everyone back to your corners."

Bill stood his ground, chest to chest with Sanger.

As Alan led Rooster to the other side of the room, she said, "Let's just tell him we know he's trouble? Tell him to leave us alone."

"What's she talking about?" Bill said.

"Nothing," Em said. "She's just a kid. Leave her alone."

Sanger raised an arm as if firing a pistol thrice in the air. "Whoa, whoa, whoa. Let's start over. Is there any coffee made. Let's all have a cup. Rooster, would you...no," stopping himself for fear Rooster might spit into Bill's. "Em, would you get us some coffee? Let's all find places to sit." He stared at Rooster and gave her a stern look, even though he knew she was only trying to help Alan.

Bill sat on the cushioned arm of the sofa. "We have a lot to do in only a few days," he said. "What about the steamer trunk. Is it okay? Is it here?"

"Yeah," Sanger said. "Right over against that wall."

"Did you open it?"

A moment of quiet, a pause long enough to be noticed. "No," Sanger said. "Never even peeked."

"Ha!" Bill said. "Don't kid a kidder. I just hope you didn't take anything out, try it on, rip the seams or something. People were a little smaller back then."

Bill approached the trunk and popped open the latches. Opening the lid, he said, "Civil War uniforms. Almost all Union. Would've been nice to pinch some Confederates. But you get what you can. A full jacket with all the buttons, patches, and the rest can bring upwards of ten thousand dollars. I won't get that for these, I don't have the provenance. My buyers get a discount for not asking questions. Someone farther down the line will forge papers of authenticity and sell at full price."

Bill ignored the boxed atomizer tucked in a corner of the trunk. Then he reached deep beneath the layers. Sanger remembered doing the same thing when he first opened the trunk, discovered nothing and hadn't explored since.

Bill looked up and said, "So maybe you didn't open the trunk. Everything seems just as it was when I folded it in."

"That's bad news," Rooster said.

"Bad news?" Bill asked.

"No," Sanger said. "No, she doesn't mean it." He opened his hands to Bill, indicating there was nothing to hide. "I don't know where she got that idea."

"Who is she?" Bill asked. "What's she doing here?"

"She's a runaway," Sanger said. "Her parents are probably worried sick but she won't tell Alan or Em or me where she lives or how to contact them."

Holding a Union field jacket, Bill stared at Rooster. He rubbed his chin and took a couple of steps away from the steamer trunk. "So, your folks don't know you're here?"

"That's right."

"Have your folks put up fliers on telephone poles, been on TV with an appeal, contacted the police?"

"Nah," Rooster said, pushing one hand away from her. "They don't care."

"Well then let's keep it that way. Maybe you could hold off on contacting them until I leave town. Just a few days."

Rooster had hoped he'd want to leave right away, distance himself from jailbait. "Sure," she said. But she thought, *Don't kid a kidder? Do old people really say that? Let's see how you handle kidding from a real kid.* She looked up and said to Bill, "Sorry about what I said earlier. Alan and Sanger have told me so much about you. Now I can see they were telling the truth. They're ready to do anything to help you out. Now that I've met you, I feel that way, too."

Bill thought there was something wrong with Rooster, like coming upon a section of pavement pushed up higher than the rest. Not right, out of line, something to trip him up. Adjusting his knapsack over one shoulder and rearranging his arms around his carryall, he said he was going to make some calls from the walk-in closet.

The four stared at each other in a profusion of silence. Em pointed to the open trunk, wondering if Bill's satisfaction was the final word about the atomizer. "He ignored the atomizer," she whispered. "Perhaps it's nothing to him. Slip the mister out now. He didn't notice, maybe he doesn't know what it is."

"What about those waiting for the trunk?" Alan asked. "What if its absence is really what starts this countdown to murder?"

"Leave it in there," Sanger said. "We just have to let go."

Within a few minutes, Bill stuck his head out of the closet and called to Em, "I need a favor of you, Em. You said you know Hugh Gardner. I need some information on him. What he's like, favorite beer, that kind of thing. Maybe you could talk to him. Use the fact that you know each other to chat with him. Come have a drink with me tomorrow night. I'll pick you up about eight."

Shit, Em said to herself. *No, this is okay. This is exactly as I've seen it. I sit with Hugh at the bar. Bill's never come with me when I've approached Hugh. He'll never know Hugh doesn't know me. Then…how do the pictures get taken? When? How much help does the future need of me? Am I to go to bed with him?* Still, recognizing opportunity when it presented itself, she said, "Okay."

Bill returned to the closet and stepped out just in time for the serving of coffee. He said, "I've got to get a move on things now. Em, I'll see you tomorrow night. Sanger, drive me out to deliver the trunk?"

"Sure…but don't you want to take your own car?"

"Don't have a car yet and I want to get it done." Bill waved a hand. "We'll deliver it and then you drop me downtown. I'm meeting with the guy I'm borrowing a car from. Then I'll be set and can get around on my own. And Em, I brought a couple of dresses for you to wear. They were your size and just laying around in Chicago, so…I left them over the chair in the closet."

When Bill wasn't looking, Em got Sanger's attention by kicking him. With palms together, she placed them against one ear and tilted her head, the international sign for slumber. She pointed the top of her head toward Bill.

Sanger asked, "Hey, where are you staying?"

"With your parents," Bill said. "They'll probably put me in your old room. Isn't that a hoot?"

"But…" Sanger stared at the floor before he could continue. "I mean, my dad's out of town."

"No," Bill said. "You don't say. Huh. Come on. You, too,

Alan. Let's carry this trunk down to the car and load it in."

~ ~ ~

Once Sanger and Bill drove off, Alan returned to the living room and said to Rooster, "Somebody, someday, is going to knock your block off if you keep taunting people."

"They all deserve it. I wish I could taunt deeper and harder that uncle of yours. We should be shoving him off his game. He's trouble, he'll get us all into trouble. Especially you."

Alan rolled his eyes. He knew teenagers, had taught school for enough years to see all kinds. And he liked them, the weird and the constrained, the pretty and the plain. He knew soon after Rooster's arrival that she was notable, parts jagged and staggered and skewed today, but she'd surely settle into a coherent whole someday. This moment, right now, he wished she wasn't so special, wanted her to toe the line and let the future unfold as they've seen. It was too late to change plans now, as if they dared take the entire future in their own hands and shape it into something it had never been. *Kill someone,* he thought. *I can do that. He deserves to die. He's selling arms, making a profit on misery.* Alan looked up and saw Rooster staring at him. "What?" he said.

She sat up straighter and answered, "I'm sorry. I think the whole time with this atomizer-future thingy, I've been seeing it only through my eyes. You all have the bigger picture in mind and I should start doing that, too."

"You give us too much credit. Look at Sanger and Em. They've got their own stuff in mind."

Rooster touched her bangs and then brought her hand down. "Not you. I didn't mean them. I can see what they're doing. But you, you're thinking of us all the time."

Humbled by her assessment, Alan remembered a well-meaning friend who, after his wife's suicide, had said, 'It's not your fault. You did all you could.' *All I could?* Alan thought. *Doesn't matter if it's true or false or something in between. It's believing it, which I don't.*

"I was told," Alan said, "after my wife died that I'd done all I could. Did everything possible. What's that say? It didn't make a whit of difference. So what's the point? Might as well have done nothing if doing it all doesn't matter. Better to believe there was more, another vase of flowers, one more talk to two am, a final measly list of what's good in the world, ignoring that we're all doomed to extinction through nuclear winter, global warming, heavy sadness, right down to the exhausted helium-filled balloons we couldn't bother to pick up as they drifted slow motion six inches above the floor."

"Don't sulk," Rooster said. "Don't do that."

Alan looked away from staring at the back of his hand. "Yeah. Okay. Where's Em?"

"In the closet trying on the clothes Bill left."

Alan lifted his head and looked at the closet door. He physically felt his avoidance of Rooster, didn't want to look at her, didn't want her to see his regret at abandoning all hope. "What did Bill leave?"

"I don't know, haven't seen it yet."

Em stepped out of the closet wearing a clingy black dress. It was very short and the thin straps crossing behind her neck highlighted the shape of her shoulders. She turned 360 degrees as her face alternated between pleasure and concern. "What do you think?"

Rooster shoved two thumbs up and said, "Cool."

"Alan, what do you think?"

Alan thought Em was happily charging into her future. He wished he could so effortlessly walk into his. But directly murdering someone was different than letting Sanger slowly die through deliberate stabs to his heart. Alan shook his head and said, "Sanger will want you to wear something underneath it."

"Yeah, won't he." Em turned fully around again and added, "You can tell?"

"I'll say," Rooster said.

"Yeah," Alan added. "I mean, if you look."

Rooster stood and took a step toward Em. "Oh, your banker will look, all right. He won't be able to help himself."

CHAPTER NINTEEN

Afternoon of June 27

In the car with Uncle Bill, the secured steamer trunk extending from the back, Sanger drove while looking straight ahead. He wanted to draw his right knee up onto the seat, turn, and talk to Bill with both hands. He wanted to ask Bill not to use Em in his plan of sleazy sex leading to blackmailing the banker. But he realized revealing to Bill any hint of knowing what's going to happen will not only make Bill suspicious, but might also deviate from the original future they'd already seen. *Original future*, he asked himself, *can that be right?*

"So," Sanger said, "you're going to stay at my parent's place?"

"Yeah, it'll be good. Catch up with your mom a little."

Sanger continued driving, struggling to keep his focus on the traffic. The silence between them lengthened, until Sanger said, "Too bad my dad's out of town. He'd've liked to have seen you."

"I don't know," Bill answered. "Sometimes brothers don't get along as well as...as in story books. Sometimes something comes between them and there's no fixing it."

Sanger said nothing but was bristling with words. *What?* he thought, *What do you mean by 'between'? Can you describe 'something' a little more?*

Sanger tapped the brakes, approaching the car ahead too quickly. Settling back, adjusting his hands on the wheel, he heard bothersome insinuations trotting over the hills in his mind, cantering, galloping through the attention he should be giving the road.

Sanger closed his eyes briefly but consciously, and said, "Have you ever been out to this place before, out to where we're taking the trunk?"

"No, never even met the guy, not in person. Talked to him on the phone, we joked a lot."

As they parked in front of the address, Bill added, "Just hang back, don't talk. We'll get in, deliver the package, and get out again. Maybe stop for a beer on the way home."

As they released the trunk from the car's trunk, Sanger said, "I've never carried my end alone. I don't know if I can keep it up."

"Give it a try. We'll see. I think you can."

Sanger noticed Bill's faith in him and surprisingly believed he could do it. At the door, Bill knocked while Sanger sat on the trunk shaking his arms. The door opened and they carried it into the house.

Bill didn't introduce Sanger and the man of the house didn't ask. Bill opened the trunk and then stepped aside. The man kneeled, placed the boxed atomizer on the floor, and went to work digging through the uniforms. As he dug he said to Bill, "It's never been out of your sight all the way here, right?"

"That's right," Bill said. "I slept with it each night."

"Got it," the man said.

The object he lifted from beneath all the uniforms looked like a specialized attaché case. He put it on the coffee table between them, took a small key out of his breast pocket, and fiddled with the latch.

Just before opening it, the man of the house pointed to the atomizer and said, "What's that?"

"Sanger?" Bill said.

"I'll take care of it."

Sanger picked it out of the trunk and held it against his waist. He wanted to ask again if anyone minded that he take the atomizer away, needed one more clarification that no one cared. Instead, while the attaché case was being opened, he placed the atomizer near the front door. On his way back he glimpsed into the partially opened case. Having never seen the real thing, Sanger suspected the gleaming metal plates were for counterfeiting one-hundred-dollar bills.

The man of the house nodded, closed the lid, and smiled at Bill. He then stood, left the room, and returned with a brown grocery bag. "We're good, then? Do you want to count it?"

Bill accepted the bag and judged its weight. "Virtue in our line of work is trust. I trust you. I'll count it when I get home."

On the way out, Sanger lingered at the door and picked up the atomizer. He held it against his ribs and covered it with his arm.

The man opened the door and said, "Let's agree to never

see each other again."

"Sounds good," Bill said with a robust swagger out the door. "Sounds good to me."

~　~　~

Evening, June 27

After having changed out of her slinky dress, Em sat in the living room, pondering her predicament. No, she was certain she couldn't explain any of this to Hugh. Nonetheless, she will wear the dress provided and then…then she didn't know. She lightly stroked her fingers over the arm of the chair. She was confident the future she'll experience will be similar to the future she's already seen. Hugh will meet her three times for the first time. Even that didn't brew any confusion. It hadn't yet troubled her. Like standing at the top of a ski jump, she felt ready to push off and let the future have its way with her.

Em wondered why the memory of flirting wasn't enough, why the expectation of doing it again wasn't satisfactory. There was something special about now, something more real when discovery's surprise was current, or anticipation's gratification only moments away.

~　~　~

Alan and Rooster also sat in the living room. They thought slowly, exchanging quiet comments, without pressure or expectation. Alan had resigned himself. The only options he saw were within a narrow range of possibilities. He will go to William Meyer's office. He will have a gun in his pocket. He will raise the gun in anger and outrage, or not raise the gun at all.

Rooster leaned and bumped Alan with her shoulder. "I wish," she said, "we hadn't sent the atomizer away. Everything's had to do with your uncle and the date you kill that lawyer. But in a couple of days we'll be past that and if we used it again, where will we go?"

"Hmm," Alan said. Of all he had learned about time in the preceding weeks, he wondered if the atomizer was really a time machine. Or was it more like a rift in time, a miniature worm hole that after June 30th will dump them to perpetually relive the past, unable to shake those cobwebs from his hair?

He cleared his throat before asking Rooster, "Does it matter if it's me that kills William Meyer, or someone else?"

"Of course it matters," she said. "What have you got, some kind of nihilism disease? Please don't start wearing black and smudging dark liner under your eyes. Of course it matters. It'll matter to me."

"That's kind of you to say." Alan paused, "But in the bigger picture? When all's said and done, what's it matter?"

"Don't be like that," Rooster said. "It's like saying what's it matter if kids are abused, if one kid is raped, what's one kid matter, one skinny kid bullied? Of course it matters. It should matter to you. It matters to me."

"You're right. You're young. But you can't let every bad thing happening in the world matter to you. There's got to be some filtering. A line drawn where it no longer matters. If not, you'll go crazy. You won't have the energy for it."

"Yeah," Rooster said, "But it's not if I can't care for it all I've got to care for none. You can't live that way either."

Alan nodded. "You're a pretty smart cookie, Ms. Rooster. I've just lived too many years, felt deflated too many times. I feel like I'm a fat peg pounded into a narrow hole. Now I'm stuck."

She wanted to touch him, stroke his arm and tell him everything will be okay. She lifted her head, looked straight at the chair across the room, and said, "When you next go to

William Meyer's office…if you go again, you know, for real, on your own or with Bill, if…" She sniffed and her neck grew warm. "You'll do the right thing, you will. I don't know what it'll be but it'll be right, right for that moment and no matter what it is, no one else can really know what it was like so how can they judge what you've done because they weren't there and you were and you'll know what the right thing was. Won't you?"

Rooster heard herself and wanted to take it all back. She'd just told him he'll do the exact thing he'd already said he was incapable of doing. She slid away an inch or two, turned, and looked directly at him. "You've done the right thing with me. It's not that you can't."

"It's just never worked out for me the right way."

Rooster wanted to tell him she remembered when everything was good for her. Those times had ended and for the last few years nothing had worked out well. She wanted to tell him she was just like him. But she knew she wasn't: she was half his age, less; his devastations had accumulated over years while hers were fewer than a dozen seasons; and he was petting hopelessness like it was an old dog, while she—*I'm not*, she thought, *I'm not hopeless*.

Rooster felt Alan's arm cover her shoulders as he said, "Hey, no sadness. What would you think if we got the mister back again? What would you like to do with it?"

Tie you up, she thought. *Break your leg. Keep you from walking arm in arm with destiny*. Instead she took a deep breath. "Everyone tells me high school won't last forever. They say there's a whole other world waiting for me. I'd like to travel to the future and see some of that. Where I'll be, what I'll be doing."

"Got to finish high school," Alan said. "And you're plenty smart enough for college."

"And pay for it how?"

"Like everybody else, grants and loans and working your way through."

Rooster raised her eyebrows. "I've got it. We'll bring back the newspaper from the day after the last game of this year's World Series? Maybe place some bets. You and me?"

"We probably can't bring back the newspaper to a time before it was printed, but we can bring back the scores."

"That's good, then. It'll help me pay for college."

"Do you know a good bookie? One you can trust?"

Rooster twisted her lips. "No. But it's a thought. Who knows? And you? If we get another chance with the mister, what would you like to do?"

"My future is like going down a dark set of stairs and I only have a few matches left to light the way. I'd like to see where I end up, how far down. If I knew…I don't know, maybe I'd find my way up again."

Rooster smiled. "I like that. Look for me. I'll leave the porch light on."

~ ~ ~

When Sanger returned from delivering the steamer trunk, he was still pleased for having snatched the atomizer from under the nose of its true recipient. He stood inside the front door with the mister behind his back, as if it was a surprise bouquet of short-stemmed flowers.

"Guess what I have?" he said, expecting them to wonder how he got away with it, what cunning magic had he pulled out of his hat?

He held the atomizer before them in one hand, using his other to encircle it with an imaginary frame. "Ta-da."

Em gave him an unsmiling, granite stare. Alan turned away, shaking his head. Only Rooster replied. "Cool," she said. "But I'd just gotten settled on never using it again. Guess I'll have to reshuffle those cards."

"Sanger," Em said. "Won't someone notice? Won't they then backtrack to where it went missing? Isn't there something dangerous at the other end of your self-satisfaction?"

"They didn't recognize it," he said, "didn't know what it was. Trust me." Sanger put the atomizer on a side table. When he turned back, he said, "And who are you to warn anyone about the dangers on the other end of self-satisfaction? You've been flirting with that all along."

"I'm not flirting with self-satisfaction," Em said.

"Danger, I mean. Flirting with danger."

Rooster leapt up and stepped between them. "Good one. Flirting. What a pun."

Alan stopped beside Rooster and added, "She's right to step between you two. Your fighting isn't helping anyone."

Sanger turned away. He thought they'd be pleased to see the atomizer again, especially Em, as she wanted her future to arrive more than any of the others. He moved toward her and said, "I thought you'd like getting the mister back. What do I have to do to please you? What do you want from me?"

"Me?" Em said. "What do I want from you? Ha. Really." She pointed at him and added, "It's you who've been upset. You who's complaining. So okay. What do I want from you? I want you to…to…I want you to quit judging me. I want you to leave me alone."

Sanger paused a moment to let pride and dignity supersede his initial desire to beseech and plead. "All right then," he said. "I can do that."

He turned away from her and then as quick as flipping a pancake, panic and desperation came to the fore. "Move out then. That's what I want you to do. Save me from bothering you on those days when I can't leave you alone. I don't want to leave you alone. Can't you see that? All of this. You. You're just a…"

"A what?" Em asked. "Say it, I know you want to. What am I?"

"You guys," Alan said as he stepped forward. "Don't do this. Don't do it now."

Sanger waved a hand between Em and himself. "It's all about you, isn't it? Wheedle, connive, finagle; twist it all around to benefit you. Get what you want, no matter how."

Em put her hands on her hips and said, "I'm approaching the banker so Bill gets the money and Alan takes it to the lawyer. We all decided to do it this way. Together. So Alan doesn't really kill the guy."

"There," Sanger said. "There you go again. Don't you know we can all see through you? Alan's situation is just a cover. If it wasn't Alan, it would be something else. You'll justify what you want. Doesn't matter what I say."

Alan put his arm around Sanger's shoulder and directed him to the kitchen.

As they went, Sanger looked back. He longed to hear her apologize and then wait through a nervy pause before forgiving her. He craved her sympathy for the worry she had already caused him. As he clenched his fists, he thought of hurting her with more examples of her selfishness. He wanted to insist she see it from his point of view. But before he got to the kitchen table, he was again unsure of himself, lost in a driving force of inadequate options.

~ ~ ~

Em walked from couch to chair to side table and back to the couch again. She thought Sanger was wrong; she was no more self-centered than anyone else. Everyone saw the world through their own needs, couldn't let circumstances dictate every decision, there had to be some selfish consideration in everything. No, not selfish. Willful. Without will, the debris of others would overwhelm her; without watching out for herself, she'd get trampled. In a social structure geared toward men, designed through the laws of men, changed only when men saw fit to... Em touched her forehead and said to Rooster, "From their point of view, they deny there's any 'me' in woman. But for men, two-thirds of it is me, me, me."

Rooster looked back at Em but didn't respond.

More confident after her moment of insight, Em continued to pace. *I'd be eaten alive if I didn't watch out for myself,* she thought. She looked at Rooster and said, "There's nothing for us if we don't grab some for ourselves."

Em turned away and spoke to the wall. "I've thought things through. If Sanger wants me, he'll have to take all of me. Why does it have to be so hard?" She turned again and said to Rooster. "Why don't men listen?"

She stared at Rooster, waiting for a response. When none came, she added, "Oh, they'll say they want a free-spirited, creative, spontaneous sort of girl, but do they? Really? They all have this mold. Nothing too much this way or that, nothing that might embarrass them because we're just extensions of them, like the car they drive or the color of their phone. Heaven forbid if anyone discovered I had sex with someone other than Sanger. How could he live with what they'd think of him?"

Em put a hand over her face and turned away because she knew she had slipped over the deep end. It was familiar, what she'd just done, pulled out the stops, revved herself up. Calmer, she said, "Is it too much to say I don't want him to tell me what to do, don't want to abandon my island of self in a sea of compromise and obedience?"

Em sat on the front edge of a chair and asked, "I'm not being selfish, am I?"

Rooster stared without expression and tugged on her bangs. She watched Em's lips move as if words were ready to leap forth. Finally Rooster said, "He doesn't want you to move out. Even I can see that. But me, me, me in men? Where did that come from? Selfish? I don't know. Everybody's got to listen some, and everybody's got to make their case in the court where they live. Sanger doesn't care about the color of his phone. He even leaves it here for us to use. Are you being selfish? Yeah, well, maybe. It's okay, though."

CHAPTER TWENTY

June 29, the day before the murder of William Meyer
Minneapolis

Time had been skittish in Sanger's apartment. A day without recognition passed without goal or accomplishment. A new day commenced and bled into the afternoon. Waiting for Bill to collect her, Em sat in the living room having a hit-and-miss conversation with Sanger. Rooster and Alan refereed. Em wore the slinky black dress Bill had left. Noticing how Sanger looked at her dress and hoping to put a stop to it, Em said, "You'd feel differently if I was wearing it for you."

"I know how I'd feel if you were wearing it for me. And I don't want some dolt with his brains between his legs feeling that way about you." Sanger flexed his hands and added, "Just don't have sex with him, Em. That's all I ask."

Rooster slapped her forehead before saying, "Sanger, she wants to have sex with him. That's what really irks you. Not that she will, but she wants to. So that milk's already spilled."

Em remembered when Sanger wanted to know everything about her. Yet she suspected there were parts he wished to ignore. He still thought calling her his very own posed no conflict when Em insisted that she was her own person, did what she pleased. *Fine*, he'd said. Or another time when she'd said she wanted to set forth without compromise, be the commander of her own scooter. *Go for it*, he'd said. But when she'd said she wanted to make her own mistakes—that had stopped him. Decisions were one thing, mistakes another. 'I can't just watch you do that,' he had said, 'no one should…' She wanted no more than they relate captain to captain rather than through his assumption that he was captain and all around him was ship.

Em didn't want to twist the knife, even though she knew she was hurting him. She preferred confining her logic to saying she must have sex with Hugh in order to fulfill Bill's plan. She understood that letting Sanger know how much she'd already thought about sex with Hugh would only serve to make things harder. "Rooster," Em said, "saying it like that's just rude and insensitive."

"I'm right though, huh?"

"Not entirely," Em said. "I mean, he's nice, I like him. If it wasn't for that, liking him, I wouldn't do this at all."

"That's worse," Sanger said. "I'd rather he was just a one-night stand. Do your thing and never see him again. But liking him, when will it end?"

Alan shifted in his chair. "Let me get this straight. You'd prefer Em pick up guys, take them to bed, and never see them again?"

Em knew what Sanger meant. He thought of love like a rationed commodity, one per person. He'd expect that if a stray dog followed her home, she'd promptly abandon her currently loved dog. And why not, who can care for two dogs at once? And who'd let her? Who of his family would approve? Whispers and sidelong glances from friends noting his inability to provide all she needed. *Crass*, she thought. *If I can't be loyal, would he really prefer me indiscriminant. What's it all coming to?*

"Them?" Sanger said. "I don't mean them, I mean him. Once. And then it's over."

Em hadn't considered seeing Hugh only once. *Does he really think he can dictate what I want? How will he ever know if he succeeds?*

"Oh Sanger," Em said. "You don't own me. You can't…I've always said, right from the beginning, monogamy's not for me. Now it's time to believe me or throw in the towel. I need to be able to live without fear I'm destroying you. We've seen the future and know how Bill gets his money."

"Have we?" Sanger asked. "Do we? It might all be illusion. I don't believe the future is already out there. We're not confined to walking in the footsteps already charted. There's nothing beyond this moment. We're all still free agents, able to do with the future what we want."

They heard a car horn from the street. Sanger was closest to the window so he looked out. "It's Uncle Bill's car. The replica antique one."

Rooster said, "You ought to make him park and come up. Even high school boys will do that much."

"It's all right," Em said. "I'll go down." At the door she added, "I'm off then. See you all later."

Only Alan answered. "Good luck."

~ ~ ~

Em danced down the stairs, pushed through the outside doors, and scooted into the passenger seat of Bill's borrowed car. They didn't talk as Bill took the short drive into downtown Minneapolis. They stopped in front of a nice bistro and paused for a look. Bill then parked the car half a block away.

"This is where Hugh Gardner has a drink or two after work. You'll need a small purse. There are a few on the back seat. Pick one."

At the door, Bill guided her with a hand on the small of her back, and said, "You look great. Come on." A boisterous after-work crowd huddled at the bar. Bill bullied his way through, towing Em behind, and ordered two beers. "Come on Em, right up here beside me. Push your way in."

Em stepped backwards, bumping a few people, while pointing to tell Bill she was going to a booth. As she turned, she read a 'Grain Belt Beer' neon sign backwards in a window. The booths were dark and intimate while the pendant lamps hanging over the bar cast cones of bright light. Twisting to look around, her short skirt rode high on her thighs. She unsuccessfully attempted to pull it down with first one hand and then the other.

Bill approach with a bottle of beer in each hand.

"What? No glass?" she said.

Bill rolled his eyes, plopped into the booth, and slid a beer across the table. "I need a favor," he started. "Your friend, Hugh Gardner. He's up at the—"

"He's not my friend. I don't really know him. I mean, I know of him."

"You said you knew him. Over the phone, you said he was coming on to you." Bill leaned across the table and lowered his voice. "What's going on?

"Nothing. I just don't know him the way you think. He might not even recognize me. That's all. But you said you need a favor. What is it?"

"I want you," Bill said while looking at his bottle of beer. "Need you to…get a few pictures together with him."

"That's it? Pictures? Like hold up a phone and shoot some selfies?"

"No, I've got this spy camera in a pen." He pointed to it clipped to his shirt pocket. "It's meant to peek out of a breast pocket and film whatever's in front. In this case, just put it on a bedside table and leave it turned on."

Previous situations like this one, previous future episodes had been dreamlike, and decisions came easy. Em now felt as though she was pulling her feet out of deep mud, dragging everything from her past with her. Less comfortable with the request than she was expecting, Em saw Bill's unsavory favor in greater context, including an aftermath. Where will this lead? Even if Sanger could understand, looking back from tomorrow, will he? "Do I have to have sex with him? Is just getting naked enough?"

"Naked's enough, sex is better. Will you do it?"

"Where?" Em asked.

"Here. I've arranged for a room upstairs."

"They have rooms upstairs?"

Bill squirmed in his seat. "Not really. But I know someone and have arranged it. It's a storage room but it's got a bed. They throw a drunk in there from time to time."

Em could barely believe Bill's gall. "And the sheets were last changed when, during the Nixon administration?" She took a long swallow of beer. "No," she said. "If I can't take him to his place, like he's married or something, I want the cash to get a hotel room."

Bill opened his wallet and placed two one-hundred-dollar bills on the table. He lifted the spy-cam pen from his front pocket and put it on top of the money. "You drive a hard bargain. There he is up at the bar. Thanks. So go do your thing."

Em slipped the money and spy-cam into her clutch purse. She paused and explored the wrinkles at the edge of Bill's eyes. "Do you want," she asked, "for me to make an appointment for us? Tomorrow, maybe."

Bill returned Em's stare with suspicion. "Why would you ask that? I already have an appointment tomorrow with him. I want you to come along. But why would you ask that? Did he say something to you?"

"No. It's just something that made sense. Shoot some snaps. Unroll them on his desk like a treasure map. That's all."

Bill rose. "I've got to be other places. I'll pick up the camera pen later."

Once Bill was out the door, Em walked toward the bar. She squeezed between Hugh and the empty stool beside him. Leaning back with her elbows resting on the counter, she knew her center buttons would be stretched and her breasts outlined by the dress's thin material. She wouldn't normally expose herself this way but felt safe, knowing Hugh as she already did.

"Hi. I'm Em," she said and touched Hugh's forearm. "Do you come here often? I don't. I mean come here often. It's nice though. And you?"

Crap, he looks morose, she thought. When Hugh didn't say anything, Em felt compelled to ask, "What's your name?" *Like I don't already know. But he doesn't know mine.* "I'm Em, short for Emerald. But nobody calls me that. Em's good enough. What's yours? You haven't said yet."

Don't talk so much, she told herself. *Let him get a word in.*

Em hiked her hips to the high round stool and pressed

both palms to the seat between her legs. She leaned forward, knowing her arms accentuated all the cleavage she could muster. "You look a little down, sad. You ought to loosen your tie, let someone muss your hair. I could do that."

When Em extended her arm toward the top of his head, Hugh pulled back out of reach. "Don't," he said. "Not right now. You should go away. I'm not in a very good mood."

"Can I help? I might have something that will help." She smiled, a flirtatious smile inviting him to lean down and kiss her. She suddenly felt foolish, like hawking get-well cards at a funeral. Embarrassed at realizing she was playing this game as she'd played it before, not as it was now, she wanted to explain herself, confess that she met him tonight last week already. They had laughed, touched, and felt the warmth of shared intentions.

"You seem," Hugh said, "like a nice person. But I don't want to pay you. You'll be better off negotiating a deal with someone else. I'm not in the mood."

"You've got it all wrong," Em said, although other than giving and getting for free, she thought he was pretty close to understanding the arrangement.

"I don't think," he said. "I wish, but no…listen, this is nothing against you. I had to put my cat down today. She's been sick for a while. I've had her for years."

Em couldn't stop a spurt of laughter from escaping her lips. She wanted to say, 'You never told me that before,' but knew there'd been no shared before and this was really his first impression of her, where she was now laughing at the affection he had for his cat. "I'm so sorry," she said. "For you and your cat, I'm sorry. But also for laughing. It came out of you so suddenly and I was caught by surprise. I didn't mean it."

"Thank you," Hugh said. "But I'm not good company tonight. I don't feel up to it. This is nothing against you. What you do is fine with me. It's me, I just can't—"

~ ~ ~

After Em went off with Bill, Rooster sat alone in the living room. She heard Sanger and Alan in the kitchen but didn't want to look at them. Her stomach was queasy and her fingertips tingled. Rubbing her hands together, she looked over her shoulder at the atomizer.

Three easy steps to be within reach. She wanted to use it again and willed herself to pick it up. Her desire to help Alan sidestep his destiny was as physical as the anxiety over a test for which she hadn't studied. When Sanger had returned with the device it was in its original cardboard container again. *When was that, yesterday, earlier today…no, yesterday. Yes.* She ripped away the homemade box and held the scrotum-like pouch in one hand.

She paused and imagined a future where the inevitability of Alan's murderous accomplishment no longer existed. All she wanted was someone else killing William Meyer, someone intimate with the story and knowledgeable of the stream of causes already in play. She saw herself raising the handgun, posing with a ninety-degree twist of her wrist, and pulling the trigger twice. She had no gun, had never held a gun, and wasn't sure she could stomach the act even though her heart was willing to try.

After she squeezed the mister's bulb, a white cloud rolled in the air before her. In it she saw a cemetery at night. Fog clung low across the ground and two tall pillars stood side by side, so close no light shone between them, their metallic sheen looking like…

*

…the doors inside an elevator. There were no columns of floor numbers, no buttons beside them. Rooster felt captured, kidnapped, and for a moment didn't know where she was. In the dark display above the elevator doors, the number 35 emerged from the black background. The elevator stopped and the doors opened.

Rooster stepped out, walked down the hall, and soon found 3580, knowing it was the office of William Meyer, Attorney at Law. Without knocking she entered. Through the reception area she saw William Meyer behind his desk.

Thumbing through papers, he looked up and said, "What can I do for you, little lady?"

"Soon," Rooster said, "someone is going to step in here and shoot you. You will die on June 30th. It will happen around sunset."

William Meyer laughed. "Well, that's nice of you to tell me, but how do you know this? Why should I believe you?"

"I'm a time-traveler from the past."

"Don't you mean the future?"

"No, from the past. I've already seen what's going to happen. I've been this way before."

"You don't say?" William Meyer shook his head and added, "I don't know how you people even get in the building."

You people, she thought, *you mean kids with crooked bangs? Or we who'll inherit the mess you've left of the world? Or one girl who knows you're scamming Bill?* Rooster understood why Alan didn't like this man. She'd only been with him once before and he was dead then, a lot less annoying. "Take me seriously. You're going to be killed on June thirtieth, near sunset."

"Well, thanks for the tip. You should go now."

"I don't want it to happen. He's my friend and killing you will get him into a lot of trouble."

William Meyer stood. "It sounds like you should be talking

to him instead of me."

He was taller and larger than Rooster remembered. She had pulled him off his desk, plunked him into his chair, and wasn't sure she could have done it, no matter how thick and luxurious his hair. *Kill him now*, she thought. *Jump on his desk, dive forward, surround his neck with both hands, and hang on like a bronco-busting cowboy.* She shook her head. *Impossible.*

"I have talked with him," Rooster said. "Now I'm talking to you."

"Listen little girl. This is an interesting story but I don't believe you. Go on, go away. I've got work to do."

Rooster backed toward the door. "You should believe me."

William Meyer came around his desk and said, "Get out of here. And if you try this on someone else, say you're from the future. From the past doesn't make any sense."

She kept an eye on him as she backed across the reception area. Reaching behind for the door handle, she twisted, pushed, and stepped backwards into the...

*

...living room, where her face was still in the white cloud emitted by the mister. She turned in a circle and then put the atomizer down. Hearing Sanger and Alan talking in the kitchen, she walked to sit with them. As she sat she said, "If we traveled from the future, back in time, wouldn't we know everything that happened in the past? I mean, this traveling into the future stuff is already hit or miss, maybe it will happen, maybe it won't."

Alan turned with concern. "What are you talking about?"

"I sniffed the mister. I was at the attorney's office and I warned him. I told him when he'll die."

"He won't remember," Sanger said.

"You couldn't have gone far," Alan said. "He'll be dead soon."

"I don't know how far. But he wasn't dead yet. I want him to know he'll die."

"Don't go down there," Alan said. "Even if your future's predicting it, don't do it."

"That's what I mean." Rooster sat up straight. "If I had traveled from the future, to the past, I'd have gone to a real time and place. History. In each time and place, only one thing happened. I'd have told him and he'd've known, then remembered, been warned."

Alan tapped a finger on the table. "I don't think it works like that. If you and the attorney sniffed the atomizer at the same time and went to the exact same time and place, you still might have experienced different things. In his future you might have walked in and said, 'Files are ready down the hall.' Get it?"

Sanger indicated a circle with both hands on the table. "We're traveling to a future that doesn't yet exist. We're interacting with people who aren't really there. How can we expect them to have any knowledge? We conjure them up. It would be crazy if bystanders in our future jaunts experienced what we're seeing them experience. They'd be struck with impressions connected to nothing, feelings out of nowhere. Déjà vu galore. That's what others would experience if they were really part of what we're going through."

"Don't feelings we can't explain happen all the time?" Rooster asked. "Maybe vague impressions are left after we're tagged in someone else's future."

"Maybe," Sanger said. "But I think there's nothing beyond now. The future isn't out there the way the past is. The future isn't there until we step into it."

"I killed him again and again," Alan said. "And I thought

about killing him more than that." He looked at Rooster. "When you saw him, did he remember or suspect that he's in any danger?"

"No," Rooster said.

Alan nodded. "The attorney won't have any recollection of you or what you told him. For him it never happened, and I don't mean never happened *yet*. You're destined to live out what you experienced, but you can't expect that he'll have a memory of it. Maybe some tiny inkling of precognition, clairvoyance, or dread. But…"

Rooster shook her head. "I think I'm starting to get it, how it happens. My consciousness was there in a future-now, not in the now-now. His consciousness was where it should have been, in the now he shares with everyone else. I was in a different now, not the now I share with you guys. So my consciousness wasn't in the same now as his even though it looked like it. So he doesn't even know we talked. Yeah, I'm starting to get it."

"Are you?" Alan asked.

"No, not really," Rooster said. "My consciousness was in a room before June 30th and it sure looked like William Meyer's consciousness was there, too. Why won't he know that? Why won't it be something that comes to him out of the blue? Something he can't explain? Something I planted in his head and will grow. A feeling of foreboding and doom."

"You didn't plant anything in his head," Sanger insisted. "He wasn't really there. We can't start thinking we're messing with people's futures just because we're experiencing ours. That would be crazy."

CHAPTER TWENTY-ONE

Evening of June 29, Minneapolis

In the bar, sitting on the stool next to Hugh, Em disliked saying it. She preferred her words matched her feelings. "I think you're getting the wrong first impression of me."

Hugh placed his hand in a wide grip on her thigh. "Am I?" he asked, thinking she wouldn't protest.

Em wasn't offended and didn't protest. She knew him and was comfortable with his touch. "We've gotten off to a bad start." She lifted his hand from her leg and wanted to curl her fingers into his palm. Instead she placed his hand on the bar and said, "Tell me about your day. What kind of work do you do?"

"I've told you I'm not in the mood."

Yet Em heard a slight break in his voice, a small avenue of access. "Then let me tell you about you. I'm good at it. I'll make you laugh."

"You're very persistent. You don't even know me."

I feel like I do. I know I already do. Why don't you know it, too? "I'm touched by the relationship you had with your cat. You're sensitive and caring."

"That's it? You're no oracle."

"Okay. I'm just getting warmed up." Em paused. "Okay. You're coming off tough right now. But it's only to protect yourself. You're clumsy at it because you don't do it much. Generally you're very open and you welcome the ideas of others."

Hugh stared. Em wondered if she was getting it all wrong. "Let me see your palm." She cradled the back of his hand in hers and stroked his open fingers. "You like your work. Not everybody does. You like the meaning it provides. You like being told what to do."

"I wouldn't go that far."

"Not in a weak way. You like when someone knows something you don't and is willing to share. You like hearing about new ideas."

Hugh leaned toward her a little and Em noticed. She thought she ought to take some chances now, so said, "You like your mom. You respect your dad. You listen to your mom. I can see you as a little kid running around and her telling you to slow down. You liked it. You like being told what to do." Em raised her eyes as if seeking a response.

"I like my mom. I like my dad, too. He was always tinkering around the house, fixing things."

"But it was your mom who touched your heart and gave you the confidence to not show off. She was the one who made it possible for you to help others and let them have all the credit."

Hugh smiled. "I don't know how you know these things. I'm either showing a lot more than I think or you're kind of spooky."

This was the moment Em had been working for. Hugh had turned the ticklish corner from indifference to interest. But thoughts of Sanger suddenly dropped like a translucent curtain. He, too, liked his mom and dad. He, too, quietly exerted his influence, day in and day out. He was as generous today as he had been when he first offered her a place to stay. She had appreciated his hospitality and thanked him once, maybe twice. Neither of them really believed their sex was given or received as payment for rent. Em knew it was Sanger's way to get her to acknowledge that their relationship was more than exchange, and her way to protect herself from that very same relationship. But still he was as generous as he had first been, and she'd been taking it for granted.

"You're just staring at my hand," Hugh said. "And that's a little spooky."

Em looked up. "It's not all picture-perfect, though. You think your mom is afraid of what lies too far from the straight and narrow. She avoids the extremes. You've picked up a few of those tendencies. You prefer a plan. Yet you're awkwardly attracted to fanciful dreamers. Without your mother's example, you'd be more willing to… Still, like her, you demand a future determined by the choices you make."

"You make me sound conventional."

"When I first saw you," referring to her future sojourns rather than her current situation, "you were enticing and exciting. You're handsome and I grew warm inside watching you. But now, this close, I'm getting a more solid sense of who you are. I like it. You're more domestic than exotic. But that's good. Dependable."

Hugh reached for his drink but didn't pick it up. "When you said you'd tell me about myself, I thought you'd be a lot more complimentary. Now I'm just confused." He took a sip from his glass. "So enough about me. What about you?"

"My story's easy. I'm a lot more foreign than domestic. Different than you, I don't especially like my parents. And they don't like me. It's easier this way because I'm not tempted to be as they are. I don't have to fight that urge."

"You sound like you didn't ever love your parents."

"I don't think I ever did. I don't remember it."

"Have you ever been around babies, toddlers, preschool kids?"

"No."

"Well, they love their parents. And it has nothing to do with the care they get. It's some innate ability in the child."

Em's muscles tightened as she found his words threatening. "And?" she demanded.

"Nothing. No and. It's just…it's just the same for all of us. We emerge into adulthood loving the way we were loved."

"No, no, no. That's crazy. Why would anyone do that?"

"Can't help it."

"No. Look at me. I'm out here full face to the world, my mother isolated herself. I talk a lot, she hardly at all. My mother praised no one. I can love just as good as the next guy. No doubt about it, when I love someone, they know it."

But her own words stopped her. *If Sanger doesn't know by now how I feel, he never will. His inability, not mine.* She looked at the floor and questioned the truth of her thought.

"And do you love someone?" Hugh asked. "Have you ever been in love?"

Wanting to get the secrecy she'd been holding off her chest, Em said, "I'm living in a man's apartment. Living with him in a, well, relationship."

"Is it serious?"

"Who knows what's serious?" she said. But again stopped herself. She wanted to explain with accuracy but worried Hugh would only hear it through his own expectations of what relationships were supposed to be. "I like Sanger," she continued. "He took me in when I needed it most. He didn't have to. He's generous and I'd like to be like him in that way. We're boyfriend and girlfriend. And although he likes to say it in that way, I'm less comfortable. We're sleeping together and he wonders how it happened so quickly. I like him but want him to better see relationships from my point of view. I've never been…oh, I'm talking too much."

"No," Hugh said. "I like it. So you don't feel like a one-man woman?"

"It's not that. I think I could be with one person, or two, for a long time. But to vow to honor and obey, I don't know about that. There are implications to promises that ought to be aired. And when people stray from those vows, it's not something to be kept secret. I just want to…we only live once."

"You are more exotic than domestic. I hope you find someone compatible."

"I'm not a terrible person," Em added. "I'm sorry. I've talked too much. It just feels like I've known you for a long time."

"Yes," Hugh said. "I feel that, too. Like we've met before and have a…trust or something."

Em leaned close and said, "Might I be the reincarnation of your cat? Or is it too soon to say something like that?"

Hugh laughed. "No. You're good." He touched her thigh, lightly this time, and added, "I've needed some help getting over her." He laughed again. "You could never replace her, I want you to know that. But there *are* some similarities."

CHAPTER TWENTY-TWO

While Em is out, June 29, Minneapolis

At nine o'clock that evening, Sanger paced, taking deep breaths, and pulling his fingers. Alan watched from the kitchen table and Rooster was nearly asleep on the couch. When the phone rang, Sanger expected it was Em reporting back to reassure him. Sanger dove for the phone, saying, "Em?"

But it was Niko, and Sanger was too disappointed to deal with it. He handed the phone to Rooster, who put it on speaker.

"I want to apologize," Niko said. "I haven't been as clear with you as I had hoped."

"Bill arrived in Minneapolis," Rooster said. "We're steamrolling into the future we've already seen. If you've got something to help us, now's the time."

"I do. But it's not easy."

"You've got something," Sanger implored, "to help us control the future?"

"Not exactly. But let's try." Niko paused, breathed, and then continued. "Some say it's we who create the future as we enter it. Remember the light through the slits experiment? The basic building blocks of our universe are both wave-like *and* particle-like. Solving this conundrum has been the work of imaginative speculators. According to the Copenhagen interpretation, our observation collapses the wave and leaves behind a solid world. Yet, the Many-worlds interpretation says that the wave-particle is the very essence of the universe and there is no collapsing of the wave to make a particle. They say every observation, choice, decision causes the universe to branch off into another universe. Both accepting the job offer and not accepting the job offer are real, yet we only see the decision we've made while the choices not made drop into a dimension we don't have access to."

Sanger, listening although pretending not to, looked up and said, "That's not interesting. And it's only helpful if you're saying our decisions determine the world and everything in it."

"I'm definitely not saying that," Niko spat back. "What kind of universe would let small-minded people dictate the shape and form of everything? How could you get more than a few ideologues to agree on anything?

"Listen. There are buildings and sidewalks and coins in our pockets that are pushed into the future without any conscious effort. Might it be that everything in existence now will also exist in the nearest future available? How can change take place in a universe constructed this way? To think we're as responsible for taking our car keys into the future as we are for our secrets is a heady task. According to the Many-worlds interpretation, my secret will exist down one branch of the future and not on a different branch. Under the Copenhagen interpretation, my secret has the potential to both exist *and* not exist according to probability laws determining likely outcomes."

"Now you're losing even me," Alan said. "If there's a point, get to it."

"Okay," Niko said. "The Copenhagen interpretation's collapsing of the wave leads straight to determinism—a future we're destined to enter holding events we're destined to endure, even if those events are random within a realm of probability. On the other hand, the Many-worlds interpretation envisions an infinite number of futures, accounting for every possible outcome of all the decisions we make, all the decisions others make, and all the decisions that don't get made at all, including a future where my secret exists, one where it doesn't, and many where it's already known. That's what decisions determine. But you need to think more about what determines decisions. In centuries past, choices were influenced by a chance crossing of a black cat, or the rumblings of an earthquake carefully mistaken as the gods murmuring their approval of war."

"I can't listen to this any longer," Sanger said. As he reached for the disconnect button, Niko quickly added, "Just this: the Copenhagen interpretation describes a sensible universe with nonsensical parts. While the Many-worlds interpretation describes a nonsensical universe with sensible parts."

Then Sanger touched the disconnect button.

~ ~ ~

Two hours after nightfall, eleven pm, after the buses ran less frequently and the traffic had thinned, Alan sat with Sanger at the kitchen table. Rooster had already fallen asleep sitting on the couch. Em was out on her date. Sanger didn't speak and tinkered with anything on the kitchen table.

As patient as could be, Alan watched Sanger's head snap up, startled and expectant, with each noise in the hall. Alan was resigned to Em not returning that night and wanted to force a sleeping pill down Sanger's throat to put him out of his misery.

Alan stared at Sanger and thought, *a fool fools no one but himself.* Alan considered Sanger's beliefs ruinous. He wagged a hand in midair between them and said, "Compromise, cooperation, even sacrifice. Sanger, these are all free will choices."

"What are you getting at?"

"You know, she's not like us."

"Who?" Sanger said.

"Who. That's funny. Em, of course. She's a big tough cookie. Gets what she wants whether outright or on the sly. She told me her former drug use was resignation to oblivion. Sounds risky. But she's no risk-taker. When you've got nothing else, oblivion's comforting. Surrender to the hands of demons and gods."

"What are you getting at?" Sanger said.

"Em's afraid."

"Ha! She sure doesn't act it."

"Oh, Sanger, you're not watching close enough. She's especially afraid of you. That you won't like her."

"Why would she think that?"

"For the same reason she's afraid some stranger at the bus stop won't like her. Or a kid in the class she audits. No reason. Other than a general background buzz that she's unlikable."

"No," Sanger said. "That can't be. She doesn't think that

of herself. She likes being with people."

"Does she? Do you really think so? I imagine her wandering around the college campus alone. She's not like you and me. We grew up in families with people who loved us. She thinks she's got no one, no one to trust. She thinks she's got this unlikable center."

"She's got me."

Alan took a deep breath. "That's the thing. As much as she wants to hide her unsavory center, she also wants to be seen. And you're refusing to see her. You've seen the way she pushes you. She wants you to take her seriously. When she says she wants to meet with this banker, you think her motivation is to hurt you. But no. That's the last thing she wants. But you won't see it. You keep pulling it back to how painful it is for you. You're going to push her to secrets to save your feelings."

Sanger got up and stood at the sink. "Are you suggesting I give her permission to have sex with her banker guy? I don't think I can do that."

"Ha! If Em was here she'd tell you permission isn't yours to give. She'd fight you tooth and nail because she thinks you're worth it. She doesn't want your permission. She wants the common respect you'd give anyone to make their own choices and their own mistakes."

Sanger turned his back to the sink and leaned against it. "Why is it so hard? I'm only asking this one thing. It's like she's throwing it in my face, doesn't think enough of me to—"

"Shut…up!" Alan said. "You've got to think differently about this. Think of it as checkers. You don't want her playing checkers with anyone but you. Why is that? What do you lose if she plays with someone else?"

"She'll fall in love."

"Em's never ever said she's only able to love one person. That's yours. What else?"

"She won't like me anymore."

"You can't force her to like you. Even if you think all women are the same, Em's not one to come around after you knock her over the head and drag her to your cave. She won't be encouraged to like you more because you're holding her as tight as you can."

"I don't know what to do."

"Take seriously what she's said about herself. What she wants. She's told you. Help her be the person she wants to be. It's really as simple as that."

"I don't even know where to start."

"Sanger, your mom loves you. Even my mom loves you. And you know it, don't you."

"Yes, sure."

"Your mom would sacrifice everything for you. It's time you took up her example and love Em in that sort of way."

"Em doesn't want parental love. She's got her own folks to—"

"No, Em's parents didn't love her. She called them indifferent. Nothing to appreciate and nothing to fight against. She's very mistrustful of affection. It's like her parents sent her onto the field of love with a brand new catcher's mitt but no practice at receiving the pitch or tossing it back. She's not a bad person, just ill-equipped."

"Yeah, yeah, I can see that. I see her for who she is," Sanger insisted.

"No, you don't. You've pleaded with her not to have sex with him. And look at you tonight; staying up late and hoping beyond hope she'll come to her senses and see it your way."

"It's just this one thing." Sanger said. "It's hard to get past."

"Well, little cousin, it's awfully late and she's not home yet. So I think you better try and let—"

A knock on the door interrupted Alan. Sanger leapt up saying, "It's her."

As he opened the door, Bill pushed his way through.

Alan said, "How did you get up the stairs?"

"The outside door was propped open. Where's Em? Is she back?"

~ ~ ~

Concurrently, Minneapolis

As they left the bar, on their way to Hugh's, Em insisted they walk arm in arm. She found him more restrained than she remembered and, adjusting her expectations, began to like it, a shy man. As they strolled, she explored all of his pockets, diving into each as if it was the deep end of a pool, touching bottom and returning.

As Hugh turned and twisted, suppressed laughter, and tried to avoid or encourage her grasp, he said, "You better be careful or you might find an embarrassing surprise. I mean, I like this and it's starting to show. Are you always this way?"

Em was pleased. Finally, a confirmation of what she already knew. *He likes me and soon we'll be...I'll be tricking him into becoming the recipient of blackmail.* Em stopped to take stock. She loosened her arms from his torso. *It was easy*, she thought, *to do what we did in my future experiences. No harm done, only the moment cared about. But they weren't real moments and I knew it. This is real. There's something very special about now, something both emancipating and consequential.*

When they arrived at Hugh's small apartment in a downtown high-rise, Em asked, "Did you bury your cat yet?"

"Cremation. They put the ashes in a cardboard urn about the size of a tea cup. I'll get something more permanent soon. Something nicer."

Em never had a pet and was touched by his concern. "I'm glad you'll do that. Keep her as a memory. Will you get another?"

"Not yet. Not so soon. There's more to a cat than alive and dead. We knew each other."

Hugh poured another glass of wine and in his slow movements Em saw his heartache but didn't really understand it. Mourning a cat was pretentious. Yet she understood mourning a relationship. They sat at his kitchen table, very proper, even though Em had eyed the couch. He could get another cat, or two. Dote on them any way he wanted. As she watched him across the table, she imagined standing behind him with her hands full on his neck, rubbing and soothing, and would do it, if this wasn't, in a way, their first date. Still, she wanted to touch him, reach across and stroke his troubled mind, run her shoeless foot up and down his calves, or... *oh just get up and rub his shoulders, I can do it, pull his ears, make him laugh.*

So she did. She felt Hugh's tight muscles as he dropped and twisted his head. She rubbed the part of his neck above his shirt's collar. As she reached around to fully remove his tie and release a couple more buttons, she whispered, "It's okay. I won't take advantage." Yet she thought she already was, knowing him the way she did, hiding it from him.

"This feels really nice, Em. I haven't...it's been a long time since someone has...since I've been this comfortable."

After a few minutes Em returned to her chair and said, "Maybe a little more later. More of, I mean, not more than." She knew they would begin a sexual relationship, had seen it in her future journeys, and wanted him to know it, too. But too much too soon would have her looking like a tramp. She wanted him to show some initiative, at least follow her obvious leads.

While sitting at the table, they didn't talk much. Em was

comfortable, relaxed in the quiet between them. Yet she worried Hugh would feel the pressure of constant talk and inadequate if he had nothing to say. She asked him about his work and he responded lackadaisically, far from the enthusiasm she remembered from her previous future jaunts. Em worried that she'd already gone too far, been too forward, expected him to be as affectionate as she already knew he could be. It was in him, that affection. All she had to do was tease it out. She reached for her wine and brought the glass to her lips. Looking up, she saw Hugh's glass simultaneously at his lips. They both smiled, caught in an illusion that brought them closer.

Em got up and meandered through his apartment, looking at photos on shelves. Working her way to the couch, she sat with her back in one corner of it. Hugh joined her and sat in the middle, as if side-saddle on a horse. Em's skirt rode high on her thighs and she wondered when he'll notice.

Growing impatient, she pushed herself to remember that she'd already been with him and he simply didn't yet know how much she will welcome his touch. *What's going on*, she wondered. *Can I tell him? What if I say—*

"I was attracted to you," Em blurted. "The minute I saw you. Do you believe in stuff like that?"

"Love at first sight?"

"Maybe. But within minutes of talking to you I felt as though I'd met you before and we already had a past."

"Something in a previous life?"

"Maybe." Em laughed. "Or our genes are lined up correctly. You smell like the evolutionary mate I'm drawn to."

Hugh furrowed his brow. "Do you believe in fate, that evolution is destiny, has destined us to be animalistic together?"

"Maybe." She lifted her head and pointed her chin at him. "Would that be so bad? I was immediately attracted to you. It made no sense, no civilized sense. I still feel it, a physical awakening of my chakras."

"Aren't chakras more of a spiritual thing?"

"I suppose. Would you like me more if I was a spiritual thing?" Em put a hand on his arm. "When I look at you, why do the hairs on the back of my neck stand on end, my skin tighten, I blush?"

Hugh didn't answer.

Em slid her fingers along his forearm and asked, "Do you ever wonder if the future already exists? That it's out there waiting and there's very little we can do to change it?"

"Back to destiny," Hugh said. "Fate. I prefer living as though that's not true. I mean, if I believed in destiny, I'd be trying to figure out what mine was. Or I'd be duped by con men and scammers who said they knew. No. That's no way to live."

"You prefer to risk the unknown? No risk, no gain. Is that it?" Em leaned forward. "The thing is, I still feel it. Something physical."

Hugh put a hand on hers and said, "I was rude earlier. Yes, my cat died but I shouldn't have been rude. I thought about you as we walked. I've never known anyone cheeky enough to reach into my pockets. You came on so suddenly. Things like that don't happen. Not to me. So to trust you seems naïve and I'd surely regret having met you, or feel this way."

Em leaned forward and kissed him. "You won't regret it, I promise." She realized she'd made up her mind without a conscious decision in sight, eliminating alternatives as if whacking weeds with a machete.

I'll disappoint Bill and rile up Sanger, but what I do next with Hugh will have nothing to do with blackmail or Alan's ability to plunk down cash on the attorney's desk.

Hugh stood and pulled one of Em's hands as he said, "This way."

Em rose and floated to the side of his body, so close only

clothing came between them. "If I said I'm getting feelings of déjà vu, what would you think?"

"I'd think you were experiencing this as though it's already happened. I'm at a loss because it feels like the first time to me." He stopped with Em beside the bed and kissed her. "Who of us is getting the better deal: you who's already seen, or first-time me?"

Em stepped back and said, "Good question. But give me a second." She returned to the living room, retrieved her clutch purse, and placed it on the table beside the bed. Rooting through the purse with one hand, she pulled out the spy-camera-in-a-pen and placed it on the table beside Hugh's phone. When she sat on the bed, she saw he'd removed his shirt. *No problem*, she thought, *I've got so little on, I'll soon catch up.*

"Come over here," Em said. "Sit with me."

With Hugh beside her, she reached for his phone and held it at arm's length. "A selfie. Just one. A remembrance." *Not for Bill, not a trick.* "Just for you and me."

"I don't have a shirt on."

"To make it fair, do you want me to drop my top?"

"No, what good is a picture you can't show anyone?"

Em took the photo and placed his phone back on the nightstand. She picked up the spy-camera and looked at it with the same dismay as if it was a disappointing pregnancy test. Then she turned the lens facing away and made sure it was off.

CHAPTER TWENTY-THREE

June 30, the day of William Meyer's murder
Minneapolis

On a chair in the living room, Sanger stared at the ceiling. Bill slept on another chair. At six o'clock in the morning Sanger heard a jiggling of the door handle, saw it turn, and the door swing open. Em stepped in on tiptoes.

Sanger made a small wave of his hand and Em said, "God, you frightened me. What are you doing up? Why is Bill here?"

"Shh. Rooster's asleep on the couch. We're waiting for you." Sanger paused. "Well?"

Em stopped in the middle of the room. She crossed her arms over the clutch purse while a loose strap drifted off one shoulder. "Bill," she said, "needs to leave."

"Well?" Sanger asked again.

"What? What." Bill stirred and then recognized Em in the room. He sat up straight, shook his head so his jowls wobbled, and added, "Give me the memory stick from the spy-cam. I need to look at it."

Em crossed her arms more tightly. "Do you have to? Here?"

"I don't have access to any other computer. I'll take the laptop in the closet."

Em tossed the spy-cam-pen to Bill and then sat in the chair he had vacated.

Sanger edged in close on the chair's arm. "Well," he said, "did you? Oh, don't answer. You probably weren't playing cards all night."

"Sanger, don't do this. In the same way that I don't want to say what I did, I don't want to tell you what I didn't do. There's a whole lot I did *and* there's a whole lot I didn't do. But you're only going to think I'm talking about sex. I don't want the rest of our conversation to circle around the pictures in your mind."

"Is that your code word for secrets? Aren't you just keeping secrets?" The nausea Sanger felt through the night returned.

"Let's talk about this some other time. I'm tired and want to get some sleep."

Sanger shook his head and said. "I guess it's obvious. Up all night. Too tired to talk. We haven't stayed up all night in a long time. Was he good?"

"Don't. Don't do this."

Bill stormed in from the computer room and said, "Em,

there's nothing on this stick. What did you do? Why didn't you record your…you know?"

"You mean it wasn't on?" Em said, holding four fingers to her mouth. "I swear I flicked the switch. Maybe I got it wrong and turned it off instead of on. Off by mistake."

"Em! There's nothing recorded."

Sanger didn't know what to think. Maybe she didn't do anything worth recording. Yes. That could have happened and now she's embarrassed to tell Bill the truth. Sanger surrounded himself with this idea and felt the warmth of newly acquired peace.

"Damn it, Em. I was counting on this."

"Leave it, Bill," Sanger said. "You need to go now."

Bill stepped toward her. "Shit, Em. You've got to come see him with me today. I've got an appointment in his office. Just your presence will put him on my side. I need this."

"Bill," Sanger said, standing. "*I* mean it. You've got to go now. She tried and…it's done now."

As Bill moved to the door, he said to Em, "I'll pick you up at 1:30. Get some sleep. Dress nice. You owe me this much." At the door, Bill added to Sanger, "I don't know what's getting in to you. Don't ever let an outsider come between you and family."

After Bill was ushered out, Sanger dropped into a chair, fingers in his hair. He looked at Em and said, "I kicked him out. I can't believe I did that. He's…family. And now I've kicked him out."

Em stood, put a hand on his shoulder, and said, "I turned the camera off before…before we did anything."

"I thought the camera was the whole point. You did it with him to get the pictures. Without the pictures, you just…did it with him."

"Would you rather we had some nice glossy eight by

tens?" In a moment she added, "I'm sorry. I didn't mean it like it sounded." She knelt on the floor beside him. "I told him about you. Told him we have a relationship. A solid one. Told him I'm not strong on monogamy but it will be harder for you. Told him if he couldn't accept that, then we wouldn't see each other again. No lies, Sanger. No secrets."

"What did he say?"

"I'm tired. Let's talk about this later. Come lie down with me."

"What did he say?"

"He's not really invested in me. For him it was a first date. He'll accept anything. I could be a single mom. Or on parole from prison. He feels we're just getting to know each other and is up for anything."

"And you? No secrets."

"I feel I've known him for a few weeks. Not much, but more than he's known me. That's why I wanted to tell him about you. I felt it was time. About time."

~ ~ ~

Later that day Alan read a book on the couch and Rooster had her few possessions spread out on the coffee table. Em slept soundly and even Sanger, anxious as he had been all night, slept.

Without looking at him, Rooster asked Alan, "Do you pray?"

Looking up from his book, Alan said, "I hope sometimes."

"Well, today's the big day. I hope you won't go to William Meyer's office. You're not going, right?"

"It's not as simple as that. Destiny feels more real to me than it does to you or Em or Sanger. More personal."

"Don't go. You don't have to. Fate is just some big

thunderstorm. All you have to do is come in out of the rain."

Alan dog-eared a page of his book and closed it. "Weather might be a random occurrence, random here and there. But if it's destined to rain on my parade, then there's something about my parade in the equation, something about me. My destiny is in store for me, I've got to live it out."

"Just don't go. Screw your destiny. Make a decision, take the bull by the horns."

"I've done that," Alan said. "I made decisions to become a teacher, to get married, to love my wife. Until I didn't any longer. That was a decision, too. I gave up on her. And although I hate to admit it, that was also a conscious decision. Not made in a day, but over a longer time, time I could have changed my mind."

"So what? Leave her alone. She's dead and you're alive and willing to follow some plan you didn't get a vote on to kill some guy you don't know and maybe spend the rest of your life in jail. How could that be anyone's destiny? Why would you even think so?"

"If I was destined for great things, you'd feel differently. And who knows, maybe killing William Meyer prevents an escalation of war somewhere that prevents the start of a greater war and saves the lives of millions."

Rooster pushed her fanny pack across the coffee table. "That's just wishful thinking."

"I'm dangling by my nails from a ledge of hope."

"You don't know that. Don't go."

When the phone rang, Alan was relieved for the break and Rooster picked it up as though it was the cause of her frustration. "Hello?"

"Ah, Rooster. This is Niko.

Rooster set the phone to speaker, placed it on the table, and said, "Just me and Alan here. Sanger and Em are sleeping.

But hey, since you're on the phone, does God set destiny? Does He know what's coming? Can God travel into the future?"

"Hmm. God doesn't talk to me but most people fall between two opinions. Some say God stands outside of time."

"Outside of time?" Rooster asked. "What's that?"

"Think of God viewing the entire universe with a mere glance. That's only possible by standing outside the confines of our universe. In that same way God comprehends all of time in an encompassing moment. God sees and knows the entirety of time in a single blink, past and future."

"So," Rooster said, "God knows what will happen with Alan tonight?"

"That's not so easy to say. When we think of God this way, He doesn't experience the universe in temporal succession. God doesn't experience the 13th century prior to the 19th century. God's understanding of time is so different than ours that for Him there is no special relevance to now. Or future or past. God has known all since the birth of the universe. God answered the prayers of Joan of Arc, who died in 1431, *and* the prayers of General Custer, who died in 1876, at the same time. To this God, Joan of Arc *and* George Custer were contemporaries. As a timeless being, God experiences all of time in one ever-present moment."

"That hardly makes sense," Rooster said.

Niko laughed. "A lot about God is like that."

Alan tapped the table. "You said there were two views. What's the other?"

"Well, the one just described causes some problems for free thinkers. Let's say sometime in my life, I'm destined to—"

"Kill a bad man," Rooster said.

"Okay, kill a bad man. As an act of free will I know I could also not kill this man. If God already knows I will kill the man, yet I want to exert free will by not killing him, I must somehow change God's mind, change something in God's mind that God has known since the beginning of time. Otherwise I have only the illusion of free will, where I do what God wills, merely believing it's my free choice."

"Okay," Alan said. "But that's not a different view. That's just a problem with the first view."

"Right," Niko said. "The other view is that God is temporal, lives within time. God experiences some events prior to other events, this before that. God exists, as we do, in each present moment, the everlasting now, and experiences now similarly to us. God grants some requests and lets others pass unheeded, just as we do. God has a special accord with now and performs his Holy acts in the present."

"So God," Rooster asked, "imagines a future to make it real and remembers a past that's already gone?"

"Hmm, I suppose," Niko said. "But God's busier than us. When it comes to time, God answered Joan of Arc's prayers before He answered General Custer's prayers because Joan of Arc's pleas passed through now and became real before General Custer's requests became real. There are time constraints as to when God can grant a request."

"I didn't think God could be limited," Rooster said.

"Limiting to God," Niko said, "but a boon for us. Freewill-wise. Instead of having a predetermined view of what will be, God knows all the possibilities of what could be—that I might or might not kill this man—and sets the stage for it to happen that way."

"Which way?" Rooster said.

"The way the universe will proceed. I can freely make choices because God has a special relationship with now. For God, time's a succession of future, present, and past. For God, of all the possibilities, it's the one chosen now that gets locked in place and becomes an indelible part of the past. It's this unique relationship with now that we share with God. So when we say free will, it's God willing to wait until now, a unique moment we share, to see what choices are made."

"See," Rooster said to Alan. "Don't go."

CHAPTER TWENTY-FOUR

June 30, William Meyer's last
Minneapolis

Em was listless all morning with nausea and fatigue. She assumed it was due to using the mister and the accumulation of disordered time. Thinking through it helped, but only a little as thinking pressured her headache to greater heights. Niko's theory of 'and' was perplexing. Everything was a particle *and* a wave? Everything was its potential *and* its actuality? *I love Sanger,* Em thought, *and I maybe love Hugh. I'm loved by Sanger and maybe by Hugh. I'm capable of expressing it and maybe I'm not.*

The Beyond Now Device

Em wanted to abandon herself and let events and emotions run their course. She wanted to love and proclaim it yet knew she was artless in the imagining *and* the actuality of its expression. Overwhelmed by a sudden craving for drugs, indifference collected at the edges of her thoughts. She imagined the courage to tell Sanger *and* Hugh how she felt. Yet unable, longed instead for the peace of sinking beneath turbulent waves while still growing a furrow in her brow.

And then there was Bill. She didn't want to be associated with Bill in Hugh's eyes, yet even without pictures she might persuade Hugh to approve Bill's loan request. Money Alan would then take to William Meyer. Money that would allow Alan to slip under his fate and not pull the trigger twice, not call the police on himself, not be dead within moments of stepping out of the building. She wanted to be seen by Sanger, see Hugh, save Alan, and if she must help Bill to do it, so be it, simply a means to an end.

There was both a chance *and* no chance at all. She preferred to believe there was a chance.

~ ~ ~

Sanger slept off and on through the morning, tossing is his bed. He had never felt so tired. His head hurt and muscles ached throughout his body. He prided himself on his ability to look at the others' situations from a distance, to hold some objectivity, even as he had to conjure mental gymnastics to keep his unrelenting jealousy at bay. *Em was doomed*, Sanger thought, *to get it on with Hugh*. When a series of events followed reason and logic, people tended to take credit for the elegant meaning of it all. When events appeared without rhyme or reason, destiny was to blame. *Shit, shit, shit.*

Sanger thought of time throughout the entire universe and

wondered if Em was a victim of enormity. When the vast collection of galaxies directed their force on a miniscule life, notions of purpose evolved; finding a place in the cosmic pattern felt a lot like destiny. *Em sees meaning,* he thought, *in all this. She's rolling along with a grand pattern, a vast paradigm where she'll show her affection, nestle in his embrace, and have no trouble saying she loves him.*

Disoriented from intermittent sleep, he suspected time was not standing still. It jerked forward and slipped past so whenever he thought of now, he had a vague sense he wasn't getting it right. *Doesn't matter,* he thought, *now's of no consequence. Fate's beyond my control. She's destined to have a place in the pattern she sees. Or she'll get dragged along by events without reason, fate. Doesn't matter. Next is what counts. Next is Alan firing a gun. Next is me as Bill's getaway driver. Next is Em in Hugh's office again.*

~ ~ ~

Rooster already wanted it to be tomorrow. The day after tomorrow was even better, the day after tomorrow would have Alan's destiny tucked neatly behind them.

She knew she existed entirely in every moment, was the accumulation of all she had been, been through, and pretended being. So too with Alan. But she didn't know how to accommodate that fullness, all she had been, was now, and surely would become. *Does Alan have a better handle on this?*

She thought of time like toothpaste. If she could just find the cap and quit squeezing the tube. Not to go backward in time but to keep it from escaping, stop dead. She didn't believe he had to go to that attorney's office, didn't have to take the gun offered, and certainly didn't have to touch the trigger. Yet she'd heard him speak of it as his destiny, a series of events certain to happen.

The Beyond Now Device

Emotions were hard enough, hers *and* his, even though she didn't know his. Time was growing as confusing as a contradictory emotion. Now. *There is only now,* she thought. *Why did another now have to come? Time could stop. Why not?* Rooster believed she could live where she was now. Nothing changing, just as it is. Couch surfing on guard outside Alan's bedroom, eating sandwiches for supper, thick coffee any old time. There was no point going any farther into the future.

Especially not the future she had seen, entering his room late one night, pressing herself on him, refusing to take no for an answer. The thought was enticing *and* repelling, tempting *and* offending.

Stop time, just in time. She imagined living in a world halted hours before Alan pulled the trigger he dared not touch, stroked her trigger on the verge of firing itself, lay with her as she stretched in satisfaction just because he was near *and… Shit,* she thought. *Don't. Stupid.*

Alan rested on his bed, listless with worry. Time will come like the Son of Sorrow, beckoning him to renounce his worldly possessions and buck up his gumption. He'll follow like a devout cultist. Bill will wait at the altar, anoint his shoulder with palm, slip a solid in his pocket, and sprinkle him with a shower of expectation. Was it time yet? How could he know? If he hadn't been to William Meyer's office, he wouldn't remember killing him. But he did remember. Just as though it had already happened. What day was it? *Come on time,* he thought, *let's get this over with. Take me away, do with me as you will.*

CHAPTER TWENTY-FIVE

June 30, Alan's day of destiny, William Meyer's last
Minneapolis

At one in the afternoon, Niko called, opening with, "Oh sure, time in the twenty-first century. Quantum mechanics. The sub-atomic world is just as real as the macro-world where we eat bad food and let emotions wash away good sense."

"What?" one of the four said.

"Just listen," Niko shot back. "The world we know, including time, depends on continuity and determinism. Things remain what they are and aren't magically transformed. And every effect is preceded by a cause. We trust a world where my and my date's clocks run at the same speed and we forgive those who are late for good reason. The double slit experiment showed the dual wave-like and particle-like properties of the atomic cast of characters. The world this describes, according to the Copenhagen interpretation, is a whirlwind of discontinuity where particles appear and disappear and 'probably on-time' is always a more accurate description of my date's arrival than 'definitely on-time'. Only as waves collapse into particles through observation does the world we imagine even begin to emerge."

"But," Alan said, "bricks are bricks and trees are trees. What keeps someone from coming along and collapsing the wave differently? Aren't you describing a world where we see what we want? Why is the world as it is?"

"You're right," Niko said. "Out here in the macroscopic world we have great agreement. But the ordinary world is made up of the atomic world. If an atom was the size of the New Orleans Superdome, then the nucleus would be the size of a golf ball. The rest of the stadium would be empty space with a wave-like cloud of hovering possibilities. It's like solid brick is composed of air and cotton balls. Crazy. That's the nature of solid space. But it's not space you're worried about. It's time, the true nature of time.

"The world seems solid. Time seems to flow. A discontinuous world of probability and unpredictability seems farfetched. True or not, look around, all that might happen hasn't, all we imagine isn't. Something is maintaining a recognizable world."

Sanger spun the phone toward him. "And you're suggesting it's time. Time keeps us from perceiving kaleidoscopic worlds where yours and mine don't match?"

"Not time," Niko said. "You. Is it so outlandish? At the

moment of conception, you are like the wave with excess potential. At the moment of birth, your wave collapses and you're one with now. Time itself turns coincidence into incident. Now turns probability into certainty. Ever-fresh nows constitute time itself. It appears to be an endless cycle. But the now you possess is the only now you'll ever get."

Without waiting for a response, Niko ended the call.

~ ~ ~

At 1:30, just as promised, Bill honked his horn on the street and Em went down to his car. In less than fifteen minutes they were pushing through the revolving door of the National Trust bank. Uncle Bill cupped one of Em's elbows and said, "I'm going to show him the pictures I've got. Keep your cool. We'll play along with him, let him believe what he wants, doesn't matter. Follow my lead. He'll be confused, won't know what's hitting him. Just don't get flustered."

Up the stairs and to his office, Em thought, *pictures? What pictures?*

As they approached, Bill said, "You're a sweetheart for doing this. Just keep your goods in mind and look beautiful. We're in a bank, you know. Let your assets earn some interest."

Even though Em had experienced this meeting before, confusion and disorientation stopped her. She said to Bill, "What makes you think he can process your loan and get it to you before your meeting with William Meyer tonight?"

"What makes you think...how do you know about that?"

For a moment Em was speechless with uncertainty. Then she said, "You told us."

"No. I don't think so."

Through the open door, Hugh recognized Em and came out, saying, "It's nice to see you again, Em. I didn't know you'd be here today. You didn't mention it."

Her fingers tingled as elation rose from sweet rumblings in her center. It had only been eight hours since she slipped from his bed. Her chest grew warm. Pushing aside loose hair, Em made and kept eye contact with him. She pressed her lips together and remembered she was the type of pretty Hugh liked.

Then she broke eye contact and returned to the present where she was sorry to have fooled him, sorry about her association with Bill. "Sorry," Em said. "We talked about so much else. I enjoyed our time together."

"I did, too."

Blush formed around the base of Em's neck as she sat in the chair beside Hugh's desk. She touched her right clavicle with her left hand and slid a piece of folded paper to him. "I didn't give you any way to contact me. I don't have a phone, so here's Sanger's number."

"Thank you. So, what can I do for you and your uncle?"

Em envied Hugh's calm, comfort in his known environment, with just an edge of workplace professionalism.

Bill paced and looked at personal objects on Hugh's shelves. Finally he said, "Show him the photos, Em."

Em lifted the clutch purse from the floor beside her and slid out a large manila envelope. Placing it in front of Hugh, she was anxious to see what they showed. She imagined him expecting a form request, a notarized document, or any of a hundred contracts on which his working life floated. Hugh's smile faded when he understood what the large, glossy photographs revealed.

Bill stood behind Em and said, "She's the picture of innocence, don't you think? Dress her up a little, slap on some lipstick—she's still just a magical image of innocence."

Hugh stuttered, "How? When? Shit. You people…"

Bill touched the back of Em's shoulder and said, "You can go now. Mr. Gardner and I have forty thousand dollars' worth of loans to discuss."

Dazed, astonished at how similar this meeting was to the memory of her future experience, Em stood and walked to the door. She didn't want to face Hugh, so never turned around, never said goodbye. At the top of the stairs she watched workers traipse from one office to another while she paused with her hand on the banister and looked to the foyer below. *That's not me*, she thought. *In those photos, that's not me. What's Bill pulling?*

As she walked along destiny's trail, Em wasn't convinced that each pebble on the path or the trees along the edge were part of destiny's rule. *Follow the road I've already seen. Or bend the future to my will. This is my now and I've got as many options as I can imagine.*

She turned and stormed back to Hugh's office, pushed past Bill, and stopped in front of Hugh. She stared at the pictures spread across his desk, alarmed that the woman in them looked so much like her. "That's not me," she said, pointing to the photos. "I didn't trick you into—"

"I know," Hugh said. "My cat's in most of these pictures. This woman picked me up at the bar weeks ago. I took her home."

"Damn you, Bill," Em said. "If you had pictures, why send me in to get more?"

"Insurance, honey," Bill said. "You can't have too much of a good thing."

Em turned back to Hugh and watched him return the pictures to their sheath. He tapped the envelope against his computer monitor as calm as ever. She knew by the expression on his face that he thought nothing of what the photos showed. Still, random and bizarre thoughts passed through her mind.

That woman in the photos is just a…just someone Bill sent to trick you. It's not that you shouldn't have, but when were you going to tell me about her? Unable to help herself, Em said, "Why didn't you tell me?"

Hugh looked up. "Your uncle sent you last night? Sent you to get more pictures? When were *you* going to tell *me*? Walking in here with these photos…searching through my pockets last night. Were you looking for a password? Something more to incriminate me? What's your plan?" Pointing to the envelope, he added, "She looks like you. What have you got going here?"

"Bill wants a loan approved," Em said, trying to deflect his accusations.

Hugh opened the top drawer of his desk, slid the envelope in and said, "This is no way to apply for a loan. I think you both better go."

~ ~ ~

Em refused Bill's offer of a ride home. Angry, disappointed, she pined for something she couldn't define. Even though she hadn't complied with Bill's plan, Hugh will still see her as having done so. She was sure he'd never want to see her again, sure to never trust her again. Even explaining time travel, destiny, the danger of time-tinkering, or the magnificence of now, wouldn't explain away the appearance of having sex with him because Bill asked her to.

Em wandered around downtown, stopped in a café, and read a newspaper without concentration. She arrived home close to six pm and found Sanger, Alan, and Rooster in the living room. She went straight to Alan, kneeled beside him and apologized. "I'm sorry. Bill didn't get the loan from the bank. I'm afraid he won't have the money to take to William Meyer."

"There," Rooster said. "Don't go."

"What happened?" Sanger asked. "How did it go?"

"Terrible. Hugh kicked us out. Nothing went right."

Sanger leaned forward from the edge of the couch. "In your sojourns, there were always photos. Were there photos?"

"Yes."

"How? Bill didn't get any this morning. Were they of you?"

"No."

Confused, Sanger leaned farther forward. "Of who then? Who did Bill have in the pictures?"

"I don't know. She only looked like me. Does it matter?"

"No money," Rooster said. "Don't go, Alan."

Alan put a hand on Rooster's shoulder and said, "Stop. I've heard you. Don't tell me again."

"Tell him, Em" Rooster said. "Tell him it's stupid to go down to that office. Why? Why go?"

"Let's get something to eat," Em said. "Rooster, you need to go for a walk, get some air. I'll order take-out and you go pick it up."

Within a few minutes, Em had ordered by phone, given Rooster money, and escorted her out the door. Just after that, the phone rang.

Sanger answered and put it on speaker. It was Uncle Bill, saying, "Hi Sanger. Put Alan on the line," unaware they could all hear him.

"Hey Bill." Alan said.

"Listen buddy. I left a carryall in the closet. I need you to bring it to me at the Capella Tower, up to the thirty-fifth floor. I'll meet you by the elevators. I need it by nine, so get there a little earlier."

"Bill, don't hang up," Alan said. "I'm not feeling so well. Let's have Sanger bring it. And meet him on the street."

Sanger showed Alan a quizzical look and waved his hands palm down, indicating 'no'.

Alan muted the phone and whispered, "You're the getaway driver. Meet him outside the building and drive him away before he goes in." Then unmuted it.

"No," Bill said. "I need someone dependable and Sanger's...what? This is too important for Sanger."

"I don't know, Bill," Alan said. "Maybe if—"

"Alan, I'm in a pinch. I need that bag or I'll face some unpleasant business. I know you know what I mean?"

"Yeah, sure, I'll—"

Bill interrupted him by hanging up.

CHAPTER TWENTY-SIX

June 30, two hours before William Meyer's death
Minneapolis

Alan retrieved the carryall from the closet and brought it to the living room. Sanger and Em gathered around. When they opened it and looked inside they saw a layer of one-hundred dollar bills settled on the bottom. After counting, $22,300, they knew it still wasn't enough to match the forty-thousand-dollar expectation of William Meyer.

"Unless," Sanger said, "Bill's got the rest on him. And this is just to top up what he's carrying around."

"Maybe," Em said.

Sanger suggested, "It's worth thinking that way, don't you think?"

"Worth it for you," Alan said. "Not so convincing for me."

"It's up to you, Alan," Em said. "You decide if you want to take this money to Bill. It's almost seven now. There's time to think."

"No," Alan said. "Let's do it. Sanger, let's take a bus downtown so we won't have your car to worry about. We'll get a cup of coffee and then deliver the money."

"Together?" Sanger asked.

"Sure. You've got to drive Bill's getaway car."

~ ~ ~

Rooster barged through the door of Sanger's apartment with a sack of food. "I've thought of something," she said on her way through the living room. She put the food on the kitchen table and stepped back into the living room, where she saw only Em.

"Where's Alan?"

"He took the money to Bill," Em said.

"What money?"

"Bill forgot some money in the closet. He called and asked Alan to bring it."

"If he's had money all along, why did he want to blackmail your heartthrob?"

"It's not like that," Em said. "He's not a heartthrob. Hugh and I have really only—"

"I mean the money."

"Oh. It wasn't enough," Em said. "But we think Bill has more, enough to make up all that's needed."

"Do you?"

"We hope."

Rooster shot her piercing eyes into the corners of the living room. Then she moved to Em's and Sanger's room, digging deep into their closet. She returned to the living room with a baseball bat.

Em asked, "What are you doing with that? How did you know it was in there? I told Sanger to keep it in the back of the closet."

Rooster held the bat in front of her with both hands around the neck. "I've been here sometimes without anyone else. I've snooped. Okay? Is Sanger's car here?"

"Yes, but not the keys. You can't drive, anyway."

"Then I'll take the bus. Crap."

~ ~ ~

June 30, 8:45 pm, outside the Capella Tower,
Minneapolis

Easily spotting Bill's borrowed car, Alan left Sanger at it and crossed the street to the office building. A light rain had been falling through the evening and as Alan turned one last time to look, he saw Sanger climb into the driver's seat. Alan entered the building and ascended to the thirty-fifth floor, thinking how uncanny it all was. Even with time's abrupt commencements and cessations bookending his future journeys, it remained difficult to distinguish a real now from any pseudo-now he previously experienced. When the elevator doors opened, Bill stood waiting, holding a crumpled grocery bag.

"Come with me," Bill said. "You'll just put the bag of money on his desk and we'll leave."

"There's not enough money here," Alan said.

"Why would you say that? You don't know what's enough."

Bill pushed Alan ahead of him along the corridor and dropped something heavy into Alan's jacket pocket. Alan knew what it was, its weight as familiar as a snow globe in his palm.

"What do I need this for?" Alan asked.

"You don't," Bill said. "Just to be on the safe side; like packing a candy bar when going to a restaurant."

"I don't want it," Alan said, even though he made no move to distance himself from it.

"I'll get it from you when we're back in the car. Don't worry."

Bill opened the office door of 3580 and pushed Alan through. With Bill prodding from behind, Alan stepped across the reception area, stopped at the edge of William Meyer's desk, and put the carryall bag on the front corner. Bill stepped close behind and placed his grocery bag on the desk. He nudged forward, but Alan had no more space to move.

William Meyer leaned back in his chair and said, "Good to see you, Bill. Is it all there?" pointing to the carryall and the brown sack.

"You know," Bill said, "it really isn't. Almost. Just a little shy of one hundred percent."

"Bill, Bill, Bill," William Meyer said as he stood. "I'm dealing with bad people. It rubs off. You become more and more like the people you associate with." William Meyer opened the left side of his suit coat, showing a handgun tucked in his belt. "There's no time left. I can't let you walk away short. What would my associates think?"

To Alan, the gun in Meyer's belt looked huge, too big for a mere human hand. Without taking his eyes off of it, he said to Bill, "You don't have more than these two bags together?"

Bill ignored Alan and addressed William Meyer. "What are

you packing there?"

"Doesn't matter. Just know that I am."

Alan felt Bill lean, squeezing him closer to the desk. This wasn't familiar. Alan had never been with Bill in William Meyer's office. Whatever happened next was not a future that had previously unfolded. He remembered pulling a trigger, firing two particles, killing William Meyer. And then he imagined not. He wondered if an observed future was set in stone. Or was it merely one stem on one branch in an infinite canopy of leafy futures?

He didn't know what the next moment would bring and understood this as a hallmark of an authentic now—regardless of confidence in prediction or how many futures experienced—Alan will enter the next moment without effort and leave it with only partial knowledge of the ramifications.

Bill stretched his neck over Alan's left shoulder. "Can I see it?" he said to William Meyer. "The gun."

"Like I'm going to hand this over to you. Do you think I'm crazy?"

"No, no. I don't want to touch it. Just show it to me. Let me see."

William Meyer rolled his eyes as he pulled the gun from his waist and raised it toward Alan and Bill.

As Alan watched the gun rise, he felt Bill touching his right shoulder. Before he even turned his head to look, his peripheral vision caught the barrel of a gun that, without warning, exploded, impaling his right ear with a sound that reverberated through his head like barbed wire across an empty oil drum. The pain was immediate and never-ending. Alan didn't understand what happened. His head filled with tornadic debris. His glasses leapt from his face. Time slowed and his eyes—one eye, left eye, as the vision in his right was eclipsed by an awful sound—saw tiny droplets of red hovering in the air, turning the room into a pointillism painting. William Meyer's gun dropped from his fingers. Then that horrible crack of noise discharged again, doubling, tripling the pain in his skull. Alan raised his arms too late to protect his ears. One arm bumped Bill's arm and the gun Bill held jumped from his hand and skittered beneath the desk.

William Meyer crumpled forward. Electric squiggles jittered around the edges of Alan's vision. Each blink refreshed the lightening. He dropped to his knees and held his right palm over his ear. Someone pulled him backwards by the collar. Looking at his hand, he expected to see that horrific noise as though out of his ear climbed a hard-shelled insect with enormous pincers. Instead he saw blood and realized he could hear nothing of the shared world around him. He was deaf to the current now, replaced by a roar, and spasms of pain.

Alan was pulled again by the collar and as he looked up and behind, he saw Uncle Bill's mouth opening and closing as if...he couldn't hear anything but the roar of red pain. He watched Bill's jaw work, exposing a set of strong white teeth. Bill stabbed the air, pointing twice to the carryall on William Meyer's desk, and screamed something so violently that Alan felt Bill's dark breath surge over his cheeks.

Still on his knees, Alan crawled away from the desk as Bill ran through the reception area. Alan stopped, needing to fully concentrate on twisting and stretching his neck, attempting to distend his head out of range of the sharp noise within.

CHAPTER TWENTY-SEVEN

June 30, 9:05 pm, outside the Capella Tower
Minneapolis

Rooster turned a corner on a downtown street. Light rain had already soaked through the shoulders of her cloth jacket. She took her post, standing with her back pressed tight to the front wall of Capella Tower. The fresh odor of humid air rose from the pavement and her hands rested on the top of her baseball bat as it stood vertical between her feet. Across the street she saw Sanger in the driver's seat of Bill's borrowed car. Convinced she and the bat could disrupt whatever murderous activity was taking place, she took a moment to develop a plan.

Turning her head to the left, Bill appeared, running from around the corner of the building to his parked car. She took a step in that direction as Alan stumbled out of the main door, head down, with his hand over his right ear. A fine spray of red covered his face and jacket. She called his name once, then again louder, and finally a third time even louder.

Alan pulled his hand from his ear and showed her the blood. "I can't hear you."

"Crap," she said and turned to look at Bill, who was already in the back seat of his car. "Go home," she said to Alan.

Enraged, believing Bill had forced Alan to shoot William Meyer, she ran toward Bill's borrowed car. She ran with the baseball bat in one hand, lurching it forward and back like the wheels' connecting rod of a steam locomotive.

At the car, with bat held high, she swung hard and struck the front windshield, causing cracks to radiate from the point of contact. Sanger leaned as far back as he could to avoid the unexpected blow. She took another swing, punching a small hole through the glass.

Bill got out of the car and moved toward Rooster. Both hands on the neck of the bat, she took a few practice swings. Bill stopped and then opened the driver's door for Sanger, who got out. Rooster threatened them both with a few more swings. Bill and Sanger backed away.

Just for show, Rooster took one last swing and broke a headlight.

~ ~ ~

June 30, mere moments later, outside the Capella Tower, Minneapolis

Rooster stepped away from the car and ran into the

building. Up the elevator and into the office where she was first overcome by the smell of gunpowder and then by the odor of blood. Already a few flies circled above the dead body of William Meyer who was motionless, face down on his desk. One fly landed and walked along his ear.

She moved closer and peeked into the carryall bag that rested on the front edge of his desk. Money. Then she looked into the grocery sack. Stepping to William Meyer's side of the desk, she opened the bottom right drawer. Lifting out a briefcase, she noticed the weight, remembered the weight, and knew it will be nearly filled with cash. She rolled tight the brown paper bag, slipped it into the carryall, and then poured the contents of the briefcase in.

Squatting, she searched the floor. On hands and knees, she crawled back to the desk. *Alan's glasses, got to get those. And the gun.* With ear to the floor, she looked under the desk, discovering two handguns. She didn't know which gun Alan had used to kill William Meyer so she put both into the carryall. Next she found Alan's glasses, messy with blood, and dropped them in.

Standing over William Meyer's body, Rooster took a deep breath but smacked her lips at the odor of blood, thick enough to taste. She looked at his ample crop of hair and remembered slipping her fingers through it to pull him and his office chair. She remembered this thing she hadn't yet done and wondered if she'll ever tell a right-minded person any of it.

Rooster picked up the carryall and baseball bat and stood in the doorway, taking another look at the crime scene. Fatigue swept over her and she left the office thinking, *Now I'm done, now I'll leave, now I'll go home, to Alan's home, now I'll get on with my life.*

~ ~ ~

The Beyond Now Device

June 30, 10:05 pm, Sanger's apartment, Minneapolis

Well after nightfall, Em busied herself by making a pot of strong coffee. There was little else she could do. The last few days had been hours through a meat grinder, where time lost its mooring to this side or that side of now. Memory of what recently happened mixed with the foreboding of what will come next.

When she sat in the living room, the atomizer was still on the side table. It was out of reach yet she imagined something comforting about sitting near it. She slid her chair, reached, and then slid her chair again. She could now touch it but instead only rested her hand to the side. She wanted to see Sanger again, soon. She wanted to know what Rooster was up to. And Alan, had they decided it was a one-in-three chance that he wouldn't shoot William Meyer? She wondered what Hugh was doing and why he hadn't yet called…when she remembered their distasteful encounter with Bill at the bank. She still wanted to see him, tonight, now, and express in detail her worry, explain about the atomizer, and what they'd come to believe was their destiny.

Yet she knew it was only Sanger who would understand. *Where is he?* Knowing but not naming who she meant, knowing, in fact, that it was Sanger she trusted, with whom she could get angry without repercussion, Sanger who must love her because she had no more surprises for him. *Where is he?*

Wanting to talk to someone, she called Niko. She immediately started talking. "Niko, I don't know where Sanger is and I don't know if Hugh will ever talk to me again."

"Who? No, I don't want to know. I can't help with that."

"How can you help, then?"

"Let me tell you all you need to know. This is the truth. At the moment of your birth you were granted a now, a special moment you'll always have with you. You won't get another."

"That's it? You've already said that. What's it mean?"

"Decisions and destiny," Niko said. "People are hungry for what destiny brings to their lives. Yet they focus on making decisions, control, and conducting life like it was a machine needing minimal maintenance. This Hugh you mentioned, are you ready to accept silence as your fate with him?"

Feeling as though if left to Hugh, she may never see him again, she said, "I left him my number, well, Sanger's...doesn't matter. It's up to him now whether to contact me."

"Your fate is in his hands?" Niko asked.

"It doesn't have to be. I could call him tomorrow. I could stop in at the bar, tell him I think he's kind and we should get to know each other."

"Why him?"

"I don't know. Does it matter?"

"In full honesty, could you tell the story of how you met? Let's say you get together and hit it off. In a few months someone asks, how'd you meet."

"Okay," Em said. "That would be a little iffy. Strange. But sure. Everyone's got a how-we-met story."

"And their telling of it is a haiku of their relationship. A lot of people describe fate or a chance meeting. A circumstance that changed their lives. Everyone wants their choice of mates to have more meaning than what tie to wear with that shirt."

"You think we want an element of fate in our lives?"

"Want or not, through your gestation period you had the be-everywhere-at-any-speed potential. Then it slowly diminished so that at the moment of birth your wave collapsed and you were given a now, fated to receive it. It's always with you. It's yours and only yours."

"Aren't we all living in the same now?"

"Haven't you been listening?" Niko tapped his table and

Em heard the clicks. "We share our nows," he added, "of course. But that doesn't make us all connected. You're perpetually becoming the you you'll eventually be. By choice if you can manage it. But even without choice, you're becoming the you you'll eventually be. No one thinks they're *destined* to jaywalk until one time it's her who slams on the brakes and reprimands him for inattention. He likes her feistiness. She likes his absorption in imagination. A relationship made in heaven."

"So fate is everywhere. I should see it more?"

"Of course not. What kind of world would that be? Fate needs to draw out that tiny discrepancy hiding in our normal selves. The street-crosser and the driver talk later over wine and she says, 'I don't know what came over me. It's not like me to yell at a jaywalker.' Without that little discrepancy there's no special meaning, nothing in the dull repetition of human experience to make that moment unique."

"You've lost me. I don't get it."

"Everyone's effort is to be the same person from one day to another. As if there's any other possibility. We get a lot of pressure from loved ones to be consistent. They think they know us that way. Yet the precious now, your personal now, needs exercise. And those around you need to know it's still you when out of character."

CHAPTER TWENTY-EIGHT

June 30, intermittent concurrent action
Minneapolis

Stunned and still unable to hear from his right ear, Alan didn't need to be told twice to leave the crime scene. The sun had set and when he turned the first corner he saw a straight street unrolled ahead, illuminated by islands of frosty yellow streetlamps. He passed a pharmacy, stopped, returned, and stepped into the men's room. In the mirror, blood dribbled from his ear and the eye on that side was bloodshot. After cleaning he peered into the mirror again. It could have been worse, it could have been he who pulled the trigger. Swaying left and right, he felt the weight of the gun slosh against his side.

The gun alarmed him. *Get rid of it. Drop it in a waste bin. Throw it from a bridge.* Yet he didn't, wanting the opportunity to return it to Bill and chastise him for the mess he'd made.

Alan meandered out of the downtown area. His ear had stopped bleeding but sound was accompanied by a gale of wind roaring with every move of his head.

When Alan opened the front door of Sanger's apartment and stepped into the living room, he felt, more than he heard, boisterous pounding on the back door that led to the landing and the outdoor stairs. He rushed through and stopped in the archway to the kitchen, surprised to see Rooster and Em squatting between the stove and the door.

~ ~ ~

After leaving the office of William Meyer, Rooster walked the streets of downtown with a baseball bat and a carryall bag filled with money. *Oh*, she added in thought, *two handguns plus a pair of glasses.* She wished she could transport herself directly to Sanger's living room where she wanted to bury herself under a blanket on the couch. It wasn't a long walk home but it was dark, she was tired, worried about Alan, and cranky. *If anyone, anyone, tries to bother me, I'll bust their skull worse than I damaged Bill's borrowed car.*

She approached Sanger's apartment building through the alley behind. At the far end, at the next street, was a bar. Plenty of people smoked in the alley while pointing and gesturing with their bottles of beer. She would prefer to ignore them, except she couldn't because they weren't always able to ignore her. Believing she'd made it undetected to the base of the stairway, she heard, "Rooster, hey Rooster."

She recognized Bill's voice and without looking began her sprint up. Unbalanced with a cumbersome bat and a bulky bag of money, she bent low and noticed the smoothly worn wooden steps. Doing more of a waddle than a run, she was hot and sweaty and her legs longed for oxygen. She stopped on Sanger's landing and knocked at his back door, the meat of the bat pounding the upper panel. "Em, Em, let me in."

It didn't take long for Em to open the door. She pulled Rooster in by the arm as Rooster said, "Shh. Shut the door. It's Bill."

Em slammed the door shut, slid the deadbolt, and told Rooster, "Not a word then, not a sound." They slid down the wall between the door and the stove.

Rooster thought her breathing would never slow, or her heart stop racing. She smelled the odor of fear rising from her body like the thick steam off a damp dog. Looking at the door, she remembered Em explaining the metal U-holders on either side, not for hanging dish towels but for a restraining bar. She pulled off the hand towels and slipped the baseball bat into them across the door.

Within moments the whole door rattled as a powerful hand on the other side pounded. "Open up, Rooster," Bill said. "How'd you get that name, anyway? I know you're in there. I saw you running up the steps. Come on."

Rooster and Em looked at each other, both making a cross with their index fingers to their lips.

Bill pounded loudly again, using the heel of his hand.

Rooster's eyes were as wide as a cat's and she pulled her bangs hard, wishing to hide behind them. She wanted to speak, but thought better of it; yet found it impossible to refrain. Anger, frustration, injustice. And she just didn't like Bill. A low growl emerged from her throat, rose, and became a roar in her mouth. "Go away." She thought she screamed it, certainly she heard it. Was that her? Rooster covered her mouth with both hands.

"I knew it," Bill said. "I knew you were in there. Open up. I just want to talk."

"No," Em said. "You heard Rooster, go away."

"Oh Em, you're here too. Good. Offer me a cup of coffee, a slice of cake. Make me feel welcome. I'm practically family."

"You not welcome and you're not my family."

"Think of Sanger then. And Alan. You're family to them and they're family to me. Do you understand what I'm saying?"

Just then Rooster saw Alan standing in the archway between the kitchen and the living room. She signaled him to be quiet.

Em took a deep breath. "Go away, Bill. Rooster and I are busy and we don't want to talk to you."

Rooster breathed hard. She heard Bill turn and take a couple of noisy steps before he backed up and jiggled the door handle again.

"Um," Bill said. "Rooster, we have to settle the damage you did to my friend's car."

"I hope he has insurance."

Bill made a disgusting nasal sound and said, "I just want to tell you this one thing. Then I'll go. It's about Alan. The police picked him up near Lake Street. They've got him at the Fifth Precinct. That's all. Just wanted to let you know. Open up and we can all go down there together."

Silence. Pause. In a minute, but seeming longer, they heard Bill clop down the stairs. Rooster got up and went to Alan, embracing him in both arms. She put her hands around his head and said, "Did the police have you? What happened in the lawyer's office?"

"I can't hear you," Alan said, pointing to his ear.

Rooster leaned to the left side of his head, her lips less than an inch from his ear, and then hugged him again.

Alan said, "A gun went off too close to my ear."

Ushered to the kitchen table, Em brought a few pens and a pad of paper. She said, "This will keep us from having to scream."

Eventually Alan told the story of William Meyer's death: that Bill fired twice using Alan's right shoulder as a brace, the tremendous pain, and the roaring static that followed.

Rooster chronicled her story of using the baseball bat on Bill's windshield, going up to the office, putting all the money in the bag and returning home. She showed them the money and then dug deep to retrieve the two guns at the bottom. Stepping away, she reached into a bottom drawer filled with old bread bags. She put each gun in its own plastic bag and returned them to the carryall.

Alan pulled a handgun from his coat pocket and placed it on the table. "I never fired it," he said. "That big gun is William Meyer's. The other should have two bullets missing, along with Bill's fingerprints on the trigger."

~ ~ ~

When Sanger burst through the apartment door, he pointed a finger and said, "Jesus, Rooster, you broke Bill's windows."

"He deserved it. He fired a gun right by Alan's ear."

Sanger settled at the kitchen table with them. He told his story, writing a few words for Alan, but even with exaggeration it didn't match the tension and suspense of Alan's or Rooster's. After he listened about Bill knocking at the back door, Sanger said, "So you think Bill lied about Alan being picked up by the police?"

"Da, yeah," Rooster said.

Sanger put his palm to his forehead. "Why would he lie? That's not like him."

"Wake up," Em said. "He's been lying all along."

Alan tapped the table. "Bill set up William Meyer. Asked him to show his gun and when it was out of his belt, shot him. No warning. Bang, bang."

"I can't believe he'd do that."

"What?" Alan waved a hand and repeated, "He set it up. Am I talking too loud? He asked William Meyer to show his gun. He wants it to look like self-defense. Right from the start, his plan was to kill William Meyer. Bill never had all the money he was supposed to have."

"Sanger," Em said. "Your uncle murdered someone. We have to turn him in."

"I can't turn him in," Sanger said. "He's family and we just don't do that."

"What?" Alan asked.

Sanger wrote, 'Can't turn in family.'

"I was there," Alan said. "I'm the only witness. If we turn him in, some strange story of how this all came about will emerge. I want us to agree it's the best thing to do."

Sanger said and wrote, "Not yet. Let's sleep on it. Decide tomorrow."

"Family or not," Em said, "you can't let him get away with murder."

"We thought Alan would do the killing. Was that your plan, to turn Alan in if he was the killer? Would you turn me in? Or Rooster?" Sanger paused and covered his face with both hands. He took a deep breath and without saying it aloud, he wrote on the paper for all to see, 'I think Bill is my father.'

"Yeah," Alan said. "He is. The whole family knows. You know how these things are."

"No," Sanger said. "I don't know how these things are. Why didn't you tell me? Does my dad know?" And then he wrote, 'Who knows?'

Alan lowered his brows. "Sanger, everyone knows. Your dad's a little squeamish about the whole thing. Look at it, your mom gets pregnant by his brother and he's left to raise a kid that isn't biologically his. But he hung in there. Bill was never going to be a family man. Your dad patched things up with your mom, loved you both all these years, and never took out his frustration on you. Still, it's not been a topic for the Christmas table."

Sanger squirmed and wrote, 'I need to talk to my parents.'

"Sanger," Alan said. "Do you appreciate the father your dad has been?"

Sanger nodded. "But—"

"No. Just take it all in, and appreciate him more."

~ ~ ~

July 1, one am, as minutes bid farewell to the previous day, Minneapolis

Em reached, took Sanger's hand, and led him to their bedroom. Fully clothed they lay on their backs. When she had last spoken with Niko, he told her about a now that she owned. She wanted to tell Sanger of this wondrous now, share a piece of her special time. She crawled over him and suddenly worried about his view of her. To counter it, she said, "I'm generous, kind, respectful, willing to help, comfortable sharing—"

"What are you saying?"

"I'm listing my good points, giving myself a little boost so I can maintain my self-respect while talking with you."

"Is it that bad?" Sanger asked. "Am I that bad?"

"You have been. I haven't lied to you. I haven't cheated on

you. It's all been out in the open. I know you're thinking worse of me than what you've said."

"It's just shorthand. I'm sorry."

"We deserve more from each other."

Sanger turned his head to face her. "Alan set me straight. He said I have to let you be you or I'd end up loving my imagination. Or at least a person not you."

"Can you do that?"

"I don't know. But I'll start by not insisting you change. If I can't accept it, I'll pack your bags and throw you out."

Em suspected Sanger of tossing a little humor. Already on slippery ground, she chose to miss the joke rather than laugh at something that wasn't there.

~ ~ ~

July 1, 1:22 am, Minneapolis

The living room was quiet and dark except for a trapezoid of moonlight on the floor before Alan's bedroom door. It shined like a bright welcome mat. The door was ajar. *Of course it is*, Rooster thought. *He trusts me and won't be surprised when I walk in.* She stepped through and saw him on his back, one arm tucked behind his head. She saw his closed eyelids and knew he couldn't hear her. Hot and humid, a pulse of sweat sprang from the skin between her breasts. *He's had a long day.* She wanted to soothe him, comfort him, share her relief that he hadn't killed anyone.

She sat on the edge of the bed, startling him. Touching his hip, she said, "You've had a hard day. Take it easy."

"I can't hear you."

She leaned across, her chest grazing his, and spoke into his left ear. "I bet you're tense."

"Yeah," Alan said. "Come around this side." He indicated

his left side and slid to his right to make space for her.

Rooster curled on her side next to him, her left hand resting on his shoulder, her lips next to his good ear. "I'll rub your back, if you want."

"No. Thanks. I'm okay."

"I'm sorry about your ear. But I'm very happy you didn't pull the trigger."

"Yeah. Me, too."

Rooster felt simmering, contradictory emotions. Exuberance rose and she pressed herself so close to him that not even doubt could bloom; followed by feeling stupid to think he even liked her. Effervescence *and* apprehension. He was kind *and* it was nothing more than chivalry. Still, touching his skin returned an immediate electrical reaction. "This feels like déjà vu to me," she said. "But it's not. Not like it was before, when I first sniffed the perfume. Not really like that at all. I mean—"

"Hey. I didn't experience what you told us about."

"Uh-hu, that's good. Back then I was going to force myself on you. Now I'm not. Free choice is the way to go. That's the big difference. Don't you think?" Rooster pressed her forehead into Alan's shoulder and slid her knees deeper into his thigh. She raised her face so her lips were only a breath from his ear and placed her hand on his chest before saying, "That's the big difference, huh? Choice."

She felt his stillness, knowing he was thinking. She hoped he'd turn toward her *and* dreaded his laugh if he called her a stupid kid.

"I think," Alan said, "forty is right around the corner for me and you're not even out of high school. I think that's the big difference."

So? she thought. *That's not the big difference.* She pulled her free hand back, considered pouting, but instead said, "Okay. I don't get it, but okay."

After a moment, she moved her lips closer to his good ear and said, "I'll get my GED. Who knows, maybe go on to college."

"That's really good," Alan said. "If that's what you want, we'll do all we can to get you there."

"Are you proud of me?"

Alan touched her head and said, "Of course. I'm proud to know you."

His morsel of encouragement brought her confidence to the surface. "It's been a crazy couple of weeks." Rooster rested her head on Alan's shoulder and relaxed. "I feel good," she said. "I feel like I can do anything. Whatever I put my mind to. Like, mistakes or not, I'm destined to do well. Fated that all I touch will turn out okay. Even if it seems put-offish at the start. Do you know what I mean?"

When Alan didn't answer, Rooster added, "I'm saying, maybe if you just followed my lead, and even though only one of us knows everything will be okay...because you probably don't feel that way...but if I knew, and you trusted my judgement, then...do you see what I mean?"

"No. Maybe you better say it."

"Can I sleep here tonight?"

"Rooster, that's not such a good idea."

"Why? Don't you like me?

"No, that's not it."

She lifted her head to better see his face. "Because you do like me?"

"Rooster, you're only fifteen. In ten years you'll be at the peak of your life and I'll be over the hill."

"In ten years we can talk again. What about now? Didn't you learn anything from Niko? We have a very special relationship with now. I'm young and willing. You're calm and accepting and—"

"And something tells me that our very special relationship with now changes over time, changes with age. You and I will never experience now in the same way, even if we're doing the same thing at the same time."

Rooster sat up and frowned. Relief *and* dejection. Heavy-hearted *and* safe enough to say anything. "There will never be another now like this one."

"What?" Alan said and pointed to his ear.

Rooster spoke louder. "There will never be another now like this one. That's something I've learned. What's wrong with that?"

"Shh," Alan said. "We don't want to wake Sanger and Em. Come down closer."

"Now is special," Rooster said. "What's wrong with that?"

"Nothing. But I don't believe there's only now. That's not the only bit of time that counts, no matter how special it is. Now is not all there is."

"The future?" Rooster asked.

"Yes. There will never be another tomorrow like the one that's coming. And it will come. And I don't want to wake regretting what we've done. I want us to still be friends."

He doesn't like me, she thought, *or maybe he does*. It was her choice, regardless of the truth, no matter what he thought, it was her opportunity to select her preference. "I don't know, old man," Rooster said. "I suppose I've got to be nice to you now because you're so old."

Rooster paused before she added, "I didn't mean that. I like what's between us." She relaxed and snuggled comfortably beside him.

"I want to see you receive your GED," Alan said.

"I'd like you to see it."

CHAPTER TWENTY-NINE

July 1, three-ish in the morning, Minneapolis

In the quiet darkness of Sanger's apartment, the phone rang. Sanger and Em jumped from their bed, thinking it was Bill. As Sanger reached for the phone, he saw Alan and Rooster come out of Alan's room. He wondered for a moment and then said. "Hello. Bill?"

"No, this is Niko."

Sanger carried the phone to the kitchen and the others followed. He put it on speaker and sat.

"I want to check in," Niko said. "Your day is coming

soon, right?"

"Niko," Em said. "We're past the worst of it and…it's the middle of the night."

"Is it? Oh, yes. Hello, Em. Did you get any use out of your personal now?"

The four around the kitchen table looked at each other. Em said to them, "Niko and I talked earlier, while you were out."

"Yes," Niko said. "And it was a good talk, too. It brought us back to where we started. Does the future already exist? Is it out there like an empty stage with a vague backdrop? Or like an unfurnished apartment, utilities already connected and you just bring your own furniture? Does choice have any sway over the content of the future? There are buildings and sidewalks and coins in my pocket that are pushed into the future without any personal effort. Can it be that everything in existence now will also exist in the next nearest future? How can change take place in a universe constructed this way?"

"What are you talking about?" Rooster asked.

"Time. And how we understand it. You see, we believe in a future defined by the decisions we make. But are we as responsible for getting my kitchen table into the future as we are for carrying a secret forward? If the future already exists, my secret is already a part of it, as is the table. Yet it feels as though the secret is mine and I bring it into the future. What else must I carry into the future? Where does my responsibility start and stop? If we're responsible for even a tiny bit of the future's content, it is an intoxicating proposition."

The four around Sanger's kitchen table rolled their eyes.

Niko continued. "We want to think the content of the future depends on rational decisions filling the future with rational events. But look at the world around us, doom and war and misplaced garbage. We're doing no better than if we had followed superstition and omen at luring a preferable future. Our curse isn't bad luck in decision-making, but an inadequate understanding of time."

"You're losing me again," Rooster said.

"We try to make sense of a future for which there is no evidence. Just a lot of potential and speculation. So let's say there are an infinite number of futures, accounting for all possible outcomes of all decisions made, unmade, by me or you, including a future where my secret exists and one where it doesn't."

"Okay," Em said. "Okay."

"Do you remember the universe as a giant rope-making machine where multiple strands of future are twisted together now, releasing a braided rope behind into the past. The strands in the future are undetectable, emitting no radio waves, and nothing in the range of visible light. Yet in their invisibility, how does one future materialize over another? How?"

"Blindly. We choose blindly," Alan said, hoping he heard Niko correctly.

"So we do," Niko said. "But we also carry with us a gist of things. And a ton of emotional content. And a set of values honed from the expanse of our experiences."

"I get it now," Alan said. "My fate was in Bill's hands all along. I just never knew it. But I should have seen it from the first time he slipped a gun in my pocket. All my life, my future has depended on the choices of others."

"True for so many. But does it matter? Time is not space, there's no up or down, no volume, no inside or outside. We don't enter the future; there's no future to enter. Now is a parent walking with child, imploring her to keep up while also admonishing her not to get too far ahead. Now is the sweet spot Buddhists spend their lives prolonging and losing and discovering again."

"Are you saying there's only now?" Rooster asked.

"I'm saying," Niko answered, "that your body, your senses, and the world around you is in now. It's only your thinking that cares to leave now's warm embrace and hark back to the past or forecast a future. Choice is the gateway drug through which we attempt to re-manage history and manipulate a life to come. It's our special relationship with now that holds the—"

"No, no, no," Sanger said. "Stop. You talk a lot. We're past our date with destiny and we have no more decisions to make."

"No more decisions to make?" Niko asked. "You know that can't possibly be true."

Sanger shook his head. "We're done." And then he ended the call.

~ ~ ~

July 1, morning, Minneapolis

After Sanger returned to bed for a few hours and got up, he found Em sitting at the kitchen table. He went back into the living room and returned with the atomizer and the telephone, placing them both on the table. When the coffee Em had started was finished, Sanger retrieved mugs and poured coffee for himself and Em.

"What's the phone for?" Em asked.

"I think it's time Rooster called her parents."

"Hmm, you're probably right."

Within a few minutes, Rooster rose from the couch where she had slept the rest of the night after Niko's phone call. Pouring a cup of coffee, she turned and asked, "Did you guys sniff already this morning?"

"No," Sanger said. "It's just here because we need to talk about it."

"And the telephone?" Rooster asked.

Sanger said, "It's time you called your mother and let her know you're all right."

"Do I have to?"

Sanger knew she did. They hadn't wanted interference while they were approaching murder. But that was past. It was time.

"Let her know," Sanger said, "that you're welcome to stay here through the summer, at least. Tell her you're safe and happy and eating well and the people you're staying with are just...just as normal as can be."

Rooster sat at the table and Sanger slid the phone to her.

After dialing, Rooster spoke to her mother without putting the phone on speaker. "Hello Mom. It's me... Yeah, I'm okay. I'm in Minneapolis... No, not yet. Maybe. I don't know when... I'm okay, really... No, no drugs, nothing like that. I'm staying with a small family... No, they're just regular folks. It's okay... Well, da! Yeah, he's the reason... No, I don't want to talk about it and I don't believe he's sorry. You should have... You keep saying that but... You're not listening."

Rooster paused and looked at Sanger and Em. She rolled her eyes and then said into the phone, "I'll be sixteen before school starts in the fall. I'm going to quit and work on getting a GED... Gen Ed Diploma. It's just like graduating, same thing... No I don't want to hear what he said last night... As if... If you start I'm going to hang up... Mom! I don't care...it wasn't the only time... I don't care what he... I'm hanging up now."

Rooster disconnected and placed the phone on the table. Without looking at Sanger or Em, she said, "That went well. At least she knows I'm safe." Rooster pulled on her bangs. "Excuses. Why do people make excuses?"

"Sorry," Em said. "But I'm glad you called."

"Yeah," Rooster agreed. "That now has passed and good riddance."

Em looked around the kitchen and asked, "Should we wake Alan?"

"No," Rooster said. "He was hurt last night. Sleep is probably good for him."

Em touched Rooster's hand and asked, "Did you guys get to bed okay?"

"No, I mean yes. I mean why?"

"Nothing. I meant nothing by it. It's just that Sanger and I went to bed before you. And when we got up to answer Niko's call, you came out of his room. Alan's usually up earlier than this. I meant nothing by it."

Sanger pointed a finger at Rooster and twirled it in small circles. "We saw you come out of Alan's room last night. You guys didn't...you know. I mean did Alan..." Sanger took a deep breath and added, "Was Alan not a perfect gentleman?"

"Sanger!" Em said. "That's none of our business."

Rooster tilted her head and said, "We're fine. Nothing happened."

Em said, "You'll let us know, though, because it's something that would interest the law and we'd all want to be prepared for that."

"Alan was hurt. I wanted to sooth him. That's all. Nothing happened"

"Good, then," Em said.

Sanger added, "Good, then."

"Don't worry," Rooster said. "Alan is quite the gentleman."

Alan soon stepped into the kitchen scratching the right side of his face. "I can hear better," he said. "Traffic and stuff." He covered his better ear and cocked his head to listen. "It's still like through a blanket but getting better." After pouring a cup of coffee he sat with the others.

Rooster put a hand on his and said, nearly sang, "Good morning Alan."

He slid his hand away and looked up to see Sanger and Em staring at him. He felt guilty, as though a secret had been revealed and he didn't know which one. "What?" he said.

"Nothing," Em replied. "It's just good to see Rooster happy."

Alan looked at Rooster and asked, "What did you tell them?"

"I assured them nothing happened between us last night. We didn't do anything."

"They don't seem convinced." He looked from Sanger to Em. "We didn't do anything."

"I called my mom this morning," Rooster said. "I told her I'm safe and I'm going to quit school as soon as I'm sixteen. Then I'll work on my GED. Everything's good."

Alan rubbed his face and said again, "I can hear better today."

"You should still get it checked out by a doctor," Em said.

"I've thought about that. In a day or two. I want any evidence of what happened to wash away. Gunshot residue. And I need a story of how something that loud got close to my ear." After a sip of coffee, Alan added, "Why's the mister out here? Where's the bag of money? What are we going to do about yesterday?"

Sanger put a hand flat on the table. "We need to talk again about turning Bill in."

"We should count the money," Rooster said.

Sanger tapped the table in front of Alan. "I don't think I can turn him in. I know he did wrong but if it was you, and we thought it would be, I couldn't turn you in."

"Thanks, but—"

Rooster chimed in, "What are we going to do with the guns? When we decide about the guns we'll be most of the way there on what to do with Bill. If we give the guns to the police, only Bill's fingerprints are on the one that was fired." Rooster touched her eyebrows as she added, "But this is just because I don't like Bill."

Em waved a hand, getting their attention. "Let's hide the guns and say nothing more about it. Let's keep the money because Bill left it behind and he doesn't know where it is. Whoever eventually discovered the body might just as well have taken the money. Bill's hardly in a position to say his money is missing. In all likelihood, the police have it. Except, of course, we have it."

"Don't you think," Sanger said, "that it belongs to Bill?"

"So?" Rooster said.

"I second what Em suggested," Alan said. "Sanger, our Uncle Bill masterminded a very rotten operation. Maybe you're too close to turn him in. I say we cut him loose: quit taking his phone calls; no more welcome here; and no one-last-plan to make things right. Agreed? Sanger, it's up to you. Agreed?"

"Yes," Sanger said.

"Okay," Rooster said. "Now, what about the atomizer?"

"Do we really," Alan said to Rooster, "want to lock ourselves in to what we see? Impulsive choices might…we should slow down, think about it more."

"Right," Rooster said, rolling her eyes right back at him. "Heaven forbid we do it just because it's exciting, imaginative, and feels good."

"Feels good?" Sanger asked. "You mean using the mister?"

Rooster ignored him and addressed Alan. "You know what I mean. It might be really different because I want to, not because I'm forced to."

"Or not," Alan said, pressing his face into his palm.

~ ~ ~

July 1, hours later, Minneapolis

Sanger sat in the kitchen while the others counted money in the living room. He resented his parents' lies and didn't believe he could maintain the deception that his dad was his real biological father. He imagined confronting them, mom and dad, bemoaning, first the cover-up, and then how his mom could have done such a thing.

Sanger pondered with his chin planted in his palm. *Em ruins everything by sleeping with her banker. Now every good memory of my dad is tainted.*

He had respected their marriage, wanted to emulate it and pattern his own future after theirs. With an epiphany that drew his mind still, Sanger felt the tether to his family loosen and the safe harbor of home inundated by a tsunami. Struggling to not lose his footing on an increasingly slippery past, Sanger thought, *I've always wanted a relationship like my parents had. Why can't it be as simple as that?*

He let his hands drop, heavy with the weight of all he believed he lost. Lifeless and forlorn, he thought, *so maybe I already have the relationship they had? Maybe a life with Em is destined all along. How much choice have I ever had in the matter?*

When Em walked past, Sanger was reminded of his upcoming trip to the bank. *Maybe I wasn't there to stop or report an abduction. Maybe the delivery of the letter was the most important factor.* Reaching for Em's hand, he asked "Are you intending to write Hugh a letter?"

"No. I'm leaving it up to him to contact me. I gave him your phone number. So if he calls, be nice."

Sanger collected paper and pen and intended to write to Hugh. He didn't know what to say, but that must have been what his jaunt to the future revealed—his hand-delivery of such a letter.

At the kitchen table with pen and paper in hand, Sanger scraped his teeth over his lower lip and periodically discovered he was squinting. He had a lot he wanted to tell Hugh not to do, chief among them was 'don't hurt her'. He might have been satisfied repeating those words over the whole page if he hadn't believed Em would tell him he had no right to treat her like a puppy being handed over to a new owner. Careful, don't hurt her.

Finally, he simply wrote: 'Em makes her own decisions.' Then he folded the sheet into thirds, slipped it into the envelope, and wrote Hugh's name on the face.

CHAPTER THIRTY

July 1, evening, Minneapolis

Em took her turn to brood at the kitchen table. She knew Sanger was stewing over his parentage problem. She assumed Hugh hadn't called because he was squeamish about what he'd gotten himself into. No, what she'd gotten him into.

A barricade inside crumbled, dropping the rubble of haphazardly made plans at her feet. If Hugh can't take a chance…if Sanger can't accept the truth…*who am I to insist it should be different?*

Each time she renounced responsibility, another gap

opened in the thought palace she wished could exist. As soon as she justified her actions, the pieces of her grand scheme fell to the floor. All the blame she pointed at others returned, making her feel self-conscious and ill. Nonetheless, she tried to fashion a complex set of ideas she could call her own.

Rooster pulled a chair and sat with Em. "You don't look so good," she said.

"I'm thinking." Em explained as best as she could. "The past is over. I don't regret any of it. Mistakes? Sure, but so what? Everybody's got to get over it. I'm not responsible for how Sanger misinterprets or Hugh judges. Without their baggage I can get on with things. I can't be really myself with them hanging around my neck."

Rooster scratched her head. "Them? Who are they?"

Em leaned forward. "Anyone," she said, "anyone who needs you to...to care...to care what they feel."

Em's words didn't adequately explain the depth of her turmoil. She knew beneath her excuses rested a cauldron of discomfort. "I can't explain it. Something deep inside is spilling over whenever I think seriously about now. It's a crowded space when I have to think about...them."

"I don't know," Rooster said. "I figure when now swells and fills with this and that and stuff that goes against the other and you can't do anything but pay attention." She paused and thought about her time with Alan the previous night, how each moment had more than one feeling, often contradictory, filling that instant with widgets and whirls. "Don't you think being smack dab in the middle of now-time...when there's just as much this as that and competing urges are on an even playing field...and someone else's feelings need to be...who knows what others feel? But then, don't you think, something else, bigger, needs to guide us?" Rooster raised her brows as high as her bangs. "But what do I know? I've never thought like this before."

In a glimpse Em understood that her turmoil was because she wanted to be with Sanger, *and* wanted to see Hugh again. *Would it,* she thought, *be so difficult? Was it asking too much?*

Em lifted her head and reached to touch Rooster's hand. "You're something, you know that."

~ ~ ~

Niko stared at the dirty dishes piled in his sink, at the disorder in his living room. There was no reason for it. He had let himself slide long enough. He regretted much of what he'd told the four in the last month yet still wanted to say more. He leaned back into his couch and watched a glow of revelation trail across his ceiling. *That's it,* he thought. *Yes, that's it.*

He tapped in the number and Em answered the phone. She called Alan and Sanger to join her and Rooster.

Niko said, "I had wanted to write a paper on your use of the device. But I did it all wrong. I talked too much when I should have been asking questions. I disregarded what you were going through. I wanted only to tell you my story about time. It was a mistake. And now I have no data, nothing to submit to a reputable journal."

"Oh, Niko," Em said. "Is there anything we can do to help?"

"No, it's too late. If anything can be too late, this is too late. There's something very special about now. Our intimate relationship with now is the only thing keeping us from tripping into a future where we don't yet belong."

"Huh?" Rooster said.

"We imagine a future," Niko continued, "and believe in its orderly arrival. We hope to shape its outcome. We trust the past to hold its contour and not to be continually rearranging itself.

Does the future already exist? As imaginative as we are, all that might happen won't, all we dream up isn't. Time doesn't flow or expire or change to become new. The now you know is the only now there is. It's the same now given to you at the moment of birth."

"I've been in now," Rooster asked, "since I was born?"

"Yes," Niko said. "Now things happen. An arm waves, a musical note transitions to another, a springboard diver performs three and a half somersaults. All happens now. There is no other time for it to happen. The movement, growth, and decay we see takes place now. It's not as if more nows are coming down the pike and all we need do is wait for the right one in order to succeed or fail or attempt or falter."

"That's what I want," Rooster said. "Get on with things. Take advantage of the moment." She looked at Alan and added, "We shouldn't wait."

"The truth about time," Niko continued, "is that now is in a perpetual state of becoming. Objects are to space as events are to time. Some events are more tightly bound to time than are other events. As an event draws nearer to the extremes, to never or always, time loses any useful meaning."

"Do you mean, don't be rigid?" Em asked, thinking of her own uncompromising view of how her relationships should work. "Express a little give and take?"

"I suppose," Niko said. "We all grasp an attitude that helps shape the decisions we make. Yet in a quest for that footing, many are fooled by glittering truth—a list of ways to always be and a corresponding list of ways to never be. A self under construction. We want to always respect the views of others. Yet not when those views spew hatred and woe. We never want to abandon our dreams. Yet self-sacrifice is nothing to be ashamed of. Encapsulated truth tempts us toward abstract extremes where we lose our connection with now. Without now, we have no connection to the real world."

Sanger looked at Em and knew he'd only been seeing the success of their relationship through his terms. And if it failed, he would surely blame her. He touched her hand, wanting a paragraph of fresh insight to pass from his fingers to hers. But knew he will eventually have to say it.

"Woo the future with hope," Niko added, "or dig in your heels with dread and worry. Doesn't matter. There is no separation between you and the course of events. Hesitancy shapes the future as much as recklessness. Joining now is all there is. Finding meaning, losing it, and discovering it again, is all shrouded in our relationship with now."

Niko heard their silence and chose that moment to say, "At one time the heavens were static and all revolved around the earth; the natural world made intuitive sense. Galileo then drew a few pictures and rounded some circles with his fingers and turned the natural order on its head, challenging the powers that had already defined how the world must be seen. But few understood or even believed him. Then Descartes came along and proclaimed all people could think for themselves. And Newton defined the laws of motion so well that even children understood.

"The ancients fought back with eternal truths embedded in values that had stood the test of time: faith, loyalty, love, appreciation. But progress marched on so human values only had value when convenient, morality became individualized without authority, and choices turned into a collection of synaptic discharges in the brain. Along the way any search for meaning became the responsibility of each of us alone. Should we put all of our marbles in the enduring truths of the ancients? Or is there a new legitimacy looming around the next discovery?"

"Niko," Em said. "Are you okay?"

"No, but I will be. I have been so wrong for so long. If we share anything real with one another, we do it now, when now is right, when now has swept hesitation aside and pushed anticipation out of the way." Niko paused and thought. Without warning, he added, "Listen. While trekking through the jungle, one person hacks a path with a wild machete while another reaches forward to push aside leaves. Every choice is asking the question: Does the future already exist? It's only an understanding of now that makes any of this real."

Em said, "Niko, we didn't know you wanted to publish something. We…what will you do now?"

"I have a new plan," Niko said, slapping the table in front of him. "I'm going to turn my hand to fiction.

Acknowledgements

I'd like to thank early readers, Joan Parks, Veronica Ringler, James Hollock, Ron Wunderlin, Jim Burpee, and Janet Shapiro, who helped shape the final version.

Along the way I emailed members of the Departments of Physics at Rutgers University, Cornell University, Brown University, University of Chicago, University of Edinburgh, University of Wisconsin, and the California Institute of Technology. I also emailed members of the Departments of Philosophy at Rutgers University, University of Nottingham, and Georgetown University. And last I emailed members of the Department of Theology at University of Nottingham and the Center for Islamic Theology at the University of Tubingen. In each email I briefly described my project and asked 'Does the future already exist?' Many people responded, too many to thank individually. Some answered the question briefly, others advised direction for further study with links to articles and topics, while quite a few wrote multiple paragraphs explaining the nuances of time and the future. I am indebted to their generosity while still taking full responsibility for the content of this book, blaming no one but myself for any mistakes and inaccuracies written within.

About the author

Independent writers and publishers depend on word of mouth to get their books recognized. If you liked this book, please lend it or tell others or approach your favorite bookstore and ask them to stock this book. If you purchased from an online bookseller, please go back and leave a critique. It will be greatly appreciated.

Independent writers face a daunting blankness of obscurity without the recognition of those few who read independently published books. I live in Minneapolis, Minnesota, USA with my wife and two cats. I have a static website of photographs at www.hollock.info/markhollock and can be reached by email at m.i.hollock@gmail.com

I welcome your thoughts.

www.ingramcontent.com/pod-product-compliance
Lightning Source LLC
Chambersburg PA
CBHW031141120726
47905CB00006B/1778